D1202251

ALSO BY CHRISTOPHER S. WREN

*The End of the Line: The Failure of Communism
in the Soviet Union and China*

*Winners Got Scars Too: The Life and Legends
of Johnny Cash*

The Super Summer of Jamie McBride
(a novel with Jack Shepherd)

Almanack of Poor Richard Nixon
(with Jack Shepherd)

Quotations from Chairman LBJ
(with Jack Shepherd)

CHRISTOPHER S.
WREN

HACKS

Simon & Schuster

New York London Toronto Sydney Tokyo Singapore

SIMON & SCHUSTER
Rockefeller Center
1230 Avenue of the Americas
New York, NY 10020

This novel is a work of fiction. Names, characters,
places, and incidents either are products of the
author's imagination or are used fictitiously as
described in the Author's Note at the beginning of
the work. Other than as indicated in the Author's
Note, any resemblance to actual events or locales
or persons, living or dead, is entirely coincidental.

Copyright © 1996 by Christopher S. Wren
All rights reserved,
including the right of reproduction
in whole or in part in any form.

SIMON & SCHUSTER and colophon are registered trademarks
of Simon & Schuster Inc.

Designed by Levavi & Levavi

Manufactured in the United States of America

10 9 8 7 6 5 4 3 2 1

Library of Congress Cataloging-in-Publication Data

Wren, Christopher S. (Christopher Sale).
    Hacks / Christopher S. Wren.
        p.   cm.
    I. Title.
PS3573.R4H33   1996
813'.54—dc20   95-26119
                                                        CIP

ISBN 0-684-81413-7

Excerpts from "Newspapermen Meet Such Interesting People"
are reprinted with the permission of Heatherfield Music.

In memory of two foreign correspondents, tough competitors and gracious friends who never lacked for courage or compassion

DON A. SCHANCHE
Died in Miami,
November 17, 1994

DIAL TORGERSON
Killed on the
Nicaraguan-Honduran border,
June 21, 1983

and of a gentle colleague

NATHANIEL C. NASH
Killed in Croatia,
April 3, 1996

"He who prides himself on giving what he thinks the people want is creating a fictitious demand for lower standards which he will then satisfy."

—LORD REITH, *first chairman of the British Broadcasting Corporation*

"If it bleeds, it leads."

—(TELEVISION) NEWS APHORISM

Hackspeak—A Glossary

A-roll—sound for a television story

B-roll—picture/video for a television story

Beat—reporter's area of news responsibility

Beta—television minicamera, sometimes: Betacam or minicam

Bird—satellite for transmitting video; on the bird

Ceasefile—agreement among reporters on a story not to file competitively

Copy—news story or other news material

Cover—video footage accompanying a reporter's voiceover

Dateline—location where a news story was gathered or filed

Embargo—time restraint imposed for filing a story

Feed—to send a radio or television story

Feed the goat—to send a story to a daily newspaper

File—to send a print story

Fill—account of a missed story from another reporter who was there

Fireman—reporter sent to breaking stories

Flack—public relations specialist trying to influence news coverage

Fuzz and wuzz—urban police reporting (from police and corpses)

Hack—foreign correspondent

HLSGP—(Hairy-Legged Swedish Girl for Peace) groupie for leftist causes

In the window—time allocated to use a satellite

Ink-stained wretch—print reporter

Laptop—portable computer

Lede—opening of a news story, usually summarizing its elements (deliberately misspelled to distinguish it from the verb "lead")

Mushroom journalist—reporter assigned to hard, thankless stories

Peg—news event or situation used to justify a story

Pool—small group of journalists covering an event on behalf of a larger press corps

Rock'n'roll—warfare and other organized violence

Rocket—message from editors alerting a reporter to a competitor's story and demanding that it be matched

Run and gun—news coverage of homicides, fires, car crashes, and other daily mayhem

Scene setter—preview of an upcoming event, such as a summit meeting

Sound bite—snippet of an interview edited for a news story

Spook—intelligence agent, spy

Spray—to shoot a news event quickly, without setting up a tripod

Stand-up—correspondent's appearance before the camera on a news story

Stringer—nonstaff reporter paid by the number of stories sent

Suit—senior news executive, especially one without field experience

Takeout—longer thematic newspaper story

Talking head—news interview, often in the studio

Thumbsucker—news analysis, often short on news; sometimes called Q-head

Voiceover—narrative accompanying video footage

Wanker—jerk, obnoxious nuisance; from British vulgarity "to wank" or masturbate

White balance—adjustment of the video picture as a cameraman moves from one light source to another

Author's Note

This book is a work of fiction. It is based, very loosely, on the civil wars I covered in Angola and Mozambique, but the characters appearing in it are unrelated to the people I met and interviewed in those countries.

Equatoria exists, but it is a province in the southern Sudan, where I also worked, and not the nation depicted here.

Finally, some of the events I write about never happened to foreign correspondents. The rest did.

1.

PORTO PARADISO, Equatoria—With no end in sight to the self-styled anti-Marxist insurgency that has ravaged this mineral-rich, war-torn land, hard-core guerrillas mounted a savage predawn raid on a refugee-packed shantytown.

Shack dwellers watched in wide-eyed horror as steel-jacketed bullets slashed through the rain-soaked tamarind leaves . . .

"Speak English?" he asked the keening widow, for who had the time or patience to learn the local dialect?

He and Alistair had shared a taxi out in search of the old woman's grief. A thousand widows make a statistic, T.K. reminded his friend, but one widow still makes a story.

"Speak English?" T.K. asked her.

Civil war in Equatoria had rendered violent death so banal that it no longer grabbed his editors back home. Where would last night's raid rank on the loftier scale of news judgment, which equated a dead American with four Frenchman, ten Russians, fifty Pakistanis, a hundred Haitians, or God knows how many Equatorians?

T.K. voiced a reporter's compassion for unfortunates trapped in the wrong place at the wrong time:

"Howdoesitfeel?"

The widow rocked back and forth on her heels in the shanty's gloom. The only reply was rain, soft at first and then more persistent, rain that drummed against the scrap wood and dripped through the plastic until rivulets trickled across the pounded earth.

"Did it sound like tat-tat-tat," prodded Alistair, "or pocka-pocka-pocka?"

The absence of children laughing or dogs barking should have alerted them to the danger in this warren of inhabited packing crates. The shanty-town was secure, the guerrillas driven off, T.K.'s source in the Ministry said, then tipped him off to the frail woman who had watched her family slaughtered last night.

"Speak English?" T.K. prodded harder. "Howdoes—"

A grenade exploding in the alley turned the world outside the plastic sheeting incandescent orange. The widow screamed, wood tumbled upon them, assault rifles dueled. Nothing was secure, and the firefight sent T.K. and Alistair scrambling for their lives.

"Bloody hell," shouted Alistair. "They're still here."

T.K. chased his friend through the torn plastic, but Alistair had vanished into the rain. An assailant colliding in the labyrinth of alleys clubbed T.K.'s knee with a rifle butt. He dropped his notebook and ran, heedless of the pain, slipping and sliding on the greasy trail.

Then the furry clouds emptied with a climactic deluge that T.K. had not witnessed before in Equatoria, until he was hobbling alone through the sheets of water.

At the fresh crack of an AK-47 rifle, he pitched headlong into the ditch. Like rivets slammed into a door, it punctuated the thunder rolling around him. Hard rain was hiding him now, battering down with a force that pocked the rising waters of the ditch in which he cowered.

He dared not raise his head. AKs were the rock'n'roll of conflict resolution in these countries where he worked. T.K. knew the racket, unless fear had tricked him this time, unless the staccato etched into his consciousness lived only within the thunder, preceded by such lightning as shredded the leaden sky.

How did he get out of this one alive? His knee throbbed from the rifle swung in the alley. There was no sign of Alistair, he had not run fast enough.

He never thought to bring the flak vest. He had bought it from a free-lance photographer scrounging airfare home for a fraction of the two thousand dollars that one cost new. Now that he needed it, the Kevlar vest lay useless under his hotel bed.

T.K. hugged the muddy slope. Rainwater swirled clumps of garbage around his chest. He could get no wetter if he pissed in his pants, which he probably had—not that anyone cared. If the world was going to end, this was the place for God to start demolishing His handiwork.

The slashing rain almost obscured the rows of wretched shacks cobbled together from corrugated metal, plastic, burlap, and scrap wood by refugees fleeing an incessant war. They dumped their meager garbage in the ditch, squatted in it themselves, until the stinking accumulation was washed away to the river by the kind of sudden storm that had covered his escape.

Something collided in the current. T.K. fought for footing, but it was not Alistair who nearly knocked him under. This corpse lacked a face. From the tattered uniform, he was once a militiaman, or more likely a bandit killed before last night's raid. Bodies went into the ditch too, to await the rains that washed all garbage into the river and down to the cleansing sea.

T.K. lifted his head above the ditch. Eucalyptus trees along the road cracked in the banshee wind. A lightning flash garish as neon illuminated a scarecrow of a man emitting a primal scream:

"Sod them all, bloody wankers!"

"Over here," T.K. yelled, and relaxed a little as Alistair splashed into the ditch, minus his eyeglasses and a shoe.

"We'll need typhus shots if we make it out of here," T.K. said. "Seen what we're swimming in?"

"Bloody worried about typhus, you reckless bastard?" Rainwater trickled down Alistair's scraggly whiskers.

The storm was letting up. A broken umbrella, black fabric whipping from the metal spine, tumbled along the empty road as if possessed. Across the road lay the unkempt remains of an airstrip, neglected since Russian engineers built a modern airport nearer the capital. Beyond the dirt runway and the tree line, cocoa-colored water splashed over cataracts defining this stretch of the wide, sullen river.

"Courage is being scared to death and saddling up anyway," T.K. shouted into the wind. He climbed out of the ditch, leaving a trail of mud as slimy as diarrhea.

"Made that one up, did you?" Alistair followed.

"I think John Wayne did," said T.K.

They trudged toward the taxi left idling back around the bend. T.K. had torn a fifty-dollar bill as his customary insurance against being stranded, and promised the other half to the driver when he picked them up.

"This might be the closest the guerrillas have come to the capital," T.K. said.

"Or might not," Alistair said, "and my readers won't queue up on Fleet Street to find out. No blood and no bodies mean no bylines."

In ten minutes they felt safe enough to stop within an untended growth of smooth rubber trees, where Alistair jotted down their escape in his notebook. T.K. envied British hacks like Alistair their shorthand, a skill given short shrift by American journalism schools.

"Fill me later?" he asked. "My notebook's back there."

Fresh shots jolted T.K. out of his fatigue. Shadows flitted among the farthest rubber trees. The insurgents went into battle better equipped now, thanks to the C.I.A. Yet soldiers also looted these remote settlements to compensate for unpaid wages or revenge some petty grudge.

T.K.'s knee hurt again as he ran after Alistair. "Sod the bastard," Alistair yelled, and stopped.

The taxi was gone, with half of T.K.'s fifty-dollar bill. If he survived this treachery, he would not patronize Mahmoud again. There were better taxis, but Mahmoud's Garage gave every journalist squeezing into its junk vehicles an individual receipt—with the fare left discreetly blank for expense account purposes.

"My Ministry source," T.K. said, "probably wanted us killed so the rebels would get blamed."

"You make them sound like chess players," said Alistair. "These wankers play checkers."

"Why not tell us the guerrillas were here?"

"There's a logical explanation," Alistair said, "and I haven't the faintest what it is, mate. I know bugger all about nothing anymore."

"Only nothing makes sense to a mushroom journalist," T.K. said.

Their old joke dissipated the tension. As a mushroom journalist, you plied your trade in the dark, and every so often someone dumped another bucket of shit on you.

T.K. stopped to listen. The taxi was returning; it must have gone to fill up the gas tank.

Instead, a squat BMP armored car hove into sight like a menacing tortoise. The machine gunner locked onto them. The commander, wearing goggles, popped from another hatch.

"Foreign press," T.K. said. "Your refugee camp's full of guerrillas."

"Impossible," the commander said in English.

"They're bloody in there," said Alistair, "because they nearly killed us—see for yourself."

The commander barely glanced at their press cards before pocketing them in his camouflage smock. "Journalists are barred from unrest areas, comrades."

"It's not an unrest area, comrade," T.K. said. "It's a frigging combat zone."

"Unrest area, comrades. Come for interrogation." The commander sank through the metal hatch.

T.K. climbed aboard after Alistair, and gave the disappearing commander a rude thumbs-up.

The gesture might mean "Okay" in the States. Out here it translated unequivocally as "Screw you," imputing, moreover, lapses in the recipient's manhood and his mother's morals.

"Want us bloody killed, mate?" protested Alistair.

The insult went unnoticed by the machine gunner, who was busy with an unruly belt of ammunition. The armored car clattered back toward the capital.

"Point that elsewhere, comrade?" Alistair asked.

"We still don't know what happened," T.K. said, "and they don't want us to find out."

Still, he could whip this into a vivid first-person account if he got back to the hotel in time. T.K. banged on the wet hatch, and dropped in a twenty-dollar bill.

"Can we get down to the self-criticism, comrades?" T.K. shouted into the armored car. "We acknowledge and bewail our manifold sins and wickedness, which we, from time to time, most grievously have committed . . ."

* * *

Cass watched the inspector rummage promiscuously through her suitcase in the customs shed. She hadn't slept since Montreal. It seemed forever ago, with three penny-pinching aircraft changes and her accumulation of jet lag. Circling in the old Boeing jetliner as it rode out the storm on the rim of dense clouds, Cass knew she should never have traipsed to the uncharted side of the world.

"So many pretty things," the customs inspector said.

Once the Trident landed, hours late, a dash through the rain left her new running shoes sloshing from puddles on the tarmac and Cass herself so sodden that the customs inspector could see through her sleeveless cotton dress. Certainly he was trying.

"And what have you brought me?" he said.

"Nothing." Cass wiped the rainwater from her pale arms. "I didn't know you."

"You know me now," the customs inspector said. "Your passport?"

When Cass tugged the passport from her backpack, a cornucopia of wallet, traveler's checks, nasal spray, spare eyeglasses, vitamin pills, tampons, hairbrush, tissues, and the meditations of Julian of Norwich in paperback spilled onto the counter. She stuffed it all back, and blinked hard to reposition an errant contact lens.

The inspector held up her passport. "How do you say this name?"

"Cassandra Marie-Clarisse Benoit."

"I see you are Canadian."

"French Canadian, or my father is. My mother's Anglo Canadian, actually, but her mother, my maternal grandmother, was Ukrainian Canadian, you see—"

"Curious," the customs inspector said. "We do love Canadians, but you are curious."

"I explained this to immigration. See, he's stamped the visa in my passport."

"He did not explain to me," the customs inspector said. "You come as a tourist? My wife's brother has a taxi, he can show you around."

"I'm a journalist for public radio, in America."

The inspector sampled her bottle of contact lens solution.

"Come to tell the truth about our poor country?"

"Don't journalists tell the truth?" Cass asked.

"Not here," the inspector said. "Americans are the worst—the C.I.A. makes them lie. Your press card?"

Cass reached into her backpack for the letter of introduction. "My editors wrote this to your ministry that handles us foreign correspondents. I present it tomorrow for accreditation."

"No press card."

"Actually," said Cass, "I'm starting out."

The customs inspector sighed and handed back her passport. "What do you have to declare?"

"Nothing really."

"Yes, you do—your charm." The inspector flashed a gold tooth and turned to fondling her underwear.

"I suppose so," said Cass. Her contact lens was wandering again.

"And for me, some little gift?" Taking her silence as assent, he dug into her backpack and found the new Sony tape recorder that would launch her new career.

"I cannot allow this in without a permit," the inspector said, "which you may apply for after you receive your accreditation, but first you must show them your recorder—how to solve our problem?"

Cass said nothing. After the roller-coaster flight, the odor of chlorine and sweat permeating the hall made her nauseous.

The customs inspector dismissed her with a wave. "Wait until we have time to study your case," he said. "You see how busy we are."

Behind her, weary passengers lined up with their oversized bundles and cardboard boxes.

"I do have a gift." Cass pulled out the stereo radio that Marc had given her for Christmas. She wouldn't be here if she had Marc.

The inspector donned the earphones, turned up the volume, and suddenly went fuzzy. "Welcome to the Equatorian People's Democratic Socialist Republic," he said. "Next?"

Crumbs, she'd lost it now. With her other eye, Cass scanned the counter for the missing lens, without result.

"Welcome to Equatoria," the customs inspector said more sharply. "Next?"

Her suitcase, packed snugly back in Montreal, would not close. She shoveled in what she could, hoping that the lost lens was included. The left-over running shorts and *Save Our Dolphins* sweatshirt went into her back-pack.

Cass had yet to reach the exit with her typewriter and suitcase, whose small wheels now refused to turn, when a young man in a baggy white shirt intercepted her.

"You may claim your luggage outside after we X-ray it," he said in charming English, and took her suitcase. Cass, clutching her typewriter, smiled back, appreciative of the first courtesy shown in this strange country.

"Thank you." She hoped he would not expect a tip.

Despite the rain, the air outside was redolent of heat and dust, not at all like the forests of Quebec. The carousel had yet to move. Other passengers flowed past but Cass waited politely, the way Canadians do knee-deep in a blizzard while they watch for the traffic light to turn green on a deserted street.

A gaunt woman with two dirty children and a baby lashed to her back materialized to beg in a strange tongue. Cass laid a few Canadian dollars in the outstretched hand. She could not afford to be benevolent, but the beggar had looked about the same age as Cass.

Fifteen minutes, then a half hour passed and the carousel did not rotate, nor had any passengers joined her. And wasn't luggage X-rayed before a flight, not after it?

She lifted the rubber curtain and peered into the baggage shed. It was empty. She rushed back inside, but the charming youth was gone. So were the police.

"Pretty lady, this way to my taxi," said a heavyset man, when she emerged.

"My suitcase is being X-rayed," Cass said.

"The X-ray is broken many months." The taxi driver shook his head sympathetically. "You have dollars to pay for the ride, yes?"

Crumbs, how naive she was to trust anyone. She felt for her tape recorder, passport, excursion ticket good for forty-five days, but the airline might let her leave sooner, if only she wouldn't cry.

* * *

Ginny sat in the lobby of the Hotel Ritz composing her thank-you note to another white male news executive.

"When I said your office would make a perfect day-care center," she wrote, "I meant only that it was large and sunny enough for a day-care center, not that it should become a day-care center."

Ginny had agreed to meet her new source on the hotel veranda because the security police staked out his office. It had taken the storm to drive her inside. She should have gone off with T.K. and Alistair, but Ginny could not bring herself to grill another grieving widow.

"And when you asked me where I saw myself in five years if your newspaper hired me," she wrote, "and I said I saw myself in your job, I didn't mean that I deserved your job, at least not yet."

The rain pelted the windowpanes. Inside, the lobby looked even bleaker, down to its plastic flowers. The rouged whores who gave the Ritz its notoriety promenaded listlessly under the ceiling fans. The drab Hotel Turissimo where Ginny stayed looked antiseptic by comparison.

"But you said your newspaper wanted more diversity," Ginny wrote, "so I assumed your job was included."

No, that wouldn't do. Ginny chewed on her ballpoint pen. The news executives who interviewed her expected minority applicants to be seen but not heard, like polite children, whereas Ginny was outspoken to a fault.

Never lie, her Aunt Edna taught her, be direct. But it did cut short a lot of job interviews.

And Ginny needed a break. Her colleagues assumed that a reporter of color would glide easily through the Third World. But government officials more often patronized or propositioned her, whether because she was black or female Ginny didn't know. Were such indignities inflicted on journalism's dewy white birds of paradise? Probably not. Their bright hair and eyes invited confidence, while Ginny roamed indistinct from her surroundings.

When Ginny looked out the door for her overdue source, a blue van had arrived. Policeman poured out like clowns from a circus car and marched into the lobby. The whores scattered.

It was their problem; she mustn't make it hers. T.K. had taught her that much. Ginny returned to her letter.

"I appreciate the time you took to interview me," she wrote, "and remain interested in a reporting position at your newspaper."

Or any good newspaper with a regular paycheck and health insurance.

Ginny was weary of juggling the handful of small newspapers she had strung together, of rewriting the news she gathered for five different readerships.

Around Ginny, the whores were screaming, flailing at the policemen who drove them like geese into the rain. She felt a jab. A policeman cursed her in a language she could not understand.

"Foreign press." Ginny looked up. "African-American, Baptist." She fumbled for her passport and credentials.

The policeman's truncheon struck her shoulder. Ginny raised her arm before the next blow slammed down. She heard the crack. Pain consumed bone between her wrist and elbow.

The police dragged her to the van where the whores were wailing. A door slammed, trapping her in their cheap perfume, the lock clicked, the van began to move.

She would stop feeling sorry, get to work, find a story somewhere in this. Ginny pulled out her notebook, but her hand could not grip the ballpoint pen.

* * *

"Get on the bird," said the disembodied voice from network news in New York. Another story looked destined for the shelf because Schuyler couldn't find the geosynchronous satellite floating for him in space.

"We're trying to feed," Schuyler shouted into the telephone.

"You lose your window if you're not on the bird."

"I've got you A-roll, B-roll, all kinds of bird shit," Schuyler told New York. "Helluva storm knocked us out."

"Any later and you'll crash," the voice said. "We've got better visuals of traffic jams on the Cross Bronx Expressway than what you sent lately. Guys in the goldfish bowl thought your last transmission was the pits, quality-wise. What happened?"

"Sure looked good leaving here," Schuyler said. "Must be too many folks breaking into television these days."

* * *

As he did most nights after filing his stories, T.K. passed up the dismal hotel food and walked down to the Cafe Peri-Peri. The hacks had staked out the concrete patio. An evening's accumulation of beer cans littered the metal tables.

"Your crew chases after massacres like they were rainbows," T.K. told Schuyler, and popped the top of his frosty can of Castle Lager.

The hacks descended on the Cafe Peri-Peri not just for a meal but for a nightly ritual at which they unwound after filing and swapped bawdy yarns about covering old wars and new famines. Antonio, the expatriate Portuguese owner, wooed them with his incendiary peri-peri sauce, crusty bread, and black market beer chilled to five dollars a can.

"This massacre's worth checking out," Schuyler said. "They say it happened near the railway junction. We've chartered a Cessna to fly up for a look."

"With shovel and minicamera?" T.K. let the cold beer trickle down his throat. The junction was already so bombed that more slaughter couldn't bounce the rubble any higher.

An empty beer can hit the stucco wall, dropping a gecko from its vertical perch. Hacks cheered the lizard's demise.

"We want to find out how many got chopped and who did it," Schuyler said. "Catch what's left on tape. That's why we bring the shovel."

A police truck cruised the boulevard, its machine gun swiveling from one shadow to the next. Under the plane trees along the sidewalk, ragged urchins poised to scramble for whatever scraps the diners might leave.

"Count me in," T.K. said. "What's my share, five hundred bucks again?"

"Alistair and Ginny took the last seats," Schuyler said.

By T.K's fast calculation, Schuyler and his crew made three, plus Alistair, Ginny, and the minder sent by the government. Six in a Cessna left no room, but he had to go too—what if the others stumbled onto something?

"If Ginny drops out, you could take her place," said Schuyler, "or fly up commercial. I hear they siphoned enough gas from the air force to resume flights."

T.K. had a boarding pass from his last flight on Equatorian People's Airways, which never showed up. And the World Bank repossessed the airline's thirdhand Boeing 707, which left the prop-driven Ilyushins. T.K. tried to avoid planes older than he was. Still, he needed a change; the same old story kept coming around here.

"Screw you," said the waiter. "Lovely grilled chicken?"

"Abednego," T.K. said, "find some frigging shrimp."

"All gone last month." Abednego passed over the plates and headed back to the kitchen.

"Peri-peri, Abednego," Schuyler called. "I need more hot sauce to make this roadkill edible."

Schuyler's request was lost in the drone of aircraft overhead. Tonight, no jetfighters screamed or helicopter gunships clattered to signal another government offensive. These sounded like Antonov transports ferrying ammunition and rations to garrisons beleaguered in the interior.

But why would Ginny drop out? She could fend for herself, but T.K. still liked to watch over her.

"She got mugged yesterday," Schuyler said, "busted her arm."

"Someone call the police?"

"They *were* the police," Schuyler said. "Swept Ginny up with the whores at the Ritz, didn't you hear?"

"I was feeding the goat," said T.K., justifying his ignorance of Ginny's plight. If his newspaper was an insatiable beast, devouring whatever he sent it night after night, the jargon for filing a news story made sense. Alistair, in his perversely English way, called it "playing kitten on the keyboard."

"What'd you find to feed the goat?" Schuyler stopped eating.

T.K. shrugged. His interview with the President had been postponed again. He loved hacks like Schuyler and would lay down his life for them, but such sacrifice stopped well short of sharing an exclusive interview.

"I went down today to customs to clear the new laptop my masters sent," T.K. said. "Some wanker stole it and left me a teddy bear."

A winsome stranger nodded sympathetically from the far side of the table, but to Alistair. T.K. did not recognize her through the curtain of light brown hair spilling across her fresh face. She sat with an open notebook, like a freshman attending her first college lecture, her pen poised like a dart.

"First you tell the who, what, when, and where of your news story," Alistair was saying, "and then the why."

The wide-eyed stranger wrote this down. "Why not put the why first," she asked, "or else it won't make sense?"

"We're covering a country in which nothing makes sense," Alistair said. "It's not our task to impose a logic that isn't here."

Alistair's friend looked too mousy for a Hairy-Legged Swedish Girl for Peace. Aid worker perhaps, or missionary. Whatever she was, Alistair would fumble his chances, which left T.K.

"But why?" she was saying. "I'd still want to know why, eh?" She caught T.K. staring and looked away with disdain.

"Abednego," T.K. yelled, "some frigging shrimp."

"Screw you," Abednego yelled back. "Lovely shrimp next month if the boats go home."

Before the colonialists departed with whatever they could haul—down to the iron rails on which small trams once plied the cobbled streets—Porto Despondo, as Equatoria's capital was named long ago by a homesick sailor, was famed for its seafood, especially the prawns and lobsters plucked fresh off the wooden boats. Its restaurants skimmed the day's catch before exporting the rest to Europe.

When the new Marxist government renamed the capital Porto Paradiso, fishermen were drafted to fight the rebels, the palm trees fringing the harbor were chopped down, the beaches were sown with mines, and the government licensed Russian trawlers to vacuum the seabed of marine life in return for Moscow's deliveries of AK-47's. Now shrimp or fish seldom got as far as the Cafe Peri-Peri, only the scrawny chickens that Antonio bought in the market at prices beyond the reach of ordinary Equatorians.

"Chicken then, heavy on the peri-peri and more beer." T.K. turned to Alistair; the stranger was enough of a looker to warrant some details.

"Cassandra Benoit," Alistair said, "it's T.K., like the 'to come' that you stick in your story when you can't find an elusive statistic. T.K., Cass is starting—"

The newcomer sniffled into her handkerchief. "I'm a working journalist too," she said. "Isn't everyone here?"

She was suspect. Practitioners of T.K.'s noble craft described themselves as reporters or newspaperfolk or correspondents or hacks or scribblers or ink-stained wretches, but never journalists unless they scuttled off to enrich themselves in public relations, when truth in packaging required them to add the modifier of "former."

And these hacks weren't working. They were goofing off in what they called a "ceasefile," which required notepads to stay mutually holstered in back pockets. Her open notebook affronted standards of decency at the

Peri-Peri. She didn't belong here, not in a sleeveless white summer dress that bared her clean limbs to potential malaria and encephalitis, while veteran hacks respected the cafe's dress code of faded jeans, multipocketed vests, T-shirts, and plastic flip-flops.

"Our delicious new colleague has come from faraway Canada to invigorate us," Alistair said. "She couldn't find a spot to jog this morning. Too many trucks, she said, and the masses stared. Where would you advise?"

"Try downtown," T.K. said. "The stoplights don't work."

"Screw you, gentlemen." Abednego emerged from the kitchen. "Who gets lovely chicken?" T.K. grabbed a plate.

"Does he always talk this dirty?" Cass swept back her long hair, and her face and arms shimmered bone-white under the string of colored lights. So many hacks had clustered around her that if the big round table were a boat, it would have capsized.

"We had to teach Abednego, okay?" said Rolf, a photographer of indeterminate Nordic origin who had squeezed in downwind of Cass. "His English's pretty focking limited."

"Then he doesn't know what he's saying?" asked Cass, ignoring the appeal, *Kiss Me, I'm Horny,* across Rolf's grubby T-shirt. She squirmed as the dinner conversation inexorably deteriorated. Another beer can hit the wall.

"Fock you, too, Abednego," shouted Rolf over the personal din of his Walkman. "Bring my shit fast, okay? I'm laying heavy pipe tonight."

"Bonking again?" Alistair asked.

"Women are like rugs, okay?" Rolf's earphones looked fused to his skull. "Lay them right the first time and you can walk over them for life."

Did he turn down the volume when he bedded his prey? Probably not. Rolf's sex appeal was one of those mysteries as unfathomable to T.K. as DNA. Rolf shaved just enough to maintain his albino stubble. He bathed only when his bathtub was not full of Dektol and the other chemicals used to process his film. His speech was unspeakable, yet Rolf was notorious for seldom sleeping alone, even when stoned.

"Wanna know my secret?" Rolf said. "Go ugly fast."

"Rolf, you stick your prick in places I wouldn't put the tip of my umbrella," Alistair said.

Rolf responded with a thumbs-up-yours.

Cass had sought refuge in an assiduous study of the dog-eared menu.

She held it high enough for T.K. to read the notice on the back: "Our drinking water is passed personally by the waiter before your meal."

"Screw you, gentlemen." Abednego emerged with more plates balanced along each arm. "Lovely grilled chicken?"

"May I please have . . . your garden salad?" Cass flinched at the ricochet of another beer can.

"Lovely garden salad?" Abednego looked stunned.

"Yes, your lovely garden salad," T.K. said. This triggered guffaws around the table.

"Ignore him, Cass," Alistair said. "Antonio's garden salad is, ah, therapeutic. I recommend it if you're feeling constipated. Avoid it otherwise, along with everything else here that isn't cooked or peeled."

Cass let the tattered menu drop. "Is the bread safe?" She turned to Alistair. "I'm rather short of money until I get paid."

She was in for sticker shock. The long-standing rule, or at least custom, was that hacks eating together divided the bill without regard to who consumed what. This avoided bickering, while elevating the tab because no one tried to eat or drink less than he paid for.

"Since it's Cassandra's first night out," Alistair said, "our treat this time, agreed?" Murmurs of assent preempted the objection that T.K. prepared to raise.

"Abednego," Alistair said, "bring our lovely new colleague a peri-peri chicken with chips and a cold lager, imported—not that piss you drain from your goat out back."

"Screw you, gentleman," the waiter said.

"Abednego, have your chef sauté my potatoes in something polyunsaturated," Cass said, "no tropical oils, thank you. And a glass for my beer, if you please."

T.K. snorted. If anyone could use a salad, it was Cassandra Benoit.

"Thank you all for being so kind," Cass said. Her eyes skipped over T.K. "In return, I . . ."

"Yes?" prompted Alistair.

"I was aerobically certified in college. We'll start a morning class at the hotel."

The hush that followed was broken only by the smoker's rasp of Schuyler's cameraman, Kobus. Had someone belched or broken wind, it would not have embarrassed the crowd as Cass's offer did.

"First I must cash some traveler's checks," she said. "What time do the banks open?"

"Don't you carry money?" T.K. emptied his beer can and winged it at a gecko, but it landed short.

"Traveler's checks are money," she said.

"Waste a day standing in line at the People's Bank to exchange them into Equatorian funny money at the worst rate? That's not what my editors pay me for."

T.K. pulled a succession of creased hundred-dollar bills from his money belt like some sleight of magic. He waved a five-hundred-dollar bill from his desert boot. "Money," he said.

"I . . . never carry that much cash." Cass blew into her handkerchief. "I have sixty dollars, maybe—forty of that's Canadian."

"American dollars are the accepted currency," said Alistair. "Or imported beer cans."

"Or AK-47's," Schuyler said. "Country's awash in them. AK goes for sixty bucks now in the black market."

Cass wrote this down too, though every hack knew about the assault rifle designed by a guy named Kalashnikov and first issued back in 1947. The Soviets dumped millions around the world, so did the Czechs, Bulgarians, and Chinese. The originals had almost vanished, but more modern versions got referred to as AK-47's too, because who wanted to check for modifications if the damned thing was pointed at you?

T.K. turned to Schuyler. "I'll take Ginny's seat if she can't go."

Schuyler, who had swallowed too much peri-peri sauce, pointed to Alistair, who gave an awkward sigh.

"I offered it to Cass," he said, "in case Ginny can't go. I thought your bad knee put you out too."

"If she's not going, I get Ginny's seat," T.K. said. "Otherwise, I've got to fly Vanessa up commercial."

Kobus gave a whistle. "First-class ride on that redheaded ass of hers."

T.K. winked back. A trip worth taking.

Cass, who had picked the chicken clean, stopped stacking lard-fried potatoes on the back of her fork.

"Do you harass all your women colleagues behind their backs?" she said.

"Vanessa is, well, a sexual commando." Alistair's defensiveness was unseemly. "She has to steal the hotel sheets because that's where she writes her notes."

"What I'm hearing are sexist double standards," Cass said. "Crumbs, you make this poor lady sound like a slut, but when your friend here"—she looked for Rolf, who had left for his plumbing appointment—"boasted of his pathetic promiscuity, you cheered him on."

"Rolf thinks he's a stud," said T.K., who thought Rolf far more of a jerk. She wouldn't know that in these backwaters, free-lance photographers were as populous and welcome as body lice.

"The difference between a stud and a slut is gender," Cass said. "Sexist code language like that is . . ."

Abednego appeared. "Screw you, gentlemen and lady. Who wants lovely coffee?"

". . . totally unacceptable." Cass kicked back her chair and led the waiter off by the elbow.

T.K. expected her to scold Abednego, though in fact they were smiling and shaking hands. Cass wrote something in her notebook and recited it with the waiter. She left him the paper and returned.

"I get Ginny's seat, agreed?" T.K. said.

Ignoring him, Cass took a swig straight from her beer can and dug into what remained of her fried potatoes. She did have an appetite.

Abednego approached, smiling at Cass.

"Thank you, dear gentlemen. Thank you, dear lady. Who wants lovely coffee?"

The hacks groaned. "What a spoilsport," T.K. said.

She slammed down her fork. "Making our waiter the butt of your twisted jokes, that's your notion of sport, eh? He thought he was being polite. He supports a wife and five kids on whatever you tip him."

"How do you know?" said T.K. "He doesn't speak English."

"He learned Spanish from the Cubans and I speak a little, so we communicated. Which is more than you and I'll do. Crumbs, I've taught fourth-graders with better manners."

Having concluded her little speech, Cass shoved back the chair, slapped her Canadian dollars on the table, and walked out.

Her exit might have been more dramatic had she not backed into the tray of dirty crockery. The top few dishes slid to the concrete with a crash that turned heads. Cass fielded the next dish, barely, and returned it precariously to the stack.

"I'm myopically inconvenienced," Cass told no one in particular. She renewed her retreat, more successfully this time.

T.K. appraised her with the hack's eye for detail. Nice enough ass but flat-chested, judging by the lack of jiggle, and too tall for Alistair though not for himself.

"So aerobics takes cellulite from your thighs," T.K. said, "and parks it between your ears?"

"Cassandra is scared because she's new," Alistair said, "and beset by foul-mouthed hacks like us."

"Let her learn to swim with the piranhas."

"She fell for the old X-ray fiddle at the airport," Alistair said.

Her gullibility proved T.K.'s point. Hacks only traveled with hand baggage. Hacks never took anything that couldn't be toted at a dead run for a mile.

"It's her first job," Alistair said, "stringing for radio. No one else wanted to come. She was teaching school in Quebec till a few weeks ago." He jumped up. "I'll escort my dolly bird back to the hotel, she's prone to collision."

"Escort your H.L.S.G.P. into bed," T.K. said, "and give me your seat on the charter."

"Don't call Cass a Hairy-Legged Swedish Girl for Peace," Alistair said. "She's Canadian, not Swedish, she isn't hairy, except for that marvelous hair of hers, and she's entitled to causes. But H.L.S.G.P.s screw for theirs and Cass doesn't, I expect—not for ink-stained wretches like you and me."

* * *

When T.K. looked in on Ginny, her arm was swaddled in a sling. Worse, her laptop computer wouldn't transmit.

"You do get into mischief without us, sis," he said. "You could have gone swimming in shit with Alistair and me."

"They dumped us in the bush." Ginny's trademark serenity had deserted her. "Took me all night to flag down a truck, driver wanted fifty dollars to carry us back."

"And the girls?"

"We drove them in too." Ginny winced as T.K. touched her arm. "Wasn't their fault. Their payoff to the cops was late."

T.K. set down a napkin with some chicken that he had brought her from the cafe.

"Which first, your arm or the computer?" he asked.

"The nuns did my arm at the Chinese hospital," Ginny said. "They don't do computers."

Irish nuns ran the brick hospital now but everyone called it after the Chinese, who built it years earlier in a failed effort to woo Equatoria out of the Soviet orbit.

T.K. ran his hands over Ginny's computer. "Software seems okay." He would have told her about the ditzy newcomer who called herself a working journalist, but Ginny had feminist tendencies herself.

"How'd your job interview go?" he said.

"I haven't heard." Ginny sighed. "I don't know if I come on too diverse or not diverse enough."

He followed the wires out to a coupler gripping the telephone handset. "Computer's okay," he said, "so it must be your connection."

"Their notion of a minority hire," Ginny said, "is someone who wore gang colors through Harvard Law School."

T.K. unscrewed the telephone and tapped the mouthpiece. Bits of dirt rattled into the wastebasket.

"Carbon buildup," T.K. said. "Try it now." The modem chimed. "You're connected, sis."

Ginny's copy flowed through the screen with nary a hyphen in sight. Anyone who dashed off sentences that good deserved to write them for one big newspaper, not have to hustle for a pack of little ones.

"It'll take me hours to do the rest of this," she said, "and file it to five papers."

"Go to bed, write it better tomorrow, and give me your seat on the charter—you can't go into the bush banged up like that."

"I do owe you." Ginny massaged her forearm.

"Only your undying love," T.K. said, "but I'll settle for your place on that Cessna. Otherwise, I've got to fly up commercial with Vanessa."

Ginny sniffed disapproval. "Not Vanessa?"

"She invited herself along. She wants to cool the striped trousers of that Brazilian diplomat—"

He caught himself in midsentence. Ginny was too much a lady.

"Set your sights higher, T.K.," Ginny told him. "You're a good-looking guy, or could be if you'd shave more often and start hanging out with grown-ups."

"I'm over the hill," T.K. said, "forty years old next month—now that's a secret, Ginny."

"What's forty years?" Ginny laughed. "I saw redwoods older than you back home."

"I'm looking at my fourth decade," T.K. said, "for a hack, that's ancient."

"Technically," said Ginny, "you're moving into your fifth decade. The first started when you were born, see, so you've been in your fourth decade for the last ten years."

"Sorry I mentioned it."

"Okay," Ginny said. "If you're that decrepit and my arm won't travel, maybe I'll give you my seat on the charter."

* * *

A telephone jangled. Jolted awake, T.K. rolled out under the mosquito net, groped for the telephone. A call this late portended humiliating word of a rival's exclusive that he could not hope to match at this hour.

"Updating your riot for us?" The foreign editor spoke as if hollering down a rain barrel.

"What riot?" It took a few moments for T.K. to sort out what hotel, what town, what country he was in. Had rampaging mobs been sacking the capital, live on CNN, while he slept?

"About this Chinese riot thing," the foreign editor said, "I need our Hong Kong chap."

"I'm in Equatoria," T.K. said, "where some bastard switched the laptop you sent for a teddy bear."

"Wanda," the foreign editor shouted, "T.K.'s turn with Scoopie Bear? Okay, that's why I called—you didn't read my letter?"

T.K.'s kneecap still ached from the collision in the refugee camp. "Mail takes six weeks," he said. "Whose sick joke is this?"

"Our publisher's. Scoopie belongs to his little granddaughter. Her kindergarten's learning geography by pouching the teddy bear on a round-robin of our foreign bureaus. They track it on the map we publish, great circulation promotion."

T.K. snickered. No one bought a paper to read about a Fed-Exed teddy bear. Readers demanded real news.

"Circulation's up twelve thousand in our primary market area since the Lifestyle section featured Scoopie Bear on Wednesdays," the foreign editor said. "It's visited Buckingham Palace with our London bureau chief, climbed Mount Fujiyama with our Tokyo correspondent, ridden a camel around the Pyramids with our Cairo—"

"So Scoopie Bear's come here to show kids the jolly side of war?"

"TV filled that niche. You take it on a picnic in the bush, have it meet lots of exotic animals."

No way. T.K. wasn't traveling with any frigging stuffed bear.

"We need photos, too, so don't fake its dateline," the foreign editor said. "When you're back, write us nine hundred words for our Scoopie Bear Scoop box. You're creative enough, judging by your expense accounts. Then pouch the bear's ass to Rio, gotta get it up the Amazon and back here before school lets out."

"Tomorrow, I'm looking for a massacre."

"Hey, no risks—kiddies'll be pissed if anything happens to their Scoopie."

"Why not replace us all with teddy bears?" T.K. said. The Newspaper Guild wouldn't notice.

"Journalism's in a new era, got to push the product, give our readers what they want."

"It's a newspaper, not a product."

"You don't approve?" the foreign editor said. "I'll tell the publisher you're too busy to bring some joy to his little granddaughter. He won't forget when he approves the next Paris correspondent. Did I tell you he wants to open a shopping mall beat here?"

Covering shopping malls, not coups or famines?

"Scoopie goes into the bush with me at dawn," T.K. said. "Tell the publisher his little bear's safe with me."

"And you keep up the heavy hitting, T.K. Slam us a home run every time you step up to that computer."

"They play soccer in Equatoria."

"Put that in Scoopie's dispatch," said the foreign editor. "Circulation can use it to build market penetration. Hey, d'you buy that parrot?"

"What parrot?" T.K. asked.

"Must be our chap in Yemen, or is it Oman? Cheers."

The sweet soprano of the news clerk chirped in even as the foreign editor hung up. "Filing late again?"

Filing a newspaper story was a delicate matter of timing, early enough for the first edition but too late for the desk editors to put pawprints all over your pristine prose.

"I already filed," T.K. said, "front-page stuff."

"It's not in our computer system," the clerk said.

The line clicked; the security police were back. Filing from one computer to another was like shaking hands. As long as the hands clasped, T.K.'s story rode an electronic highway from his laptop to the mainframe at his newspaper across the world. When the handshake was broken, even momentarily, the signal died. It happened whenever the police tapped into his telephone, now that the East Germans were no longer around to supervise the repression.

"They're screwing up my line tonight. I'll dictate to the recording room, okay?"

"She's having a baby," the news clerk said. "No one replaced her because of the downsizing. If you can't resend by computer, maybe telex or fax it."

T.K. printed out a copy on the printer rigged to his laptop computer and ran down the stairs to the hotel lobby.

The reception desk was deserted. "Dear guests," said the notice taped above the counter. "We bear no response for your values if they are not reposed with us."

Off the lobby, the telex machine remained swaddled in chains, despite someone's attempt to split the steel links with an ax. Anything of value got chained down in Equatoria.

T.K. looked for the fax machine bought by the hotel management to gouge more money from journalists. His hopes plummeted.

The aerobics-certified, myopically inconvenienced feminist from Quebec crouched over the machine, handpiece tucked between her shoulder and a damp tangle of honey-brown hair. The red and green wire entrails running from her recorder into the fax machine weren't cooperating, judging by the desperation with which she pushed the buttons.

"That's a fax," T.K. said.

She waved him off as if swatting an insect.

T.K. raised his voice. "How long you going to take?"

"Hush." Her free hand fluttered again. "I'm feeding Recording Central."

"Feed them a telephone, I need the fax."

"Telephone in my room doesn't work. Five minutes, maybe ten, eh?" she said. "Return to your place in the queue."

T.K. glanced at his watch. He would miss the first edition. He muscled her aside and grabbed for the handset.

"Takes just a minute," he said.

Her tape recorder careened off the table and onto the floor, nearly dragging down the fax machine. He never saw her running shoe before it lashed out in reprisal, catching the tender cartilage under his kneecap that got slammed out at the squatter camp.

The agony buckled him over. Flashes of pain coursed through his extremities. When he could stand, he found himself staring down into slate-colored eyes. A smoldering anger was bottled up behind her eyeglasses. Even her small nose looked inflamed.

"That was unprofessional." She snatched the handset, pressing it against her belly like a quarterback protecting a football. "So unprofessional."

"Why not aim for my—"

"I didn't expect you had any," Cass snapped.

T.K. fell back in confusion while she retrieved her tape recorder. She redialed and began again. After a few false starts, she slammed down the handset.

"Go ahead if you're so important. My luggage was stolen, I lost my contact lens, and now I'm missing my first deadline." She sniffled loudly, whether from self-pity or clogged sinuses he wasn't sure.

Warily, he stepped up to the fax machine.

"You've taken it apart, for crissake," he said.

"Never helps to blaspheme." Cass chewed on a long strand of her hair while T.K. rebuilt enough of the fax machine to send his article. Even so, he hobbled away with some remorse.

"The telephone in your room might work if you unscrew the mouthpiece and tap out the carbon dust," he said. "They tend to plug up here."

"I don't need your advice." Her sweatshirt proclaimed Cass as the sort who braked for dolphins, not for him.

"You're a long way from Quebec."

Cass hesitated. "Shawinigan," she said, "but I was teaching school near Montreal."

"Who's milking the cows back in Shawinigan"—T.K. did not hide the sarcasm—"until your fourteen-day excursion ticket runs out?"

"It's valid for forty-five days." She tossed the freshly washed hair back from her face. "And Shawinigan has aluminum smelters and paper mills."

She wore what looked like a wedding ring, but on her right fist.

"And I presume," Cass said, mentally dismembering him through her smudged spectacles, "you became a foreign correspondent to perpetuate your adolescence?"

2.

PORTO PARADISO, Equatoria—Bullets whined through the tamarind leaves as the brutal insurgency here entered its sixteenth year without any sign of peace between the pro-Marxist government and its guerrilla opponents.

A lull in fighting that followed the failure of the government's latest offensive was broken . . .

———————

T.K. had boarding passes in hand, but the time he hoped to gain by leaving at dawn for the airport was lost waiting for Vanessa. He slept badly after his run-in with the news twink, and Ginny hadn't called. The sun cleared the horizon and the taxi driver was cursing by the time Vanessa appeared in Vuarnet sunglasses, concealing the likelihood that she had just woken up.

"I was filing," said Vanessa, who never apologized.

His stomach contorted into the familiar knot. What pillow talk had she gleaned from her Brazilian diplomat?

T.K. put her suitcase in the front seat; Vanessa wasn't the backpack type. What had she found to file?

Vanessa never explained either. Accepting T.K.'s hand, she stepped into the taxi. What a pity that Cass wasn't there to see the company he kept. Vanessa was so blue-eyed and petite that you wanted to park her in your pocket, though you might find your wallet missing later.

The taxi pulled away, and Vanessa spread across the back seat her hairbrush, makeup kit, and other utensils of her morning ritual.

"They're like tarts in a brothel, aren't they?" she said. Vanessa was at it again, belittling the writers at her magazine who toiled like alchemists to transubstantiate her gummy prose into hard copy.

"They sit around all week in those cubicles, don't they?" Vanessa had T.K hold her mirror while she pursed her lips and traced on some gloss, then set to thickening her eyelashes.

"On Friday nights," she said, "they bang away and the editor keeps popping in like a madam? And the weekend's one big douche, isn't it? Turkeys, my dear, while we soar like eagles."

T.K. had flunked his tryout at news magazine writing and envied those who could do it, but not at the risk of offending Vanessa on the cusp of a dirty weekend. She had a few miles on her odometer, but in the candlelight glow of an evening power failure, Vanessa could still trigger a hormonal buzz in the gonads of her male competition.

The route to the airport passed through a capital once celebrated as the Paris of the Equator but now fallen on hard times like a consumptive whore. Infectious decay spread across the neglected facades, peeling away the colonial rococo ornamentation, exposing swaths of crumbling brick. Telephone poles in fading barbershop stripes lined the street like skeletons strangled by the sagging wires. The balconies of passing tenements overflowed with junk—a bent bicycle, a broken icebox, lines of flapping laundry. Through an open window blared a tinny radio.

It was early, but men desperate for a day's hire were congregating on street corners. Under the arcade, a trio of amputees in cast-off uniforms leaned together on crude crutches to share the dregs of a bottle of raw moonshine called lombo. A woman bathed her children in water spilling from a broken pipe. Other women lined up to fill their plastic buckets. The departing colonialists had poured cement down the pipes of the high rises they left behind.

The taxi passed a grubby intersection denuded of a billboard that once depicted smiling workers in stride below a slogan: "Socialism is the future!" Refugees had torn it down one night to turn into shanties.

"If your dark curls were mine," Vanessa told T.K., "I'd forbid them to snip off a single lock, you dear child, not one lock." Her fingers parked T.K.'s shaggy hair behind one ear, then the other. "They make you so romantic, like Frédéric Chopin, but every woman must tell you that."

Every woman never had, only Vanessa, so why disillusion her?

A traffic light swung lifeless at the intersection, where barefoot children competed with two dogs and a goat for desiccated garbage. The wall beyond was littered with the graffiti of officially mandated optimism: *VIC ORY OR DEAT IS C RTAIN.* And *LIV THE STRUG LE OF THE PROL TARIAT.*

The wall hid a hard-currency store stocked with French cognac, Danish beer, American panty hose, and Japanese VCRs reserved for the party elite, while the proletariat queued up elsewhere to struggle for rationed cornmeal and cooking oil. The self-proclaimed popular democratic republics that T.K. covered invariably revealed themselves as neither popular nor democratic nor republican.

Vanessa produced a brochure. "A new luxury hotel opened on the way to the railway junction, it says here."

"Can't be," T.K. said. They'd go broke paying off both sides.

"Supposed to open last month, it says, overlooking the river. I couldn't phone through, so we may have to share." Vanessa fixed him with her brazen blue eyes.

"No problem," T.K. told tonight's busty little roommate, if all went as planned.

The taxi arrived at the airport, where T.K. outraged the driver by paying in local dinars. Vanessa left her bags for T.K. to carry.

"Write down my share," she said. "I'll pay you later."

"Whenever." T.K. needed the money, but why risk his chances with Vanessa by fussing?

Now that the airline was flying again, a host of travelers overwhelmed the check-in counter. Some had camped there long enough that they huddled inside blankets or brewed porridge on portable stoves.

"Now be assertive, T.K.," Vanessa said.

He squeezed behind the counter and found the agent, a harried man in flip-flops. T.K. waved the boarding passes, which had cost him fifty dollars under the table downtown, and proposed taking Vanessa directly to the plane.

"Your passes are blue, comrade," the agent said. "Today's are yellow."

"Please exchange these, comrade?"

"No more yellow, comrade."

T.K. palmed a fresh fifty-dollar bill with the blue passes. "Anything you can do, comrade."

"We've had two cancellations, comrade." The agent pocketed the fifty dollars and pulled two yellow passes from a stack inside his drawer.

"Write my share down," said Vanessa.

The airport metal detector was still broken, which spared T.K. the bother of explaining why he carried enough steel in his hip to set off the alarm. A policeman poked into T.K.'s pack and Vanessa's bags, whacked their laptop computers together to confirm no explosives were inside. He felt T.K. from armpits to crotch, and put Vanessa through a more thorough fondling before waving them out to the tarmac.

The only aircraft was a patched Ilyushin-18 with fresh bullet holes in the tail. Passengers milled about.

"Boarding passes, comrades?" the pilot called from atop the rickety ramp. A rainbow of cardboard waved back.

"I don't know our color today, comrades," said the pilot, who wore a shirt with ragged epaulets. Ignoring the shouts, he consulted a formidable stewardess beside him, but she shrugged.

"We shall resolve this democratically, comrades," the pilot said, "with a footrace, twice clockwise around my plane. Winners board first; the rest must wait for the next flight, so do not lose your boarding passes."

Far from complaining, some passengers seemed to have done this before, judging by the head starts they took.

"One, two, three, go, comrades!" the pilot cried.

T.K. struggled to stay abreast, with Vanessa hanging on his arm.

"Around the wing, comrades, not under it," the pilot said. An old woman taking the shortcut hit a stationary propeller and caused a pileup. At the back straggled those passengers unwilling to jettison their boom boxes, sacks of cornmeal, and poultry.

By employing his elbows, T.K. found himself on the ramp. Vanessa, last seen in the final sprint, called from a few steps below. "Assert yourself," she pleaded.

A reassuring odor of high-octane gasoline wafted from inside the cabin. It belied rumors that Equatorian Peoples Airways cut its scarce aviation fuel with palm oil.

"Seats full, comrades." The stewardess blocked the door before T.K. could reach it. "Coffins for next four passengers only." The wooden coffins being loaded from the other side and shoved down the aisle looked empty enough, but preowned.

"I didn't pay to sit on a coffin," said T.K.

"Step aside, comrade," the stewardess said. "Next flight tomorrow." The crowd behind T.K surged forward.

"Coffin's fine, comrade," said T.K. A seat belt wouldn't help on this flight anyway.

"Assert!" Vanessa's shriek rose from somewhere down the ramp.

"Can my girlfriend sit on my lap?" T.K. asked.

"Fiancée," screamed Vanessa. "Wife, goddamit!"

"Can she sit on my lap, comrade?" T.K. couldn't envision Vanessa as anyone's wife, least of all his. He pressed a bank note into the stewardess's hand.

It must have been more than T.K. intended, for the stewardess ejected the passenger from the nearest window and placed him on a coffin with his crate of ducklings. T.K. crawled into the vacated seat, of a kind contoured to excruciate foreign reporters taller than six feet.

Vanessa, hauled aboard by the stewardess, squeezed onto what remained of his lap. "Let me reimburse you," she murmured.

As T.K. watched the losing passengers being pushed back across the tarmac, Vanessa rewarded him with a wet kiss. His odds of scoring had soared from fair to excellent.

"That's the down payment," Vanessa breathed into his ear. Her legs entwined, however involuntarily, around his. Her perfume enveloped him.

* * *

With a mighty shudder, the Ilyushin banked and plummeted through the clouds as though antiaircraft flak had clobbered it. Habit was prompting the pilot to evade potential Stinger missiles, which had closed every other airfield in the interior. The air pressure dropped, babies stopped suckling and bawled, T.K.'s ears popped.

The ground rushed up to demolish the old aircraft. With disaster imminent, the pilot yanked up the wing flaps. The Ilyushin bounced into its landing before the left front tire blew apart. The plane spun around and thudded to a stop, one wing snagged by a fence protecting the terminal shed. Ululations of thanksgiving arose from the passengers.

Through his window, T.K. saw the protruding tails of MiG jetfighters and the sagging rotors of Hind helicopter gunships parked behind earthworks. Trash had filled in the fighting trenches. Soldiers slumbered under the torn netting of an antiaircraft gun emplacement. It was one of those armies where manning defensive positions became a suicide mission.

Outside the corrugated metal shed, a swarm of travelers jockeyed for a place on the flight back. Many were peasant women straining under baskets of potatoes, pineapples, and bananas. The government's inability to move even a truckload of food had promoted a brisk commerce in cheap radios and cassette recorders traveling up-country and fruit or vegetables back down.

The stewardess pried open the door, admitting a blast furnace of heat. A brace of donkeys pulled the ramp up to the plane. At the runway's edge waited more coffins, double-stacked and nailed shut.

Vanessa could not climb off T.K.'s lap until the empty coffins were passed out. T.K. followed her down the ramp, stamping his foot to restore circulation. Once again, he carried her bags.

A husky blond man in a flowery sport shirt mingled with the milling crowd.

"He looks American," T.K. said. "I didn't see him on our flight."

"Who," Vanessa asked, "what, when, where?" But the blond stranger had disappeared.

The shed felt stifling, as though the air were sucked out. Vanessa proposed waiting outside in its shade while a cyclist pedaled T.K. downtown to find a taxi. The only automobile in sight, a rusting Mercedes, was being engaged by the crew-cut blond man whom T.K. had glimpsed at the airport.

"Going near the railway junction?" T.K. asked. "We could share."

When T.K. approached, the blond man whipped on his sunglasses. "Who's 'we'?" he asked in an American twang. "Peel the onion."

"Two American reporters," T.K. said, "checking out a massacre."

"Down where the rubber meets the road?" The blond man was scouting locations for a soft drink plant himself, he said, but eliminated the junction after collateral damage took out the power plant and local work force.

"Come play in my backyard some other time," he said. His Mercedes left T.K. covered in red dust, wondering what spooks really did out here.

T.K. inspected the market with its pots beaten from artillery shells and pig tallow soap. The imported whiskey bottles looked so ubiquitous that even a teetotaler could guess they were refilled with tea.

A man weaving cricket cages shook his head when T.K. asked if he spoke English. So did a woman selling flyspecked fritters from a towel and a barber cutting hair under a tree.

By the road, T.K. came upon a panel beater hammering on a dented automobile. T.K. mimed riding in the car. The workman pointed with his mallet to an old Toyota minibus. Its driver sprawled across the seat so lifelessly that T.K. wondered if he had died.

"Speak English?" T.K. tickled the driver's nose with a ten-dollar bill.

The driver's good eye snapped open.

"How much to the railway junction?"

"No more railway, comrade." The driver stretched himself awake. "The masses liberated the rails."

"Take me to the junction anyway."

The driver shut his good eye and opened it again. "You buy me a new motorcar when we hit a mine, yes?"

"Heard of this new hotel?" T.K. stuck Vanessa's brochure through the window.

The driver nodded. "Before the halfway station."

So there was a hotel, maybe a decent restaurant, clean pool, cold beer, a king-sized bed upon which to sport with Vanessa. Tourists who knocked new hotels never had to cope with the alternatives where T.K. toiled.

"How much to get there?" T.K. said.

The driver shrugged. "Forty thousand dinars."

T.K. wasn't sure how much that was, with the rate of exchange wobbling about these days.

"Too much," he said. "Fifty American dollars?"

"Each way, comrade?"

"The return's your problem," T.K. said, "and I want a receipt."

The driver pointed to the empty fuel gauge. "Plus dinars for petrol."

T.K. divided his dinars between the driver and some onlookers who pushed the minibus to the gasoline pump.

He returned to the airport, but Vanessa was gone. A child in a cast-off T-shirt ran up holding a page from a reporter's notebook. "From the lady," he said.

T.K. reached for the note, but the child hid it behind his back. "Ten dollars," he said.

"One dollar," said T.K.

"Lady says five dollars."

"Two dollars."

"No." The child began to cram the note in his mouth. T.K. handed the boy five dollars and took the paper. He recognized Vanessa's scrawl.

"Dear T.K.," she wrote. "I ran into an old friend who offered me a ride, only room for one, you won't mind because your inner journalist's so clever. CU XXXOOO V."

It occurred to T.K. that Vanessa and the blond man might be acquainted and that she had paid back none of the money spent on her behalf.

As a rule, T.K. rode up front in taxis, unless the driver looked speed-happy, stoned, or prone to accident. This time, T.K. climbed in back.

"First I pick up my wife," the driver said. "She visits her mother."

"Not on my fifty bucks."

"Only two minutes."

The taxi wandered through the town, breaking a half hour later into unfamiliar countryside. Eventually, it stopped in front of a shabby stucco house.

"Maybe two minutes," the driver said.

After another fifteen minutes, T.K. went inside. The driver was drinking tea while a pregnant woman dressed two small boys.

"They're not going," T.K. said.

"Only to their grandmother," the driver said between sips. "They ride with me."

The driver drove back through town, his view mostly obscured by a child wriggling on his lap. The other boy sat wedged between the driver and his wife, who was nursing an infant that had materialized at her breast. A near collision with an oxcart made T.K. relent.

"Put the kids back here," he said. They scrambled across and began to quarrel. The driver turned up his radio.

Where the town's outskirts yielded to open savanna, a wooden pole between two rusting oil drums blocked the road. A soldier popped up from behind rotting sandbags and blew on a whistle. The taxi screeched to a halt.

The soldier wore a peaked cap with flaps down his neck and shiny sunglasses. One cheek bulged as though a golf ball were wedged inside. He waved them out of the minibus.

"Army demands our documents." The driver patted his pockets and shrugged. "Two minutes." He backed around and sped off, leaving his wife and children under T.K.'s involuntary protection.

A beefy soldier emerged from the dugout. He packed another narcotic leaf into the cud he was chewing and walked around T.K., inspecting him like a goat for sale.

Khat ranged far from the Horn of Africa as nature's amphetamine. Soldiers manning checkpoints out here usually whiled away the time smoking the local marijuana, sometimes laced with cinnamon, or popping mandrax barbiturates. But khat left you jittery, clogged, and unable to sleep. For T.K., that meant a roadblock defended by cranky, constipated insomniacs.

"I'm an American newsman," T.K. began, "meeting my colleagues." A hack didn't admit to traveling alone out here.

"Who buys you, newsman?" A leafy stream of khat juice aimed at T.K.'s desert boot expressed the soldier's opinion of foreign journalists. Splat.

"A half-million readers buy my newspaper, Captain."

A star on each epaulet marked the soldier as a lieutenant, but bullies at roadblocks never objected to being promoted.

"But who buys you?" persisted the lieutenant.

"My editors rent me by the month, Captain," T.K. said.

"What kind of newsman are you," the lieutenant said, "that nobody wants to buy?" He compared T.K.'s press card with the passport. "This says American," he said, "but your passport says Ireland." Splat.

"My ancestors are Irish but I write for an American newspaper, Major."

T.K.'s American passport stayed concealed inside his jacket, because the army blamed America for arming the rebels.

"Camera, newsman?" The lieutenant let fly a blob of khat that stunned a scorpion curled translucent in the dust.

T.K. produced his Pentax. "A spy camera," the lieutenant said. "Where is your camera for television?"

"I'm a newspaper reporter, Major," T.K. said.

An even larger soldier festooned in bandoliers of ammunition brought a fresh sprig of khat to his leader. A lens on his sunglasses still bore the sticker *Made in Hong Kong*. T.K. was weary of sunglasses in Equatoria.

"Americans are rich, they ride in big motorcars, but you hire a taxi, to meet another spy?" the lieutenant said. "What's in your bag?"

T.K. emptied his backpack on the red earth. The lieutenant sifted the contents with his boot. He picked up the old computer and shook it.

"Radio transmitter?" Splat.

"Laptop, Colonel." T.K. turned on the computer and typed something for the lieutenant.

"What does it say?" The lieutenant stuffed yet another leaf in his mouth.

T.K. read from the screen. "The quick brown fox jumps over the lazy dog's back, the quick brown fox jumps—"

The lieutenant flung the computer on the ground. "Do quick brown foxes mean terrorists in your code? Are we the lazy dogs on whose backs you instruct them to jump?"

He turned on T.K. "On your knees or we cut you to size—you are too tall." T.K. knelt; he had no choice.

"Who is the lazy dog now?" the lieutenant demanded. "Walk like lazy dog, newsman, make dog noise." Splat.

T.K. barked on all fours until the soldiers lost interest. The lieutenant yanked at his poncho; the teddy bear spilled out.

"It belongs to a friend, Colonel," T.K. said, kneeling again. "My employer, his granddaughter."

"No newsman travels with this—what does it hide?" The lieutenant pried the bear apart with his bayonet. Handfuls of cotton stuffing scattered in the wind.

The lieutenant tossed aside the eviscerated teddy bear and squatted down, revealing a flapping sole on his worn boot. He poked some envelopes with his bayonet.

"From my many fans," T.K. said, "forwarded by my newspaper." The letters had been in his pack for weeks, but this was not the time to open them.

The lieutenant pushed them aside and held up a small yellow canister. "For invisible messages?" Splat.

"Sprinkle it on your clothes and insects disappear like magic, Colonel." T.K. regretted his imagery.

"Magic?" The lieutenant tasted the powder with his finger and pocketed the can. He also scooped up most of the chocolate bars and the cigarettes that T.K. carried to burn off leeches and barter for favors.

"Up, newsman, you are too stupid to spy," said the lieutenant. "But you must carry a big camera like the foreign journalists this morning." Splat.

T.K. paused from refilling his pack. What foreign journalists?

"Four men with a camera and a girl." Splat.

That had to be T.K.'s friends, though Ginny would resent being called a girl.

"They went back to fix the motorcar," the lieutenant said. "They come again tomorrow."

T.K. wiped khat saliva off his laptop. He turned it on but nothing happened. He dared not complain.

A roadblock was no place to loiter. T.K. was about to walk back to town when the taxi reappeared. The driver waved his papers but the soldiers paid no attention.

"Toll," the lieutenant said, "is fifty dollars."

T.K. held out ten dollars, which the lieutenant took. "Farewell, my newsman," he said, and bestowed a kiss that left khat juice trickling down T.K.'s chin. A soldier lowered the pole.

The taxi climbed toward the hills through groves of eucalyptus and banana trees. Goats and poultry scattered on the road as the driver took the curves without braking. The small boys had fallen asleep against T.K. The infant was slurping. At the top of the highest hill, the driver turned off the ignition and shifted into neutral.

"What are you doing?" T.K. shouted. The minibus accumulated speed downhill.

"Save petrol." The driver, clinging hard to his steering wheel, nearly missed a hairpin turn. "And bandits shoot when we go slow."

The taxi eventually coasted to a halt in the next valley, where the driver had some trouble restarting the engine. T.K. held a wet baby while the driver's wife opened her door to throw up.

At last, a sign welcomed him: *Every Room with Beauty-full Widow at Our Holiday Hotel: Coming Soon.* But hadn't it arrived?

The driver turned onto a rough dirt track, which ended at a deep hole half filled with water and oozing with verdant slime. T.K. climbed out. Only mosquitoes lived here.

"Where's the hotel?" he asked.

"After the war started," the driver said, "the masses took the pieces home."

"Why didn't you tell me there's no hotel?"

"This is the place of the hotel," the driver said, "though the hotel is not yet . . ."

"Not yet what?"

"Not yet yet."

"We'll keep going," said T.K.

"First, I take my wife and children to her mother in the hills. I return in two—"

"I don't want to hear it."

"Two hours," the taxi driver said. "You will like my wife's mother, she prepares us a tasty cup of tea."

"Drop me at the main road," T.K. said. "If I'm still here when you return, stop."

The minibus drove off with the baby nursing and the boys quarreling. Jerking his thumbs-up, T.K. bade them good riddance. He extended his hand to measure the gap between sun and horizon. Only a few hours remained till dusk in this deserted place. T.K. looked both ways down the road, while an old song percolated in his head:

> Newspapermen meet such interesting people,
> Behind the story now it can be told.
> I'll tell you quite reliably off the record
> About some charming people I have knowed . . .

Sitting on the grass, he mentally filled an obituary column with the newspapers where he had worked. One after another, they hemorrhaged and went belly-up. What buffeted him was no worse than the luck of others in what had become a lean profession, but clinging to the wreckage, T.K. felt like some Typhoid Mary of newspapering, though each new employer accepted his failures as testimony to his grit, not miscalculation.

> Hold the press, hold the press,
> Extra, extra, read all about it,
> It's a mess, it meets the test . . .

Some months after his wife, weary of unpacking and repacking, of arranging dinner parties for which he failed to arrive, traded him in for a more intimate relationship with her psychiatrist, T.K. landed on a large Midwestern daily. Before its earnings revealed the first inevitable drop in advertising lineage, the Moscow bureau chief eloped with a nymphet from the Bolshoi Ballet. T.K. applied for the vacancy on the advice of an ex–foreign correspondent who shuffled around the newsroom in trench coat and scuffed wing tips. Nothing short of an ax murder or sex scandal, advised the faded hack, jump-started a stalled career like a foreign assignment.

"But you don't even speak Russian," the managing editor said.

"Only French and Spanish, and the German's gone rusty," said T.K., who as a natural monolinguist knew none of these. "I'll be candid, it could take me days to whip my German verbs back into shape."

So T.K. found himself toiling in lands afflicted by more economic disaster than the newspapers he helped drive under. He filed from countries bankrupted by colonialism, capitalism, and socialism, sometimes simultaneously, which landed him inevitably in Equatoria. He became a hack.

> Oh, newspapermen meet such interesting people,
> It's so much fun to represent the press.

But foreign correspondents sent to the developing world tended to remain there. T.K. didn't find poverty or disease exotic, yet he welcomed his niche. If his byline was not illustrious, it was all he owned. Without it, he might not exist.

* * *

Dust devils danced in the late afternoon. The tiny tornadoes swirled down the red dirt road, scooping up twigs, leaves, and an incongruous food wrapper. Dust devils had some meteorological explanation, but to T.K. they seemed possessed spirits, dead hacks perhaps who had faked their datelines and now wandered this dry plain as a warning to reporters like himself.

At last he heard the putter of an engine. T.K. waved his hand and a truck stopped. The driver climbed down, leaving the engine idling. He wore a ragged shirt, torn trousers, and shoes without laces.

The truck was the most battered T.K. had seen, even in a country with a knack for keeping derelict vehicles in motion. Fire had charred the chassis. The windshield and doors were gone. A cigar-shaped fuel tank jettisoned by some MiG jetfighter was lashed to the flatbed.

Beside the driver sat an old man in a khaki jacket with brass buttons. He clutched a worn Bible. A haggard woman and a child sat back with the fuel tank and scrap metal.

"Speak English?" T.K. said. "I go to the railway junction." He chuffed like a locomotive.

But the driver shook his head. "You may ride until we turn east," he said.

The seat was missing, so T.K. sat on a crate beside the old man. The driver sat on another crate, working a gearshift improvised from a broom handle. The truck seemed to run on patches and promises.

"We harvest the wasted metal," the driver said. "We follow the battles and gather it to sell to others who send the metal back where it came from, across the sea."

T.K. pulled his notebook from the pack under his feet. The scavengers made a story. "Howdoesitfeel?"

"Soldiers shoot at us, they say we take what belongs to the people, but no people want so many mines and bombs."

The scavenger spoke good English.

"I was a mechanic at the Scottish mission before war drove away the missionaries," he said. "The guerrillas stole our cows and goats, the army stole what was left. Soldiers poisoned one water hole, guerrillas another, so God led us into the wilderness like the Israelites."

T.K. asked if this pious old man was his father.

The scavenger nodded. "My wife rides with our son. Our other children have died from mines in the ground."

The road ended in a crater. But the scavenger only downshifted and jockeyed the truck onto what remained of the adjacent railway. They clattered past boxcars and gondolas rusting in tall grass, a locomotive toppled like a butchered leviathan. When the truck seemed about to come apart, they stopped at a stucco building pocked by shrapnel, looking as though a can opener had pried off the roof.

T.K. climbed out and stretched. This must be the midway station. Before the war, freight trains laden with copper from mines in the interior stopped here to take on water and coal before the winding descent to the coast.

"We rest here tonight." The scavenger dismounted and helped his father down. "Tomorrow we turn east and you go north."

He drew a rusty AK-47 with a splintered wooden stock from under his seat and slammed in a rustier magazine packed with cartridges. Leaning the rifle against a tire, he opened the truck's hood and let steam erupt from the radiator.

T.K. picked up the AK-47. The weapon had brought as much pride and misery to the wretched of the earth as any other invention of the twentieth century. Discolored wooden grips protruding below the metal trigger assembly and beyond the adjustable gunsight were grimy with use. Cyrillic letters stamped into the metal identified the rifle as made in Russia or Bulgaria. Proprietary initials—M.H. or H.W.—had been scratched into the wooden stock. When did the last owner die? T.K. propped it back against the wheel, but not before confirming that the barrel inside was shiny. However decrepit, the rifle could still kill.

"May I photograph your father?" T.K. asked. The scavenger spoke to the old man, who nodded and pressed his jacket with gnarled hands.

Opening the lens to accommodate the gathering dusk, T.K. focused his Pentax while the old man stood at attention with his Bible.

"I'm an American newsman," he said.

"My father is a preacher," said the scavenger. "God sends him to spread the Good News. What news were you sent to spread?"

"I report to the world what happens," T.K. said.

The scavenger translated for his father. "Have they not their own sorrows?" asked the old man. "How can knowing our sorrows make them better?"

"The more people know, the better they become." T.K. adjusted the camera for the waning light, and clicked a few more frames. "We cut down trees to print a newspaper that will share the knowledge we collect."

The old man caressed his Bible. "How many trees must be cut down to share your knowledge?" he asked.

"Maybe two hundred thousand trees to print Sunday newspapers across America," T.K. said.

"Your newspapers would eat our forest." The old man talked faster than his son could translate. "We would have no shade or protection from the wind, nowhere to hide when the soldiers come, floods would steal our fields and leave us without enough to grow. Is what you know worth a forest?"

"If we tell people how to protect what's precious," T.K. said, "they will save more trees than we cut down."

The parchment face brightened. "So you do make people better," the old man said. "When they read what you know, they no longer want to burn our villages or steal our crops or take away our young men, that's why you come?"

"Not exactly," T.K. said.

The scavenger's wife wore a faded cotton dress and a knitted beret. She stirred the cornmeal over a fire while the old man led the family in a hymn, then she ladled out the porridge. When it came T.K.'s turn to eat, he offered some money, but the old man shook his head.

"Elders like my father sat once under the big trees to discuss their differences," said the scavenger, "until foreigners gave guns and bombs to the children. Now no one needs the wisdom of old men."

After supper, the woman covered the blackened pot with a large stone against animals and carried the chipped enamel plates and cups down to the river. While the old man read his Bible by firelight, clouds on the horizon glowed impossible hues of rose and pink and acacia trees flattened into stark cutouts against the vivid sunset. It was the sort of evening sky that his father had conjured up for T.K. on the prairie of his Illinois childhood.

"We sleep in the forest," the scavenger said. "Snakes live in the station, and bandits. The forest is safer."

T.K. had heard about the ragged gangs of army deserters and other outlaws who fed like vultures on the carrion of war. For them the scavenger had taken out his precautionary AK-47.

The scavenger stamped out the fire. He broke the truck's silhouette with a few branches. T.K. helped carry the family's tattered blankets into the woods. He spread his own poncho some distance away under a wild fig tree.

As he lay on his back, a carpet of stars winked down through the branches. Bats flitted among the trees. In the distance, a thunderstorm rumbled. A night breeze kept the mosquitoes at bay, so his netting became a pillow.

Alistair, Ginny, Schuyler, and his crew—what if they failed to appear? But worry succumbed to the serenity of this spot. A rising moon threw long shadows among the trees and washed the railway in silver. His foreign desk or his ex-wife or her lawyer or a flawed civilization would not find him here. T.K. could afford to wait another day.

* * *

T.K. awoke to a strange hand over his mouth. The scavenger knelt in the dark, gripping the battered AK-47. His terse whisper made it more frightening.

"We are in danger."

At first, T.K. heard nothing beyond the nocturnal grinding of the cicadas, but then a quarrel among strange voices, a captive woman's plaintive wail and raucous male laughter. The red glow of a cigarette cloned itself into many. Armed specters shuffled down the railway.

The driver vanished to protect his family. T.K. was alone.

The underbrush crackled. Someone was tramping into the woods toward T.K. And something crawled up his jeans, but he could not afford to scratch. Moonlight would betray him.

When the bandit looked about to step on T.K., he propped his SKS rifle against a tree, dropped his baggy trousers, and, squatting, voided his bowels with a grunt and answering break of foul wind. His hands seemed to graze the poncho when he reached for leaves to wipe himself. T.K., lying close enough to count the buttons on the torn army jacket, gagged at the stench. The bandit buttoned up, shouldered his rifle, and ambled back to his gang drifting toward the ruined station.

Somewhere, the captive was screaming like a banshee. After a few minutes, she fell silent. T.K. swatted at his jeans and dragged his poncho under a more distant bush. It was a long time before he drifted back to sleep.

* * *

He awoke to the clean fragrance of dawn. The family was loading the truck and anxious to depart.

"I heard a woman last night," T.K. said.

"We prayed over her and the child," said the scavenger, "but the animals may dig them up again."

He had packed away his assault rifle and held a shovel. T.K. asked if there was more than one victim.

"You did not hear the bandits who passed us," said the scavenger. "They were arguing whether the woman's unborn child would be a boy or girl. To settle the wager, they cut open her womb."

The scavenger spoke listlessly, as if such atrocity was routine out here. T.K. inquired about the massacre.

"The railway junction." The scavenger nodded. "I heard the soldiers took many people to the river and shot them for helping the guerrillas."

"How many?"

"Too many to pray over. I heard it, I did not see it."

The family shared the last of the porridge, then sat with eyes shut as if summoning strength for their journey. Again the scavenger refused T.K.'s offer of money. The old man placed his hands upon T.K.'s head and prayed.

"My father sends you, too, with God's protection," the scavenger said. He cranked up the truck and boosted his father into the cab, then his wife and son onto the back.

After the truck had rattled out of sight, T.K. walked over to the station. Morning shadows filled the pockmarks in the stucco. Overhead, a jet aircraft trailed a pencil-thin fluff of white across the sky.

He would have entered the station, until he saw the fresh grave. He retreated into the tall grass and spread his poncho to dry. Dew still webbed the blades of grass. Something bit again inside his jeans. He shook one leg, then the other, dancing until the biting stopped.

Opening his pack, T.K. came upon the letters. His ex-wife still dotted her name with a cartoon face. He began with another letter, from someone called Tiffany.

"Our teacher asined a report on Equatoria!!! I asked to do Italy because I luv pizza but Italy isn't developing enuf she sez. My father whose always in my face showed me yr story. PLEEZ send everythin I need NOW!!! Do kids there eet pizza? Also on race-ism for another project not du til next week. This report's du Friday so PLEEZ!!! P.S. How can I become a fourin coraspondant?"

The next letter bore the logo of his own newspaper.

"To the news staff:" it began. "In this period of declining advertising and rising newsprint costs, we must all learn to be thriftier with our expenses.

So while no one expects you to hitchhike or sleep on the ground, we do ask that you adopt the following economies . . ."

This too T.K. set aside.

He had saved his former wife for last. The envelope yielded a photograph of a glowing couple in red parkas and goggles, brandishing skis at the camera. The photo was printed on a long green paper decorated with Yuletide holly scribbles.

"Dear friends," read the letter below. T.K. felt promoted. "When you read this, we will have lots of fresh powder outside our Vail condo. Last June, we attended Darryl's medical school reunion at Yale, where he's not the only one fed up with Freud. Now it's Darryl's turn to go to Jill's reunion at Sarah Lawrence. Jill's jewelry, from shells we harvest together on our Caribbean weekends, is selling beyond her dreams, with orders from as far away as Darien, CT. Darryl surprised Jill with her own BMW after she stole the Saab on his squash nights to commute to fund-raising meetings for the Civic Opera. Who says life isn't fair? Despite our busy schedule, we found an amusing auberge in Provence to cheer up Darryl after his international symposium on depression. We can't divulge its name because someone would ruin it by printing it in a newspaper."

T.K. pinned the happy couple and their skis on an acacia thorn. He would have discarded the other letters but he had forgotten to bring toilet paper.

The dust devils came to dance as the day turned hot. T.K. pulled off his shirt. A pale leech clung to his belly. His cigarettes were gone and pulling it off would cause infection. T.K. watched the leech engorge itself on blood and fall away. Something else was biting his groin again, but he couldn't find it and scratching brought no relief.

Outsiders who envied foreign correspondents their life of romance overlooked the prickly heat, the foul water, and the insects. T.K. had slept on some hotel mattresses so infested with fleas that he bedded down on the floor.

It was past noon. Where were Schuyler and his crew, Ginny, and Alistair? Was T.K. missing some big story that had turned his friends around, sent them racing back to the capital where a big guerrilla offensive was under way? That must be why Vanessa had disappeared. The entire haggle of hacks would be there pumping out their copy, capturing the world's front pages and evening news programs while his own frantic editors sought him in vain. Perhaps they had already dispatched a replacement from one of the European bureaus, writing off T.K. while he wandered ignorant on the brink of the world, as worthless to his newspaper as his busted computer. If only he'd thought to bring along his short-wave radio.

He was ready to start walking back, when a reassuring racket broke the drowsy calm of the afternoon. An old Land Rover bobbed into sight, white towel flapping from a branch wedged behind the spare tire. T.K. relaxed. He recognized the makeshift flag of noncombatants, recalling times when journalists got spared if they went about identified and unarmed.

Alistair was driving while Kobus, Schuyler's lank cameraman, leaned against the cracked windshield, exploring the landscape through the lens of his Beta minicamera. T.K. jumped into the road and waved.

Alistair braked for the stop and climbed out. "No shock absorbers, but it does run," he said. "New carburetor too—we lifted it from a Japanese TV crew while they were off filming water lilies."

"I haven't missed anything, have I?" T.K. pulled on his T-shirt.

"Only bloody nothing." Alistair shook his head. "We parked our government minder, had the pilot do a few rolls to get him puking. We left him in the district resthouse with a bottle of Scotch—he seemed grateful enough."

Schuyler dismounted with his crew. Still no sign of Ginny.

"We hired the Rover empty," Alistair said, "and the petrol depot wouldn't accept dollars, can you believe it? We had to buy eggs first."

At the mention of eggs, T.K. was suddenly hungry.

"Cass took our dollars to the farmers' market to buy eggs," said Alistair, "which she sold to the state store for dinars, which we used to get petrol. Resourceful, no?"

T.K. jerked Alistair forward. "What's that news twink doing here?"

"Cass sold eggs at her grandmother's farm as a kid," Alistair said. "Must be why I'm smitten."

"And where's Ginny?"

"Ginny had to drop out," Alistair said, "and Cass so wanted to come."

Had Alistair forgotten what they survived together? When hacks pooled their resources and stamina, such teamwork acquired the emotional parameters of marriage. T.K. had been jilted.

"Instead of calling me, you pommie bastard—"

"Commonwealth ties and all," Alistair said.

"—you gave Ginny's seat to some bubble-brained amateur and left me here in the bush?"

"You could stack pennies on her cheekbones," said Alistair, "or walk barefoot through her smashing hair—what color would you call it, not quite blond and not quite not."

"Betrayed me, you limey sonofabitch, for a dishwater-blond radio bimbo?"

"She's no bimbo, she's bloody smart," Alistair said. "I think I'm in love, mate."

"You always think you're in love," T.K. said. Alistair's sex life was as pathetic as his own, which was to say that both of them hadn't had any for a long time.

"I'd drink her bathwater," Alistair said. "I'd eat kippers off that tight little tummy."

"You dump that ditzy Canuck or I'm not working stories with you ever again, Alistair."

Alistair gave this brief thought. "I'm bloody well going to miss you, mate," he said. "Those long legs run all the way up to her ass."

"They usually do—you're hornier than Rolf."

"He wanted to come too, if it's any consolation," Alistair said.

That was only because Rolf thought of the railway junction as another dateline where he never got laid. T.K. would have kicked the crap out of his old buddy Alistair but he needed the ride.

Schuyler walked up, taming his windblown mop of prematurely white hair with his palms. T.K.'s mistrust of television reporters did not extend to Schuyler, who once subsisted for United Press International before deserting to triple his wages in television. In an age of electronics, Schuyler, like T.K., could still remember a newsroom of pastepots and pencils.

"I don't know how much more of my crew I can take," he said. "I thought we'd have a race war on the way up."

Kobus was an ex-Rhodesian, like many free-lance cameramen floating around the backwaters. Sipho, his sound engineer, was South African.

"Give the Zulu the bloody sticks," Kobus called.

"The Boer wants our tripod," Sipho told Cass. He was roly-poly, with an even rounder belly. "Sun fried the Boer's brains."

They kept sniping as they walked off on a quest for fresh footage. "You should be in Natal herding your cattle," said Kobus.

"My grandfathers sat on thrones," said Sipho, "while you hairybacks were fornicating with your dogs."

"I tried to split them up once but they refused," Schuyler said. "Kobus said Sipho was clever, and Sipho said Kobus thought African. Cass lectured Kobus on the drive up, and Sipho told her to butt out. She called Kobus racist for advocating white balance, you know, adjusting the minicam so the picture won't come out green. She's sweet but she's got a lot to learn."

Cass hopped out last, though not before snagging her tape recorder on a side-view mirror. She wore the sleeveless white cotton frock, as though they were traveling to sip lemonade at a garden party. Her slender arms glistened with suntan lotion and perspiration. Aviator sunglasses masked her myopia. Behind the mirror lenses, prescription of course, she showed no surprise at T.K.'s appearance.

"Where's your ladyfriend?" Cass said, exuding more confidence than a day in the bush warranted.

"She couldn't keep up," T.K. said. "I thought your excursion ticket expired."

Schuyler, who had strolled into the tall grass, returned with the toy bear. "Yours, T.K.?" he said. "I'm afraid I sprayed it when I peed against that tree."

"He's so cute," Cass said. "Oh, but he's hurt."

"Back off Scoopie Bear." T.K. snatched it away. "He's mine."

"Intwepid foweign cowwethpondent twavelth with vewy own teddy bear," Cass lisped. "Like Winnie-the-Pooh, eh?"

"Scoopie Bear is my publisher's granddaughter's," he said. "I'm bear-sitting it for circulation promotion."

"Can't you try harder than that? Crumbs, you call him Scoopie Bear."

She broke into infectious laughter that urged T.K. to join in, at his expense.

"Crumbs?" he told her. "Why can't you say 'shit' like any normal reporter?"

With billowing skirt and a flash of thigh, Cass swung her leg up on the Land Rover and stretched forward as if preparing for a race. Instead, she pulled a boxy case from the jumbled gear and sought out the shade of the old station.

She did not deserve the last word. T.K. shoved the eviscerated bear into his pack and followed.

"No hack wears a dress in the bush," he said.

"In case we meet someone important to interview," she said. "Besides, my suitcase was stolen, and Alistair said to travel light."

Under the Montreal Expos cap, her nose was layered white with sunblock, but the sun had elicited a dusting of exquisite freckles across her cheeks and shoulders.

"What's that?" T.K. pointed to the case at her feet. Typewriters went out with Edsels, as any real hack knew.

Cass pulled off her cap and shook her light brown hair vigorously. A few twigs fell out.

"I'm a stringer, not a staffer, so they didn't give me a laptop. Six, seven." Cass counted out the strokes of her hairbrush. "Besides, I present my stories better when they're typed. Nine, ten. One can grow too dependent on technological fashion."

"Fashion?" T.K. said. Computers had revolutionized his noble craft.

"Twelve, thirteen. Where's your electric outlet here?"

"Rechargeable batteries last for hours," he said.

In the sunlight, the gray of her eyes looked flecked with sea green. "But what happens," said Cass, "if everything goes out, like forever?"

"Most unlikely," said T.K.

Cass's insouciance was betrayed by her fingernails, which were bitten to the quick.

"What malaria pills did you bring?" he said. "Chloroquine, mefloquine, they won't work out here."

"Twenty-seven."

"You don't have any. Insect repellent?"

Something was chewing at his groin again, but T.K. could not afford to lose face by scratching.

"Thirty-one, thirty-two."

"Mosquito net?" he asked "Poncho? Flashlight?"

"Thirty-nine, forty." She brushed the hair down over her face and started again.

No press tags festooned her slender neck. "First assignment overseas?" he said.

Cass peered at T.K. through the curtain of long hair. The tips were bleached butterscotch, remnants of a botched dye job.

"I lined up some radio stringing," she said, "and paid my way over, yes."

"With no professional experience."

"Reporting looks easy enough," Cass said, "like writing home to tell your mother what's happened."

T.K. snorted. Would she describe a Renoir or Matisse as some paint splashed on a canvas?

Cass tossed back her hair and studied him with the exasperation of a laboratory researcher who finds a rat too dumb to navigate the maze.

"When I taught school," she said, "I learned to explain everything so little minds could understand."

"That doesn't make you a newspaperman . . . woman . . . person."

"At least a radio reporter doesn't consume dead trees," Cass said. "You need a haircut, you know."

"Some women think it looks romantic," he told her, "like Chopin." He didn't credit Vanessa, because she had ditched him.

"You?" Cass found this so ridiculous. "Crumbs, you wouldn't know Chopin's Polonaise-Fantasie from his Sonata in B-flat Minor."

Having flaunted her erudition, Cass packed up her hairbrush and walked back to the Land Rover. Alistair had stretched out in the shade and fallen asleep. Kobus and Sipho were still off shooting. Schuyler leaned against the Rover, deciphering his notes.

"Know much about Chopin?" T.K. asked.

Schuyler shrugged. "I thought you were happy with the Grateful Dead."

Print hacks who chided Schuyler for defecting to television still turned to him for advice. The electronic wizardry of his new profession gave Schuyler the reputation of a fixer.

"Some wanker dropped my laptop at a roadblock," T.K. said. "Take a look?"

Schuyler laid the computer on the Rover's hood, flipped open a screwdriver on his Swiss Army knife, and probed the computer's recesses until the screen lit up.

"Switch got sheared off," he said. "Use a paper clip—maybe Cass has one."

But Cass had wandered off to the river with her soap and towel.

"Wedge the paper clip here where the switch was," Schuyler said, "wiggle it, and your laptop should turn on."

Schuyler held the switch with his knife blade while T.K. tested each key: QW RTYUIOPASDFGHJKLZXCVBNM. "All okay, except my E, dammit."

"Some dirt under there," Schuyler said, "or your key's broken. We won't know until I take it apart somewhere inside—too much dust out here."

"How can you file from Equatoria without an E?"

"Use a dash or asterisk," Schuyler advised. "I did that when I lost a U once in Duluth. Warn your editors first, they're so easily confused."

"Where's your bug powder, Schuyler?" T.K. asked. "A soldier took mine and something's living in my shorts."

Schuyler tossed him a small can. "Don't use it all," he said, "and don't show me what you've got. Douse somewhere else."

T.K. walked to the river, stepped out of his jeans, and dusted his underpants with insecticide. Something fuzzy with manifold legs jumped to his crotch. T.K. backed around a bush, hoisted his genitals, and dumped on more powder.

"Swallow frigging this," he told it. The centipede fell away and T.K. let out a celebratory whoop.

There followed a splash behind him. Cass rose startled from the river, naked as Venus and not as flat-chested as he thought.

"That's so revolting," Cass said. She stopped scrubbing her dress and lunged for shore. Water hyacinths bunched around her long legs.

"Alistair," she yelled, "your friend's exposing himself."

"Schistosomiasis," said T.K., who was preoccupied more by her glistening navel.

"It's called flashing," said Cass. "You're so sick."

He struggled to avert his eyes, and lost. "Snails in the water carry it," he said, "nastier than malaria."

"I don't see them." Turning a flawless back, Cass peered into the river. "I think you're making it up, eh?"

"Think what you want, just don't swim in fresh water this close to the equator. There's enough parasites in there to kidnap your liver."

"Perhaps you know a bit more about this," she said. "Turn around while I go ask Alistair."

Cass tugged on the damp dress and brushed past him, her nipples against the diaphanous cotton as pert and appealing as puppies' noses behind a pet shop window.

"And do stop playing with yourself," she said. "For a working journalist, it looks very unprofessional."

"Journalism's not a profession," he called after her. "It's an honorable trade, a noble craft."

Professions were for wimps.

3.

HIGHLANDS DISTRICT, *quatoria—Survivors watch*d in horror from b*hind th* tamarind tr**s as doz*ns of m*n, wom*n,
and childr*n w*r* massacr*d in a mountain villag*, victims of
a savag* r*b*llion that has d*vastat*d this onc* p*ac*ful nation.

Th* gov*rnm*nt forc*s and th* insurg*nts both d*ni*d
r*sponsibility for th* massacr*, but a w*ll-plac*d sourc*
id*ntifi*d th* kill*rs . . .

The day that followed their spat dawned sunny and hazardous, a day in
which Cass nearly got T.K. shot and wound up sleeping with him, though
hardly out of choice.

She had disbelieved T.K.'s warning about bandits. "Making it up, eh?"
Cass said when he tried to explain the new grave inside the station. T.K.,
who slept again in the forest, did not dissuade her from bedding down with
the others inside a derailed boxcar. Cass seemed capable of bewitching Alistair into leaving him behind.

When T.K. rejoined them at dawn, Cass was charring tinned sausages
and bread over a fire, though she would not wash up afterwards, dismissing
this as men's work.

"Confirmed the massacre," Alistair told T.K. while they cleaned up. "Scores slain."

"Alistair!" scolded Cass. It was already turning hot, but she looked much too cool and collected in her white cotton dress. "He's not in our pool," she said, "we've embargoed our scoop, remember?"

Pool? Embargo? Scoop? Alistair had given his news twink a crash course in hackspeak.

"It isn't that exclusive," Alistair said. "A colonel we met had seen an army report about guerrillas killing the families of soldiers at the junction. Cass got him on tape."

"He would say that," said T.K. "I've traveled with some battlefield scavengers who told me the army did it."

Even Cass paused to listen to his account of what sounded like rough companions.

"When we get to the junction," T.K. said, "I know where to start looking." He had no idea, of course, but he was not about to be stranded in the bush again.

They managed a dozen miles before the Land Rover stopped at the brink of a bridge dropped into the fast brown water by a few well-tamped limpet mines. An unexploded packet of plastic explosive dangled by a green cord from the twisted steel. Some yellow detonator envelopes littered the dirt. With no other way across, they spread a map on the vehicle's hood.

"We could wade it," said Cass. She twisted her light brown hair into a braid, and snapped the rear tabs of her Montreal Expos cap around it. Retrieving a rubber band from her lips, she finished the braid with a jacaranda blossom she had picked.

"If the quicksand and mines don't get you," T.K. said.

"Messy, those land mines washing downstream." Alistair rattled the map. "Where are we?"

"At that bridge." T.K. tapped the map with his finger.

Cass leaned across to contradict him. A bead of sweat rolled into the gentle hollow of her breasts.

"But the map shows a bend in the river," she said, "and there isn't any here. Who has the compass?"

There followed an awkward silence.

"Then we'll put a stick in the ground," said Cass, "and the angle of shadow—"

"Just point the hour hand of your watch at the sun," interrupted T.K. "Bisect the angle between that and twelve to find north."

"That angle points south," said Cass. One of her gray eyes had yesterday's sea-green flecks, yes, but today the other inclined more toward slate blue.

"Only when you're north of the equator," T.K. said. "We're just south of it."

Actually, Equatoria wasn't that near the equator. The colonial scapegrace who claimed its discovery in the nineteenth century had bestowed the misleading name to let the merchants who bankrolled his expedition assume that he had penetrated well beyond the coastal fleshpots.

Cass streaked on more sunblock from a plastic tube. Exposing her freckling shoulders to the tropical sun was foolish. T.K. could prove it by pressing his fingers against the delicate skin. Instead, he accepted a swig from the can of beer that Sipho was passing.

"What are you drinking?" she asked. With hair pulled back, her small ears stuck out beguilingly, combining with her wide eyes to give Cass the demeanor of an inquisitive gazelle.

"Our last beer," Sipho said. "Fancy a sip?"

"Crumbs, at this hour?"

"Fluid intake," Alistair said. "Essential out here in the bush."

Sipho wiped off his hefty recorder, shook out the fluffy mop at the end of his long shotgun microphone. Then he kicked Kobus, who was sleeping in the shade of the Land Rover. "Rock'n'roll time," Sipho said.

Kobus stretched, exposing a bony rib cage. His farmer's tan ended at the neck and elbows. "Without my nose for rock'n'roll," he told Sipho, "you'd be home herding cattle."

"The only thing your nose could find us is a truffle." Sipho's laugh exposed a few missing teeth. "Or a minefield."

Cass produced the disposable sort of camera that tourists point at each other. "Photo, everyone," she said.

"She had us doing this yesterday, man," Sipho told T.K.

"Closer everyone, leave room for me." Cass set her camera on a rock, clicked the timer, and rushed back into the picture. The camera tumbled, popping the flash at the sun.

"Again?" Cass set the camera upright and ran back, more successfully.

"Get this Mongolian pig fuck on the road," snapped T.K. "We're hacks, not sightseers."

He climbed behind the wheel, though no one asked him to drive, and started the engine. The others were barely aboard before he backed the Land Rover toward a track heading into the hills.

"What's all this got to do with pigs?" Cass asked Alistair, who had grabbed a seat beside her.

"That's what we call a press gang bang," Alistair said, "so many hacks jumping on a story that they ruin it. Mongolian pig fucks are held regularly."

The scrub vegetation gave way to thickets of bamboo and, still higher, a scattered grove of pine trees rising from the thick underbrush. An incongruous granite boulder crowned the nearest hill.

T.K. checked his mirror. Alistair, his arm snugly around Cass's shoulder, was promising her a bacon cooler. She wrinkled her nose at the thought of all those nitrates.

"Bacon cooler's what Australian hacks call a bloody good story," Alistair said. "Some bloke's reading his paper over breakfast and he gets so involved he forgets the bacon on his fork. That's a bacon cooler."

T.K. would have added that a bacon cooler required a dateline exotic enough that the reader couldn't pronounce it. He knew a hack from the *Financial Times* who grabbed China datelines starting with X for twenty days straight. But Z was okay, or Q if it wasn't followed by U.

But Cass would ask why a dateline, if it was about places, wasn't called a placeline, and T.K. didn't know.

"It takes rock'n'roll to get you prime time," said Schuyler, who preferred to do his stand-ups atop the kind of wrecked locomotives bound to be lying about the railway junction.

Cass preferred Chopin, she said, too new to realize they were talking about fighting.

"They called it boom-boom in Vietnam," Alistair said. "But so many photographers go deaf sleeping in their Walkmans that they can't tell a mortar from a grenade anymore, so we call it rock'n'roll."

They exaggerated to impress Cass, though not much. For all the profession of war's immorality, there was an initial high to covering one: sweeping over the treetops in a helicopter, hearing the gunfire patter, watching howitzer puffs on the hillsides. War turned abhorrent once people were killed and mutilated, homes and livelihoods smashed to rubble, and pastures cratered into moonscapes. Yet all too often journalism, in tidying up this chaos, failed to convey the random terror of combat that tore into a reporter's gut and hollowed the heart with cold fear.

"If it bleeds, it leads," Schuyler said. "Got to give the viewers what they want."

Flushed from the brush by the Land Rover, a band of furry gray monkeys scampered across the rough road, toward a mountain stream that threw a rainbow mist as it tumbled over the rocks. Here and there at the edge of the forest grew flowers as bright as the jacaranda blossom in Cass's braid. Across the shining river to their backs, in a country where there was no war, verdant tea plantations crowned distant hills like manicured hedges.

T.K., at the wheel, felt the exhilaration of being the first to explore these exotic hills—at least the first American reporter, certainly the first from his newspaper to grab a dateline up here.

But why was no one else traveling the road? "Too frigging peaceful," T.K. said.

"Can't you speak without using that word?" Cass said. "You only say it to upset me."

"'Frig'? You ought to try it."

"I won't say it for you, and sure as sugar don't expect me to do it for you."

She wasn't worth sorting out, but T.K. sifted the dustbin of his memory for one of Rolf's baser aphorisms.

"Women are like linoleum," T.K. said, and waited for Cass to rise to the bait. Even Sipho and Kobus stopped arguing and listened.

She snapped like a gullible young trout. "What's that supposed to mean?" she said.

"Lay them right the first time—"

"That's so swinish."

"—and you can walk over them for life."

"Let me out." She pronounced it "oot" like a proper Canadian. Neck flushed, Cass jumped off before the Rover had rolled to a halt.

"You don't talk like that in print," she spat at T.K. "Or on the air," she told Schuyler and his crew. "If your editors won't tolerate gutter language, why should I?"

"You could step on a mine if you try to walk back," Alistair said. "There's a war on."

Cass rose on point like a ballerina. "Buried here?"

T.K. rummaged through the numerous pockets of his photojournalist's vest, the one that carried him safely through the Horn of Africa, for something to lure her back. If there was a mine here, she'd find a way to step on it. He did not relish sweeping up whatever was left of her.

He tossed her his last square of chocolate, like a softball to a child. Cass fumbled the catch, but instead of throwing the candy back, she ate it, licking flakes of chocolate from her succulent lower lip.

"Swinish," she repeated, but climbed back in, as far as she could from T.K. "Sod off," Alistair told him. It was that kind of trip.

"Equatoria has a world-class collection of mines," said Alistair, letting his arm slither across her shoulder, "millions, and nobody marked where they're buried—that's why the farmers are afraid to plant their crops."

Land mines were indiscriminate weapons, which is why they terrified hacks like T.K., too.

"I thought they're supposed to put up signs," said Cass.

"The signs make great roofing," Sipho said.

After a few more miles, the lush hills with their infinite hues of green, the bright blue of the sky, and the yellow of the savanna stretching far below on the plain dissipated Cass's sulk.

"Those pines could be in Quebec," she said, cradling Sipho's long microphone to keep it from bouncing. "But what's that tree over there?"

"Tamarind," said T.K.

"Tamarind trees grow in India," Cass said.

"Tamarinds grow here, too," T.K. said. "Schuyler, got some cigarettes? Mine were grabbed at the roadblock."

But Cass refused to pass the crumpled pack forward; her personal space was not going to be polluted.

"I don't smoke them, I push them," said T.K. Was there anything he and this news twink agreed upon?

Schuyler explained how they carried cigarettes to barter with the locals. "Someone's less likely to kill you after you've offered him a smoke," he said.

"Unless he wants the whole pack, man," said Sipho.

Behind a field to their left emerged the first thatched houses of a village. But no children were playing, no farmers were harvesting the ripe corn.

Hoes and scythes lay scattered in the stubble. Something was wrong. Instead of turning, T.K. accelerated.

"Mind the dog," shouted Kobus, who was panning with his minicamera from the front seat. The road was too rutted for T.K. to swerve; he slammed on the brakes, but not fast enough. The gaunt yellow dog dropped a worn shoe from its mouth as it catapulted into the brush.

"You hit it," Cass said. Still holding Sipho's microphone, she jumped out to help, and looked up.

"The shoe," she said, "there's still some kind of foot in it."

"Dog bites man?" said Alistair. "No news there."

The breeze shifted, wafting in an acrid odor of cordite. From behind the nearest shack stepped a teenager with an AK rifle braced against his shoulder. More country boys with hard faces, black scarves tied around their heads, and ammunition pouches harnessed over their ragtag uniforms aimed Kalashnikovs into the reflection of T.K.'s rearview mirror. Some of the assault rifles had the magazines taped back to back for faster reloading.

"Here's your guerrillas," T.K. told her.

"Can we interview them?" said Cass, too green to hear T.K.'s heart pounding.

"Drop the mike," he said, "they think it's a gun." He waved his dirty handkerchief and climbed out of the Land Rover, slowly.

A guerrilla wearing jeans and an incongruous Red Sox T-shirt skewered the squealing dog on his bayonet and flung it against a thorn tree. The dog twitched. The other guerrillas laughed. The sadism on display did not encourage T.K. A hack who'd been grabbed in Lebanon told him once that the first hour in captivity was the most perilous.

"They're almost children," Cass whispered.

T.K. pulled her hands out of her pockets. Children could kill you sooner than grown-ups.

A guerrilla grabbed for the minicamera, but Kobus smiled and shook his hand, holding the Beta well back. T.K. and his companions were hustled down the road toward the village.

A woman sprawled at the entrance of her house, blood still soaking into the ocher dust. From under her body stuck out a small pair of lifeless legs. Cass paused to stare and cross herself, until a guerrilla's rifle pushed her back into line.

Flames licked the blackened beams of the largest building. Other houses burned with the stench of phosphorus grenades. Kobus limped beside T.K. The minicam's red light flickered; the bastard was filming this.

They passed more villagers contorted in sudden death, jelly spilling from crushed skulls, teeth overbiting lower lips like headhunters' trophies, the downside of rock'n'roll.

In the center of the square was splayed the remains of an old man. His stomach had been slashed open and the slick coils of intestines strung out. The genitals were hacked away. T.K. had heard of ritual executions like this.

Unsure what to do next, the guerrillas hustled the journalists inside a small stucco church with a corrugated metal roof.

"We have a picture like that back in Natal." Sipho pointed to the Jesus poster near the small altar. Target practice had perforated the blue eyes, the blond beard, the white robe, the outstretched hands. From a corner of the church came the waterfall sound of a guerrilla urinating.

Cass, her face ashen, sat on a bench.

"I can almost understand them." She strained at the wisps of conversation. "It's like a kind of patois—hear how they palatalize their consonants?"

"They're debating whether to shoot us," T.K. said, "and you want to know how they pronounce it?"

"I can reach out to them," she said.

The guerrillas searched the captives in turn and lashed their wrists. When they tied T.K., he flexed his hands to steal more movement. They found his American passport in the vest, but not the Irish one.

Cass let the rope bind her hands too tightly. When the guerrillas reached Kobus, he clutched his minicamera so firmly that they tied his fists around it.

And then Cass astonished her captors, gliding among them, smiling bravely, experimenting with words in English, French, Spanish that they might understand. They gawked at her braid and smooth limbs. Misinterpreting the curiosity, she stood on display like a healthy young thoroughbred while they took turns stroking the twisted mane of honey-colored hair that ended in a jacaranda flower.

"Get over here," Alistair pleaded, but a guerrilla shoved him back into the wall.

"We're learning to trust each other," said Cass, by now uncomfortable with the curiosity. A big guerrilla with a livid scar across his scalp rubbed against her.

Cass sought to reassure her captors that everything was okay. Forcing a smile, she jerked her thumb upward—screw all the insurgents and their mothers, too.

The big guerrilla shoved her to one side of the church, knocked off her cap with his Kalashnikov, grabbed her braid, and shoved down her head. His comrade, stockier, with rocket grenades cramming his harness, pried the gold ring from her finger.

T.K., spread-eagled against a wall with the others, watched over his shoulder. She wasn't his problem. All they could do was try to clean her up afterwards. So he felt estranged from the banal voice rising within him.

"Cigarette?" he asked, and turned around.

No, he needed to save himself, even as he was drawn toward Cass and what would follow. His own bound hands scooped up Schuyler's crumpled pack of cigarettes from the contents piled on a bench.

Controlling her by her braid, the big guerrilla had forced Cass onto her knees. His rifle barrel violated her dress. He pulled her face into his soiled trousers.

"Cigarette?" T.K. sidestepped a guerrilla's attempt to halt him. Alistair and the others would have followed but for the guerrilla, who cocked his AK-47 and backed them away. T.K. was alone now, but he had not reckoned on Cass.

Her tormentor fumbled at his trouser buttons, and neglected her braid. She sprang up, colliding under his jaw accidentally, but with such force that other guerrillas flinched. Their snickers erupted into derisive laughter.

"Cigarette?" interrupted T.K. His hands trembled.

Humiliated, the guerrilla slammed the Kalashnikov into T.K.'s face instead, driving him back onto his knees. Blood filled his mouth. He raised his immobilized hands in supplication. Cass looked on aghast.

The butt battered at his face. Blood dribbled into one eye. He could no longer stand. A blow to his ribs left him gagging for air. The Kalashnikov clicked off safety.

He would not die cringing. T.K. looked down the barrel into hard eyes bracketed by incongruously effeminate lashes. He repeated Cass's inadvertent obscenity with both thumbs, and braced for the bullet.

From the door came a shout. The guerrilla muttered and lowered his assault rifle. A small man wearing leather boots and a pistol holstered high on his belt trotted up. He slapped the guerrilla with the stump of an amputated arm.

T.K.'s knees buckled.

"But who are you?" the one-armed commander asked in English.

"I want my wedding ring," Cass sobbed. Under the commander's cold stare, the other guerrilla delivered up the ring and was stump-slapped in turn.

"Your husband, yes?" The commander looked from Cass to T.K. He nodded, though she meant nothing to him.

"We do not separate husbands and wives," said the commander. "We respect families. That is why we fight—for family values."

"We're foreign journalists." T.K. stood unsteadily. "We heard rumors of this."

"Of what?" the commander demanded.

"How government soldiers murder these villagers," T.K. said, "because they support your Patriotic Alliance."

"You are truly a journalist, for that is what has happened." The commander smiled. "You are welcome to Free Equatoria."

"Thank you," Cass said. "Might you untie us now?" The rope had mottled her hands, in which she now clutched her ring.

The commander motioned another guerrilla over to cut their ropes.

"But we must bind you more tightly if you abuse the hospitality of Free Equatoria," the commander said. "Proceed to passport formalities."

One of the guerrillas gathered up the passports from the bench. He took a large rubber stamp and ink pad out of a canvas ammunition pouch, and swatted each passport with the stamp, as if he were crushing an insect.

T.K. watched the guerrilla despoil one passport after another. When the Ministry of National Guidance caught sight of the ersatz visas, it could accuse them of consorting with the rebels and pull their accreditation. It hardly mattered for Cass—she'd be going straight home if they got out of here—but T.K. would need a clean new American passport.

The guerrilla put all the passports and press cards in his canvas pouch and gave it to his commander.

"We'll radio the contents to our base," said the commander, "to confirm that you are what you say. We do not shoot journalists who tell the truth."

Cass was busy restoring some dignity to the torn dress, oblivious to a red welt left by the Kalashnikov's gunsight. T.K. slipped his vest over her shoulders, only because he didn't want Cass attracting more oversexed guerrillas, and tucked her recorder into one pocket. Her spare tape lay on the bench; he scooped that up too.

"We leave before the puppet soldiers come back," the commander told them. "We must hide you where they can never find you."

Outside the small church, the guerrillas had loaded a truck with sacks of grain, blankets, and other loot taken from the village. Their commander nodded first toward the truck, then toward the Land Rover.

"You must travel in our lorry," he said. "My men will follow with your motorcar."

Guerrillas piled in around the journalists. Nausea washed over T.K. but he dared not close his eyes. He could not see the big man who wanted to shoot him. Having lost face, the troublemaker would likely return.

Reprieved from her ordeal, Cass looked contrite enough. "I messed up there, I always do."

"You're bad luck." T.K. wanted to shake her and hug her too, like a mother who catches a toddler playing in the street, to make her nevermore wander this backwater where bare limbs and cleavage would be misinterpreted.

Cass had stood her ground though, he'd give her that. She bumped against him as the truck took a winding road out of the village.

"They won't harm us anymore?" she asked.

He didn't know. "We've seen too much," he said.

"What I'm seeing is your face, and it's a mess." Cass probed the swelling with her fingers. His vest accentuated her fine arms. "I'll have to clean you up. How's the rest of you?"

"Maybe a rib cracked, just sore otherwise."

She pressed a handkerchief to the lip of her canteen, until T.K stopped her.

"Don't waste water, we'll need it to drink."

"You're feeling courageous," she said.

"Courage is being scared to death and saddling up anyway."

"What macho hero of yours said that?"

"Emily Dickinson."

"Feminist poetic introspection?" Cass sucked on a corner of the handkerchief and with her saliva daubed at the blood coagulating across his cheek. "That's why you protected me?"

"Some of those corpses looked raped."

"I'm trying to thank you," she said. "You risked your life for me, and pretend it happens every day."

"It does, somewhere."

"Do you always expect the worst?"

"I'm seldom disappointed," he told her.

Cass added more saliva to the handkerchief and rubbed harder. Tiny lines radiated from the corners of her gray eyes. She wasn't the flower child she looked.

"That's your wedding ring?" He needed to know.

"I heard some women correspondents wear these so they won't get bothered," she said.

It was well that Cass wasn't married. T.K. would not have a grieving spouse to console once she got herself killed.

The truck twisted through a rut, and she jabbed the deepest gash. T.K. flinched; the pain was emerging.

"I'll have to finish you later, Thomas," said Cass.

"It's T.K."

"But that doesn't make sense, not for Thomas Robert." Cass bit her lip. "I looked at your passport when the guerrilla stamped it."

"Just butt out—"

"Crumbs, will you really be forty next month?"

"—of my life, Cass."

"Once we're out of here, I promise," Cass said. "But we're wasting time being enemies."

She was right; there were enough around. It was time to act like allies, even if they'd never be friends.

"Your braid," he said, "it's got to go."

Obediently, Cass moved to unravel her hair.

"No, cut it off," he said. "I think it's what turned them on. They'd regroup for a gang bang, then swap you to some mercenaries for booze and cigarettes. But first, they'd have to kill the rest of us."

"They're so young," she said. "And they talk so softly."

"They were young once, maybe, but the war's beaten it out of them," T.K. said. He was traveling with a pack of jackals now, and packs were dangerous.

Cass handed him the fat Swiss Army knife from his vest pocket. "Use this," she asked.

He found the tiny scissors from the combination of tools and snipped at the braid with its crushed flower. She bowed her head while he severed each strand, uncomplaining even when the truck lurched.

"Crumbs, why are you leaving it for them?" Cass said.

T.K. had tossed away her braid with such casual deliberation that the wind whipped it back into the truck. The guerrillas vied to claim it. The winner tucked the trophy inside the back of his cap. The glossy braid flopped from side to side as he wiggled his hips seductively. His imitation of Cass delighted his comrades, but not her.

"They were fighting over my hair," she protested. "That's so revolting."

"Not as revolting as if you were still attached to it," T.K. told her.

It was dark when the trucks halted somewhere inside the rain forest. The guerrillas motioned the journalists down and lined them up. Kalashnikovs clicked in succession. Had they been brought here to be shot? But the guerrillas were only clearing the chambered cartridges. They slung their rifles and, grabbing blankets and food from the village, led the way into the forest.

The column moved among tall trees rising like pillars of a dark cathedral. Traces of moonlight trickled through the filter of tangled limbs, branches, and leaves overhead. The moss yielded underfoot, a vast, spongy carpet. Vines hidden like hunters' snares snatched at their bodies. They waded a stream only knee-deep but flowing so fast that T.K. nearly fell in. Around him drifted shadows with assault rifles.

Ahead, Cass moved gracefully, catching branches before they slapped him in the face. Kobus, limping, lagged until an older guerrilla prodded him with a rifle.

The moon lit the way once the trees thinned out. They marched for another hour, until they arrived at a hollow in the hills; it was the night's encampment. The old guerrilla herded the journalists to the shelter of a rock outcropping, and built a small fire under it. Then he stepped back, squatted with his Kalashnikov against his haunches, and watched them. In profile, he resembled T.K.'s old city editor a few newspapers back.

"He must be sixty," said Cass. "He should go home."

"They need him to cover their retreat," T.K. said. "He'll stand and fight because he's too old to run."

The guerrilla left and returned with a pot of water and another of stewed meat and rice. T.K. rolled some rice and meat into a ball and popped it into his mouth to show her how to eat it.

Cass tasted a fragrant handful. "What's this?"

"Puppy dog," T.K. said. "Had a doggie as a kid?"

"You're disgusting." Cass stopped eating and walked away from the small fire, though not too far.

"Why tease her?" Alistair was angry. "She nearly got raped."

"And nearly got us killed," T.K. said. "You want to tell her we're eating cane rat? She'd barf it all over us."

"You could say it's, well, a nice roast?"

What would Cass do when their captors ran out of rats and boiled up some pit vipers?

"I'm misinformed," T.K. said. "Alistair says it's roast beef."

"I don't see any cows," she called back from the shadows.

"You've got to eat something," T.K. told her. "There's hot water here to work on my face later."

"If you behave," she said. Cass came back and tilted him toward the fire to examine the deep gash that exposed his cheekbone.

"You need a couple of stitches here," she said. "I have a needle, but no suture or anesthetic."

"Try some dental floss in my vest," he said. "You Girl Scouts know how to use that."

"I'm a woman," she snapped, "and this is going to hurt."

The piercing pain of the needle caused him to pass out. When he opened his eyes, Cass was cradling his head in her lap while she bathed his face.

"Broke your nose once, didn't you?" she said, and scooped more warm water from the pail with her hands.

"It doesn't look that bad," she hastened to add. "My brothers broke their noses playing hockey—very macho I suppose, if you're fourteen years old."

The guerrilla commander padded out of the shadows. "I would send our medical orderly," he said, "but your wife gives you more loving care. The soldier who struck you will be punished for disgracing our cause."

"Things happen." It was painful for T.K. to talk.

The commander squatted on his haunches and warmed his one hand over the campfire. A cool wind had shifted the smoke in T.K.'s direction, scattering the mosquitoes.

"Where is your pretty pigtail?" the commander asked.

"I cut it off," said Cass.

"My men behaved like children," said the commander. "The next time one neglects his duty, I must have him shot; our struggle demands discipline. I radioed my base about you all. If you have told the truth, you will be free to go."

Sometimes hacks groveled not just for their scoops, but also to stay alive. "You are married too?" T.K. asked.

The commander watched Cass push the button on her recorder before he answered. "I have not seen my wife for more than a year," he said, "but her letters worry me."

"I'm so sorry." T.K. sighed in a tone to invite his captor's confidence.

"My daughter is now twelve years," the commander said, "but already she outgrows school under the trees at our base. She is too clever for her teachers. Our alliance's leader—he was once a doctor, you know—is compassionate as well as brilliant. He arranged to send my little girl to a school outside the country, but my wife refuses to be separated from both her daughter and husband."

"Let us pray your victory comes soon," coaxed T.K.

"I have fought for twenty years, first against the colonialists and now against the Communists. My wife was a nurse at our base hospital when the mortar bomb took off my arm. I am prepared to sacrifice my other arm but not my daughter's future. War's tragedy is that it extinguishes not just lives, you see, but also talents and possibilities."

The commander smiled sympathetically at Cass.

"I can't understand what you're an alliance of," she replied.

"What?" The commander turned belligerent, as if atoning for his earlier candor.

Shut up, Cass, T.K. told himself, but she couldn't hear him.

"You call yourselves a Patriotic Alliance, but who's your allies—besides the C.I.A., I mean?" said Cass. "Don't you and the government come from opposing ethnic groups?"

"A Communist lie. Some of my men are related by clan to the oppressor, yet they fight alongside us. Now, I must attend to their welfare." The commander stood up. "Give me your tape—this was not an interview."

T.K. wrested the recorder from Cass and fumbled for the cassette. "Don't argue," he told her.

The commander pulled out strands of tape and threw the tangled cassette into the fire. "You would be unwise to try to leave tonight," he told them. "And put out your fire so it will not bring the gunships."

Cass watched her tape crackle and shrivel. "You had no right to give him my interview," she snapped at T.K. after the commander withdrew.

Schuyler interposed himself. "You two call a truce till we're out of here. We have another long hike tomorrow."

"As if Communists mattered anymore," she said.

"During the cold war, the labels stuck so easily." Alistair moved in to console her. "Villains and heroes were Communist and anti-Communist, and readers drew appropriate conclusions. Who cared if the local poobah devoured children so long as he was anti-Communist? Now the scoundrels we cover have split into neo-Communist, pseudo-non-Communist, quasi-anti-Communist like the commander here—no wonder the reader gives up."

"Then drop the Communist part," Cass said.

"How?" said Alistair. "Communists sell papers—not as briskly as Nazis, but they still sell." Alistair cast a wistful glance in Cass's direction before joining Kobus and Sipho, who had stretched out near the fire and were bickering goodnights to each other.

"I suppose the guerrillas expect me to stay with you." Cass made it sound distasteful.

"Unless you'd prefer them," T.K. said. Tonight, he and Cass were stuck with each other.

He wet down the fire with the water until only a few embers glowed. A young guerrilla dumped a tarpaulin at their feet.

T.K. waited until he left, then sat down beside Cass and shook out his handkerchief. "Hide it," he said softly, "where they won't find it."

The tape fell into her hand.

"Switched tapes?" said Cass. "You're incorrigible."

"Don't walk off again," he told her. "They've put the youngest kids on guard. They're scared enough to shoot at anything that moves."

"You know a lot about wars," she said.

"I covered a few."

"Then who killed the villagers?" Cass asked.

In the ebbing glow of the campfire cinders, her eyes had become dark pools under the even brows. "You told the commander it was the army, but his guerrillas didn't seem that upset."

"If I said it wasn't the army, the commander might have shot us," T.K. said. "That elder hacked apart in the square had a guerrilla trademark."

The insurgents liked to make villagers watch while they carved up their elders. It drove home a message that this government couldn't protect anyone. But the army was capable of atrocities too.

There was no monopoly on truth out here, he told her. People would look you in the eye and tell contradictory stories. All you could do was report both sides and step out of the way.

"I expected things to be clearer," said Cass. She held up a tiny pill. "Your vest pocket's full of these."

"Swallow a couple," he told her. "They prevent malaria."

"It tastes bitter." But Cass washed the pills down with a sip of water.

"That old man, that woman and her child lying out there with no one to bury them," she said, "wouldn't you like to do for those people what you did for me today?"

"People will kill each other whether we're there or not," he replied. A crusading hack was a hazard, not to mention a pain in the ass.

"A journalist who absolves himself from moral responsibility can't be much of a journalist," Cass mused. "I want passion in my reporting."

She rolled over on her elbows to confront him. "Why did you bother?" she asked.

"Someone had to protect you," he said.

"I mean, to become a journalist?"

"There's no heavy lifting involved," T.K. said.

"Crumbs, but you work hard at not working hard," Cass said. She stretched out on her back. "I'm glad I'm not a man burdened with your machismo—your lot would drive any wife nuts."

"Schuyler's married, well, kind of separated, a minor spat."

"How minor?"

"Sarah set fire to his passport, complained he spent too much time away. She married Schuyler hoping he'd become a rabbi."

"Alistair?"

"Always falling in love," T.K. said. Cass was too absorbed in herself to notice.

"Sipho's family's in South Africa, but he never seems to go home," T.K. said.

"And Kobus?"

"Likes marriage enough, tried it three times."

Cass looked up into the starry night. "We have skies like this in Shawinigan, but where's the Big Dipper?"

"Not this far south," he told her. "Orient yourself using the Southern Cross there."

Watching it hanging over the trees brought back the Croce del Sud, the hotel in Mogadishu where he stayed on his first trip to Somalia. He would have shared his nostalgia, and told her about the fresh tuna and pasta under starry skies in the cool courtyard, but why would she care? Anyway, the hotel closed down when the country fell apart.

"And you?" she said. "Is there anybody you care enough about to commit yourself, without reservation?"

"Not anymore," T.K. said.

"I was fortunate to have found someone like that," she said. Her hoarding of the details twinged at T.K.'s gut.

But Cass revealed only her weariness. She now switched mindlessly into French, whispering some confidence that he could not understand.

The flailing of a giant eggbeater interrupted her. An arc of red rain flashed across the forest. Just as abruptly, the red rain stopped, the racket faded.

"Tracer bullets," he said. "Helicopter's looking for our guerrillas." This wasn't Shawinigan after all.

He stamped out the last embers so thoroughly that he had trouble finding her. "Let's go sleep together," he said.

"Do it, here?" She gave a nervous laugh.

"Not like that, just keep each other warm," he said. And holding her would convince him that he'd survived. The guerrillas might come calling again if they realized she didn't belong to him.

T.K. pulled some small branches together into a mattress, folded the tarpaulin on top, and surrounded it with a ridge of pine needles. Snakes liked warmth too. Needles might not stop a snake but he couldn't think of anything else and he didn't want her keeping him awake.

Cass slipped between the canvas without quite touching him. "Watch yourself," she said. "I earned a yellow belt in karate once."

"Just go to sleep, will you, I'm exhausted." T.K. drifted off into a muddled nightmare that had him racing about on deadline, unable to find a telex or a telephone or even his story to file because Cass kept hiding them.

He slept hard for a few hours before the throbbing pain jarred him awake. She had backed up against him under the tarp. She was breathing so softly that he could hear a jackal somewhere. She must have snuggled up for the warmth, though she clutched his arm around her, like a tot with a favorite toy.

He had not aspired to sleep with her, not even like this. Someone with her clean looks could and would find better. He burrowed his nose into the nape of her neck and tasted it. She thrashed a little, as if resisting an insect. He should warn her that perfume or scented soap attracted mosquitoes. The telltale jasmine in her sweaty fragrance, the sturdiness of her hip jammed into his groin, the plumpness of her small breast under his hand, reproached him for having traveled alone so long. Unable to go back to sleep, he held her until first light revealed a pair of children with AKs crouching like predators in the mist, watching Cass and him.

The child guerrillas had vanished by the time she stirred and pushed aside his numbed arm. Had she sensed his botched kiss? She seemed unperturbed.

"You're rather sweet when you're asleep," Cass said. She combed out her hair with her fingers. Some fair wisps that had escaped his Swiss Army knife fell over her face.

"But talk about sexist, you want to tie my shoelaces together so you can catch me when I trip."

She opened the tiny scissors on the combination knife and set to work trimming her hair more evenly. He offered to help, but she resisted.

"Don't treat me like some damsel in distress," she said. Leeches from the forced march left red streaks down her bare legs. A few fresh ones had attached themselves.

"Sure fooled me," T.K. said. He patted down his vest for a loose cigarette and lit up.

"And don't get ideas about sleeping together again," Cass said, waving off his cigarette smoke. "I need a new man in my life like a dolphin needs a tuna net."

The engorged leeches obligingly dropped off as T.K. tapped them one by one with the glowing cigarette. She had the taut calves of a serious runner.

"You were tolerable yourself last night," he told her, "with your mouth shut for a change."

4.

PORTO PARADISO, *quatoria—Th* Unit*d Stat*s *stablish*d
diplomatic r*lations with *quatoria today, *nding y*ars of cold
war animosity caus*d by form*r Sovi*t support for th* pro-
Marxist gov*rnm*nt and cland*stin* Am*rican backing of insurg*nts in th* tamarind-studd*d bush . . .

Blue smoke from the breakfast fires mingled with the mist. The guerrillas were breaking camp, followed by Kobus and Sipho with their minicamera and recorder. Alistair had joined T.K. and Cass for root tea and stale
bread sent by the guerrillas when the commander returned.

"We cannot feed you properly, so you may leave," he said, "but you must
tell the world about the women and children you saw murdered by the
Communists, and why we fight for peace."

Hesitantly, Alistair asked about the Land Rover.

"We must pay for what we take, so how can we afford it?" The commander returned their passports. "Come back and enjoy our hospitality in
Free Equatoria. My fighters now take you to your motorcar."

The hike followed a game trail spangled by sunlight that filtered through
the leafy canopy of the forest. In the distance, wet slabs of cliff gleamed in

the sun. Cass had lost interest in T.K. and bounded ahead with Sipho and Kobus.

Alistair fell into step instead, whining about how T.K. had wrapped himself around her last night like a python around a lamb, the randy bastard. "She did do a smashing job on your cheek," he said.

T.K. would have told Alistair that he could have her, but Cass was not his to give. "Don't make her our problem," T.K. said.

He did not remember the route last night as being this rugged. Even in daylight, they made hardly better time. Every few hundred yards, they halted while the guerrilla walking point knelt and disconnected a trip wire hidden in the tall grass. After they passed, the guerrilla behind them reconnected each wire. The entire trail was mined.

At last, the lead guerrilla pointed with his Kalashnikov to the clearing beyond the leafy trees. T.K. recognized the livid scar, and for the first time, on the guerrilla's belt, the loop of shriveled ears proving how many he had killed. T.K. had seen such trophies flaunted in the Horn of Africa.

Cass, who had fallen back, noticed it too. "What's that?" she asked.

"Dried fruit," lied T.K.

"Crumbs," said Cass, "it looks more like dried ears to me."

By the time they reached the road, a thickening layer of clouds blanketed the sun. The guerrilla escort had disappeared. The publisher's teddy bear now perched on the steering wheel of their Land Rover, behind the truck. His wits dulled by fatigue, T.K. trudged toward the Rover until Sipho barred his way.

Sipho and Kobus were whispering and T.K. understood. Why would the guerrillas abandon a Land Rover, with their reputation for hijacking such vehicles. The key was still in the ignition. He led Cass behind the hard spire of a termite hill on the far shoulder. Schuyler and Alistair had dropped off the road themselves.

With her fingers, Cass tested T.K.'s face like a ripe melon and seemed satisfied. "These stitches can come out in a few days," she said.

Sipho and Kobus were circling the Land Rover.

Cass pulled away. "What's going on?"

"Precautions." T.K. pressed her head down. "Sipho was an A.N.C. guerrilla once; Kobus was Rhodesian Light Infantry, till a mine took off his foot."

"That's why he limped last night?" she said. "He never complained."

"Figured they'd shoot him if he straggled."

"I ask a lot of dumb questions," Cass said.

"No such thing as dumb questions," T.K. told her, "only dumb answers."

Kobus had slipped under the Land Rover while Sipho probed between the seats, moved around to the hood and gingerly pried it open. Sipho called softly to Kobus, who handed across a large pocketknife.

Sipho jumped to his feet, grinning as he waved the teddy bear like a trophy. So that's where they hid it. Kobus engulfed him in a hug and shoved his fingers into Sipho's tight hair.

"Nervy little bugger." Kobus laughed, "You did this in the old days, didn't you?"

T.K. dashed with Cass to the Land Rover, pulled her aboard. Alistair was behind the wheel.

"Bye-bye, bear," Sipho said. He pitched the teddy bear into the woods and ducked. The explosion collapsed a tree and showered dirt onto the road.

"Had it wired to the ignition," said Kobus, "shoved enough Semtex up its ass to blow us to hell. There's more under that lorry, Sipho says, clever 'oke, I reckoned our Zulu herdboy would blow us up."

"If I let you Boers disarm it," said Sipho, "we'd be dead."

"Maybe the commander ordered the guerrillas to defuse the booby trap and they disobeyed," Cass said. "Or maybe he planned it all."

"Down," called Sipho. They weren't away yet.

The old Land Rover gathered speed, and a Kalashnikov popped behind them. The final bullet pinged on the rear bumper as Alistair accelerated into the curve.

"A bit slow," said Alistair.

*   *   *

The Land Rover barreled down a road now revealed in daylight to be carved into the precipitous flank of a wooded ravine. They were putting the guerrillas well behind.

Since they left the forest, the sky had darkened. Though the heavy clouds presaged rain, what fell instead was hail that pelted the Rover and occupants with ice fatter than marbles. Alistair pulled over under a big indaba tree, waiting for the hail to stop.

He reached over and fondled Cass's ankle. "Well done," he told her. "You could have collapsed on us."

Cass basked in the compliment. "I'm glad I asked my editors for permission to come," she said.

"Permission to do your job?" Alistair recoiled in mock horror. "Never ask your editors what you can do, ask only what they can do, like upgrade you to first class or pouch you the latest salacious best-seller."

"What do editors know?" agreed Schuyler. "They'll only think up ways to waste your time."

"And if they do," Alistair said, "fine them."

"Fine them?" Cass slipped on the wrinkled shirt that T.K. had provided from his pack, without quite thanking him.

"When they cut your story or change your lede, you must fine them," Alistair said, "and if they wake you at night without good reason, you must fine them heavily."

Cass supposed that her editors would object.

"How," asked Alistair, "when they don't know? A double order of grilled lobster on your expense account, that's a fine. Or an overpriced bottle of imported wine—fluid intake's essential out here, you know."

"Tuck it under taxis," T.K. said.

"You must always control your editors," said Alistair, "while they think they're controlling you."

The clouds dissipated. Alistair stretched and restarted the engine.

"I need five minutes at the village for cover shots, man," Kobus said. "What I shot from the hip yesterday was marginal."

"The Boer wants his visuals in focus this time," quipped Sipho.

They had bagged the dateline—did Schuyler's crew plan to resmolder the ruins? Still, Kobus and Sipho just saved his life. "Five minutes," T.K. said, "and then let's travel, we've used up our luck."

"Don't you ever worry about getting killed covering wars?" Cass asked Kobus.

"No bloody need," he said. "Just worry about the bullet with your name on it."

"Cameraman I worked with in the Gulf," Sipho said, "told me he only worried about bullets addressed 'to whom it may concern.'"

Fetid decay permeated the devastated village. The square looked smaller, outscaled by corpses bloating in the heat.

Cass turned so queasy that T.K. expected her to faint. Instead, she climbed out of the Land Rover and began telling the tape recorder what they saw.

"Where are you going?" she asked T.K.

"Body count." He might have taken Cass along, but she'd have little appetite for what Rolf called "flies-in-the-eyes."

In the weeds beyond the village, he found two women, then a third, lying yards apart. From the torn dresses, they looked raped before their heads were smashed. How could he try to explain cruelty like this?

He started losing count at thirty corpses, but more had to be out there. As he squatted beside an old woman, he was jabbed from behind. He stood up slowly with hands high, and turned around to see a long stick pointed by a boy barely five years old.

A girl only a few years older rushed from the woods to snatch away her brother. T.K. followed at a distance, wary of an ambush.

The children stopped beside a woman curled into a fetus against the trunk of a wild fig tree. The girl pulled her brother's thumb from his mouth and replaced it with a piece of hail harvested from the grass. While the distracted boy sucked on the ice, she knelt down and fanned off flies crawling over the woman's eyes. The girl looked up with a child's trust, inviting T.K. to resurrect her mother.

T.K. knelt and examined the woman. She had died in the night quietly enough, judging by the single bullet hole in her back. There was nothing he could do.

Gently, he closed her eyelids.

"Speak English?" he asked the children. They had to understand that he was not among those who murdered their mother, that he had come to enlighten his readers over their coffee, bran flakes, and low-fat bagels. Whatever he wrote could never undo the horror, but it was better than silence. You couldn't walk away from something like this.

Yet why should the world care when the enormity of evil was trivialized in video games and afternoon talk shows? Angered by the impotence of his tongue, T.K. took the last dollars from his money belt and divided them between the children, though they were worthless here. Then he did walk away, out of the dark woods into sunshine as bright as he could remember.

"What did you find?" Cass called from the edge of the village.

"Get Kobus," he said. "Don't come yourself."

"Why not?"

"A woman got shot in the back running with her kids, not a pretty sight."

"Not pretty for me," Cass said, "but pretty enough for Kobus to show millions of television viewers, eh?" She brushed past him, and returned with the children in tow.

"At least," he said, "they didn't rape her in front of the kids."

"Don't you feel anything more?" Cass said.

"My grief won't bring her back. You can't do your job if the horror captures your spirit."

"We'll take them with us," she said.

T.K. shook his head. "I counted thirty bodies. That means dozens of villagers are still hiding. They'll come out when it's safe, they know these kids."

"The children could starve first."

"That's worse than getting dumped in a state orphanage, or on the streets? The girl could sell herself to survive. Maybe her little brother'd pick pockets. Or do you plan to ship them back to Shawinigan?"

"I just might," Cass snapped, "and first I'm finding them something to eat." She looked at the scorched huts around her.

The children bolted into the woods at the sound of an armored car careening into the square. A squad of men in blue dismounted.

"We could get away," Cass said.

"Where?" T.K. said. Blue uniforms were worn by field police, the manifestation of tenuous authority. T.K. took out his passport, the Irish one unsullied by guerrilla graffiti, and walked toward the armored car. A dead guerrilla lay lashed over one fender like a hunting trophy.

"Foreign press," T.K. said to a policeman wearing grimy sergeant's stripes. "Speak English?"

Cass followed with her Canadian passport. *"Bom dia, buenos días, bon jour,"* she said, and smiled sweetly.

The sergeant reciprocated with a stiff bow. He retreated to study their passports. Other policemen were bringing in Schuyler and his crew, and Alistair.

"Your passport's Irish," Cass said, "but you're not."

"Anyone with a grandparent from Ireland can ask for one," T.K. said. "It's handier than an American passport because nobody hates the Irish out here."

He sidled up and lifted the chin of the guerrilla ripening on the sun-scorched metal of the armored car, elbows still trussed behind his back. The bullet had drilled into the forehead at close range and mushroomed out behind an ear, enough to confirm that he was captured, then killed. He looked young enough to have parents worrying about him.

A shout from the sergeant startled T.K.

"They want us to help," he told Cass. "You mind our gear before they grab it."

T.K. covered his nose against the rank odor and helped pile the decomposing corpses in the center of the square. Policemen dragged in more bodies, though not the children's mother.

It took an hour to stack the bodies tightly enough that a single jerrican of gasoline could soak down the pyre. The bodies were jerking like marionettes within the flames when the sergeant led the way to the armored car.

"I think he wants us—" T.K., gagging at the stench, couldn't finish his thought.

A policeman even younger than the dead guerrilla helped Cass into the Land Rover. She tried not to look back.

"Muchas gracias, obrigado, merci beaucoup, spasibo," said Cass, and rewarded the policeman with a smile that left T.K. jealous.

"Oui, sí, da," she said.

"How many languages do you know?" T.K. asked. The Land Rover followed the armored car down the road.

"I'm Quebecois," she said, "so I grew up speaking French, but my grandmother taught me some Ukrainian, and I studied Spanish and Portuguese at McGill. What languages did they teach you at—where's Lake Forest College?"

"It must be in a forest by a lake."

"But isn't that where you went?" Cass said.

T.K. didn't reply. She must have pried it out of Schuyler.

Cass was unapologetic. "Journalists who poke into other people's lives have no cause to complain when it's done to them," she said.

"Good fuzz and wuzz back there," Schuyler said.

It puzzled Cass. "Fuzz and wuzz?"

"Cops and corpses," T.K. said, "like someone who was but isn't anymore."

"I started out on fuzz and wuzz for an affiliate in Chicago," Schuyler said. "Catch a homicide early enough and you'd get it on the news at noon, three o'clock, prime time at six, sometimes eleven. That's legs."

Cass wrinkled her nose and stretched.

"I did fires, car crashes too, and nearly your Prime Minister," Schuyler told Cass. "He flew to Chicago to give a speech on free trade. But I got diverted to a double murder in the burbs."

The police station sat at the crossroads of a rough intersection. A barbed wire fence festooned with rusty cans surrounded the shabby concrete buildings. Pebbles inside the cans rattled in the breeze. A concrete watchtower looked abandoned but for a machine gun poking through a slit. The moat outside the barbed wire had filled with garbage. Geese pecked at the dirt inside the gate.

Atop one of the gateposts was mounted a bleached skull to ward off evil spirits, guerrillas, and whatever law-abiding civilians remained. Even without an enemy in sight, the station looked under siege.

But T.K.'s eyes were drawn to a battered truck parked just beyond the gate. Dried blood had darkened the boxes for seats, and the broom handle gearshift. The young policeman pointed his finger at T.K. and pretended to shoot.

Inside the station, the dank concrete walls were decorated with a couple of fading posters. One warned of mines in sundry shapes and sizes. In the other, a bleached blonde with enormous breasts sat on her haunches, coyly exposing an armpit to the camera.

Behind a graffiti-scarred desk sat the captain. He looked up and tugged a blue jacket across his paunch. A pistol was jammed into his waistband. Cass explained their arrival with bits of French, Portuguese, and Spanish before he interrupted in rough English.

"No journalists without escort," the captain said.

"Tell him our minder fell ill," Alistair told Cass, but she was glaring at the blond pinup.

"Sexy, yes?" the captain said.

"Degrades women," she said.

The captain nodded along. "And sexy, yes?"

When Cass began to explain the fallacy in this, the captain cut her off with a cough. He shuffled their passports and press cards as if preparing a hand of poker.

"No pictures without an escort," he said. "Show me the permission for your camera."

Kobus handed over a creased certificate. The captain traced the words with a dirty fingernail.

"This one expires," he said, shaking his head. "No new permission? So we confiscate the camera."

Sipho reached for the minicamera on the desk. "Sun fried my friend's brains. Entrust the camera to me, a comrade of color."

The captain pulled the camera away. "Apply for it in the capital, in triplicate."

Cass rapped on the desk, her indignation portending fresh disaster.

"Now see here," she said. "Keeping their camera is so unfair—you haven't confiscated my tape recorder and Thomas has his—"

"Shut up," T.K. said. Life wasn't fair. Why did Cass think otherwise?

"Tape recorder?" said the captain. "Present it for inspection." He pushed the buttons. "No permission, perhaps you smuggle it—we confiscate this, too."

"I can't work without it." Cass recoiled. "I can't afford another. Please."

"Perhaps I return it," the captain said, "upon payment of a small fine."

"How much?"

"One hundred dollars." The captain watched her face. "With surcharges, a total of two hundred dollars."

"I don't have two hundred dollars." Cass wiped her eyes. "I barely have fifty, and that's Canadian."

"You are so pretty, we find a solution." The captain grabbed her arm and whispered in her ear.

Cass pulled back. "Not for a tape recorder I won't," she said. "Aren't you ashamed?"

"Three hundred dollars it must be, including storage fees." The captain held the recorder to his ear. "Will this play reggae tapes?"

"Help, anyone." Cass looked at her companions.

"My money rented the Land Rover," Alistair said.

"Thomas," Cass said, "please?"

T.K. rifled his pockets, but his remaining dollars were left with the orphans. Cass looked so miserable that finally T.K. removed his desert boot and shook it.

"Change for a five-hundred?" he asked.

At the request, the captain laughed as though T.K. had told a smutty joke, and pocketed the bank note.

"I need a receipt," T.K. said. Otherwise he'd have to stick this under taxis again. His newspaper took such a parochial view of bribes.

The police captain scribbled on a piece of paper and shoved it across the old desk.

"Though you wound my pride," he told Cass, "I content myself with your smile."

Cass struggled to oblige.

"A big diamond smile." The captain held the tape recorder beyond her reach.

T.K. read the receipt: "$500."

"It's not signed," he said, "and there's no official stamp."

"Sign it yourself—we are too poor for stamps, we are not paid many months. Now leave before I confiscate your motorcar, it is a month's walk to the capital."

When they turned to leave, T.K. asked about the old truck.

"Stolen from the state," said the captain. "We shot one thief, now we hunt the others."

They filed from the station. Alistair shooed a slumbering policeman out of the Land Rover.

"You got those visuals," Kobus said. Sipho was grinning at having switched videotapes so easily.

"If we charter back before dark," Schuyler said, "we can make prime time."

But T.K. stood in silence before the battered truck, staring at the old man's Bible. His five hundred dollars should have ransomed lives, not a superfluous tape recorder. The butchers in blue might have left the scavengers alone. He closed his eyes and saw the elder carved alive in front of his people, the mother shot in the back for hustling her children to safety.

It was the hack's paradox of which he despaired too: A story wasn't worth covering unless you cared, but if you cared enough, you became unfit to cover it because you were no longer objective.

Cass tugged at T.K.'s sleeve. "We're going before that dreadful policeman wants my tape recorder again."

T.K. turned on her. "You're not worth five hundred dollars."

"Crumbs," she said, "it's not my fault you had that big bill you enjoy waving. I'll pay you when I can."

The armored car escorted them out of the police station and back to the main road. This story was competitive now, but it would do T.K. no good if the others chartered back to file while he was left stranded on some obscure airfield.

"I'm doing you a favor, look at me." T.K. pushed his airline ticket at Cass. He was getting nowhere with her anyway, and who would be expecting her dispatches?

"You pay me back two hundred bucks and give me Ginny's place on the charter," he said. "Bargain, right?"

Cass sniffled.

"Leave her alone," Alistair interceded. "What's a few hundred dollars to upset you?"

"It's me she owes, so butt out," T.K. said. "Waiting an hour or two for the commercial flight won't hurt her."

Cass pulled off T.K.'s shirt and flung it at him.

"And don't go whining to Alistair," he told her, "because you don't have a choice."

*   *   *

"Heard of a reporter named Cassandra Benoit?" asked the new American ambassador back in the capital.

The ambassador, an amiable oilman who earned his posting by contributing to the last presidential campaign back home, rummaged among his pockets as if he had mislaid a lottery ticket, though what he produced looked more like a diplomatic cable.

Cassandra Benoit? T.K. pretended to match the name to a face. "I think I met her up-country—she stayed on when we flew back last week, but she's not American."

"My Canadian colleague who watches this place asked for help on her whereabouts. They don't maintain an embassy here, you know. Miss Benoit's one of his nationals. Can I assure him she's bright-eyed and bushy-tailed?"

"Bushy-tailed when we left her," said T.K., though hardly bright-eyed, remembering the news twink's snit when he parked her with that ungainly typewriter at the airline waiting shed. "She'll turn up."

"When she does, tell her to call home," said the American ambassador. "I've got enough problems keeping my own nationals out of jail, or the morgue. Next time you stop by the embassy, T.K., I'll break out some bourbon and branch water."

The ambassador slapped T.K.'s back and handed him a ballpoint pen with *Compliments of The United States Embassy Equatoria* stamped in big white letters, the creative kind of use of taxpayer dollars that built the national deficit.

"I ordered a batch of these for the locals, but you take one," the ambassador said. "You skinny little bastards in the press'd steal them anyway. I never met a reporter with enough pens."

As a hack, T.K. avoided the company of diplomats, unless they knew something. A clean passport unsullied by guerrilla stamps and a high-cholesterol fix in the snack bar had lured him this time to the newly opened embassy.

"Thanks for running interference." T.K. held up his pristine passport. Now he only needed a new working press visa from the Ministry. "Sorry about losing the old one in the bush."

"I cleared you for our snack bar today," said the ambassador. "You're having lunch with our, ah, cultural attaché?"

The spook looked fleshier, his crew cut bushier. A faded tattoo on his burly forearm displayed a mermaid impaled on a dagger. He had telephoned after T.K. returned from the bush, to propose they swap impressions. Now he handed T.K. an engraved business card: "Commercial Attaché," it announced.

"Don't call me at this number, it's not secure," the spook said. "Use the other one, though it's not secure either."

His fingers tapped out a code on the buttons of a steel-jacketed door marked *Restricted Area: Authorized Personnel Only*. What lay behind the door—code room, surveillance equipment, escape tunnel?

"Usually the press isn't allowed in here," said the spook.

The steel door swung open and T.K. found himself poolside at the snack bar, with its diet colas, potato chips, pizzas, hot dogs, Twinkies, candy bars—the kind of junk sustenance deemed essential to the conduct of American diplomacy abroad and delivered duty-free in the diplomatic pouch.

"Let's chow down first, peel the onion later," the spook told T.K.

Like so many hacks, T.K. loathed the little nirvanas built to cushion American diplomats from the miserable world outside the iron gates. He resented the treats they refused to share from basement commissaries stocked with frozen orange juice, sugared breakfast cereals, canned chili, boxed milk, and other made-in-America foodstuffs hoarded as carefully as classified documents lest a Mars bar or Coke fall into unauthorized hands. He resented their obscene station wagons, washer-dryers, and air conditioners shipped over at taxpayer expense, the snack bar, videocassette library, pharmacy, and mailbox from which ordinary Americans luckless enough to travel without official maroon passports were barred. He resented the cost-of-living differential paid to American diplomats—twenty percent extra in Equatoria—for living in conditions no worse than what American hacks were accustomed to. He resented being grilled like some terrorist by Marine Corps receptionists with acne and cottonmouth drawls.

Yet T.K. swallowed his pride. For a hack, there were times to bully, to banter, and to beg. So he let the spook buy their cheeseburgers while T.K. pumped him for details of the massacre.

The spook rambled, but on deepest background, not for attribution, affirmative? "I can confirm knowledge of a depopulation of the community in question," he said, "with significant collateral damage incendiary-wise."

So someone slaughtered civilians and burned the village; T.K. knew that. "But who did it," he asked, "soldiers or guerrillas?"

"The indigenous population was ascertained to be rendering assistance to the insurgency, which resulted in a high rate of noncombatant nonviability due to a temporary lapse of uniformed discipline."

"I lost you there," T.K. said.

"The army found the villagers helping the rebels, so it went in and kicked ass, couldn't control its boys."

"How do you know?"

American ground-sirloin juices dribbled down the spook's thick fingers. "Technical means," he whispered.

"You're telling me some spy satellite a hundred miles in space . . ."

"Amazing, huh," said the spook, "high-tech stuff."

". . . saw people getting hacked in a remote village and identified the killers?"

"Incredible detail," the spook said. "That billion-dollar bird can catch you scratching your ass and tell you where it itches. Trust me, I'm way out of line telling you this much."

A reporter became captive of his sources, unless like T.K., he was savvy enough to milk their expertise at arm's length. But what the spook just told him sounded too good to check further.

"About these rumors of drilling for natural gas off the Skeleton Marshes?" T.K. changed the subject. "Did your satellite catch anything there?"

"I'm not witting on that." The spook shook his head. "Bird would have picked it up. Now, peel me your onion."

T.K. trod a slippery slope. He knew hacks who hung around spooks in hopes of wringing out information. More often, they got wrung out themselves. It only fueled malicious rumors about his noble craft whoring for the C.I.A.

"Let's walk the cat back," the spook said.

"How far?" asked T.K.

"Down to where the rubber meets the road. What's it like in the mountains these days?"

"Too many corpses—sure the guerrillas didn't do it?" If the spook was correct, T.K. had to get back and rewrite his story.

"Trust me," said the spook. "Gunships, Hind-24s?"

"Cow's jumped over the moon on that one." T.K. had watched the red rain with Cass—where was she?

"Any tanks, maybe T-72s?"

"I'm no military expert," T.K. said, "but I'd bet the dish ran away with the spoon here."

"Say again?" The spook's eyes narrowed.

Baiting this viper was reckless. "The dish," T.K. said. "If your satellite can read someone busy butchering civilians, it can tell tanks apart."

"Cloud cover blinds the bird." The spook leaned forward. "On your next trip, keep a weather eye out. Could be worth your while."

"My paper already overpays me," T.K. said.

"You newsmen get around, great cover."

And a reporter caught in flagrante with the C.I.A. would never work again in honest journalism. Anyway, hacks didn't have time for collateral spookery.

T.K. crumpled his paper napkin and stood up.

"Thanks for the cheeseburger," he said. "What do you really do here?"

The spook picked at the skin flaking on his sunburned nose. "You're not doubting your most reliable source on this scoop?" he asked.

* * *

Fifty dollars tucked inside his new passport bought T.K. a fresh press visa at the Ministry of National Guidance with few questions asked. He returned to the hotel with a glow of achievement, the first since he'd made the news twink give back his rightful seat on the charter.

Then he bumped into Vanessa in the hotel lobby.

"Why, you're back," she said, "and alive."

Vanessa had avoided him since his return. Now she pecked the air at his cheeks and launched a preemptive tale about being lured off by her old friend, escaping his dishonorable intentions, and making her way back to the district airport to find T.K. gone. She removed the Vuarnet sunglasses to attest to her sincerity, and something like tears misted her blue eyes.

Touching—so why did Vanessa leave a farewell note? "You owe me four hundred and thirty dollars," he said, and showed her the tally of expenses in his notebook.

Vanessa reciprocated by pressing into his hand a photostat of a poem in a language that T.K., and doubtless Vanessa herself, could not read.

"Let this bring out your inner child." Vanessa was into inner childishness these days. "You met the rebels?" she asked. "Were they fierce? Anything on tape?"

T.K.'s head gave two nods and a shake, since Cass hadn't returned.

"Let's find your guerrillas." Vanessa's eyelashes fluttered that it could be worth his while.

"No thanks," T.K. said. Whenever he hoped to stick it to Vanessa, she always stuck it to him first.

"I'm waiting on my interview with the President of Equatoria." He immediately regretted his boast.

"The President?" Her eyes turned diamond-hard. "When, today? Where, here?"

"Imminent, they said, but it's exclusive."

"Well, they promised my exclusive was imminent too," Vanessa said, and she trotted upstairs to her telephone.

T.K. looked about the lobby for his colleagues and saw none. Had he overlooked some key briefing or missed a catastrophe that everyone rushed off to cover? Had the Armageddon for which they assembled started without him? All he could hear was the chatter, in Urdu for all the sense it made, of a pair of young reporters who had arrived while he was up-country.

"Four eight six at sixty-six megahertz," said one with gold studs running up his left ear, "DX, four megs RAM, Pentium upgradable."

"What's your pitch?" asked the other, who wore his baseball cap backwards.

"Point two nine, multiscan, noninterlaced."

"Dynamite pixels," the back-hatted reporter said. "My four eight six really needs a local bus. I wish some news would happen so I can show off these killer apps I installed."

"Check out the new V-34s," said the ear-studded one. "Doesn't your mouse feel greasy here?"

"I wipe it down with gin from the bar."

T.K. walked away disgusted. He could remember when hacks swapped tips on what kind of bribe would motivate the telex operator. You lavished a few discreet dollars, francs, deutsche marks, pounds, pesos, lire, rupees, rand, baht, kuna, dinars, tugriks, dirham, kwanzas, or kwachas on the operator, maybe slipped him a little extra to pull the plug on your competition's copy, and your own dispatched itself. That left time for T.K.'s generation to wax passionate about women they had known, not computers. Was the fate of his noble craft to be cyberwonked?

Kobus walked out of the hotel bar without his minicamera, confirming that nothing was happening after all. Over by the bulletin board where press advisories got posted, Schuyler was unburdening himself to Ginny, who had the misfortune to look like a good listener.

"They'll parachute a Bigfoot on top of you, too, now that this story's growing legs," Schuyler said.

"Schuyler's network's sending in a field producer," Ginny explained to T.K.

"You could use some help," T.K. said. "You guys work late every night."

Schuyler's unkempt white mane made him look like a crazed scientist about to run amok. "Field producers can be useful," he said. "They'll set up stories so you get on the air more. But the one they're sending me jerks around crews like he invented television. T.K., any word from Cass?"

"Ask Alistair," T.K. said. "She wouldn't tell me."

To save Cass money, Alistair had stored her few possessions in his room, hoping that the hotel would be full when she returned.

"That's the Canadian hack you dumped?" Ginny asked.

"A strictly commercial arrangement," T.K. said. "I bought her seat back on the charter, Ginny, she's just a news twink, not a hack."

Cass only had to wait for the next flight, yet his speculation on her whereabouts turned ugly whenever T.K. looked in the mirror at the scar healing across his cheek. The nun who removed the sutures at the Chinese hospital remarked upon how nimbly Cass had wielded her needle.

"Is tomorrow worth covering?" Ginny asked.

"If you're a hack," said T.K., "tomorrow's always worth covering."

"She means the hangings," Schuyler said. "I don't like it, but we've got to stay competitive."

The advisory was typed on a smudged letterhead bearing the Ministry's crossed Kalashnikov and sickle:

"In response to public outcry over the treacheries of the puppet rebellion, a hanging of traitors is scheduled tomorrow after the angry masses find them guilty at a trial in the national stadium. All hangings to be held at the old parade ground north of the capital, not the new parade ground in Liberation Park, where the Women's Development Brigade expose their well-digging equipment. A press bus to the mass trial and hangings departs at 10 hours unless there is a delay, when it departs later."

To this was appended the usual rhetorical flatulence: "Victory or Death: Whichever Comes First. Socialism is the Future, the Future is Socialism."

The government usually disposed of opponents more circumspectly. Hanging them publicly seemed cruel and immoral, which meant all the hacks would be there, and that meant T.K. had no choice but to go too.

"Suppose we stayed home?" said Ginny.

"You don't get many mass hangings anymore," said Schuyler. "If it wraps up early enough, we'd feed the bird for prime time. Remember when the Liberians shot their Cabinet for the press? This'll be another feeding frenzy."

"Anything else happening?" Ginny asked.

"A briefing on progress in food self-sufficiency," T.K. said. "It's been canceled."

"Guerrillas might try to rescue the prisoners." Schuyler sounded wistful. "Good visuals."

Alistair had wandered up. "Sounds like my kind of story," he said. "Shy Di Quits Elvis Love Nest to Deplore Gallows Mayhem, Nazi Link Suspected."

"You print hacks can afford to be cute," Schuyler said. "You'll watch my rough cuts or rewrite the wires. But what if CNN's out there sending it live? If I don't have it and the other networks do, I'm in trouble with the suits back home."

"Set up your camera," T.K. said, "and disapprove."

"But what if," Schuyler continued, "they're slipping the rope around some poor bastard's neck on that scaffold and he shouts: 'Give me liberty or give me death'? Helluva sound bite if he does it in English. The other networks would have it on tape and I wouldn't if we're not out there. Got to give the viewers what they want."

"Public hangings were acceptable for centuries," said Alistair. "Wish Cass were here, she'd be our conscience on this."

T.K. didn't; Cass would whine about being used or she'd wave a sign demanding abolition of capital punishment. Alistair's lapdog crush was clouding his cynicism.

"But what if the *Post* covers it," Schuyler said, "or the *Times*? Your editors read them."

T.K.'s flippancy gave way to fear. It was the knee-jerk competitiveness that unnerved him, the assumption that if one reporter uncovered a morsel of news, everybody else was obliged to pile on. He dreaded the "rockets"— wake-up messages dispatched in the night—ordering him to match or advance some story that he hadn't even heard. Why hold out? There was nothing much else to do.

"I was going to stay and do expense accounts," Ginny said, "but if you're stooping to the occasion, I'll have to go too."

"Remember how the old hacks bragged about the courage not to file?" T.K. said. "What happened?"

"One hack's courage looks like another's screwup." Ginny laughed. "The editors assume you got your ass whipped again."

* * *

Before leaving for the hangings, T.K. ate breakfast. A foreign correspondent always ate breakfast, because you never knew when the next meal would come.

He ate early, which left time to sit at his computer and craft an overdue message to his foreign editor.

"R*gr*t to r*port untim*ly d*mis* of publish*r's granddaught*r's t*ddy b*ar, who was dis*mbow*l*d at army roadblock and subs*qu*ntly d*mol-ish*d as gu*rrilla booby trap. B*ar's r*mains unr*tri*vabl* as casualty of war. It could hav* b**n m*."

No, candor would hardly further his career. He tried a new, more successful version:

"Pl*as*d to r*port Scoopi* B*ar got bigg*st bang from fun safari tog*th*r. Dynamit* photos, too. Alas, h*alth authoriti*s quarantin*d SB for six w**ks du* to *pid*mic raging in r*gion visit*d. This giv*s publish*r tim* b*for* SB's r*turn to hav* littl* granddaught*r and h*r playmat*s in-oculat*d for following dis*as*s: smallpox, chol*ra, typhoid, polio, h*rp*s, and h*patitis strains A and B. *mbassy doctor warns of contagion risk if childr*n hug, kiss, ch*w on SB. Sounds ov*rcautious to m*, but why tak* chanc*s? Ch**rs. T.K."

He was about to send this when he remembered to add a postscript: "R*garding unworkabl* l*tt*r on my k*yboard, for which I'v* b**n im-provising '*,' wh*n do I g*t my n*w laptop?"

The other networks had hired a truck, but T.K. found Schuyler and his crew on the bus, reasoning that its driver would know the way to the old parade grounds.

Two trucks ahead were exhibiting the condemned men, kneeling and co-cooned with ropes. Wooden placards listing their alleged crimes hung about their necks. A policeman stood by to yank the ropes if some victim hid his face from the street. But most passersby did not stop and stare. They quickened their gait as if terrified of being ordered to change places.

The bus missed the turnoff to the national stadium because the driver was busy overtaking an army truck with the effrontery to pass him. Rather than lose face by turning back, the driver sent word that he knew a shortcut to the hanging ground.

"So how late are you?" T.K. asked Ginny, who had beaten him to the window seat despite an arm still cast in plaster.

"Four months, nearly five," Ginny said. "Help me with some receipts? My papers won't advance any more till I send them my expense accounts."

"Buy blank receipts down at the market and fill them in yourself," T.K. said. "Everybody does it."

"I save my receipts," Ginny said. "Then I can't find them."

"Organize yourself, sis," T.K. advised. "Write down how much money you have at the beginning and end of the month. Then stick the difference on your expense account."

"Beer's five bucks a can here, no bean counter will approve that."

"You can't stint on fluid intake out here," T.K. said. "I tuck it under taxis."

"Cass would have hoarded every receipt," Alistair called from the seat ahead, "and sent expense accounts daily to her radio masters." He spoke as though she were dead.

"She's flown home to Canada," said T.K.

"Not Cass, she's too bloody competitive," Alistair said. "She'll be back to haunt you."

T.K. hoped not. Had Cass accompanied them to the hangings, she'd have made herself a vocally self-righteous pest, whining the sort of disapprobations bred in the bone of so many Canadians. He wished Cass anywhere else, like Shawinigan.

The bus hummed with conversation, none of it about the hangings. Ginny was performing higher mathematics with a pocket calculator and jotting down totals on her cast. In back, Rolf and another photographer argued the respective merits of khat and dagga. Somewhere in between hummed the cyberwonks.

"Technology," one wonk said, "will make war so interactive that you won't have to leave your computer—"

"Ride the information highway to the battlefield," added the other. "Real-time electronic networking with combatants—"

"Virtual body counts via electronic bulletin boards in the field hospitals, hey, technology's nearly there—"

"Yeah, but how many gigabytes would you need—"

As they prattled on about CPUs and EPROMs, broad bands and fiber optics, T.K. wondered whether to solicit volunteers for a search party to find Cass. But Alistair had exhausted his praise-singing of her and dozed off. Schuyler was quarreling with Barry, a testy Associated Press veteran with a penchant for baiting television correspondents.

"What you lard between the hemorrhoid commercials wouldn't fill one newspaper page," Barry scoffed. "The world news in twenty-one minutes, including the weather?"

Schuyler stood his ground. "What'll you print hacks do when people stop reading? No one writes letters anymore—how long before they stop reading them, or anything else? They'll need their news from television."

"And every time you do a stand-up," Barry said, "you should hope those viewers read a newspaper, because you've got three hundred words to tell them everything you know."

Blaming Schuyler was unfair. His crew worked as hard as ink-stained wretches like T.K. and took more risks, but then he had to stroke the network suits to get on the air. And if the story grew legs, there'd be eight-hundred-pound gorillas with pretty faces parachuting in to Bigfoot over his turf.

"Remember the famines in Ethiopia, the massacres in Rwanda?" Schuyler reacted with the umbrage of a cordon bleu chef told that the customer wants ketchup for the *pommes frites.* "It was TV that grabbed the world, not your wire copy. Yet my suits won't give anything prime time until it's been in the *Times.*"

"When I worked in Washington," Barry said, "the White House worried about what was on the network evening news, the networks worried about what was in the *Times,* and the *Times* worried about what was at the White House."

When the bus passed the Red Storm Tallow Factory for the third time, it became clear that it would soon get dark and they were no closer to watching anyone hang than when they started. At times, the driver stopped to ask directions of someone on foot or on a bicycle. At first they pointed in another direction. Later, they just shrugged.

The pungent odor of dagga wafted from the gaggle of free-lance photographers in back. T.K. could not see Vanessa; maybe she finagled a ride out with the hangman.

More worrisome, the *Post* and *Times* weren't aboard either. Had they driven out separately? Were they colluding on a story that would keep T.K. up all night in the glare of rockets incoming from his foreign desk?

He felt queasy about the hangings too, and not just for the morality of watching someone die. If nobody came, it was no worse than if everybody showed up. The worst scenario had a single TV crew videotaping hanged men twisting against a spectacular sunset while the rest of the foreign press drove around in a Flying Dutchman of a bus whose shock absorbers had long since expired. His gut twinged. T.K. was a candidate for ulcers.

"Nearly there," exclaimed Ginny. "My expense accounts, I mean."

The driver, who no longer pretended to know where he was going, braked for a pair of men blocking the road. The brawnier one banged on the door, bounded aboard, and put a pistol to the driver's head. T.K. hadn't realized that bad driving was a capital offense.

The gunman's companion followed with a handful of grenades.

T.K. pressed Ginny into her seat, he could handle this. He made his way up the narrow aisle.

"Tell them we're late for a hanging," T.K. said.

The gunman turned and shoved the pistol against T.K.'s stomach instead. The sour stench of lombo filled his breath. A thread of spittle dangled precariously from his lip as he ranted.

"He is nothing if not intensely handsome, brooding champion of national water polo team," explained the driver. "It makes a fortnight since calculates he to defect."

"Who's his pal?" T.K. asked. The hijackers weren't dealing from a full deck of cards.

"No one if not suave, canny manager, who moonlights as brother-in-law. Propose they to defect to you."

"I'm not a country," said T.K. He had never seen anyone juggle hand grenades before.

"The bottom line is you become no-brainer in event you do not spring to assist," the driver said. "My gift of gab is much polished from old copies of *Time* and *Newsweek,* yes? And modern English they should know."

"Tell these wankers to find an embassy and defect to it," T.K. said, "not me."

The gunman's hairy forearm tightened across his throat. The photographers surged forward.

"Look this way, okay?" Rolf yelled. "Have your raghead pal hold his focking gun higher. Beautiful."

T.K.'s captor struck a theatrical pose for the clicking cameras.

"Can't they defect during a match abroad?" T.K. asked the driver. "That's how it's usually done."

"A fortnight ago," the driver said, "no fewer than half-dozen of his jolly, hard-charging teammates left to defect at largest water polo match to dazzle Europe. Nest egg trickles too little for his ticket. So his sleeves he rolls up, with conventional wisdom favoring reunion with chums tearwise by week's end."

T.K. labored to keep the dialogue, and himself, alive. "To claim political asylum," he said, "they need some well-founded fear of political persecution."

"Fear of persecution is always well-founded in Equatoria," the driver said. "But our champ hides agenda to become item with L.A. chicks farthest out in swimming pool, like the Charlie's Angels tube-jiggling for us potato couches."

Pistol steel pressed against T.K.'s neck; these guys would fit right in on the Santa Monica Freeway. "Tell them California's no fun anymore, earthquakes everywhere, pollution's ruined the swimming."

"Sweat not, assures he," said the driver.

Kobus crawled up with his minicamera. "A little room, chaps." The Beta's baleful red light glowed.

Rolf flipped open his Nikon. "Don't spook your raghead, T.K. Don't let him pull the focking trigger till I change film, okay?"

The driver enjoyed the drama now that he was no longer its focus.

"Our uninvited guests opine your American paper pays big bucks for the life of its ace reporter," he said, "in ballpark of one million dollars."

They knew nothing about American newspapers. Paying a ransom for one battered-shoe reporter would invite crazies worldwide to grab every hack in sight.

"Alistair, good buddy, spell me?"

But Alistair said it served T.K. right for stranding Cass. "Howdoesitfeel?" he said.

"A little help, sis?" T.K. asked Ginny, who was checking the columns of numbers written across her plaster cast. "I bet he'd listen to you."

"And steal your first-person exclusive?" Ginny said. "This can't go on. Either he shoots you or his friend drops a grenade or—"

Ginny rose. "They're not blowing up my expenses."

Watching Ginny make her way forward, the hijacker shoved the pistol against T.K.'s jaw. Would his obituary cite aging Hollywood reruns as cause of death?

Ginny whispered in the driver's ear. He nodded, his mouth opened, his eyes widened. He shouted a translation to the hijacker, who released T.K. and lowered his pistol. The juggler reined in the grenades,

"What did you tell them?" T.K. asked.

Ginny merely shrugged.

The driver clapped his hands for attention. "Into the American Embassy prepare this dynamic duo to crash my bus and bargain for asylum," he said, "so they invite us to flee."

The driver led the stampede out the door.

T.K. stood on the dirt road, watching the bus fade into the dusk. The hijackers had looked suspicious from the start, that big gun and no sunglasses.

"Don't use the pictures, guys?" T.K. asked.

"You looked so focking scared," Rolf said. "It's all we got, everyone else got the hanging."

"Marginal visuals, man," said Kobus. "You weren't even sobbing."

It was dark when they waved down a passing army truck and piled in for the ride back to the Hotel Turissimo.

T.K. had squeezed in next to Ginny. "What did you tell them?"

Ginny paused for a deep breath. "That you're a running dog for the C.I.A., a cat's paw for Wall Street—"

"Sonofabitch, you didn't."

"—and if you're not released, your paymasters'll take away the green cards and taxi licenses from his clan's immigrants in New York and deport them—"

"They believed you?" As conspiracy theories went out here, it didn't sound bad.

"—and order a nuclear air strike on his ancestral village," she said. "Stop fussing, they let us go."

The hacks straggled into the hotel lobby. Some made it no farther than the bar.

"My suits will be all over me tonight," Schuyler said. "I bet the other networks led with the hanging."

Barry of the A.P. walked over to reassure him. "The story never grew legs," he reported. "The mob at the stadium flipped over their truck—no one hurt though."

"Thank God," said Ginny.

"Of course some free-lance photographer got his face kicked in," said Barry, "but who counts them? Read this."

He held out an item ripped from the Equatorian Press Agency wire ticker:

"Today's hangings will be canceled indefinitely. Submitting to the will of the revolution, all renegade-saboteurs performed vile self-criticisms and were paroled to their neighborhood committees following a verdict of mercy from the masses, who confirmed their guilt but asked the state be spared the cost of rope."

A press advisory followed:

"The Ministry of National Guidance schedules a briefing for foreign correspondents at 900 hours tomorrow on the virtue of punctuality. Accreditation renewed for those attending only."

Ginny slapped her notebook shut. "If we'd gotten there, they'd be hanged," she said. "But we got lost, so they're free."

"Don't tell Cass I went," said Alistair, and turned on T.K. "Where is she, you reckless bastard?"

5.

PORTO PARADISO, *quatoria—Und*r pr*ssur* from Unit*d Nations m*diators, th* pro-Marxist gov*rnm*nt tonight agr**d to
a c*as*-fir* with th* r*b*ls who hav* fought a long gu*rrilla
war with cland*stin* C.I.A. backing.

Th* c*as*-fir*, announc*d as bull*ts ripp*d through th*
tamarind l*av*s of this war-ravag*d country, will l*t th* insurg*nts op*n a liaison offic* und*r U.N. prot*ction in th*
capital . . .

What extraordinary lapse of judgment prompted Rolf a few nights later
to proposition Ginny down at the Cafe Peri-Peri—too much beer, bad
dope, a full moon?

The photographer had squeezed his chair in next to Ginny while Alistair
regaled the table with another of his war stories.

"All the hacks stayed at the Commodore Hotel while Beirut collapsed
around us," Alistair was saying, "because they took personal checks and the
phones worked. Once I was eating breakfast out by the pool and stray
shrapnel landed in the egg yolk of the *L.A. Times.* The manager apologized
for the neighbors, moved us indoors, poached Don a new egg."

T.K. tried not to listen because Alistair threatened not to speak to him again until Cass reappeared.

On the other side of the table, Schuyler insisted to Barry that television visuals, far from exaggerating the violence at hand, sought to place it in proper historical context.

"Conceive of this country rushing headlong into the sixteenth century," said Schuyler, who was forever plumbing the metaphysics of television journalism.

Someone's empty beer can dropped another gecko on the stucco wall.

"Conceive of the Hundred Years War in Europe being reenacted with machine guns," Schuyler said.

Abednego the waiter reappeared with a fresh round of cold beer. T.K. reached for the last can but Alistair, the bastard, grabbed it first.

"They kept a parrot in the Commodore bar," Alistair said, "taught it to whistle like incoming artillery, scared the hell out of blokes back from the Israeli border."

Rolf pulled his chair snug against Ginny's, slipped an arm around her waist, and whispered in her ear.

"But then Islamic crazies invaded the Commodore," Alistair said, "trashed the liquor supply. When they started kidnapping hacks, the clientele checked out. Even a well-run hotel has its limits."

So had Ginny, though Rolf managed to complete the sexually explicit part before she kicked away the legs of the chair he was rocking on. After Rolf had bounced a time or two on the concrete, Ginny told him to stop whining.

"You only landed on your head," Ginny said.

Rolf picked himself up and left, mumbling something about focking bitch, okay? T.K. did not join in the general derision, immersed as he was in his own remorse.

Cass had not deserved the vagaries of Equatorian People's Airways he had inflicted upon her. His own travels through the backwaters of the world had toughened T.K. to flights that never arrived or departed, to the menace of dark alleys and seedy bars, the bureaucratic absurdities of immigration and customs formalities, the lightning humiliation of food poisoning, diarrhea, or sunstroke. Cass was too callow to cope in such alien surroundings, and not because she was a woman. Look how self-sufficient Ginny was, or

Vanessa. But the naïveté in Cass's wide eyes solicited the familiarity of all species of human sharks.

In truth, T.K. was feeling even sorrier for himself. The crowd at the Peri-Peri had failed to amuse him. Even the stories they told sounded the same; only the names and datelines changed. He placed his contribution to dinner on the table before the outrageous bill escalated further, and walked back to the hotel. He meant to go to his room to write, but he wound up sitting in the bar for another beer. It wasn't enough. What he wanted was a steak, but mostly tonight, he craved a woman.

Briefly, T.K. wondered what Ginny would be like, but he stifled this renegade fantasy. A friend like Ginny was more valuable than any lover, and Rolf's mishap hardly emboldened T.K. As for Vanessa, not that he was her sort, she had returned to her Latin diplomat, and Cass, not that she was his sort, had yet to resurface.

A popular misconception about foreign correspondents had it that in between hustling for visas, hopping on and off airplanes, chasing stories and contriving ways to file them, they somehow found time to get laid with extraordinary frequency. Perhaps there were beats where the groupies were obliging and uninfected, but not where T.K. was assigned to toil. He ordered another beer instead.

As he sucked on it, T.K. opened his notebook, still damp with the day's sweat, and flipped through the pages, deciphering old notes on an overdue story he meant to file. He arrived at a page that, in contrast to the scribbles preceding it, offered a single observation: "Brass."

T.K. recognized his handwriting but not when the enigmatic word appeared or why. Had he scrawled it down while running late for a briefing, or fumbling in the dark, or returning from the Peri-Peri after too many beers?

Did "brass" mean spent cartridges he had seen lying in the gutter after a mysterious gun battle one night near the Defense Ministry? Or the paunchy generals employed there? Perhaps it described the belt buckles worn by the marine guards at the official opening of the United States Embassy, after it abandoned the diplomatic fig leaf of being merely an interest section of the Swiss Embassy? Did "brass" refer to the trumpeter who played off-key when the Republican Guard band wandered through "The Star-Spangled Banner"?

Maybe "brat"? No, Cass Benoit wasn't back yet.

Now he remembered. Rolf had boasted about finding some antique engraved brassware in the market and flogging it back in Europe for big deutsche marks. T.K. jotted a reminder to buy some too, and promptly forgot. It was too late now.

He closed his notebook and was about to go upstairs to his bleak room when his musing was interrupted.

"Keep a focking eye on my Gunn?" Rolf was back.

But hacks didn't carry guns. T.K. glared up and saw Rolf's magnificent companion. His eyes panned from her pale blond hair down to her nutcracker thighs. Fate must have dispatched this willowy Amazon as recompense for T.K.'s appalling run of luck.

"Gunn's her name," Rolf said, "okay?"

"Gunn," repeated T.K. It sounded no terser than "Cass," yet as a name, it left a metallic taste.

"Keep Gunn amused while I focking develop and wire my pix, okay? I don't focking trust her with the other hacks, but you never get laid." And Rolf walked off.

Rolf's parade of compliant playmates had never passed this close. Accepting a chair, Gunn sized up T.K. with predatory blue eyes from under her floppy platinum bangs. T.K. pumped the limp hand that she extended.

"Delegate," she said.

"Delegate?" T.K. hadn't heard that euphemism.

"To our congress of peace-loving forces," Gunn said. "You're a journalist like Rolf?"

T.K. groped for a civil response. "Up to a point."

"Then you will inform the world," Gunn said, "of our nonnegotiable demands for peace."

"Wouldn't miss it." T.K. had no such intention. This government scheduled its spurious conferences to squeeze money from foreign admirers and other useful idiots.

"Friend of Rolf?" he asked.

Gunn sighed. "Our hosts placed me in the old Cuban guest house, where my roommate snores so, though she is politically committed otherwise. She flies back to Stuttgart tomorrow and I take my own room."

"You need a one-night stand—ah, accommodation?" T.K. shifted his chair closer. "You'll have a beer first, wine, whiskey?" Imported stuff in the bar cost ten dollars a shot, but T.K. was working against a new deadline here.

A shot of vodka cost fourteen dollars, as he learned after Gunn belted down forty-two dollars' worth.

"Is your journalism progressive?" she asked. "If so, perhaps I stay with you. Rolf is not gracesome."

Gunn had H.L.S.G.P. stamped all over her, but her strong calves swaddled in sandal rawhide did not look objectionally hirsute. Why waste her on Rolf?

"But *I* am gracesome," T.K. said, "gracesome and progressive."

The sun had gilded Gunn so thoroughly that in another ten years the cinnamon sheen of her skin would look as parched as a crocodile handbag. But not tonight.

T.K. slipped his arm around her sweaty shoulder.

"Like you, I fight to save the world from fascism, racism, sexism"—he took up a hard sell—"activism."

"How?"

"As a foreign correspondent," T.K. said, "I write angry articles for a big American newspaper. Would you like to come up and read my clips?"

Gunn yawned. "Newspapers are boresome."

"You look terribly tired," he said, "and my clips are upstairs in my room."

"Newspapers lie."

These precoital pleasantries were hard slogging, but T.K. pressed forward. "Any particular lies in mind?"

"Journalists make it up."

"Making up quotes is too hard for me," he said. "I find it easier to steal the words people speak."

Gunn gave his remark a lot more thought than it warranted. "Newspapers lied," she said, "that Americans landed on the moon."

"Our astronauts did land on the moon. Didn't you see it, on television?" No, she would have been too young.

Gunn uncrossed her legs. She had no use for underwear, either. "Photographic deceits," she declared.

His greedy fingers caressed her skin. "But we watched American astronauts defying gravity," he said. "And speaking of gravity, we must find you a bed for the night."

"Deceits performed by the C.I.A.," she said, "to make Russia think America was on the moon."

"We'd be more comfortable continuing this in my room."

"The Democratic People's Republic of Korea," Gunn said, "is the only nation that refused to sell its labor to capitalists—you came?"

"Hope to."

"I came three times," Gunn said, "as a delegate. The North Korean comrades showed me their 'juche,' which is why they will reach the moon first."

"'Juche,'" T.K. repeated. She must sunbathe topless to achieve such butterscotch cleavage.

"'Juche' was the Great Leader's instruction on self-reliance." Gunn let T.K. rub her long neck. "He inspired Korean patriots to practice 'juche' by eating only twice a day. That's why your naughty C.I.A. poisoned him."

The Great Leader's demise, as T.K. recollected it, resulted from a geriatric heart attack, but this was not the time to quibble. T.K.'s hand wandered into the soft nape between her shoulder blades.

"To discredit the universal truth of Marxism-Leninism," Gunn was saying.

"I shall atone," he whispered, "but upstairs."

"'The people's strength is inexhaustible,' the Great Leader instructed us," Gunn said, "'and their inexhaustible strength is invincible.'"

"That's so poignant. How about some 'juche,' in my room?" T.K. remembered the condom in his wallet. It resided there, undisturbed, the wish list of some schoolboy fantasy.

"First we exchange sexual histories."

He was almost there. The small logbook that Gunn produced looked like what the U.S. Army had issued T.K. to record parachute jumps, but hers overflowed with notations in Swedish.

"Show me yours," Gunn said, "before we make each other naked. Then I arouse you with heroic instructions of the Great Leader while we screw."

Keeping a scorecard was new to T.K., who hadn't much to record of late.

"Mine's oral."

"That we list too," Gunn said. "When did you last exchange body fluids?"

"Denouncing isms gives me no time to record fluid exchange."

"I feel the throb of your progressive commitment," Gunn purred. "You are not like Rolf, he only wants sex."

What T.K. wanted by now was a sirloin steak, medium rare and smothered in crisply fried onion rings. The prospect of a mindless bounce with Gunn had been diminished by the admission price of hearing her ideological bombast declaimed between thumps. It was not mere sex that T.K. desired, but a woman worth waking up next to.

"If you exchange sexual histories," T.K. said, "Rolf must have wired his photos by now. Let's go find him."

* * *

A few days later, first news of Cassandra Benoit arrived, though the hacks could not agree on what it meant.

The message was printed on the greasy brown envelope containing a cassette tape for Stephens, the correspondent for the British Broadcasting Corporation. It said: "PLSHELPSENDBACKSOONESTBENOIT."

"Why the BBC and not us?" T.K. asked as he studied the envelope.

"Why not you's obvious," Schuyler said, "but why not Alistair or me? I think she wants the BBC to feed her tape to her public radio masters. They do it in London for lots of clients."

"No, there's a code here pleading for help, fairly screaming that she's in trouble," said Alistair. "The note wants something." He turned the paper over. "See the grease—Cass'd only use biodegradable soap."

Sipho snatched away the envelope.

"No, man, it's like this," Sipho said. "'Please help send . . .' Meaning the tape. 'Back soonest . . .' Meaning she'll see you later."

"She's wandering out there," Alistair said, "disoriented, frightened, bumping into things. She doesn't know what she's writing."

"Not so disoriented that she can't flog a tape to the BBC," T.K. said. "What's on it?"

"One side's her account of our stay with the rebels. Terrific sound bites, Stephens says. The other side's from the Skeleton Marshes."

"Impossible," T.K. said. The Skeleton Marshes encompassed mangrove swamp and scrub brush along the remote southerly coast. Apart from unconfirmed rumors of natural gas offshore, the malarial marshes were worthless. They had become a no-go area for journalists after guerrillas routed the local army garrison.

"Her reporting's so vivid," Schuyler said, "the BBC wants to use it too— that's why Stephens came to ask me about Cass."

When Kobus and Sipho headed for the Skeleton Marshes, T.K. recalled, they got detained at a roadblock for two weeks. Cass couldn't have made it, because the road was also heavily mined.

"She'd have to pass though the capital to get from the highlands to the coast," Alistair said. "Cass would have stopped to see me, unless she flew directly."

"The airline hasn't gone there since the guerrillas got Stinger missiles," T.K. said. "She's back in Canada, faking her datelines."

"Then why send a Russian to deliver her tape to the BBC?" Schuyler asked.

"Doesn't make sense either," T.K. said. "Russian advisers pulled out months ago."

"Some stayed as mercenaries. Stephens said the bloke looked Russian," Alistair said. "We'll find her."

"Where?" T.K. asked. The highlands and the coast lay at opposite ends of the country. "She's flown home before her excursion ticket expired."

"And left her tape here?" Alistair elbowed T.K. less than playfully. "Russian mercenaries abducted her to the Skeleton Marshes. We'll get a ransom note in Russian next."

* * *

Within a week, a real story—the government's cease-fire with the insurgents—distracted T.K. from his concerns about Cass. The announcement was one of those fortuitous stories capable of writing themselves onto the front page.

T.K. sat at his laptop computer, stirring the facts into an explanation of the government's promise of free elections, then folding in details about how soldiers and guerrillas who had grown adept at slaughtering each other would merge into a mellow army of national reconciliation—not that he would have bet a penny on either scenario.

He was wondering whether to move a little higher the government's offer to let the rebels open a liaison office in the capital, when his thoughts were jangled by the frantic rings that signaled a telephone call from overseas. It must be his foreign desk, asking how soon he would be filing.

But no, the caller identified himself as an assistant professor at some journalism school whose whereabouts in the United States T.K. could not place.

"I'm feeding the goat," T.K. said.

There was a pause. "I'm calling Farrow, the foreign correspondent," said the caller, "not the goatherd."

"That's me, on deadline. Can you call back?"

"Our journalism review has deadlines too, and you're in it. The media can't duck its responsibilities."

"Media's plural," T.K. suggested.

"My computer analyzed the media's coverage of C.I.A. meddling in your country," said the professor. "I fed twenty-five articles into my computer and crunched them, factoring in story position, length, impact focus."

"That's nice," said T.K., "but I need to file—"

"*Los Angeles Times* mentioned the C.I.A. in the context of Equatoria six times in February, *New York Times* and *Washington Post* did it five times, yet my computer readout shows nothing about the C.I.A. under your byline. Why are you covering this up?"

"I wrote something on the C.I.A. in late January." T.K. tried to recollect. "Or was it early March?"

"So my statistical analysis doesn't lie—you ignored the C.I.A. in February. You're not looking so professional, Mr. Farrow."

"I wrote my takeout in February, but my paper didn't have room till March because of a big scandal at city hall."

"So my correlation coefficients prove that you didn't exist, Februarywise."

T.K. asked how January or March looked.

"Statistically, we've done February," the professor said. "If I did January and March, I wouldn't have time to teach my journalism courses."

"A promising option," T.K. said.

"Don't sneer at we who mold tomorrow's journalists. The media isn't well served by you."

"Aren't well served."

"What's your null hypothesis?" the professor asked.

"My null what?"

"Null hypothesis, your bias, your point of view, your motive for writing."

"My null hypothesis," T.K. said, "is that if I keep telling my editors what happens here, they'll keep paying me."

But the professor had hung up. T.K. had been distracted from storing on a floppy disk what he had written. He groped for the save key, but his finger fumbled even as the lights blacked out, only for a few seconds but long enough to erase the screen.

He had crashed. It was no consolation that outside in the corridor, the other reporters howled at the power failure like hungry jackals outrun by a plump antelope.

T.K. plugged into his battery pack, convinced that his clever laptop, that prodigious marvel of silicone chips, liquid crystal, and funny-colored wires, would have spared his story. Something must have survived. Could such toil in the cause of truth vanish as though it never existed? Or was divine retribution being visited upon him for his abandonment of Cass, who even now lay ravished in some shallow grave? He ran through the combinations of commands on his plastic keyboard, but the screen remained blank, a testimony to the perversity of inanimate objects.

He could seek out the young cyberwonks, but he wouldn't understand whatever they advised and he balked at confessing his ignorance. T.K. was not superstitious, but his gut told him that some malevolent spirit now inhabited his computer, scrambling its keys to rob him of his rightful share of the world's creativity. Was death like a computer failure—a limitless void emptier than nothing, expunged of whatever footsteps he might leave behind? He kicked the wastebasket across the room and sat down to re-create his article from memory.

It was another hour before he finished, taking pains to save each sentence as he wrote it. Before it could vanish again, he dialed up a telephone line and dispatched the article to his newspaper. But having fed the goat, he was nagged by a hunch that while the ingredients were there, his re-creation lacked the historical sweep, political insight, linguistic style, and sophistication of the lost article.

He would redeem himself by writing a fast sidebar analyzing the prospects of the fragile truce. A thumbsucker was easy enough; it didn't matter what you wrote as long as you referred to countries as nations and made it all sound terribly authoritative. A knock interrupted his thoughts. Reluctantly, he rose to open the door.

There stood Cass.

Lean, tanned, windblown, she evoked the tousled insouciance of the aviatrix Amelia Earhart in some old photograph. Cass counted out ten wrinkled twenty-dollar bills into his hand. "That's your two hundred," she said. "I just sold my pieces to the BBC."

Her light brown hair was cut like a rough helmet, as if a pot had been placed over it first. Wads of tape held her broken spectacles intact.

"We were getting a bit concerned," T.K. said.

Cass smiled with suspicious lack of resentment. "The airline ran out of fuel again, but everyone was frightfully kind."

"Who's everyone?"

"The airline staff, for starters. When my flight was canceled, the ticket agent found me crying and invited me home. She'd been a teacher until there was no money to pay her salary. She took me back to her old school to meet the kids, then we rode a bus to her family's village, on a mountaintop."

"So you're all right?" he asked. Cass looked none the worse for wear, in fact rather better.

"The village militia stocked up on hand grenades," Cass said, "to roll down on intruders. They took me out and taught me to shoot an AK-47, such a kick."

She interrupted her recollection of another day spent with a woodcarver who made artificial legs for children crippled by mines, and fished something out of her pocket. "Use it yourself," she said.

T.K. found himself holding the tattered airline ticket. "But how'd you get back?" he asked.

"I hitched a ride on an Aeroflot plane chartered by the World Food Program. The Russian pilots let me sit in the cockpit. They delivered food to these little airstrips and they sold liquor, bicycles, black market stuff, on the side because they hadn't gotten paid themselves."

Cass's spectacles separated at the bridge and dropped off her sunburned nose. T.K. snatched them before they hit the floor. Looking into her smudged lenses was like peering through the bottom of a gin bottle at a lilliputian world. To call Cass nearsighted was to say Saudi Arabia owned oil wells.

She retrieved the pieces and pressed the wadded tape more firmly into place.

"They broke when we crash-landed in the Skeleton Marshes," Cass explained, "after bullets hit the tail. I pigeoned my cassette out with the Russian mechanic who repaired the plane. Did you know an oil consortium started drilling for gas offshore?"

"The government's denied that."

"The engineers I met there from Elf Aquitaine didn't, eh?" Cass shrugged. "I rode back with a food convoy. Stopping at all the little villages took another week."

Why did she spin so tangled a web? Not only were the Skeleton Marshes inaccessible, but hacks got detained at roadblocks, as T.K. reminded her.

"Not on Red Cross convoys," she said. "I guess they took me for a nurse. Do you know the drivers actually sell donated food off the trucks? I talked to people wearing grain sacks who ate berries and grass to survive. A doctor told me the national per capita intake's only sixteen hundred calories a day. That's barely seventy percent of the minimum—"

"Whoa," said T.K. "They didn't all speak English."

"Of course not. So many colonial armies occupied Equatoria that people speak a patois derived from French and Portuguese. The Cubans left them military terms in Spanish. Their patois bridges regional dialects. What's so amusing?"

It was remarkable that T.K. hadn't noticed before. Her top row of teeth would have qualified for a toothpaste commercial, but the bottom row had turned unruly, one too few or too many, as if Cass's orthodontist had tired of perfection halfway through and taken up root canals. As a flaw, it made her look a little less uppity.

"Their grammar's easy," she said, "because the verb goes at the end, like Latin. Down on the coast, you can understand them better. In the highlands, their consonants get palatalized."

She held up her black notebook. "It's full of their vocabulary. Everyone I met helped; they never before met a foreigner who wanted to understand them."

"Your Russians didn't speak English," he said, "or patois."

"Fortunately, they could understand my grandmother's Ukrainian," said Cass. "Amazing, isn't it, how a childhood language comes back. Did I mention what the pilots said about new landing fees—"

T.K. interrupted her. "Government's announced a truce with the rebels. I suppose you want a fill on it?"

Cass shook her shaggy head. "The general who drove me to the hotel spoke lovely French, he'd been at the talks. They nearly collapsed over exchanging prisoners, but you know that."

T.K. didn't. "You staying with Alistair?" he said. Cass would do that just to spite T.K.

She shook her head again. "He's frightfully sweet, but the hotel found a room for me."

"I guess you won't need us anymore," he said.

"Guess not," said Cass. "If I joined your hack pack, I'd never get my reports filed. Those nights wasted down at that dreadful cafe with your drinking and swashbuckling. Crumbs, I'll bet your stories even read the same."

"I'll unbuckle my swash."

"You only interview people because they speak English, not because they know anything," Cass said.

She had a rather wide mouth too, T.K. noticed, the faster to talk with, and in too many languages.

"If a dozen of you got together and invited your local friends to lunch, you couldn't fill thirteen chairs," she said. "What'll you do when people discover they don't have to talk to reporters? I'll get more done if I'm not trailing about"—she pronounced it "aboot"—"as your mascot."

It was not turning out the way T.K. wanted. "Without us," he said, "you'll keep tripping over your microphone."

"Not necessarily," she said. "I've learned how to travel light and I know how to listen. I'll beat you again."

"When's the last time?"

"We whipped you Yanks," she said, "in the War of 1812."

"The Americans defeated the British," protested T.K. "Didn't we?"

"I'll do it again," Cass said. "Eh?"

* * *

It did not take long for the first incoming rocket from the new Cass Benoit to land.

"When the managing editor drove to work, he heard some reporter poaching your turf on the radio." The message from T.K.'s foreign editor filled his computer screen. "The eyewitnesses she interviewed say guerrillas massacred your villagers. Pls confirm your version that government soldiers did it. Interest here because so much American aid went to the guerrillas. Regards."

T.K. scrutinized the message like some diplomatic communiqué. Did the foreign editor trust a radio amateur more than his own reporter? What did "poaching your turf" mean? And the foreign editor usually signed off with "Cheers," or when he was very pleased, with "Bestest." What degree of disapproval did "Regards" signal?

Some reporters isolated by distance unraveled while dissecting ominous nuances in otherwise benign messages from home. T.K. was too seasoned. He sat down to give his editors the courtesy of a prompt reply.

"If you ?hink i?'s ?ha? *asy," he wrote, "g*? off your fa? ass*s and com* ?ry cov*ring ?his shi?hol* yours*lf. O?h*rwis*, g*? ou? of my fac* and l*? m* do my job!"

Having vented his spleen, T.K. purged this from his computer screen, as was his habit, and turned his talent to crafting something more acceptable. It took a half hour to distill it into three sentences, still not totally to his satisfaction.

In an age of computers, modems, and electronic mail, it was no longer necessary to crunch messages into the cable jargon that old-timers used to save time and money. T.K. did it anyway, as befitted faraway datelines, letting editors infer that their correspondent was a crusty old hand dashing off his response, when in truth he had honed it as a poet might a sonnet.

"Assum* yr msg r*f*rs Cassandra B*noi?, gr**n young s?ring*r n*wly arriv*d. I ?ook h*r up-coun?ry, so advis* sk*p?icism of h*r v*rsion whil* I sor? h*r ou?. B*noi? *ag*r bu? no r*por?ing *xp*ri*nc*!" He signed in kind: "R*gards," and added a postscript:

"No?* ?ha? now ?h* l*??*r b*?w**n S and U in ?h* alphab*? is brok*n on my lap?op, following ?h* loss of l*??*r b*?w**n D and F. I'm subs?i?u?ing '?' for ?h* la?*s? los? l*??*r un?il you s*nd m* n*w compu?*r soon*s?."

Once he had sent the messages, T.K. took the precaution of walking over to the embassy to reconfirm the story with his source.

"Can't you tell the kid's been used?" The spook was not happy to see T.K. "Swallowed the government line, hook and sinker."

"If I could peek at your satellite photos—"

"What satellite?" the spook said.

"You told me a satellite watched—"

"Want to play in my backyard," the spook said, "then let me play in yours."

T.K. returned, looked up Cass's room, and banged on the door. There was no answer. Leaving a note would make him look desperate, so he didn't. Instead, he met Ginny.

"Talk later?" Ginny said. "I got a callback on the massacre. This new Canadian reporter promised me a fill."

"She got it backwards," T.K. said, "and blamed the rebels. I got a solid source confirming the army did it."

"I'm not taking sides," Ginny said, "but she did meet some survivors who told her the villagers were killed because they hid grain from the guerrillas."

"You'd take her word over mine?" he asked Ginny. "You're a hack like me."

"I aspire to something higher," Ginny said. "You're cute, T.K. but when did you last watch a bird or write a poem or do anything but bitch about turning forty?"

"I finished the first chapter of a novel."

"So has every other reporter," Ginny said. "Cass is right, what a dysfunctional crowd you are. I never looked at it that way."

T.K. was unconvinced. Even if Cass's sources did hold up, she was a one-trick filly. Editors didn't remember a reporter for a single story. Daily journalism forced you to prove over and over how good you were; by that criterion, she had to fail.

The trouble was, Cass didn't have enough sense to quit. She picked herself up and kept coming. T.K. turned on his computer the next morning to find another rocket from his foreign editor:

"Thanks your confirmation that guerrillas did the massacre. We'll stay with your version. Benoit's better at features because I just heard her delightful account of Equatoria's two-track economy running on dollars and beer cans, with market interviews. Awaiting your version. Tks."

Tks? Not even "Regards," much less "Cheers" or "Bestest." What did it portend for T.K.'s career?

Everyone knew the dinar was so debased that cans of imported beer circulated as rival currency; at least every hack in the capital knew that, which is why T.K. hadn't bothered to write it.

Scoops were a nuisance, especially when they weren't T.K.'s. Readers didn't fret over some article featured in another newspaper that they never read. His editors did, though, and they paid his salary. With a sigh, T.K. put aside a worthier analysis of ideological tensions inside the government, and trudged down to the candonga.

The market stretched more than a mile along the sandy bluff overlooking the port. Whatever stalls existed had long ago deteriorated or been stolen. Instead, the merchandise was displayed on canvas tarpaulins, plastic sheeting, blankets, or bare earth. Portable radio–cassette recorders were stacked next to truck radiators, screwdrivers alongside jars of instant coffee, medicine with tires, bolts of bright cloth with canned fruit and other booty doubtless from the warehouses ringing the port below.

The capital's economy survived in the bedlam on the bluff, not downtown in the sad state stores with their empty shelves and barred windows. Women walked the market's narrow paths balancing cases of imported beer on their heads. Children tugged at T.K.'s sleeves, hawking individual cigarettes from crumpled wrappers.

A pair of likely pickpockets bumped into him. T.K. felt for his wallet, safely tucked inside his khaki vest. How did Cass manage to traverse this precarious terrain without getting robbed or sold off herself? Was it luck or freckle-faced naïveté?

T.K. roamed the market in search of anyone who spoke more than rudimentary Pidgin English. Around him wafted the competing aromas of vanilla, cinnamon, and diesel fuel. He extracted one minimal quote from a man hawking inflatable pink rabbits and another from a peddler who flashed open his overcoat to display grenades hanging like stolen wristwatches. Under an awning beyond the pens of chickens and ducks, a few AK rifles and a grenade launcher leaned against a color television set in its original box.

When a trader hailed him in passable English, T.K. stopped to inspect the wares. Within the tarpaulin's profusion of batteries, lipstick tubes, and bootleg tape cassettes nested a quartet of slender malachite bangles trimmed with silver, more delicately finished than the clunkier bracelets abounding in the market. To prime the trader's tongue, T.K. began to bargain. Once he owned them, T.K. wasn't sure what do with the bracelets. They would have looked elegant gleaming on Cass's sleek arm if she weren't such a pain in the ass.

Still, Equatoria's parallel economy was not a bad story. T.K. was jotting down some notes about beer cans trading like negotiable commodities when he spied Schuyler.

T.K. had the sort of arrangement with Schuyler that print reporters informally strike up with television crews. He tipped off Schuyler to visual stories he encountered. In return, Schuyler let T.K. watch rough cuts of what Kobus and Sipho collected before their tape was edited down and fed to the satellite.

"One of the network suits heard Cass," Schuyler said, "and sent us out to shoot beer cans. We'll get this on the evening news since they ordered it. Want a lift to the dollar store?"

Schuyler led T.K. to an old truck, into which Sipho was loading the camera and sound recorder.

"Bought it here this morning," Schuyler said. "The guys have been after me to get one since the bus hijacking. It's still cheaper than Mahmoud's taxis."

"You got rocketed on Cass too?" T.K. joined Schuyler in the cab. Why didn't editors watch TV like patriotic Americans instead of eavesdropping on public radio? Cass proved how dangerous a little knowledge could be.

"It used to be only the *Times*," Schuyler said. "Now it's radio, too, and public radio at that. Maybe I should feed Cass my story ideas; then we could have our pieces ready to go once she reports them."

The next morning, T.K. found Didier, the Agence France-Presse correspondent, dousing an unfiltered Gauloise in his breakfast coffee.

"A.F.P. wants me to match Cass's landing fees," Didier said, "and I can't find her. What do you know about it?"

"Landing fees?" T.K. said. A faint bell rang.

"Cass reports the government's charging the aid agencies a hundred and fifty dollars a ton to fly their grain into those dirt landing strips," Didier said. "She reports people go hungry because some agencies won't pay."

Air delivery of grain already cost seven hundred dollars a ton. The government couldn't be greedy enough to make it worse. "Don't tell me your editors listen to her in America," T.K. said.

"She recycles her reports in French for Radio Monte Carlo. Cass began stringing for them, too. Her Quebecois accent is *très* adorable."

"Cass is soufflé journalism," T.K. said, "all air and no substance."

"The Aviation Ministry confirmed her story, after first denying it. Minister said the fees will go to upgrade airport facilities. I think they go to his Swiss bank."

So that bimbo savant had gotten it right.

"Embarrassing, *n'est-ce pas?*" Didier said. "Whoever heard of callbacks from adorable radio stringers?"

The cyberwonks worked up a scheme to monitor Cass by dialing into her electronic mail, until they found she didn't own a computer. Another plan to bug her telephone was scrapped because Cass was too frugal to call her desk to discuss stories.

Only once did she turn to T.K. "May I ask you . . ." she began. So she did need his help.

"Ask away," he said.

". . . for a pen? I lost mine somewhere and I'm late for an interview with the Energy Minister."

T.K. gave her his pen. The odds were against getting rocketed on whatever Cass reported about energy in a country that had none.

Sure enough, when he scanned his incoming electronic messages a day later, a rocket was waiting from the business editor:

"Public radio correspondent Cassandra Benoit says a Western oil consortium hit big natural gas deposits off coast of Equatoria. Benoit quotes her sources as saying the companies bought peace by sharing royalties with both government and rebels. Pls file your story under Skeleton Marshes dateline soonest. Regards."

T.K. promptly messaged back. "?h* Sk*l*?on Marsh*s ar* compl*?*ly off-limi?s to for*ign corr*spond*n?s. B*noi? w*n? ?h*r* accid*n?ally b*caus* sh* go? los?."

The business editor replied overnight. "Benoit scooped you by getting lost? Suggest you try it." He signed off with "Haha." It had gotten that bad.

T.K. calculated when her excursion ticket would expire and started crossing off the days on his calendar.

It was hard to keep Cass out of mischief. She declined to dine with the pack, visiting the Cafe Peri-Peri only to give Abednego his English lessons. Though she had paid back everything she owed T.K., she remained thrifty with her money. Cass disappeared most evenings into a circle of local friends, carrying her black notebook and a plastic shopping bag of food-stuffs from the dollar store.

On Thursday nights, Cass walked to the Chinese hospital to help the nuns make soup for street children cast adrift by the war. Some hacks took her absence from the Peri-Peri as a breach of solidarity. But the nightly rockets suggested that her maverick habits were paying off.

"You can't even relax over a beer while that news twink's running amok," T.K. complained to Schuyler after another opaque government news briefing.

"Didn't you say Cass and Ginny wouldn't hit it off?" Schuyler said. "They're starting to work stories together. A feminist nonaggression pact."

"Omigod," said T.K. What Cass didn't know, Ginny would. They could leave him dead in the water.

"I think Cass already has," prompted Schuyler.

Perhaps Cass, with a little firsthand reporting and more luck, somehow called it right after all, while T.K., the seasoned hack, let a single source, and a spook at that, stampede him into believing in a satellite as though it were the tooth fairy.

If so, his newspaper needed a correction. He sat down at his computer to row back as deftly as he could:

"My massacr* s?ory fron?*d a f*w w**ks ago holds up nic*ly, wi?h jus? ?h* minor*s? chang*. *vid*nc* now sugg*s?s ?ha? gu*rrillas kill*d ?h* villag*rs, no? soldi*rs. P*rhaps a v*ry small corr*c?ion may b* in ord*r."

Like buried back in the death notices.

"Thanks for correction, which we're running on the front page," replied the foreign editor. "Lots of room tonight because nothing happened today."

T.K. knew what it meant: a box in fourteen-point type informing 534,000 readers how badly he had screwed up.

* * *

A few nights later, the foreign editor roused T.K. from a deep sleep. Had the country's President been assassinated (and would anyone notice)?

"Loved what you wrote about Scoopie Bear riding the elephant," the for-eign editor said. "We cut out the epidemic bit, don't want to scare our young readers."

"Sewage backed up in the storeroom where Scoopie's in quarantine," T.K. said. "He'll be dried out enough to send you in a month or so."

"The publisher hadn't considered the health thing," said the foreign editor. "You keep Scoopie Bear, maybe give it to an orphanage, rip off any tags first so it can't be traced."

"Won't his little granddaughter be heartbroken?"

"Between us, the publisher just ordered her a new bear from FAO Schwarz."

"Where's the laptop I asked for?" T.K. said. "We could do a deal."

"It's yours. Now, about this Benoit," the foreign editor said. "She's pushed you back to your own goal line, and it's fourth down, so punt her the hell out of there."

"I got a one-on-one interview coming with, get this, the President of Equatoria."

"You playing the man or the ball, buddy boy?"

"Last time I looked," T.K. said, "she was a woman."

"When I drove home last night," the foreign editor said, "Benoit was sorting out your civil war—how the colonialists used to play the clans against each other, how it took the superpowers to send in enough guns for them to slaughter each other big-time. Benoit explained it just like she's writing a letter home."

T.K. watched the fan turning slowly overhead. Clan frictions were clear enough to anyone in Equatoria but she kept reinventing the wheel. Let Cass file her emotions. T.K. would file facts.

"Give me a few weeks to talk to some clan leaders."

"Focus group," the foreign editor said.

"I don't follow." T.K. looked at his watch. His foreign editor would be fined heavily for calling this late.

"Sit your clan leaders down in a room with a few cases of beer, tape their pent-up emotions hanging out, make a great story."

"They'd butcher each other, me too, if someone threw a grenade," T.K. said. "Two hundred thousand killed in this civil war. U.N.'s estimate, not mine."

"You're our utility outfielder," the foreign editor said with a sigh. "So we look forward to your clan piece for the Sunday paper. Meaning, on the desk here Friday. Hang on, will you?" T.K. heard intense chatter at the other end.

"We're tipped to a plane crash overseas," the foreign editor reported. "You near it?"

"I didn't hear anything."

"Check it out with Benoit, buddy boy? She'll know. Cheers."

Every morning thereafter, T.K. rose dreading what Cass might have filed to distract him from the three-part series that he was preparing on the current state of Equatoria's Workers and Peasants Party. Invariably, Cass had.

"You're fraternizing with the enemy," T.K. told Ginny. He failed to sound lighthearted. Cass was easier to digest when she was asking him questions.

"Technically it's sororizing," Ginny corrected him. "Fraternizing refers primarily to men." They were leaving another unhelpful news conference.

"She's out to nail me."

"Cass is out to nail all of you. Don't take it personally—competition's the lifeblood of journalism."

"It's the curse, Ginny. It makes nice people do nasty things."

"Notice how reporters use two kinds of interviewing styles?" Ginny asked as they walked back to the hotel. "There's the tell-me-or-I'll kill-you and there's the tell-me-I'm-an-orphan. You and Cass come from the second school. Walking insecurities, both of you—the two of you have more in common than you'll admit."

"Alistair's her type," T.K. said.

"It's gotten him nowhere," Ginny said. "I suspect Cass had a crush on you once."

"I doubt that," said T.K., though the notion flattered him.

"I employ the past tense," said Ginny. "The hard time you gave her would piss off Santa Claus. Cass'll make you cry aunt. But your strengths are her weaknesses, and vice versa. You'd bring out the best in each other if you stopped trying so hard to dig up the worst."

Something more distressing was happening. T.K. had considered Cass comely enough, notwithstanding her myopia and bouts of clumsiness. Now her success elicited an artless sexuality. She replaced her patched eyeglasses with new contact lenses that enhanced the pastel of her eyes. For all the blocking cream she applied, the sunshine buttered her skin and streaked her light brown hair. On hotter days, she forwent a bra under her T-shirt. She even forgot to bite her fingernails.

T.K. was not the only male to notice. Cass had become, the hacks agreed at the Peri-Peri, a class piece of ass. "I'd plow into her knickers," Rolf said, scratching wistfully under his *On Your Knees, Bitch* T-shirt, "but she pretends she's too good for me."

When Cass walked by, T.K., whose head swiveled as fast as Alistair's, wondered what he had overlooked and for how long. The bemused condescension with which he once treated her had metamorphosed into heavy lust.

It was inevitable that she would go too far, though T.K. failed to anticipate the recklessness of her revenge.

"Forty years old already?" read the note slipped under his door overnight. "Enjoy your present."

He hadn't forgotten. Today was his birthday, the start of his fifth decade. He hadn't felt like a horny old man until Cass's note arrived. Where was her present?

Rolf alerted him. "Focking bitch," the photographer was mumbling out on the stairway. "Focking bitch."

It did not take much to set off Rolf's garbage mouth but Cass must have run out something that had burned them all. He asked Schuyler over breakfast.

"What's the vilest, most despicable thing you can conceive of?" Schuyler said. "Because Cass just did it."

T.K., who had done a few vile, despicable things in his life, was hard put to single out the worst.

"She's reported on the black-market exchange rate and how it's manipulated," said Schuyler. "We're all getting rockets, but this time on our expense accounts."

"But that's taboo," T.K. said. "It's the one thing nobody writes about."

"Civilization dictates you don't crap where you eat," Schuyler said. "What's wrong with buying a few dinars on the black market and billing expenses at the official rate? If your newspaper knew, they'd probably say okay."

T.K. did not panic. His editors paid him to chase good stories, not goof off in banks, especially in banks that would not even change dinars back into dollars.

"You can't announce you're using the black market," T.K. said. "So what if we wind up with a few bucks? Everyone does it."

He recalled the night that Kobus paid for the beer at the Cafe Peri-Peri to celebrate the stiff customs duty slapped on his new minicamera.

"Okay, more than a few bucks," T.K. said, "but what she's done is immoral."

Alistair was unable to defend Cass. He mumbled that she was too inexperienced to grasp the existential nuance of expense accounts.

Cass had forfeited their respect. If anyone needed a few extra dollars, she did. T.K. returned to his room, turned on his laptop, and dialed into his electronic mail.

Her birthday present was conveyed through the managing editor himself:

"Delightful piece on public radio this morning from Cassandra Benoit about Equatoria's exchange rate, which she says is making journalists rich. Please file same for us. Incidentally, the absence of bank receipts with your expense account puzzles us. We know a correspondent of ours wouldn't stoop to the black market, because we'd fire him. But we expect to see documentation for all expenses in the future."

T.K. looked on the bright side. The managing editor had signed off, "Cheers."

6.

POR?O PARADISO, *qua?oria—*qua?oria's Pr*sid*n? ?oday
admi??*d holding s*cr*? n*go?ia?ions wi?h ?h* insurg*n?s
who hav* fough? for a d*cad* and a half ?o ?oppl* his quasi-
Marxis? r*gim*.

As bull*?s ?or* ?hrough ?h* ?amarind l*av*s ou? in ?h*
coun?rysid*, ?h* Pr*sid*n? disclos*d ?o ?his r*por?*r ?ha?
bo?h sid*s w*r* m***?ing b*hind clos*d doors *o ?hrash ou?
?*rms for a p*ac* . . .

When T.K. arrived in the whitewashed presidential compound, the Republican Guard was feeling up Vanessa. She smiled at him with resignation
that grown men would exploit these little body searches to satisfy their
puerile curiosities.

T.K. spread his arms to be frisked for weapons himself. "Change dollars?" whispered the searcher.

With rakish red berets and gold braid on their tunics, the Republican
Guard swaggered about like schoolyard bullies, brandishing machine guns
or fiddling with rocket grenades.

"Whatever are you here for?" Vanessa asked T.K. while yet another
guardsman groped her for good measure.

"My interview with the President," T.K. said, "but they told me it's exclusive."

"I must have requested my interview eons ago," said Vanessa. "Do you want to piggyback on me?"

"No," T.K. said, "we'll piggyback on each other."

Uneasily, they shared a paneled reception room stuffed with turgid political pamphlets and wilting ferns. T.K. examined the framed photographs of Equatoria's President and his hapless choice of friends. The President grinned as a metal star was pinned on his lapel by the demised Soviet leader Leonid Brezhnev, toasted North Korea's equally defunct Kim Il Sung, shook hands with Libya's Muammar Qaddafi, and hugged Cuba's Fidel Castro.

In another photograph, the President saluted a parade of soldiers. The setting looked familiar. Shadowed by Vanessa, T.K. went back to check the photograph he had just passed in the hallway. It was the same photo, except that now three bemedaled generals stood alongside the President. T.K. returned to the waiting room, where the generals had metamorphosed into a fuzzy patch in the other photograph.

"You see how our Uncle led the masses to liberation?" said a squat man in a safari suit who called himself the President's policy adviser. Vanessa and he seemed unusually well acquainted.

"I thought the President sat out the anticolonialist war in Czechoslovakia," T.K. said.

"He liberated the masses from Czechoslovakia." The adviser handed T.K. and Vanessa glossy booklets. "It's all in this summary of his selfless career."

"This says your President is forty-nine years old," said T.K., "but other estimates I've seen put his age between sixty-six and seventy-four. Which is correct?"

"Yes," said the adviser, and ushered them into the air-conditioned office. By the doorway hung the same photograph, except that a trio of schoolgirls bearing floral bouquets now occupied the fuzzy patch next to the President.

"What happened to the generals?" T.K. asked.

"Resigned," said the adviser, "for reasons of health."

Behind a polished wooden desk sat the President of the People's Democratic Socialist Republic of Equatoria. He was staring at a large television set, on which a blonde cupped her pointy black brassiere and blew kisses at the camera. Behind her, a couple of barechested men pounded at guitars. A song pulsed faintly.

The President's trademark white beard looked more unkempt than in the photographs but the same toothy smile invited confidence. Reluctantly, the President looked up to nod at T.K. and briefly ogle Vanessa. With a wave of his remote control device, he froze the blond singer, leaving one leather-sheathed leg hoisted in midair.

Vanessa shoved T.K.'s tape recorder aside with her own on the polished desk.

"I can see how busy you are, Excellency, so I won't take but a few minutes of your valuable time," Vanessa said. "May I begin by inquiring about your economic plans, or more specifically, the absence of any?"

"Let a hundred flowers bloom—" the President said without taking his eyes off the stalled rock video.

"Bloom for his new five-year plan," the adviser said, "which leaves our socialist economy prudently in place while charting a bold but voluntary course toward a free-market system. Both coexist so that we may experiment with what works best. If the free market fails to deliver the butter, the state must supply the guns."

"Does it work?" asked T.K.

"Let practice be—" The President turned up the volume again. The television set throbbed.

"Be the sole criterion of truth for your World Bank and International Monetary Fund when they lend us money," shouted the adviser. "Surely you read Uncle's brilliant essay on this in your journal *Foreign Affairs*."

T.K. hadn't. "Now that socialism's failed—" he said.

The President clicked the remote control. The song vanished, the singer went snowy. "Wrong," he said, "it is capitalism that failed—"

"Our Uncle trenchantly observes that capitalism has failed," the adviser said, "to take full advantage of our excellent tax holidays, low wages, export-processing zones, and discreet offshore banking."

"But Excellency," Vanessa said, "how can capitalist exploitation coexist with your socialist command economy?"

"And the President disdains to be addressed as an Excellency," said the adviser, "believing that such titles perpetuate feudal divisions of class. He modestly prefers everyone to call him Uncle, in deference to his charismatic wisdom, or if you prefer, Liberator-for-Life."

The President strained for a thread to his thoughts. "Conceive of socialism as our spaceship soaring into the heavens of prosperity and crashing in other peoples' countries—"

"He points out that the ship of socialism crashed in other countries due to pilot error, not structural failure," said the adviser. "That is why he declares our country open for joint ventures with your multinational corporations, assuring full repatriation of profits after three years."

"Blame the workman—"

"The workman, not his tools, for ideological errors," the adviser said, "and ours work cheap for you."

"And how much longer will this take?" asked the President.

"That's why you dumped Marxism-Leninism at your last party congress?" asked T.K.

The President looked for a nod from his adviser.

"Marxism-Leninism deviated from true Marxism in that it gave rise to isolated violations of socialist legality," the adviser said, "while true Marxism crystallizes the collective experience of the toiling masses with the distilled insights of the revolutionary vanguard."

T.K. asked what that meant.

"Your questions will fall away once you grasp the dialectic between the socialist struggle and the profit incentive," the adviser explained. "It's in Uncle's eloquent thesis, 'Perpetuate the Revolution for the Time Being.'"

"We can't interview a thesis," Vanessa said, "even if it is eloquent."

"It's written for the most illiterate peasant, so the press should be able to understand it," the adviser said. "Because our party vanguard exists to serve the broad masses, Uncle points out, it can never be vanguardist, which means strikes at your factories here become dialectically impossible. This is clear from our Uncle's monograph, 'Let Everyone Serve the People at the Same Time.'"

The President clicked his remote control device at T.K. "Aren't they done?" he asked his adviser.

T.K. flipped through his meager notes. The interview for which he had waited had yet to produce any rocket to scorch Cass.

"A final question, Mr. President," he said, trying hard to think of one. Vanessa rescued him.

"Why did you let the United States open an embassy," she said, "and invite in Western business? Is it because the rebels are winning more—"

"You ignore the dialectic—" the adviser said.

"No no no no," snapped Vanessa. "I want to hear it directly from this dear, wise man." Her blue eyes impaled the President like a butterfly on a board. "Why won't you negotiate with the Patriotic Alliance?"

But the President's eyes had closed, his head drifted onto his chest. The adviser shooed the reporters toward the door. "Uncle is late for his Cabinet meeting."

Vanessa drew a Nikon from her handbag. "One teensy photograph?"

The adviser shoved T.K. out the door. "She'll be right behind you."

T.K. pressed his ear against the corridor wall in time to hear Vanessa tighten the parameters of her question: "You're talking to the Patriotic Alliance, aren't you?"

The President replied inaudibly. Vanessa's voice soared to decibels capable of shattering plate glass. "Are you negotiating," Vanessa screamed, "because your aid from Russia and Cuba ran out?"

Something akin to a sob followed from the President. Vanessa, adept at firming what men said or did, plunged onward. "Then you have no alternative but to negotiate with your enemies?"

Wisps of the presidential confession filtered through the wall. "Yes . . . weeks . . . U.N."

"For weeks, where, the U.N.?" Vanessa's questions required no amplification.

T.K. scrambled back to inspect another photograph as Vanessa emerged trying not to look smug. She tolerated a furtive caress from the presidential adviser. Behind the closed door, the music resumed.

"That was a very long photograph," said T.K.

"Film snagged." Vanessa was rushing for the hotel. "Nothing in that interview, was there?" she said.

"Nothing worth filing," said T.K., who was crafting in his mind a first sentence muscular enough to clamber its way onto his newspaper's front page.

* * *

The next day, T.K. went to his computer to see whether his interview led the paper. He did not find it on the frontings sent daily. In fact, his exclusive had gone altogether unmentioned.

"My in?*rvi*w with *qua?oria's Pr*sid*n? unsigh?*d on ?oday's fron?ings," he messaged his foreign desk. "I assum*d i? would mak* fron? pag*, in vi*w significan? admission ?ha? gov*rnm*n? h*r* s*cr*?ly n*go?ia?ing wi?h r*b*ls. Pls *xplain ov*rsigh?"

He signed off with "Ch**rs." No point in sounding churlish about his desk's lapse of judgment.

Part of being a far-flung correspondent was having as little contact as possible with one's editors. But by that night, he was driven to telephone and inquire what became of his major interview with the reclusive President of Equatoria. A long pause followed.

"This earthquake thing in Turkey," said the foreign editor, "and the season's first no-hitter. How about our new pitcher—is the bonus baby worth two million bucks or what?"

Under relentless questioning, T.K. pointed out, the President had spilled his guts about talking to the rebels.

"Sorry, it didn't grab the readership."

"You never ran my interview."

"We ran it by the young readers' advisory board," the foreign editor said. "They missed the local angle."

"What local angle? Equatoria's on the other side of the world."

"I know—the kids couldn't find it on the map."

"You let brats decide what makes news now?"

"Publisher's idea," the foreign editor said, "to woo the young movers and shakers into the product, T.K. Our demographics are graying."

T.K. had heard newspapers disparaged as rags, fish wrappers, even birdcage liners, but nothing sounded quite so insulting as calling them products.

"We'll try to run your interview," said the foreign editor, "if you trim it, say, to twelve inches. Our space budget's been cut because of newsprint costs, publisher's memo says they're going through the roof."

From three thousand down to six hundred words for an interview with a sovereign head of state? If T.K. refused, Vanessa, with her weekly deadline, could beat him after all.

"What we need is the kind of enterprise I heard on the radio this morning from this Benoit?" the foreign editor said. "Your guerrilla leader's made a deal to store American toxic waste in return for payoffs to a Swiss bank."

Where the hell did Cass dig it up?

"I'm ahead of her on that one," T.K. said. "Consider it filed."

"Tomorrow," the foreign editor said. "If not, you hire this Benoit on retainer before the *Times* or *Post* do. If she's as good as she sounds, we might put her on staff."

T.K. reminded his boss that this Benoit had never written a newspaper story.

"There's software does that now," said the foreign editor. "Feed in your notes and the computer spews out a story. Our sports desk's testing it."

"Maybe computers will replace us all," T.K. said.

"Not this Benoit," the foreign editor said. "She cute?"

"No. And what happened to my new laptop?"

"Sent it out yesterday," said the foreign editor. "Expensive as hell, but we're sick of deciphering your copy. You'll find waybill details in your E-mail. Cheers."

What T.K. read in his electronic mail the next morning prompted a rapid response:

"Som*on* dispa?ch*d ?h* n*w compu?*r to *cuador. I'm in *qua?oria, ?housands of mil*s away. R*?ry soon*s?."

* * *

He had drunk too many beers at the Peri-Peri the night before, but T.K. forced himself to rise indecently early. He put on shorts and running shoes borrowed from Schuyler. Ignoring the queasiness of a hangover, he awaited Cass outside the hotel. He didn't plan to do this again.

Every reporter dreamed of access to an omniscient source. Cass must have hers inside the government, or some embassy, or how could she stay so far ahead of the pack? Her stories never described anyone as concerned or thoughtful or feisty, immediate giveaways to a reporter's sources. Sour quips circulated about her sleeping her way into exclusives, like Vanessa. Cass hadn't shown much interest in sex, so who was feeding her? It was enough for T.K. to waylay Cass when she emerged for her morning run.

"I'm very busy," she said. "You'll have to talk while we jog."

"I just did five miles." T.K. sucked in his gut and gave the fib as much credibility as he could muster.

"Jogging, eh?" she said. Cass wedged one leg on the porch railing, and stretched forward to grab her toe.

"I'm impressed," she said, "because your T-shirt isn't sweaty. If you're in such good shape, another five or ten miles more won't matter, eh?"

She finished stretching her other leg, bounced up and down a dozen times, and took off down the street, her heels kicking out an eggbeater stride.

When Cass ran, her clumsiness transcended into an unfettered graceful-ness. Her hips swayed, her hands flopped limp-wristed. But he would not let her humiliate him again.

Cass let T.K. pull astride for a second lap around the littered square, with its patches of weeds and the generic statue of Lenin leaning into the wind, one hand tucked into his lapel and the other outstretched as if hailing a taxi.

"Just tell me—" T.K. began between gasps.

"Can't talk until the training effect kicks in." She pulled away and up a long hill to the unfinished monument to the Martyrs of Socialism, its ex-travagant spire pointing like a vulgar middle finger.

T.K. stayed with her for almost two miles. But the running shoes bor-rowed from Schuyler were a size too large and slipped on stones damp with dew. Without looking back, Cass jogged in place until T.K. caught up. Then she veered off down toward the harbor, where the sand spit, sheathed mostly in cracked asphalt now, curved into a peninsula denuded of most of the original palm trees.

T.K. welcomed the respite of a downhill stretch, though it made his knee ache. "Wait," he called.

But Cass loped into a dirt alley, leapt a drainage ditch, and turned back up the hill. T.K., in pursuit, missed the far bank of the ditch. He scrambled to his feet, shoes sodden. With each step now, he gasped like a drowning man. Pain within his hip seared his body.

He was limping by the time he regained the hilltop. His nemesis had dis-appeared. She must have finished toying with him and sprinted back to the hotel. Bent over, T.K. sobbed for breath.

Behind him sounded derisive applause. Cass was sitting, laughing, on the monument's concrete parapet.

"Better than expected," she said, clapping in time to her words, "for someone of your age and condition. What do you want to ask me?"

"Forget it, I wouldn't get a civil reply." He headed back down the hill.

She scrambled down and fell into step. "But you've earned a civil reply," she said. "What do you want to know?"

"How you do it, Cass—you've been beating my ass."

"Oh no, Thomas." Cass could not suppress a smile. "I'd say I've been beating every part of you, eh?"

"Who's this informed source feeding you?"

"Calling someone a source sounds so pompous," she said. "I mean, you wouldn't write your mother, 'I met the most informed source today.' If it's a diplomat or official you talked to, why not just say so? And if they're not informed, why quote them?"

"So we've agreed it's a diplomat or official who tips you off over lunch, or is it somewhere else?"

Cass scoffed. "When a woman comes out on top, you men just can't accept that she's smarter or quicker—no, she has to achieve it on her back. What are you trying to pry out of me?"

"Toxic waste," he said. "A little help, that's all."

"Why should I trust you?" she said.

"Don't trust a hack who won't try to steal another hack's sources," he said, "and you've turned into a hack."

Cass seemed touched. "That's so sweet—you really do mean we're colleagues?"

"No colleague of mine," he said. "You're cutthroat competition."

"Crumbs, that's the nicest thing you've called me." Her eyes shining, Cass grabbed his arm and wrapped it over her shoulder as if propping up a drunk.

"Your shirt's soaked and you're still dripping." Her free hand caressed his heaving belly. "So you want my toxic waste notes," she said. "What's in it for me?"

"How about a retainer, fifty bucks a month for a little legwork—it'll spruce up your résumé." She did not need to know the idea came from his foreign editor.

But Cass only laughed at his offer. "One network offered me five hundred a month to tip them off to my stories before I file them. What good's your name on my résumé? Maybe I'll start with that T-shirt you're wearing, the tie-dye reminds me of a rainbow."

"I sweated for this," T.K. said. He recalled the hot sun, eighty thousand screaming bodies, no water or sanitation. Cass seemed impressed.

"Refugee migration?" she said.

It had been a Grateful Dead concert back home, but why tell Cass? "It got me through the Horn of Africa," he said. "How about I lend you my nice flak vest?" She'd collapse under the weight of it.

"And ruin your fun covering wars?" Cass said. "I don't expect to get that close."

"Pretty malachite bangles?"

"That's so sexist. Yes or no?"

"A grateful widow sewed this shirt by hand, in a cave in Eritrea."

Her teasing fingers flicked away the sweat beading his forehead. "You need a haircut," Cass said. "You heard my terms."

"My tie-dye for your toxic waste." T.K. winced. "I don't trust you."

"Which makes us good cutthroat competition, because I don't trust you either," Cass said. "Bring it to my room after my shower, then I'll fill you in."

T.K. reminded her that she was busy.

"Because I'll be with you," she said. "I had plans with Ginny but she's flown out to have her arm fixed."

He thought of covering the amnesty for defecting guerrillas that the government was staging for some U.N. visitor, but suddenly Cass seemed more important.

They passed Lenin still bidding for his taxi. "Let's eat breakfast first," she said. "Do you really consider me a hack?"

"You'll only eat my breakfast, too."

She held his arm until they reached the hotel. "You told me once that a hack always eats breakfast," Cass said, "because she doesn't know when she'll eat again."

* * *

Though T.K. had glimpsed her room before, this was the first time that Cass let him in. Correspondents wallowed in squalor on the road, but nothing as willful as this. True, her bed was made, a daily chore that eluded T.K., and her clothing neatly folded, excluding the panties and socks from her run, now strewn across the cracked bathroom floor. Across the shower tile was printed a reminder in lipstick: *DO NOT SWALLOW THE WATER!*

"You told me a grateful widow sewed this for you in Eritrea." Cass held up the T-shirt newly taken off his back. "The label says it's made in Hong Kong for Banana Republic."

"They must have bought her out." T.K. waited for Cass to try it on. "That's my part of the deal—where's yours?"

"Only a minute, eh?" Her tone implied that it might take longer.

Newspapers had accumulated in piles around her room, books sprouting paper markers, magazines peeled open to pages underlined, with "N.B.!" scribbled in the margins. Cass must have squirreled away every scrap of paper since her arrival over a month ago. The mess was dumped under headings in French: *"politico-économique," "socio-politique," "histoire colonialiste," "l'oppression des femmes."*

If Cass declined to reveal her sources, it must be because she couldn't find them in this mess. It lacked only the coffee stains, the paper cups varnished with congealed chili, and the surreptitious cigarette butt to complement his old desk back in the newsroom.

Taped haphazardly around the walls in her slanted handwriting were lists of Equatorian vocabulary to memorize, with the longer words broken down phonetically.

A Quebec flag with white cross and fleurs-de-lis on a blue field hung over her desk, alongside some photographs interrupting the vertical clutter. One showed an amiable older couple, doubtless her parents, sitting in a canoe. In another photograph, Cass posed among schoolchildren swaddled in parkas. In the third, Cass, cradling skis, her long hair spilling out from under a knit cap, was laughing while a handsome athlete nuzzled her from behind.

While Cass rummaged through her papers, T.K. sidled up to her desk, upon which lay a stiff white letter embossed with the logo of an American television network. Why was TV sniffing around her?

"Stop reading my mail," Cass told him.

"It's upside down."

"That's how you were reading it, upside down. Your lips moved."

T.K. did not deny it. A reporter taught himself to scan the desks of officials he interviewed. So the network liked her.

"One of their vice presidents heard me on the radio, that's all," Cass said. "He has a silly idea that I should try out for television—he claims the network wants more women on camera. He's having their crew here videotape an audition. I'll bet nothing comes of it, eh?"

But T.K.'s eyes had been drawn back to the last photograph. She and her handsome athlete were wearing bibs with black numbers and standing in the snow. T.K. could not imagine the coltish Cass in a ski race.

"Some old lover?" he asked.

"Very much so." Cass could attract a dozen such lovers, but T.K. was left without the prurient details.

"Finished poking into my life?" she said.

"For the time being."

Cass produced a grimy photostat of a letter labeled "Confidential," from Grandma's Tidy-Up Environmental Waste Management Corporation.

"May we bring to your attention that the nation you are about to liberate has been significantly underpolluted for some time," the letter said. "This will leave you with insufficient influence at international environmental conferences. Our company is uniquely positioned to remedy such neglect by accelerating your country to the waste emission levels of enviable industrial powerhouses like Shanghai or Bratislava, in a discreet offshore arrangement that can generate a significant positive cash flow to your cause. . . ."

T.K. concealed his fascination. "Fake," he said.

"Not necessarily," Cass said. "A friend of mine got it from her cousin when he deserted the Alliance."

Cass had plunged in without the trepidation of a seasoned reporter, who would know better than to run out a story based on a single letter of dubious origin. Even if the details were true, confirming them demanded persistence and ingenuity.

"I called the number on the letterhead and it was Grandma's Tidy-Up," Cass explained. "I asked the secretary when they sent payment to the Alliance's bank account and she put her boss on. He said he couldn't discuss it by phone; he assumed I called from the Swiss bank because I started out speaking French."

"He told you that?" T.K. probed for the flaw.

"When I asked the date of the transaction, he yelled at me and hung up. Want to bet a dollar there's spent nuclear-fuel rods involved?"

T.K. could only find a five-dollar bill. "But you don't know that."

"My brother does," said Cass, taking the money. "Did I tell you he's with the Royal Canadian Mounted Police? He phoned a contact of his in your F.B.I., who confirmed that Grandma's Tidy-Up is being investigated by some federal grand jury for dumping radioactive waste. His contact put me onto someone else at the Environmental Protection Agency in Washington, who told me Grandma's Tidy-Up is banned from government contracts because it got caught dumping toxic waste at sea."

"But you still didn't ask the Patriotic Alliance?"

"Only their Washington representative by phone," she said. "He confirmed the date of a meetings with Grandma's Tidy-Up. He got cross when he realized I wasn't the company secretary. But he didn't deny it."

"You should have gotten it on tape," T.K. said.

"But it is," she said, "all of it. Alistair lent me something that plugs from the handset into my tape recorder. But my brother's friend and the others in Washington didn't want to be quoted." Cass shrugged. "I did the best I could, Thomas."

She had nailed the bastards, and better than T.K. would have done. For an airhead, she had too many brains.

"Not bad," he said, "for someone who's a news twink, a stainless steel news twink it turns out, and a menace to fax machines, a good reporter maybe, but a very frustrating woman." He did not characterize the frustrations as overwhelmingly sexual.

"That's sweet, Thomas." She handed him her notes and tapes.

"There's an amnesty for guerrillas today," T.K. blurted. "I could take you, if you're not busy?"

It sounded like his first date back in junior high school—a movie matinee followed by an ice cream soda with two straws.

"The United Nations will be there," he pressed. "In fact, its Special Representative. Might make a good story."

Equatoria was crawling nowadays with representatives from every nook and cranny of the United Nations. Like locusts, they descended on fact-finding junkets with their retinues of staff, pigged out at government banquets, and flew off again loaded with teak souvenirs, leaving behind ineffectual promises and large bills. It added up to no story at all, which was why T.K. had almost decided not to go.

Now he waited for Cass to turn him down. "I'd like that, Thomas," she said instead. "Let's jog it, eh?"

"Very funny, Cass. I'll find us some wheels."

T.K. went back to his room. From her notes and tapes he mined enough nuggets that she overlooked to advance his catch-up story. He owed her some attribution.

"According ?o r*por?s circula?ing h*r*," he wrote, and stopped. Too misleading.

He changed this to: "According ?o *vid*nc* mad* availabl* by inform*d sourc*s familiar . . ." No, that wasn't specific enough.

He tried again: ". . . by r*por?*rs knowl*dg*abl* abou? . . ."

T.K. cursed Cass and cleared his computer screen of evasive attribution.

"?h* s*cr*? arrang*m*n? was firs? disclos*d by Cassandra B*noi?, a public radio corr*spond*n? who mad* availabl* ?h* docum*n?s from h*r inv*s?iga?ion."

Her name didn't look that embarrassing under his byline, so T.K. promoted Cass to the second paragraph.

* * *

When Cass emerged wearing his T-shirt, she found T.K. straddling a menacing black motorcycle.

"Rolf owes me," he said, "so I borrowed his bike."

At the dare of a wild motorcycle ride, Cass shrugged and swung on behind.

"What could Rolf possibly owe you?" she asked.

"I lent him my room." T.K. handed her Rolf's helmet. "He knows these, ah, two sisters and he doesn't want them meeting in the same bed."

Dramatically, T.K. gunned the hand throttle. The motorcycle lurched and died. "Rolf says it's hard to start."

"That's because you went straight into third gear," said Cass. "Step with your foot first, then nudge up that funny bar and step down. And don't race your throttle."

The motorcycle started without faltering. Cass's lanky body stored an annoying excess of trivia.

"You read motorcycle manuals too?"

She laughed into his ear. "I helped my brother rebuild his Harley-Davidson."

"I thought Mounties rode horses."

"That's another brother with the Harley—he's a wildlife biologist."

"How many brothers should I worry about?"

"Four," Cass said. "Sometimes you remind me of them, that must be why I put up with you, eh?"

It was not quite what T.K. wanted to hear, but an opening nonetheless. Her fingers dug at the belly under his shirt. "Low-impact aerobics can work this off," she said.

"Love handles, for your convenience."

"No thanks," Cass said, but she hung on tight. "Rolf needs to check the timing on this—hear what I mean?"

T.K. couldn't hear anything beyond the mighty purr of the motorcycle. Cass's helmeted head bobbed against his shoulder, her thighs gripped his own. Wind fluffed the pale down on her arms, locked around his waist.

"I bet Rolf paid lots for this bike," she shouted.

T.K. could have told her about Rolf's prize-winning grab shot of the toddler bawling over its dead mother in the Rwandan rubble. Rolf peddled it for a news magazine cover. Flies-in-the-eyes, as he called his specialty, sold well. But Cass would ask what happened to the kid, and T.K. would have to explain that Rolf didn't know, or care.

"Isn't Rolf coming to the amnesty?" Cass asked.

T.K. shook his head. "Like I said, he met these two sisters—"

A cloud of dust overtaking him forced T.K. to ease up on the throttle. He pulled off the rutted road and let an armored personnel carrier pass before it ran him down.

"What's a perp walk?" Cass asked abruptly.

Before he went overseas, T.K. covered perp walks, when cops escorted the perpetrators of a crime from jail to court, giving the media their first good look. But that had nothing to do with Cass.

"That's how your nose got broken, I heard, at a perp walk," she said. "You blocked some cameraman and he hit you with his Betamax. Sipho thinks it's why you're not partial to television."

T.K. didn't reply; she did her homework. He banked the motorcycle onto a track leading to where the amnesty ceremony was taking place. The press cards cleared him and Cass through the roadblock. He parked the motorcycle at the edge of the woods.

A sagging canvas tent had been set up in the clearing but the heat appeared to have driven everyone outside. The armored personnel carrier that nearly drove T.K. off the road was parked alongside. A gunner in a padded helmet sat in the turret, rearranging his ammunition belt.

Fewer than a dozen guerrillas, sullen, frightened men, milled about the center of the field. They wore not uniforms but cast-off civilian clothing of the thirdhand sort collected by religious charities. Some went barefoot, with the callused feet and splayed toes of peasants more used to field work. These were part-timers, with none of the defiance that marked the hard-core fighters who had detained T.K. and Cass.

The weapons surrendered had been dumped in a pile: old SKS rifles, a vintage AK-47 with a blue plastic stock, a rusty grenade launcher, a few bayonets. The newer weapons must have been cached out in the bush.

A platoon of field police in blue uniforms lounged on the grass. One po-liceman bestirred himself and toted a bucket of water to the guerrillas, who lined up to take turns drinking. The muddy water dribbled down their open shirts. They looked hungry as well.

The armored personnel carrier hatched its cargo: a dignitary emerged wearing a flak vest over her pink sari. The Secretary-General's Special Representative had arrived to do modalities.

She began to speak, turning not to the guerrillas or the field police, who comprehended none of her English, but to a television camera that had pre-ceded her out of the armored personnel carrier.

"Media?" T.K. felt a tug at his sleeve.

"I'm the spokesperson for the Secretary-General's Special Representa-tive." A redheaded ferret of a man introduced himself and slipped T.K. a copy of the speech under way.

". . . watching old foes embrace as new friends fills me with spontaneous admiration for your valour in choosing an honourable path to peace. (*Pause for applause*) Your very presence tells me you yearn for the United Nations to do here what it has done to so many other war-torn parts of our globe."

The guerrillas looked more interested in the cans of food being brought from the tent. Cass was practicing her vocabulary with the police com-mander. T.K. shielded his eyes from the sun with his notebook. How long would this take?

The Secretary-General's Special Representative's spokesperson handed T.K. another piece of paper, listing the speaker's educational degrees and other qualifications for addressing guerrillas just in from the bush.

"What are you finding out?" T.K. asked.

"How robust our presence should be," whispered the spokesperson. "Does a failed state like Equatoria need peacemaking or peacekeeping, peace enforcement or merely peace building? Madame is defining our strategies before she briefs the media at the airport upon her departure. I could offer you a separate interview. Sshhhh."

The spokesperson gripped T.K.'s arm as the speech climaxed.

"I bring you uplifting news. (*Pause for applause*)," the speech read. "When I return to New York, I shall press for the creation of a committee to recommend a feasibility study for the Security Council to mandate the timely funding of UNEQUALFOR, a United Nations Equatoria Liaison Force, to consider your needs. (*Pause for hearty applause*)."

T.K. jammed the crumpled speech into a pocket of his Levi's. The last thing this screwed-up country needed was another acronym.

"UNIFIL UNOMIL UNOMIG UNIDIR UNAMIR," confided the spokesperson, "UNPROFOR UNPREDEP UNIKOM UNOMSA UNMOT UNMIH MINURSO."

"I don't speak the local language," said T.K.

"Acronyms," the spokesperson continued, "are the key to successful peacekeeping. Some of our member nations still can't tell the difference between UNTAC and UNTAG, or UNTSO and UNCRO. It's why they stopped paying their peacekeeping dues."

Her speech over, the Special Representative handed out a can of food to each guerrilla, much like a college president conferring graduation diplomas.

"The government asked the United Nations to preside over their reconciliation feast," the spokesperson said.

T.K. picked up one of the clunky brown cans from the carton. It looked like the C rations that he ate in the army years ago, though the label was pasted over with something in Thai, or maybe Ethiopian. He located an expiration date; it had lapsed while these rations were circumnavigating the globe.

Upon opening the cans, the guerrillas turned surly. Thumbs-up insults were exchanged, shoving started.

"Sonofabitch, you die," someone yelled in English passable enough for Schuyler's crew to run on the air without subtitles.

The Secretary-General's Special Representative screamed and beat a quick retreat with her spokesperson to the womb of the armored personnel carrier. It swallowed them up and churned off, depositing a layer of dust over the disputants.

T.K. could not see who flung the first can or fired the first shot, because he hit the ground, reaching out to pull Cass down too, except she wasn't there. Bullets snapped overhead like whips. If he survived this food fight, T.K. could file a vivid eyewitness account of the amnesty's dissolution into atavistic ethnic hatred. Or perhaps it was really a guerrilla trap, or a police massacre, and Cass, never having heard a shot fired in anger, was trapped out in the middle.

T.K. shouldn't have brought her. He had visions of Cass's brother in the scarlet tunic and spurs tracking him down relentlessly by dogsled or however Mounties got about these days. T.K. raised his head to find her. The concussion from a smoke grenade blasted dirt into his face. He could not see for the grit in his eyes. He called out to Cass through the smoke; she was still his responsibility. There was no reply.

Instead, a firm hand seized his shirt and hustled him rudely by the collar, head downward, out of the clamor and into the adjacent woods. The brambles tore at his hands and face before his protector steered T.K. behind the cover of a large tree.

"You're slowing down, Thomas." She turned up his face to wipe his eyes. "Lucky I came too, eh?"

He looked at Cass, who had just saved his ass when he ought to be saving hers. It was ignominious to be rescued by a news twink, though she was cutthroat competition now, which made his deliverance less embarrassing.

Brambles had scratched her hands too and dust mixed with the sweat streaking down her cheeks, making Cass look unconscionably spunky.

"I tried to warn you," she said, "when I realized what they were saying. Open wide now, that's better."

The shooting finally stopped, but T.K. left his head embedded in her lap, letting Cass clean the last of the dirt from his face.

"You heard them calling off the cease-fire?" His hand lingered against the softness of her arm. Perhaps the time had come to make his move on her.

But Cass was laughing. "Their quarrel was over cans of beans—they considered it some American delicacy. The guerrillas accused the police of keeping the best cans for themselves. You must have realized that."

She dropped his head and jumped up. "Do you know this war began with a village dispute over water rights?" she said. "I checked it out."

Cass had sprinted through gunfire to save him from more than harm. She saved him from another front-page correction. She showed pluck.

T.K. loathed pluck in a woman.

* * *

When they left, two policemen were tending a wounded guerrilla; the others had escaped back into the bush. The rest of the policemen were busy eating up the C rations. T.K. revved the motorcycle, taking care to nudge the funny thing as Cass instructed. He was heading back the way they had come, when Cass proposed her detour.

"Turn right over there," she said, "and I'll show you some of my sources."

Squatter shanties popped into view with the random pattern of a patch-work quilt. T.K. knew where he was now. He and Alistair nearly got killed out here just about the time Cass arrived.

Some women washing their clothes in the drainage ditch caught sight of Cass and waved. These couldn't be her sources, though she implied they were. After all, what did they know?

The afternoon thunderstorm was gathering, turning the fleecy clouds dark. He pulled a tarpaulin over the motorcycle, and swaddled it with Rolf's chain and padlock—not that it did much good where men got killed for a pair of leather shoes.

"The venereal disease and HIV rates are ghastly out here among the refugees," she said.

"Then tell your sources not to screw."

"It's the only recreation they can afford, eh?" For the first time Cass spoke of sex. "At least there's a family-planning program now."

T.K. had already reported the new program funded by the aid agencies. In fact, he spent a day watching women line up at the clinic to be fitted for in-trauterine devices, and depart content with bags of cornmeal. The doctor whom T.K. interviewed explained it all in English more intelligible than the obscure dialects spoken by Cass's sources. For a change, he had scooped her.

"I know," he told her. "I've filed it."

"You did?" Cass professed surprise. "I couldn't make sense of it."

She consulted her notebook. "The average woman gives birth to more than eight children—that means a population growth of three point three percent a year, even with a life expectancy of only forty-six years," said Cass. "So why do they all suddenly want IUDs? I'll share my statistics when we get back."

Cutthroat competition didn't share, but why tell Cass?

Ignoring the drizzle, Cass hunkered down to chat with a couple of urchins in their patois. T.K. grabbed a wriggling boy with distended belly and reddish hair.

"Kwashiorkor," he said. "Lack of protein causes this malnutrition."

"You sound like a doctor." Cass looked up at him.

"I covered enough of it," he said. "Your squatters will have cholera, too, unless they dig latrines downstream from where they wash their clothes."

"Let's help them." Cass had yet to learn that a reporter was not a social worker.

"And intrude into their lives?" he said. "That's creating news."

"But we create news all the time," she said. "Look at the crowds that television crews or photographers attract. We intrude into people's lives anyway, so why not leave them better off?"

The drizzle stopped, but instead of sunshine, more clouds swept in with rain from the sea. An old woman called from one of the shanties. Cass returned the greeting and clapped softly.

"Traditional sign of respect for elders," she said. "See how it opens doors."

Sure enough, the old woman beckoned them through the plastic flap. The bleak interior was pin-tidy, with glass windows. They sat on a tidy blanketed cot while she heated a scorched enamel teapot over a few twigs. The board walls were papered with birth control posters depicting happy parents doting over a single fat child.

"She's with the family-planning program, she says," explained Cass, "a sort of midwife."

Cass plied her with questions unintelligible to T.K. The toothless old woman winked with the vacant socket of her left eye as she replied in the patois.

"Now it makes sense," Cass announced at last, and directed her superior smirk at T.K.

"Those women you interviewed who got fitted with IUDs in return for food?" Cass said. "They come back here and she takes the IUDs out. They give her part of their corn, she says; it's how she can afford glass windows."

"That's family planning?" T.K. said. Midwives were supposed to deliver babies, not prevent them.

Cass translated the old woman's rambling reply. "She says families can plan for more sons to support them when they get too old to work. Promise not to write it, Thomas, these people are getting fed and the U.N.'s happy."

T.K. nodded. As for following his earlier story with this, he did not relish another retraction.

"Don't aid agencies give these squatters any other food?" he asked. "Some powdered milk would help those kids."

Cass translated again. "It goes to the army or the black market, she says, so the refugees accept whatever God and the family-planning program provide."

The old woman offered a cracked cup of steaming root tea. Cass took a sip and passed it to T.K. The bitterness brought back their night together in the bush.

"Can she prove the food's diverted?" T.K. asked.

"Some relative—I don't recognize the word she uses—goes down to the port to find work. He says there's a warehouse where the government hides stuff." Cass touched T.K.'s arm. "What if we saw what they've hidden?"

"It'd take weeks to get permission," T.K. told her, "and they'd empty it first."

"What if we just showed up?" said Cass. "She can draw us a map."

"You've the guts of a burglar, Cass, which is why you'll end up like one, in jail."

Cass consulted her notebook. "The man who told her was, let's see, her younger sister's daughter's husband," she said. "Their families are so intricate that there's a different word for each relative."

"We'll come back and interview him. Here's my card." When T.K. opened his wallet, a condom spilled out.

Distastefully, Cass retrieved the condom between two fingers. "So juvenile—how long was it hiding in there?"

"Weeks, I dunno, months, donate it to your sources." Ignoring Cass's disapproval, T.K. found a calling card, but it wasn't his after all so he put it back.

Outside, sunshine had broken through the clouds. The children were playing on Rolf's motorcycle.

Cass had the midwife's crude map. The rain had pasted her T-shirt like a second skin. T.K. savored Cass soaking wet, but not the madness that possessed her gray eyes.

"I'm going into that warehouse," Cass said. "Want to come?"

The afternoon's firefight left her cocky. T.K. knew the elation, it was dangerous because it left you careless.

"No," he said, "you can get yourself expelled or shot alone."

"Over powdered milk?" Cass shivered against him as the motorcycle picked up speed.

"There'll be more than milk in there. Kleptocrats like these deal in everything from diamonds to dope."

The motorcycle passed the ditch in which T.K. once cowered, just before Cass trespassed into his life.

"Do you enjoy being cynical?" she asked.

"Sure," T.K. said. Cynicism inoculated you against despair, or madness.

Halfway back to the capital, he stopped short of a furrow newly dug in the road, big enough to hide a land mine capable of incinerating them. He made Cass get off and, cautiously, wheeled the motorcycle around the disturbed earth, telling her to follow in the treaded track.

An old man was pushing a black bicycle toward them. His bulk sagged against the handlebars. The shirt was stained a port wine color. His grizzled head was bowed as though the old bicycle were too heavy.

"Probably drunk," T.K. said.

"He's not drunk," Cass said, "he's dying."

The cyclist did not greet them. He lurched past, sobbing with the exertion of his steps. A sliver of metal protruding from his back glinted in the waning sun.

"Speak English?" T.K. asked.

The cyclist paused over his bicycle. He looked up, muttered something hoarse and incomprehensible. Beneath the glaze of sweat and blood, his nose had been splayed open, as if by a machete. He seemed oblivious to the metal embedded in his back.

"He was cycling home to his family and an army truck passed," Cass translated. "Soldiers riding in the back threw something like a grenade to scare him, he says, and it exploded. We've got to help him, Thomas, there's no one else."

The bicycle clattered when T.K. pried the man loose and maneuvered him to the roadside. In his stint as a police reporter, T.K. had seen corpses ventilated with stab wounds, but this one didn't know he was dead.

"Can't you take it out, Thomas?" Cass asked.

It wasn't what his editors paid him for, but T.K. picked at the shrapnel. It did not budge. He gave the steel a more decisive yank. Brighter blood than what encrusted the man's face trickled through his teeth.

"Keep this up and we'll kill him," T.K. said. "It's too near his heart."

"Let's take him to the Chinese hospital."

"Not on a motorbike."

"I'll stay," Cass said. "You go and send the ambulance. You can still make the airport briefing."

"No, you go. I'll try to keep him alive."

Their companion, legs twisted under him, impassively watched Cass kick the motorcycle into gear and wobble out of sight. T.K. sat by the roadside, clasping his patient. A fresh pull on the shrapnel only brought more blood.

Rolf would have posed this punctured wretch against a sunset, clicked off an award-winning photograph, and walked away. But T.K.'s patient trusted him, which didn't do either of them any good. Thank God she wasn't here.

It was dark now, and his reverie was broken by the crunch of approaching steps that paused at the furrow in the road, like those of a trapper come to check his snares. Or perhaps it was some scavenger after scrap metal who might pull up the mine and blow them all apart. T.K. hugged the comatose cyclist tighter.

A night wind had blown up, carrying T.K.'s memory back through the years to the first time he found himself this witlessly scared. He was standing in the door of a C-130 as its four engines cut back to 125 miles an hour. He was watching the jumpmaster's face twist like putty in the wind as he leaned out to inspect the drop zone 1,250 feet below. He was hooking his yellow static line to the cable overhead, praying he wouldn't lose his life before he lost his virginity. Then with the other cherry jumpers pressing so hard behind him as to block off saner escape, the door light flashed from red to green, and he was leaping into emptiness while the prop blast tried to slam him into the fuselage, shouting to four before the opening shock racked him from neck to crotch and the canopy fluttered overhead, swinging him like a pendulum until the sand of Fort Bragg rushed up to punish his legs. He was seventeen years old.

Safer than crossing a highway, the army recruiter had promised, but it frightened T.K. every time. Yet the next jumps made the fear more familiar, teaching him that sometimes doing nothing was riskier, like sitting here in bandit country propping up a human pincushion.

There was scratching now down at the furrow. T.K. tried to will himself to stop shaking. It was movement that could give them away, even in darkness. After a long time, the steps resumed and faded into the night. The two of them had gone unnoticed or spared, by whom T.K. didn't know.

When the time had come to lay his patient down to die, T.K. heard the ambulance. A nun rushed over in her nursing apron, followed by the driver and Cass.

"Is he alive?" Cass asked. She made fast time.

"I can't tell anymore," T.K. said. He helped carry the cyclist to the ambulance, and propped him upright until they were safely on more solid asphalt.

Blood smeared her hands. "I got it over the motorbike," Cass said. "Rolf'll be frightfully cross."

"Considering what he's left on my sheets, no."

"Who would throw a grenade for sport?" she asked.

"Whoever had the decency knocked out of him," T.K. told her. "It happens all the time here and nobody cares."

"I care," Cass said. "You care too." She traced the healing scar on his cheek with her fingers.

"Don't worry," she said. "I won't tell."

7.

CORRECTION: An article last Sunday about a recent massacre in Equatoria misidentified the alleged perpetrators. The survivors have described their attackers as guerrillas and not government soldiers. Our correspondent also misnamed a species of local flora. Tamarind trees are not indigenous to Equatoria.

The next morning, T.K. dressed in his gig suit, the blue poplin one for interviews with dictators and such. It took two tries to knot his necktie over a fresh white shirt.

When the cyclist was wheeled into surgery, Cass had insisted upon waiting for the outcome. So T.K. drove Rolf's motorcycle back to the hotel, telephoned her room twice, and finally went to bed. He woke up worrying what she'd do next.

He gave her another couple of hours to sleep. Then he went out and banged on her door to intercept whatever reckless notions Cass had about going it alone.

She answered wearing a towel that exposed her slim shoulders. Her eyes, ringed with fatigue, grew wider as she surveyed him.

"Crumbs," she said, "I didn't know you owned a suit."

"And I don't know why I'm dumb enough to do this," he told her.

"So you'll go with me into that warehouse? Only official visitors wear suits here." Cass pulled on her glasses. "You even shaved—rather a turn-on." Why did she always leave him feeling defensive?

"We're getting in there for a story, not one of your good deeds," he said. "See you downstairs in a half hour, and don't bother to bring your press card."

Cass showed up on time, bespectacled and prim in a white blouse and dark skirt, looking not at all like a reporter.

"So you condone misrepresentation," he said.

"It's not misrepresentation to look nice," she said. "My mother says it's always better to show up overdressed."

"They still might recognize us for a pair of hacks," he said. "We'll turn back when I say so."

"Good manners from you could fool them," Cass said, "and your Irish passport."

T.K. had the passport in his pocket. He haggled with a taxi driver and pointed him toward the port, navigating with the makeshift map. Cass kept closing her eyes.

"Hung in there all night, didn't you?" T.K. said.

She sat up. "He's alive thanks to you, Thomas. You kept him from bleeding to death."

"You fetched the ambulance. I just propped him up."

T.K. had to wake her when the taxi stopped near the warehouse, where the map had put it. He tore twenty dollars in half and told the driver to return for the rest in an hour. The vacant streets baked in the somnolent heat of high noon. The bureaucracy was on siesta, or so he hoped.

They walked the last few hundred yards. "If we pull this off," she said, "we could embarrass the government into distributing any milk in that warehouse."

"They can snort what's in there as far as I'm concerned," T.K. said, "as long as we report it first. Bring any kind of ID, just in case?"

He studied the plastic identity card she produced from her schoolteaching in Quebec. The photo made Cass look about fifteen years old. "You were cute," he said.

"I hadn't met you yet," she said.

They walked slowly in the midday heat to a gate set in the barbed wire fence. Inside the sandbagged sentry box, a policeman dozed with a towel over his head to block out the sunlight.

T.K. set to work on the heavy metal gate, slipped his hand through to muffle the open padlock. He and Cass walked to the warehouse as softly as soldiers on patrol. The heavy doors would not open, but Cass found a smaller door on the side that creaked when she tried it.

They glided into the dark interior like dancers on point. Two policeman were napping on burlap sacks near the door. T.K. followed Cass to the first pile of grain. Clasped hands stenciled on the sacks identified them as gifts from the United States of America.

"Leakage," T.K. whispered. "An aid rep told me forty percent of the grain here never reaches people who need it."

"Theft's more like it," she said.

"International agencies call it leakage, to avoid offending the thieves. Here's your powdered milk."

They moved behind the smaller sacks that formed a partition of the warehouse. Adjacent pallets held cartons of Japanese television sets and video recorders.

"Here's what they're really hiding," T.K. said. He led her past the hoarded piles to a partition at the far side of the shed.

A dozen four-wheel-drive vehicles—Toyota, Nissan, the odd Jeep Cherokee and Land Rover—sat parked in a row. Some were still white, others mottled camouflage with black and green streaks that smelled of fresh paint. With his hand, T.K. traced an outline of the insignia of the United Nations High Commissioner for Refugees newly peeled from one Toyota. Like everyone else, he had believed the stories of guerrillas hijacking such vehicles, until now.

T.K. expected diamonds and dope, not a chop shop spray-painting hijacked cars. And why store them with grain and powdered milk?

He scooped up an empty paint can before Cass could trip over it. "See how full this place is?" he asked.

The cavernous warehouse wasn't full at all. Yet the freighters out in the harbor ran up heavy demurrage charges because the government claimed there was no space to store grain. If this warehouse sat half empty, it catered to a more limited clientele than hungry refugees.

Cass pulled out her pocket calculator. "Start counting," she said.

"Grain's about six bags high, eight deep, another eight or ten across." T.K. worked across to the powdered milk. "How do you count a pyramid?"

"Didn't they teach you geometry in school?" she said. "How wide's the base? Break it down."

Cass fed his tallies into her calculator: Four hundred and twenty bags of grain at fifty kilos a bag made twenty-one metric tons. At least three thousand bags of powdered milk at a kilo a bag made three tons. Plus seventy-three VCRs, sixty-eight TV sets, and twelve four-wheel-drive vehicles in transition from white to camouflage.

When they were done, Cass produced a new disposable camera. There wasn't time for snapshots; they had to slip out before the guardians of this loot woke up.

But Cass pointed her camera and snapped the grain sacks, powdered milk, and four-wheel-drives. "Evidence," she explained, "for when the government denies it."

A door swung open, flashing a ribbon of daylight across the concrete floor. A new pair of policemen entered.

"Merde," said Cass.

One policeman kicked his sleeping colleagues awake. T.K.'s watch showed one o'clock; he had not anticipated the change of shift. The old guards stretched and stumbled out, leaving the door barely ajar. Their replacements fell into step on an inspection tour of the interior.

T.K. pulled Cass into a gap between the stacked grain sacks. She fitted on top of him with a snugness that seemed indecent.

"If I hadn't taken my photos—" she whispered.

"We'd have met the cops on the way out," T.K. said. They might still get away, but he didn't know when or how. If they waited till dark, the compound would be floodlit and more closely watched.

But Cass, after the long night at the hospital, was dozing off again. Her breasts flattened against his chest, her hair tickled his nose. It took the slamming of a Jeep door to wake her, and a youthful voice, giddy with delight.

"Vrooommm. Vrooommm, vrooommm."

Cass raised her head above the parapet of sacks and lowered it as cautiously. "He's pretending to drive, his friend's in back," she breathed, as if sharing a secret. One of her legs had jammed into T.K.'s groin.

"Vrooommm. Eeccchh. Whhhhrrrr." The front wheels of the Jeep twisted in the dirt. The other policeman shouted.

"Something about an hour more," Cass whispered. "I think the painters must be returning then."

The Jeep engine turned over, emitting a whoosh of air. Cass pushed up against him with her arms. He had fantasized before about climaxing under her, but not like this.

"Hear the air-conditioning?" Her lips brushed his ear like a kiss. "I'll bet they're taking a nap."

He could not afford to let Cass nap too. But her eyes were wide open now, flirting with him, nose to nose.

"Let's do it." She pressed her mouth so near T.K.'s ear that he expected to feel the wetness of her tongue. "I'll go first, hide behind things."

Her weight slid free of him. He counted to ten and followed. Meticulously, they withdrew. Cass collided softly with a grain sack, knocking her eyeglasses to the floor. She groped for them in vain, then resumed the retreat until she had cleared the door.

He retrieved her glasses on the way out, following her into the white sunlight, watched only by a dog with xylophone ribs from the thin shadow of the warehouse.

"Bet they keep a list of their deliveries in that office," Cass said. She was euphoric.

"Greed gets you caught." T.K. put the spectacles back on her nose. "Just walk out like we belong here."

A bellow of outrage stopped them short of the gate. A policeman rushed toward them, buttoning his trousers.

"He's asks what we're doing," Cass said, "I'll feed him an alibi."

"Don't let him understand you," T.K. said. "He didn't see us leave the warehouse or he'd have yelled before. We've just arrived, for all he knows."

The policeman scooped up his Kalashnikov from the sentry box.

"USAID food warehouse?" T.K. asked. "USAID? Food?"

Cass rattled away in French, faster than sounded possible in a foreign language, but then, French wasn't foreign to her.

T.K. searched his wallet for some financial distraction, but no, it was too late for bribes. He extracted a calling card instead.

The policeman studied the card, saluted, and stepped aside. T.K. rewarded him with a blue ballpoint pen from the United States Embassy.

"We come back tomorrow." T.K. pronounced all six syllables slowly.

The policeman saluted again as they walked out the gate. By the time T.K. turned around, he was back in the sentry box, shouting into a telephone.

Cass wanted one more photograph. "To prove we found the warehouse," she said.

"Let's go," T.K. said. "Our taxi's still waiting by that tamarind tree."

"It's a quinine tree." Cass put away her camera and chased after him. "I took a branch to the university," she said. "It's a quinine tree—the botanist told me tamarinds don't grow here."

T.K. steered her into the taxi, and handed the driver the other half of his twenty dollars. They made their getaway through still-deserted streets.

"We'll file this when we both say so." He cupped her chin with his hand. "No double crosses."

Cass paused. "They'll catch us first—you gave that policeman your calling card."

"Embassy spook's, actually," T.K. said. He had forgotten it was in his wallet.

"Crumbs, you framed the C.I.A.?"

"The government won't protest this unless they want to admit corruption." His shoulder welcomed her drowsy weight. "That's a quinine tree, you say?"

*   *   *

Invading the mystery warehouse proved easier than filing their joint exclusive. Like cooks quarreling over a stew, T.K. and Cass could not agree on what they had and whether it was seasoned enough to serve.

He knew the risks: Wait too long to file an exclusive, and someone else would beat you to it. But file it too soon, without enough pieces nailed down, and it could fall apart or, worse, blow back in your face.

"We'll confront the government with what we found," he said.

"With so much donor fatigue, they'll only deny it, eh?" Cass replied.

So T.K. made the rounds of aid workers, asking what they knew about missing grain and four-wheel drives. Cass had her urchins watch the warehouse for what moved in and out. And when T.K. was ready, Cass still wasn't.

"The Norwegian aid guy told me their vehicles are always getting stolen," T.K. told her one night, "and the government says it can't stop the guerrillas from grabbing them."

"You talked to Lars; eh?" Cass said. "Cute blond guy with pectorals, used to be a ski racer?"

T.K. ignored her attempt to irritate him. "U.N.H.C.R. lost four vehicles in a week, Lars says; their rep did a report on it, just took it to headquarters in Geneva."

"Then we don't know yet, do we?" Cass said. "And we have to interview the minister handling foreign aid."

It had been almost two weeks now, thanks to her fussiness with details.

"A reporter can't know everything," T.K. said. "You have to get it right enough so lawyers won't come after you and no one goes to jail who doesn't deserve it."

"I'd like to get it right enough," said Cass, "that I don't wake up at night wondering how I could have done it. Remember, it was your idea to hold off and file together."

T.K. played to her guilt, evoking a scene of hollow-eyed waifs dropping like flies without the powdered milk in that warehouse.

Cass peeled a banana. "I thought you wanted your scoop, not one of my good deeds." She bit down hard.

She was flaunting his trophy T-shirt again. Did she sleep in that thing?

"In my Lanz nightgown," she said.

"Can I come watch? Flannel turns me on."

"My bedtime's not a spectator sport." Cass scooped up her notes and flounced out of his room, leaving her banana peel and his draft of their investigation, which now looked as riddled with holes as Emmentaler cheese.

They were getting along no better as a team than they had as cutthroat competition, though T.K. breathed in her scrubbed fragrance whenever Cass propped her chin on his shoulder to read his laptop screen. It was the coziest he could hope for; any illusions he had about collaborating his way into her bed were fast waning.

When the telephone rang, he snatched it up. It might be Cass agreeing that they file after all. No such luck.

"A real home run you slammed us," said the foreign editor. "Story had sweep, scope, color."

So his toxic waste piece had run, though T.K. had not seen it on the frontings. The story had come from Cass, but he could not afford to correct a compliment.

"How about doorstepping this European Union thing in Venice?" The foreign editor was never much for details. "I had to send our Rome chap to the Sicily bombing."

"Yes, yes." T.K. would find room on the next flight out. He needed a break from his new cutthroat competition.

"Tourist season's over, so you shouldn't have a problem with flights," the foreign editor said.

This observation puzzled T.K. Spooks, mercenaries, hacks, aid workers, H.L.S.G.P.s, yes, but no one came here for the tourism. The line clicked and took on a fierce echo, signaling a police attempt to change tapes.

"By the way," shouted the foreign editor, "I'm stopping on the way back from Leningrad, or Saint Whatever-the-Shit-They-Call-It-These-Days. Book me at the Ritz. And reserve us a home run for dinner, three crossed forks in your Michelin guide."

"The Ritz happens to be a whorehouse," T.K. said, "and if the Michelin man came here, he caught dysentery."

"So this isn't our Paris bureau," the foreign editor said.

"Not really."

"Where's Paris?" The foreign editor's voice faded.

"It's me, T.K. Can I go to Rome anyway?"

"You're more valuable to us where you are." T.K. heard papers rustling. "Refresh me, where's that?"

"Equatoria. Toxic waste."

"Oh yes, the assistant managing editors are vetting your toxic waste. Once they agree on what the lede should be, we'll pop it onto the front page."

"Agree? That'll take weeks."

"Maybe your lede's really in that next to last paragraph," said the foreign editor, "the one that begins, 'Also, in other developments . . .'"

"But Cassandra Benoit filed her toxic waste," T.K. said. He'd fine his editors, fine them heavily for this.

"You staying on this Benoit's back?"

T.K. remembered the water glistening on Cass's pretty shoulder blades when she bolted from the river.

"Trying hard," he said.

Before T.K. and Cass could consummate their investigation, it was buried in her toxic waste fallout.

Let Cass fight her own battle this time, thought T.K. as he walked into the news conference called by the Committee for the American People's Constitutional Right to Know.

Waiters bearing trays with fish skewered on toothpicks circulated through the tidied-up ballroom, in which the hotel normally stored canisters of cooking gas. Two tables with relatively clean white tablecloths held cans of imported beer, bottles of cola and tonic, French wine, pretzels, potato chips, and other junk delicacies that T.K. had not seen since he left the States.

The flack from Washington, D.C., stood out in a blue shirt with a white collar, red power suspenders, and the only necktie in sight. Sleek-headed and redolent of cologne, he greeted T.K. like a classmate at a college reunion. Pulling on half-rimmed glasses swinging from a dainty chain around his neck, he scanned the name tag his assistant had pinned on T.K.

"A real pleasure," the flack said. "I read all your columns."

"Articles," said T.K. "I'm a reporter, not a mere columnist. You're flacking for the rebels?"

"Their consultant, and the cease-fire allows us in. You ask tough questions." The flack was undeterred. "A real pro who won't take any bullshit, right?"

The warm glow of celebrity suffused T.K., but only for a moment. Reporters who yearned to be admired by people they covered got bought at fire sale prices.

"Join some of us for a buffet supper after the briefing?" the flack said.

"I don't dine with my sources," T.K. said. "I get paid to dine on them."

The flack punched T.K. a little too playfully. "Excuse me, tough guy?"

The pain in his mending ribs evoked Cass. Who could blame her for hiding from this public relations juggernaut that had flown in to discredit her? She would not find much support from the other hacks after whistle-blowing on their expense accounts.

Flacks ranked just below spooks on T.K.'s social register. Lie down with dogs and you'd get up with fleas.

"Sit down, mate," said Alistair. He handed T.K. one of the beer cans wedged between his knees.

"I thought you weren't speaking to me." T.K. took the beer and an adjacent seat. A respectable hack didn't accept anything he couldn't eat, drink, or screw in an hour.

"That's over, mate, she's leaving," said Alistair. "This time, I'm really in love."

T.K. grabbed a fistful of pretzels atop Alistair's glossy folder, which was emblazoned with *The Committee for the American People's Constitutional Right to Know*. In fact, the Constitution didn't give the American people the right to know anything, only the right for reporters to try to tell them—not that anyone cared. This committee was the creation of a public relations firm from Washington, D.C., plumping for an austere band of bush insurgents.

"So who's leaving?" T.K. said.

"I'm lapping up that Swedish tan of hers like it was café au lait," said Alistair. "Nipples like bonbons, T.K., she was wasted on Rolf."

A faint bell rang. But hadn't Gunn already left?

"She thinks I worked in North Korea," said Alistair.

"You mean it's Cass leaving?" T.K. had forgotten the countdown on his calendar.

"Excursion ticket runs out tomorrow, remember?" Alistair said.

The flack from Washington had waylaid the *Chicago Tribune*. "Love your columns," T.K. overheard him say. "I hear you're a guy who asks some tough questions." He punched the *Trib* in the arm, and loped over to the lectern.

"We'll begin if you gentlemen of the press are ready—ladies of the press too." The flack's stentorian baritone startled some reporters into putting down their drinks. "Our bar will reopen after this briefing, with a little buffet. And once you've filed, we'll be showing a video of the Super Bowl." He acknowledged a mere ripple of enthusiasm. Who cared about watching the rerun of a sports event from six months ago?

The flack consulted his gold Rolex. "But we're here to work hard before we play hard. Staci here—"

"That's Staci-with-an-*i*," piped the dark-haired assistant.

"Staci has some background material to give you on the Equatorian Patriotic Alliance's eighteen-point peace plan. Feel free to call us with questions at our operations suite on the sixth floor. Or just stop by to say hello and join us in a little nightcap."

T.K. waited for the flack to announce next that Staci would be turning tricks in the back of the operations suite. But she only walked down the aisle distributing folders as glossy as Alistair's.

T.K. riffled through the handouts: "Six Veritable Truths About Equatoria's True Revolution." "Ten Despicable Lies Spread by Equatoria's Communist Despots." "Eighteen Precious Paths to Peace in Equatoria." The kit included a photograph of the guerrilla leader, the Doctor, wearing his pistol, a map showing Equatoria as mostly guerrilla-held, and a color foldout of the Patriotic Alliance's flag.

"The bull rampant on the flag symbolizes the Equatorian people's industriousness, virility, and stamina," it explained. "The flag's background colors symbolize red for courage, blue for loyalty, white for purity, green for hope, yellow for fertility . . ."

"But you don't need it from me," the flack was saying, "because you want it straight from the shoulder of this little freedom fighter, Colonel Omar, who directs the Patriotic Alliance's new liaison office here. How about you reporters in front let these fine photographers get their good pictures before you ask your hard questions?"

At the sound of the flack's two hands clapping, a small man blinked into the harsh lights, looking more like a schoolboy called to deliver a report that he forgot to prepare. The colonel's green uniform was dressed up with red-and-black shoulder boards. In place of the guerrilla's usual canvas boots, he wore tasseled loafers.

Reluctantly, the colonel accepted the speech, typed and double-spaced, with portions underscored in red. Even with lip-synch encouragement from the flack at his elbow, he stumbled over the jargon of denial: ". . . Communist propaganda calculated to deceive . . . baseless fabrication without foundation . . ."

Calling Cass's story a baseless fabrication without foundation made the hacks sit up. Had she gotten her story right?

The flack applauded again when the colonel thrust back the speech, as if he had only rented it, and scurried to one side of the podium.

"A lot there for us to ponder," the flack said. "The colonel will be available for sound bites with you networks later. First I'll open the floor to questions. Staci has the microphone—state your name and news organization. Yes, the lady in front?"

T.K. raised his hand too. With a nod, the flack jotted his name down on a pad.

"My question's in five parts," said Ginny. "First, did the Alliance's leader agree to accept toxic waste when he comes to power?"

"Why don't you ask Miss Benoit where she heard such nonsense?" The flack smiled. "Oh good, there she is."

Cass stood at the back of the hall, wearing her old spectacles, looking vulnerable. From her large notebook, she extracted a piece of paper that quivered in her hand.

"Didn't representatives of the Equatorian Patriotic Alliance meet on—" she began.

"Wait for the microphone," the flack said.

"Thank you, Staci. My question is—"

"Name first, please."

"I'm Cassandra Benoit, and my question is, do—"

"Hold the microphone farther away," said the flack.

Cass juggled the microphone with her notebook. "Is this better?"

"Question?" the flack said. "Mustn't keep our Super Bowl fans waiting."

Stand and fight, Cass. T.K. fidgeted in his chair. The bastard's sandbagging you.

"What I'm asking is," Cass stammered, "I mean, are you saying the Alliance . . . no one ever met anyone linked . . . to discuss . . . anything toxic?"

"That dog won't hunt, as we say back in Virginia. Couldn't you give this decorated war hero the courtesy of your attention?" The flack professed disappointment. "Or didn't you want to hear the truth?"

It was an old politician's ploy to evince disgust with a reporter's question, to imply that it was posed out of stupidity or incompetence. Even good reporters could be intimidated into silence, and Cass unraveled.

"Speak up," said the flack.

"If you just hush, I'll rephrase my—"

The flack interrupted again. "As a former journalist myself, I must say your reporting's been pretty superficial. I wouldn't blame the Doctor for taking legal action."

"But I don't—"

"Miss Benoit, isn't it the dark complexions of these fine people that you really object to?"

"Oh, I'd never—" Cass looked appalled at the suggestion. Her notebook slipped from under her arm. She tried to catch it, but the cordless microphone skittered off across the aisle and under the chairs, emitting deafening squawks through the amplifiers.

T.K. would have fed her his question, but Cass was on hands and knees now, trying to retrieve a microphone beyond her reach. She gave up and beat a graceless retreat from the room.

The flack snickered. "It seems she let herself get too close to the story," he said. It was the snidest way of implying that the reporter could not be objective.

Ginny was on her feet. "The second part of my question is—"

"You had your turn," the flack said. "Give your fine colleagues a chance. Yes. You over there?"

From his patronizing politeness, the flack expected T.K. to play a walk-on in this charade.

"Thank you so much." T.K. opened with perfunctory courtesy. "Now that you've trashed a good reporter, can we focus on what she reported?"

"Hold your microphone—"

"You wrote the colonel's speech, so tell us," T.K. said, "when did your client arrange to dump toxic waste?"

"Question's been answered, we're short of—"

"We'll take what Ms. Benoit has reported, point by point." T.K. paused. He forgot what Cass's points were.

"Another question in the back?" the flack said.

"The third part of my—" Ginny began.

"Point by point." T.K. tried to phrase a new question with the requisite presumption of guilt. A good question never asked if wrongdoing had occurred, only when.

"Mr. Farrow, isn't it the dark complexions of these fine—" The flack played his last shabby card.

"What color will they be after they water their crops with your toxic waste," T.K. shouted, "bright blue?"

Don't stoop to his level, keep shoving incriminating questions in his face.

"Answer my question. Get your butt back with that mike, Staci," T.K. said. "When did the Patriotic Alliance—"

The flack's joviality evaporated. "I've given you a heads-up, read the guidance we distributed."

"Nothing here about your client's plans to turn this poor country into the world's largest garbage dump."

"We'll miss our Super Bowl."

"Screw your frigging Super Bowl and answer my question." T.K. didn't remember his question anymore.

"No point in continuing this silliness," the flack said. "We'll have a media-alert statement later, and some video B-roll for you hardworking guys from television. And hardworking gals. Mr. Farrow, I'll straighten you out with your publisher. You can forget about our buffet supper."

"Answer my question!" T.K. yelled.

"I'll take a last one," the flack said, "on another subject. Yes, the gentlemen with the glasses?"

Alistair jumped up. "Thank you. About these lovely photographs in your press handout . . ."

The flack untensed, only for a moment.

"Does your Doctor's big pistol," Alistair asked, "compensate for some sexual inadequacy?"

* * *

Cass would not unlock her door until T.K. identified himself.

"It's your tuna net," T.K. said. "That nervous?" he asked, once she had opened up.

"Of course not," she said. "Just scared."

"Courage is being scared and saddling up anyway," he told her. "Who said it?"

"Camus, maybe Sartre?" She laughed. "Soap's in the bathroom if you're here to wash out your mouth, eh?"

A new photograph had joined the cluster over her desk. It showed T.K. at the guerrilla campsite, warming his scraped hands around the mug of root tea. He looked wearily into her camera, face swollen and hair rumpled, like a shipwreck survivor.

"It's there because I like the composition, that's all," Cass explained. "It has very little to do with you."

The composition was terrible, of course, badly off-center, and the photograph itself not quite in focus. T.K. did not know whether to feel flattered or betrayed. He looked too vulnerable, as though she had captured his soul on 400 ASA Kodachrome.

"What's this about you bugging out?" he said.

"My excursion ticket's over, remember?" she said, "which puts me on an afternoon flight tomorrow."

"Don't." He seized her by the shoulders, and let go, awkwardly. "Running off now makes it look like the flack was right," T.K. said. "You're going to stay and fight."

"He vilified me in front of practically everybody," Cass said.

"When reporting's this good, someone's always going to vilify you," T.K. said. "Worry when they can't thank you enough. You did fine back there."

"Liar," she said. "You can be frightfully sweet when you're not busy hiding it. I'm still leaving."

Cass was the most annoying woman T.K. knew, and worse, the most appealing. "Go ahead, throw away what you achieved here," he said. "I gotta go file."

"But you're coming back?" she said. It was the first time that she had expressed any interest.

"Nevermore," he told her.

Back in his room, T.K. dispatched a proposal that his editors risk running his overheld toxic waste story now that every other news organization in the world was onto it. Then he put on his battery-powered headlamp, the one he wore to file on deadline when the power failed, and walked down the back hall to the archaic fuse box. When he yanked out the fuse, the hotel went dark.

The nightly blackout was about due anyway, so who would know the difference? T.K. groped his way to the flack's buffet and filled two plates with food, heavy on the clean lettuce since Cass was partial. He scooped up a bottle of wine from the ice chest. Before his escape, he interred the borrowed fuse inside a bowl of chicken salad.

T.K. felt not unlike a miner as he headed upstairs balancing his culinary loot. His headlamp illuminated the way down the hall to Cass's room.

"Room service," he said. "You ordered the après–news conference supper for two?"

She greeted him barefoot, wearing a sensible cotton nightshirt and toweling down her wet hair. When the electricity died, Cass had lit her own candles; they suffused her room with an intimacy that he had never associated with the Hotel Turissimo.

"You've been up to mischief," she said. "It's in your eyes."

"I know you Canadians prefer your Labrador muscatel sipped through straws," he said, "but tonight we make do with a 1989 sauvignon blanc from the flack downstairs, with apologies for being such a wanker."

"You stole it, eh?"

For a tablecloth, Cass spread a dry towel on the floor. From her bathroom, she produced a couple of glasses for the wine, which he pried open with his Swiss Army knife. He sniffed at the cork. "Nervy, but with a long finish," he assured her.

Cass swirled the sauvignon around the glass before tasting it. "Formidable," she said, accenting it like the French. "I thought you'd be watching the Super Bowl."

"The video replay of the Super Bowl is postponed," he told her, "due to the blackout."

"For how long?"

"How long would you like?"

Having wolfed down her food, Cass measured T.K. over the rims of her eyeglasses. The wine had mellowed her into a mood almost kittenish.

"'Let her learn to swim with the piranhas.'" Cass did not look angry as she recalled it. "You told Alistair that when you met me, eh?"

"As it turned out," T.K. said, "the piranhas had to learn to swim with you."

"Thank you," Cass said. If it was sarcasm, she hid it well.

She let him refill her glass and knocked the wine back. "Some hack you are," she said. "You never asked why I quit teaching to come out here."

"The truth emerges."

"You guessed I was married, eh?"

T.K. hadn't. To the handsome athlete in her photograph, the one he was jealous of?

"Yes," she said. "Marc was killed soon after our wedding. That's our ring I wear, on my other hand now."

Cass looked suddenly frail. "How—" T.K. began.

"Marc loved to ski the fresh powder. He took me off piste to find some and we triggered an avalanche."

T.K. had never thought of Cass as a survivor like himself.

"One minute he was ahead of me, the next he was gone under all that rolling snow," she said. "I was too busy saving myself. It took three days to find his body."

"He could have gotten you killed," T.K. said.

"It wasn't his fault," she said. "I was racing Marc and fell out of my bindings. He skied back for me and the snow gave way."

Shadows thrown by the candles flickered across the ceiling. The delicate down along her forearms glittered for T.K. like spun gold.

"I get too competitive," she said.

"So I noticed."

"I came apart after his death," she said, "ending up in the wrong beds, doing things I wasn't proud of, until one day I found myself getting scraped out at some clinic and I thought, what if nothing better happens to my life? Crumbs, why am I telling you this?"

He reached for her hand. "That's what your cutthroat competition's for, to confide in."

"So I came out here, as far away as I could get from his memory. I was so scared and you made me stick it out, didn't you, just to spite you?"

"If I could do it again," T.K. told her, "I wouldn't."

Cass laughed. "Not even the part I deserved?"

She reached up and for the first time kissed him deliciously on the mouth, lingering long enough for her fingers to trail lightly across his neck.

"That was overdue," she said.

His tongue went for her lower lip, but she turned away. Rebuffed, he collected the dishes while she flaunted her nubility.

Cass tossed back her hair, yawned and stretched, put her eyeglasses on and pulled them off again. Only dregs remained of the wine. His gaze was drawn back to the nipples teasing him through her sensible nightshirt. He yearned to spread her on the spot, among the landfill accumulation of *"histoire colonialiste"* and *"l'oppression des femmes."*

"I'll go put the fuse back," he said. "Hope no one ate it."

"You're sneaking off to watch the Super Bowl," she said.

"That's so pathetic." He mimicked her.

"I don't care," she teased back, "since I'm leaving tomorrow."

"Send a postcard."

"Stay," she commanded in a tone more appropriate for cocker spaniels.

"Expect me to hang around all night?"

"You did out there in the bush."

"There's a fundamental problem now," T.K. said, "which is that you turn me on, Cass, you've been doing it for weeks."

"Thomas, you can be frightfully sweet." Sitting on the bed, Cass parked her spectacles on the bedside table and rummaged in a drawer. "And sometimes frightfully dense."

She looked up, mischievously, and extended a cupped hand.

"You'll be needing this back," she said.

He caught the condom that had slipped from his wallet in the squatter camp. Whatever she said next before her nightshirt crumpled to the floor, he heard it in French.

Watching his miracle unfold, he did not need to comprehend it. Her arms, luminous in the candle glow, felt silken under his touch as she drew him into her bed, and deep into herself.

When he mounted her, Cass erupted with the incandescence of a Roman candle. She yelped, her fingers raked his spine, she nipped his shoulder. He plunged deeper and released the aching loneliness in copious spasms. Her gift had transcended any fantasy.

He lay between her thighs, dazed and utterly spent. Beneath Cass's straight-arrow priggery, linguistic pedagogy, and motorcycle mechanics, he had plumbed a lasciviousness that seemed to awaken for him alone.

Her fingers completed the task of undressing him. "I came first," she murmured after they had lain together awhile in postcoital languor. "Beat you again."

"What'd you say in French before we made love?" he asked.

She arched her splendid back while he stroked her. "That men are like linoleum," Cass whispered in his ear, "lay you right the first time—"

"Don't—" T.K. said.

She pushed him over on his back, nuzzled his chest. "If you knew what I really said, you'd be insufferable." The scent of her wafted like an aphrodisiac.

"We should have done this sooner." T.K. counted her vertebrae, very slowly.

"Oh, not before I'd scooped you."

"You've scooped me every night to get my attention?" he said.

Her fragrant hair brushed his face while her fingers explored the contours of his body. She found the slick pockets of scars across his hip and abdomen.

"How'd this happen?"

She lifted her head to look down and turned to inquire, though not before kissing him.

"A long story," he replied, "long ago."

"My flight doesn't leave for twelve hours."

"You're not leaving."

"I will if you don't tell me." Her head fell back against his. "If we're going to be lovers, let's keep no secrets."

"Mine's not much of a secret," he said.

"I owe myself not to get involved with another man who puts his machismo first," she said. "No one deserves that twice in her lifetime."

Through the soft skin, he felt Cass shiver. He had not thought of her as someone who would care, not about this.

"It started with a practical joke," he said, "that landed me in Vietnam. But then I always outsmart myself."

"A soldier? You don't look old enough," Cass said, forgetting her derision when he had turned forty.

"Seventeen was old enough to get drafted where I came from," he told her. "I didn't want to shoot anyone, so I became a medic. I volunteered for airborne too. I didn't like jumping out of planes, but I needed to be with guys who did. They'd be tough enough to help me survive."

"But how were you hurt?" she persisted.

"Toilet paper," he told her. "White's the color for mourning in Vietnam, you know, not black."

"Don't joke," she said, "not about this."

"After I finished jump school at Fort Bragg, we had to stage a big airdrop for some visiting South Vietnamese generals. I told my buddies we ought to turn it into an antiwar protest, take up lots of toilet paper, fill the sky with white streamers. We raided the barrack latrines, stole every roll we could find. The Vietnamese would figure it out and our generals wouldn't."

The telephone rang but Cass didn't answer it. She was listening too intently.

"After my canopy opened, I pulled the roll out from under my reserve chute, grabbed an end, and unfurled. We had dozens of white streamers floating over Fort Bragg with our subliminal appeal, 'The Eighty-second Airborne Division says shove your war.' A lot more persuasive than all those beards and sandals who marched on the Pentagon."

Cass tried not to laugh.

"The colonel couldn't prove it was me, not with so many paratroopers in the air," he recalled. "But my sergeant guessed. He cut me new orders and I found myself standing on the tarmac at Bien Hoa, Vietnam."

"That's when you got wounded?" Cass asked.

"The war was winding down for us Americans, but not for the poor bastards who lived there. So I was issued lots of toothbrushes and dental floss and sent off with a patrol to win hearts and minds in some hamlet. The hearts and minds ambushed us first."

The nightmare spilled out again: His sergeant, six days away from rotating home, gutted by the claymore mine he had tripped. T.K. unable to reach him for the crossfire of AKs from the treeline. Rosie cut down next, guts spilling out faster than T.K. could push them in. T.K. slipping an M&M into his buddy's mouth—lying that it was a painkiller—but the blood washing it out. The new kid screaming on the radio for mortar support but screwing up the coordinates, and the firebase pounding what was left of the patrol. Then silence, but for the cicadas and footsteps swishing through the long grass and the deliberate point-blank shots.

Cass listened to it all, even the part his other women never heard, how the cartridge scorched his neck when it popped out of the AK that put the final bullet in Rosie's face.

"I had so much blood on me that they didn't kill me," he said, "took my pistol and left the toothbrushes. The next morning, a chopper crew was zippering me into a body bag when they decided I was alive. When I see a corpse now, I think it could have been me down there."

Her hand cupped the scars, as T.K. had when he tried to stanch the hemorrhaging many years ago. "I understand," she said.

"You can't," he said, "because I can't. The real practical joker was the army, sending me to teach flossing to guys in black pajamas who wanted to kill me. My tears ran out in that hospital. I haven't cried since."

Cass had raised herself on her elbows, memorizing his face.

"My ex-wife's shrink told her the trauma made me distrust authority,"

T.K. said. "The bastard never met me. Enough shrapnel's left in my hip to set off detectors in airports and I still don't know which side put it there."

"All will be well again," Cass told him.

"When I was a medic," he said, "I wanted to go back to college and become a real doctor. But I became a reporter because I didn't want the responsibility."

"My father's a doctor," she said. "It's the kind of thing you accept."

"In Saigon, I watched the foreign correspondents drinking on the porch of the Continental Hotel, talking about what they'd covered. I wanted to become a spectator like them, to be free to watch and then excuse myself from the killing, to satisfy my curiosity at someone else's expense. It seemed the world's best job, still does, orbiting out here like an astronaut."

"But a journalist has responsibilities," she said. "That's why I became one, to make people care."

"Let yourself care," T.K. said, "and you'll screw up every story you're sent to cover." He had revealed too much of himself.

"Now listen to me," she said. "Sin is necessary, but all will be well and every kind of thing will be well."

The candlelight set the fluid curves of her back aglow. Her smallish breasts fell unfettered with a peachlike plumpness against his chest.

"I don't call this sin," he said.

"Julian of Norwich means whatever went wrong will be set right."

"An old friend?"

"Older—she was an English mystic six hundred years ago. I read Julian's revelations last year when my life was a mess. I learned to believe her because I'm with you."

"We're survivors," he said. "That's all that counts in most of the world."

"What counts is resurrection," she said, "and you're going to learn the joy of it. Crumbs, I'm sleepy."

He took it as a signal. "I'd better leave."

Cass stretched against him with the contentment of a cat. "You'd better not."

They lay clinging to each other. "What would they think of us?" he asked after a while.

She raised her head.

"My readers, your listeners," he said. "Would they trust us if they knew we're as battered as the countries we write about?"

Cass did not answer. She only crawled onto him and reached down to prime him—not that he needed it.

"My turn on top," she whispered, as if sharing a secret, and began to rock him. "Now don't be in such a hurry."

He awoke some hours later to find the candles burned out and the lights on. A promise of daybreak had slipped in through the window. The ceiling fan hummed with the power restored while they slept. Cass had backed up tight against him, skin moist on skin, hugging his arm to her belly as she had out in the bush.

He looked around the cluttered room. Cass told him she was leaving today, yet she never started packing.

As he studied the thick lashes closed over her eyes, tried to count the freckles bridging her nose, he found himself swelling against the cleft of her. He would have rolled her over and entered again but she was sleeping too sweetly. Gently, he unpried his arm, slid out of the bed to turn off the lights, and knocked her spectacles from the bedside table.

"Where are you going?" she asked drowsily.

"To cancel your flight." Her tooth marks indenting his shoulder confirmed that for a change he had not dreamed this. "You're staying if I have to tie you to the bed."

"Sounds fun." Cass sat up and tossed the disheveled hair back from her face.

"That office doesn't open for hours," she said. "Can't you procrastinate?" She dragged him back onto her moist loins. "For a hack, that's so unprofessional."

* * *

Cass was still asleep when T.K., back from the airline office, wandered into Schuyler's room. Two walls were stacked nearly to the ceiling with electronic gear on which lights winked against the black metal. Talking heads beamed or froze on the garish color screens of a couple of tiny monitors. A television crew traveled with more luggage than T.K.'s ex-wife.

The rest of the room was littered with open bottles of beer, either empty or partly so, with greasy dinner plates crusted with dried egg yolk from which the odd crust of bread protruded. Sipho, who was editing at a small console, gave T.K. a wave. He wore a crisp white T-shirt over his jeans. *For-*

eign Press, it announced. *Don't Shoot.* The phrase repeated itself in French and two more languages that T.K. didn't recognize.

"Sipho's idea," said Schuyler, who was wearing a quadrilingual T-shirt himself. "We had a bunch made up in Hong Kong and flown in with our videotapes," he explained. "Copied a T-shirt that Kobus wore covering Beirut."

"Only twenty dollars," Sipho called without looking up from his work.

"What's the family rate as your illegitimate brother?" T.K. said.

"Okay, our weekend discount for whites," Sipho called, "forty dollars for two."

"Guaranteed to repel bullets," Schuyler said. "We'll make a fortune peddling our magic to other hacks once the truce breaks down."

T.K. ripped back the Velcro tape sealing his inside pocket and pulled out a couple of bank notes. He ordered a large for himself and a medium for Cass.

"I tried your room twice about the briefing, and no answer," said Schuyler. "And you lost your hangdog look. How come it took you both this long?"

T.K. didn't quip back; Cass was off-limits now. He caught the T-shirts that Schuyler tossed him.

"What briefing?" His night with Cass had cost him the big story. "Can I watch your rough cuts?"

"Relax, you didn't miss anything." Schuyler regarded him with a bemused grin. "Government accused the rebels of violating another ceasefire. We sprayed the briefing and ran. We're passing up the bird."

"Where's your new producer?" T.K. asked.

"Gone." Schuyler did not suppress a grin. "Medical evacuation."

"Is it permanent?"

"Hope so," Schuyler said. "He wanted to split up Kobus and Sipho, said the tension between them wasn't creative and Kobus couldn't move fast with a metal foot."

"You got him run over?" In the capital, accidents could be arranged for about three hundred dollars.

"That would be wrong," protested Schuyler. "We just took him to the beach and let him splash in the sewage while the sun boiled him like a lobster. Then we bought him a salad at the Peri-Peri and plied him with lombo. And Rolf took him to the Ritz to get laid. I don't know what did it—typhoid, food poisoning, sunstroke, or the clap—but he left here flowing from every conceivable orifice."

"Your network will send a replacement," T.K. said.

"That's why we burned his press card. The Ministry won't accredit anyone new until they get the old card back," Schuyler said.

Kobus darted in. "Where's my camera? And the sticks? Demo outside."

"Burning an American flag again?" Schuyler shrugged.

"American flag," said Kobus, "but this time they got women ripping it with their teeth and chewing it. CNN's out there." Kobus was followed by Sipho with his microphone and recorder.

"That's prime time." Schuyler sounded awed.

"That's why they do it." T.K. followed Schuyler to the window. The hotel driveway was filled with shabby people led by a man with a bullhorn. The flack from Washington was there too, watching placards distributed from a truck.

"What's it mean," asked Schuyler, "beyond the flag chewing?"

"The local audience for Cass's stories, I guess."

The television crews had gravitated to the placards obligingly printed in English:

SCIENTIFIC SOCIALISM EQUALS CASSANDRA PLUS ELECTRIFI-CATION OF OUR COUNTRY.

RUNNING JACKALS OF THE WESTERN PRESS: STUDY THE SELF-LESS CONTRIBUTIONS OF OUR CANADIAN CASSANDRA

LET COMRADE CASSANDRA BE OUR NORMAN BETHUNE.

T.K. found Cass down in the lobby. She was shaking her head at the man offering her the bullhorn.

"Who's Norman Bethune?" T.K. asked.

"A Canadian surgeon who went to China to help the Communist guerrillas," said Cass, "and died of blood poisoning. What about him?"

"Oh great." T.K. took the bullhorn thrust into her hands. "You're not their cheerleader."

"His friends walked all the way here, he says, and won't leave till I meet them."

"This rent-a-crowd got trucked in." T.K. shoved the bullhorn back at the organizer. The Washington flack glided in, without his antique Super Bowl video.

"Hi there, tough guy." The flack pumped his hand. "Loved your questions, straight from the hip."

"Where's your toxic waste rebels?" T.K. asked.

"Yesterday's agenda."

"You cater mayhem from both sides?"

"While we're here, yes, we do a little consulting for the government, too," the flack said.

"Double-billing for a civil war doesn't keep you awake nights?" T.K. asked.

"Love your dispatches, Miss Benoit," the flack called out. "May we borrow you for a minute?"

"That's so ridiculous." Cass turned away.

"A real professional, Miss Benoit. I respect that, even if we don't always agree. Maybe later?"

The flack went off to corner a camera crew. "We've lined up someone who speaks English," he shouted. "And Staci has some complimentary video-news releases."

"It is rather flattering," said Cass.

"Reporters thrive on flattery," T.K. told her, "but don't accept it from crowds of more than three unless they pay you an honorarium."

"It's time to run our warehouse story," she said. "I've talked to someone who's filled in the details."

"You held out on me," he said.

"Because I didn't trust you, not before last night."

"You're learning," T.K. said, and kissed her.

* * *

The Center for the Pursuit of Conflict Resolution and Human Rights turned out to be a rented room behind an Indian dentist's office. A plaque identified the tenant as Mukhtar Phuqqa, M.A. (Incomplete) Oxon., Consultancies by Appointment.

"But why?" Cass was saying as T.K. walked in. "Why?"

Mukhtar Phuqqa, a rotund man with insufficient hair combed carefully across his bald spot, had cleared enough newspapers from the sagging sofa for Cass to sit down.

"We need a second liberation from our past," he was telling her. "One can no longer blame all our problems on the colonialists, however wretchedly they behaved. Aid money flows out to Swiss banks as fast as your donors send it in."

When Cass identified Phuqqa as one of her sources, T.K. did not recognize him among the usual dial-a-quotes. Phuqqa rose to shake T.K.'s hand and found him a seat atop a yellowing pile of *International Herald Tribunes.*

The office, which would have looked brighter had the windows been cleaner, overflowed with old newspapers. A tiny radio blared pop music, masking conversation from whatever microphones had been planted by the security police. Bottles of a clear liquid filled the windowsill.

"I asked Mukhtar," Cass said, pronouncing his name with a click of tongue against her cheek, "about what we saw in the warehouse. The government claims to have captured the Jeeps from the guerrillas, but no one believes it. Talk on the street is that they belong to the aid agencies."

"Gifts for the generals who suppressed the mutiny last month in the north," Phuqqa said. "You heard about it?"

T.K. hadn't. "They get four-wheel-drives to keep them loyal?"

"They're supposed to buy them at the official dinar equivalent in hard currency," Phuqqa said. "But by paying with black market dinars, they spend a few hundred dollars, and can resell the motorcars for a big profit."

Cass turned a fresh page in her big black notebook. T.K. had failed to persuade her to switch to the thin notebooks that he jammed in his rear pocket.

"Mukhtar used to be a journalist too," she said.

"Only by fax machine," Phuqqa said, "but many people read my weekly faxes because I included all the soccer news. Our party newspaper, *Truth of the Masses,* only manufactures battlefield victories and bumper harvests. The police closed me down for publishing official secrets—the losses of our national soccer team in the World Cup. When I got out of detention, I had no fax machine or telephone. Say, I hope you don't smoke?"

He gestured at the bottles along his windowsill. "Petrol for my little moped is so rare these days that I store what I can find here in my office."

Phuqqa was the first Equatorian T.K. had met who was willing to criticize his government in fluent English and at dictation speed. How did he survive?

"Embassies like yours pay me honoraria for briefing their visiting delegations," said Phuqqa. "We attract more of them these days. I think it's because we carve our teak so magnificently."

Cass was undeterred. "And the grain, Mukhtar," she said, "tell Thomas about the grain."

"Twenty-two tons," Phuqqa said, shifting T.K.'s attention back to his notes. "The train left the port full and arrived at the refugee distribution center empty. You saw some of the grain in the warehouse. The rest went to the black market—so my army friends tell me."

T.K. was distracted by the graceful arch of Cass's neck over her notebook. Had his nibbling caused that bruise? He must try to graze at her nape more circumspectly.

"If the grain had fed our soldiers, it would not go wasted because they might stop stealing from the peasants," Phuqqa was saying. "Empty bellies caused the mutiny."

T.K. rejoined the conversation. "The rebels must not seem so bad."

Phuqqa turned up the radio before replying. "You Americans always fail your dialectics. Because we have such a wretched government, you assume whatever replaces it must be better. How often does a good government follow a bad one? In China, the Soviet Union, Iran, Cuba? New rascals kick out the old ones and the masses still go hungry."

"Mukhtar told me the leader of the Popular Front isn't even a medical doctor," Cass said.

"His supporters bought him a mail order degree from California," Phuqqa said. "You would not want him removing your appendix during his mood swings. I knew a physician who treated him. My friend was found later in a crocodile pond. The Doctor can be charming and lethal, too, like our spitting cobras."

"Mukhtar says the Doctor received guerrilla training from the Chinese," Cass said.

"Many revolutionary fighters were trained in China because the West refused to help," Phuqqa said. "How much happier my country would be if America had learned that a revolutionary is not always a Communist and a Communist is seldom a revolutionary."

T.K. glanced at his watch. He had to leave, but this source was worth seeing again. He had a parting question.

"How can the Popular Alliance afford a big public relations firm?" T.K. asked.

"There are rumors," Phuqqa said, "of diamonds found in the river to the north, of gold mined by captured soldiers. One does not inquire if one disdains to swim with crocodiles."

Dr. Phuqqa rummaged through the chaos of his desk for a piece of paper. "This is my sister's number," he said. "One of her children will fetch me."

In the street, T.K. hailed a green taxi with a cracked windshield. Cass had explained once that drivers broke the windshields themselves to discourage thieves from ripping them out.

"Where'd you find him?" T.K. asked.

"I overheard some correspondents laughing about not pronouncing his name on camera," said Cass, "so I looked him up. It's the name he was born with, eh?"

The taxi turned a corner and nearly plowed into a student protest. The university was not the political hotbed that flourished in other developing countries. The children of government and party officials enrolled as a draft dodge, demonstrating from time to time to force a postponement of looming examinations.

The students were venting their latest grievance by smashing the windows of shops and parked cars.

"UNEQUALFOR go home," they shouted.

"But they haven't arrived," said Cass.

T.K. had nothing against a good riot, which usually wrote itself, given the reliable mix of truncheon-wielding police, volleys of tear gas, and protesters responding with rocks or dragging injured comrades into doorways. He just didn't like being trapped in one.

"Keep down," he told Cass.

The rampaging students surrounded the little taxi. A bearded youth peered through the windows. "UNEQUALFORs," he shouted.

His comrades rocked the taxi, back and forth in an expanding arc that knocked T.K. and Cass against each other.

"UNEQUALFOR go home." The students pummeled the taxi. The windshield was shattered by an ascetic youth in an Eric Clapton T-shirt, who beat on the precarious glass with a length of pipe.

The taxi achieved gravity-defying angles before it flopped onto its side, sliding Cass atop T.K. A grinning student clambered onto it, waving a cigarette lighter. The ascetic drummer applied his pipe to the rear window.

"UNEQUALFOR go home," chanted the students. *"Idi domoi. Vaya a casa.*" The taxi driver hung on to the wheel and watched his livelihood trashed.

A canister thumped against the roof, the protesters scattered, the taxi filled with tear gas. Cass was coughing.

"Cover your mouth," T.K. told her. He opened the door, now overhead, boosted himself through and pulled her after him.

Her eyes were shut tight. "It's in my contacts."

He led Cass across the street, propped her against a wall, pressed a hand-kerchief against her runny nose. The students had run away. T.K. returned to the taxi and hauled out the driver feet first.

A truck with police in gas masks rumbled past. A grenade bounced off T.K.'s thigh and spewed an acrid new cloud.

T.K. pressed some dinars on the driver, who was nursing a nasty gash across his forehead. "Keep the change," he said. He retrieved Cass and steered her free of the tear gas.

"Congratulations," he said. "You've just been initiated as a hack."

She flipped one tainted lens, then the other, into her palm. "What'll we do," Cass said, dabbing at her swollen eyes, "if we're not around to pull each other out?"

8.

PORʔO PARADIIO, *quaʔoria—A! a fragil* ʔruc* conʔinu*d ʔo hold in ʔhil counʔry'! long civil war, ʔh* Uniʔ*d Naʔion! agr**d ʔo l*nd a conʔing*nʔ of p*ac*k**p*r! ʔo lup*rvil* ʔh* pr*paraʔion of fair and fr** *l*ʔion!.

Bull*ʔ! whil!ʔl*d ʔhrough ʔh* quinin* l*av*! in ilolaʔ*d incid*nʔ!, buʔ boʔh lid*! r*affirm*d a commiʔm*nʔ . . .

The Ministry of National Guidance was irate enough about the fuss that their disclosures of diverted grain and aid vehicles attracted overseas that T.K. and Cass were summoned to learn about the responsibilities of the press.

They sat side by side on two straight chairs like schoolchildren summoned to the principal's office while the Deputy Minister rummaged among his papers.

"The press must shine like a beacon, inspiring and leading the broad masses." The Deputy Minister gave a little whinny. "Yet you prefer to wallow like a mirror, distorting the filth in dark corners."

"Mirrors can't wallow," said Cass, staring back through her spectacles. "And if dark corners are filthy, shouldn't they be swept out?"

"You abdicate your duty as journalists," said the Deputy Minister. "Your irresponsible reports portray us as a bankrupt regime that rides about in luxury sedans while the masses walk."

T.K. nodded agreement.

"Dialectically impossible," the Deputy Minister said. "How can the government neglect the masses when we are indivisible from them, Miss Benoit? And the People's Democratic Socialist Republic of Equatoria is not bankrupt, Mr. Farrow, merely overdrawn."

But T.K.'s eyes had wandered to the air conditioner in the Deputy Minister's window. How much had it cost? Maybe T.K. could find one for Cass's room, to make love under.

"Your fabrications about American grain being sold on the black market are not merely groundless but without foundation too," the Deputy Minister said. "The masses nearly starved because of you."

T.K. had not expected his congressman to introduce a resolution halting all food aid. Fortunately, more venal interests prevailed.

"We know of your carnal misbehavior, too," the Deputy Minister said. "If you keep abusing our hospitality, we must ask you to go."

"Expel us?" Cass sat upright.

"You leave us no choice," the Deputy Minister said. "Imagine what an expulsion would do to your reputation."

T.K. knew that expulsions were the price paid by hacks who did their jobs, that far from being a disgrace, expulsions got worn like badges of honor. But Cass, with her Canadian conscience, looked so miserable that T.K. took the offensive.

He dropped his head into his hands and counted silently to ten. Having invited the Deputy Minister's curiosity. T.K. rolled his eyes heavenward and sighed.

"We acknowledge and bewail our manifold sins and wickedness," he intoned, "which we, from time to time, most grievously have committed, by thought, word, and deed, against the broad masses of Equatoria, provoking most justly your wrath and indignation against us."

Cass's despair turned to incredulity. She stifled a smile.

"That's better," the Deputy Minister said, cupping his ear and leaning forward.

"We do earnestly repent, and are heartily sorry for these our misdoings," T.K. said.

"The remembrance of them is grievous unto Mr. Farrow," said Cass. "The burden of them is intolerable."

"Have mercy upon us," T.K. said. "Forgive us all that is past and grant that we may hereafter serve and please you in newness of life."

"That's what I call self-criticism," the Deputy Minister said. "Yes, Miss Benoit?"

"We have erred and strayed from your ways like lost sheep," said Cass. "We have followed too much the devices and desires of our own hearts."

"Let this be a final warning then," said the Deputy Minister. "You both may go."

The billboard across the street from the Ministry had replaced its time-worn slogan *THE FUTURE IS SOCIALISM* with an apocalyptic new one: *UNEQUALFOR IS COMING.* Dueling graffiti had been appended below: *Where Is UNEQUALFOR?* and *UNEQUALFOR Go Home.*

T.K. and Cass were well down the street before he could hail a honking green taxi breaking out of the noonday traffic jam. Once they were inside the taxi, Cass leaned against him and giggled.

"Crumbs, you were reciting the Anglican confession," she said. "Sometimes I include it in my bedtime prayers, but never like that."

"I thought it was Episcopal," T.K. said. "Useful, though, when you get detained at roadblocks."

"You seemed to know it by heart," she said. "You must have been a choirboy once—oh, that's so sweet."

"One word about this, Cass, and I'll ship your ass back to the guerrillas, that's a promise."

A vendor running alongside thrust his coconuts through the taxi window in a vain attempt to make a sale.

But Cass shook her head. "I can't afford to get expelled," she said, "not when my career's beginning."

"They never expel hacks from Equatoria. They need the dollars we bring."

"We could be the first."

"It won't happen," T.K. told her, "believe me."

* * *

It was on a government tour to the model pig farm that Cass and T.K. first quarreled about the audition tape that would drive them apart.

"Warmly welcome, foreign friends," hailed the government minder.

The minder sent to supervise the journalists sat up front in the bus with an agricultural official and his box of statistics. Ginny had stayed behind, awaiting a telephone interview for another job. Alistair had abruptly flown back to London to be dosed for what he described in a whisper as a staphylococcus infection, and please don't tell Cass. Rolf maintained down at the Cafe Peri-Peri that Gunn had bestowed a dose of gonorrhea on Alistair, which served the focking bastard right, okay?

So T.K. signed up Cass for the outing, because hacks went to places that didn't interest them to see things that did, such as whether the government was observing the truce. The pig farm lay in a closed area that encompassed a tank division and an airfield, the sorts of attractions that got a reporter traveling alone accused of espionage.

"I told you I was terrible." Cass solicited T.K.'s reassurance.

"Your television audition?" T.K. was not unhappy to hear about her poor performance.

"I had to tape it about twenty times before they had a wrap," she said. "I stared at the camera and kept fluffing my lines."

The government minder ordered photographers to put down their cameras whenever the bus passed another gun emplacement. Soldiers were dozing under tattered camouflage netting. Other soldiers, stripped to baggy underpants, paused from drying their uniforms on the coils of barbed wire to wave at the bus as though relatives were aboard.

"I guess I'll stick to radio, eh?" she said.

"Why not, people listen to you," T.K. told her. "You can line up some radio stringing wherever I'm posted."

"It doesn't work that way." Cass bristled. "We might be sick of each other by then."

"Not with all we've got going for us."

"I'm Canadian and you're American," she said. "I read Julian of Norwich and you quote John Wayne. I adore the Montreal Symphony and you dig the Grateful Dead. I want to try television and you're happy newspapering. What going for us did you have in mind?"

"We're both left-handed," T.K. said, "and totally compatible in bed."

"Love affairs don't go anywhere," Cass said, "and a career does."

At a roadblock, old men and boys wearing mud-colored uniforms boarded the bus to check credentials. There were countries where T.K. carried wads of press cards, extracting whatever promised to placate each new squad of paramilitary highwaymen. But the soldiers here, grateful to escape the sun, paid scant attention.

"You could marry me, you know." T.K.'s heart pounded when he heard himself propose it.

But Cass only shook her head. "I'm frightfully fond of you," she told him, "but I've done marriage and it almost did me."

Cass held up her press card for inspection by a soldier who looked too young to shave.

"You haven't picked the world's safest line of work, eh?" she told T.K. "You'll chase one good dateline too many, and when you get yourself killed, well, you're not dragging me down with you."

"You forget I'm indestructible," T.K. said.

"So was Marc and his death nearly destroyed me. I make a wretched widow."

"No story's worth getting killed for," T.K. told her, "because you can't even file it."

But Cass did not withdraw her hand when he insisted upon holding it. Only in retrospect did he recognize their quarrel for the warning shot it was. The animosity had dissipated by the time they reached the pig farm, a few miles past an air base.

T.K. assumed that it was a farm. The first view was of long rows of white barracks built near enough the river to pollute it. *Red Utopia Swine Husbandry Institute,* read the sign on the metal arch through which the bus passed. The compound was surrounded by barbed wire with gaping holes.

Cass pressed her nose against the window. "I don't see any pigs," she said.

"They're probably inside those sheds." T.K. still held her hand. "Pigs turn you on?"

"I put up with you," she said.

They were ushered into the reception room, where a plaque boasted that Cuba's Fidel Castro considered paying a visit to the farm once, but didn't.

On another wall, Lenin marched arm in arm with Equatoria's President while grinning peasants waved sheaves of corn. The painting was so inept that the artist panicked and omitted everyone's feet, which enhanced the kitsch value enormously if T.K. could persuade someone to sell it.

The farm manager, who wore a long white coat more befitting a research chemist, led the visitors to lunch of bread and herring pried out of oval tins donated by well-intentioned Lutherans overseas.

Cass asked about ham. "Our pigs are not for eating," the manager told her. "They are property of the masses."

Some farm workers with accordions performed a postprandial concert of folk music while others danced with AK-47 rifles. Eventually, the briefing got under way in a stuffy reception room, where the statistician set to boasting of the government's agricultural successes.

The photographers reloaded their cameras in blind faith that a better photo op would follow. Rolf, having changed tapes in his Walkman, was engrossed in a comic book. T.K. dozed off with Cass's head against his shoulder.

He awoke to the subject of pigs.

"Our production target is twelve percent higher than last year's target, which we overfulfilled by five percent," the statistician was saying. "So our current five-year plan could exceed the last five-year plan by eight percent, and exporting thirty percent of this production would generate an increase of zero point two percent in gross domestic product, assuming that population growth is maintained below a ceiling of two percent."

"And how many pigs is that?" asked Cass.

The statistician sipped from a glass of water on the podium. T.K. wanted a glass himself. The sweet orange-flavored drink at lunch did nothing to slake his thirst.

"One performs one's arithmetic from one's base year of 1990," the statistician said.

Cass took out her pocket calculator. "How many pigs did you say there were in 1990?"

"The swine census was destroyed when the puppet traitors burned our archives," the statistician said. "What I can confirm is that the swine throughout our country today number forty eight point seven percent more than in 1990."

"The guerrillas claimed you were storing grenades in your archive," said T.K., "that's why it blew up."

"And why does production keep rising?" interjected the farm manager, though no one had asked. "It rises thanks to the boundless enthusiasm of the peasants and scientific advances shared by our comrades in Cuba. You know of course that a boar ejaculates up to a liter of semen into a fertile sow during a copulation lasting forty minutes."

Rolf dropped his comic book and grabbed his camera.

"Applying scientific new techniques," the manager said, "our boars now woo our sows serially for ten minutes. Electrical stimulation allows us to impregnate thirty-four percent more efficiently—any questions?"

T.K. might have asked how much the wretched painting in the next room cost in dollars, but Cass raised her hand first.

"Where are the pigs?" she said.

The farm manager and the statistician looked at each other.

"I thought the point of visiting your piggery was to see some pigs," Cass said.

"The swine are resting," said the manager. "To disturb them would interrupt production."

The Ministry minder jumped to his feet. "We must board our bus before tonight's curfew keeps us in the countryside," he said, "or you'll miss the chance to inform the world of this scoop."

"There's nothing to file until we see some pigs," persisted Cass. "Where are they?"

"Our host agreed to take your question, Miss Benoit," the minder said, "he didn't agree to answer it."

The manager pushed a small buzzer. Several farm workers appeared in rubber boots smeared with manure. They held metal batons.

"Focking cattle prods," announced Rolf, and swung his zoom lens at a pursuer. The others raced him through the door.

"Yes, onto the bus, good," the minder said. "I have conveyed your gratitude, foreign friends, for the excellent luncheon."

Once aboard, Cass rubbed her jeans. "Do they really use those things on dumb creatures?"

"They just did," T.K. said, "and I've solved their secret of rising swine production."

"Uh-huh?" Cass unbuttoned her jeans a notch and peeked down at the bruise.

"They stand over the boar with an electric prod and stopwatch. When his ten minutes are up—"

Cass cut him off. "That's so revolting," she said. "Plausible enough, but revolting."

And T.K. couldn't file it for a family newspaper. He had nothing to show but a dateline for an article that had yet to coalesce, unless the pig sheds concealed surface-to-air missiles. He had propped the computer on his lap to punch in his thoughts, when the bus hit a pothole.

"Damn," he said, "my S just broke."

"You may use my typewriter," Cass said.

He'd never be that hard up. T.K. composed a new message to his foreign desk:

"Pl*a!* no?* ?ha? ?h* l*??*r af?*r R ju!? brok* on my lap?op, !o I'm forc*d ?o u!* an *xclama?ion poin?. Any !igh?ing of ?h* n*w lap?op you mi!rou?*d? Ch**r!."

With a squeal of brakes, the bus skidded into the drainage ditch. The headlights transfixed a motley knot of refugees huddled together on the road.

"Visuals," exulted Schuyler. Kobus and Sipho were already heading down the aisle, beaten to the door by the photographers who emptied the bus as though it were burning.

"Not on our itinerary," the minder protested.

By the time T.K. disembarked with Cass, camera crews and photographers had cordoned off the refugees, bathing them in a halogen glare.

"Speak English?" Reporters jockeyed photographers for a view. *"Parlez-vous français?"* asked Didier. *"Italien?"* A Japanese reporter took up the cry: *"Dareka, nihon-go ga dekimasu ka?"*

"No photographs, closed military area," the minder howled in vain. The statistician had wandered off to help the driver pack rocks under a wheel protruding into the ditch.

The photographers closed on the refugees like jackals. Rolf found an old man wearing a piece of carpet stitched crudely into a vest. Dried blood matted his white hair. His callused hands stretched forward in supplication.

"Focking great photo!" Rolf said.

"Where's Cass?" T.K. said. "She'll understand."

The others parted to admit her to the scrum. Cass clapped her palms softly for the old man. Flattered by the gesture, he chattered back. Tape recorders swung at arm's length between the old man and Cass.

"Government trucks removed them from their village," she said, "after guerrillas stole their harvest." She turned back to listen, oblivious to the questions from the others.

"Who's the refugees?"

"When'd they come here?"

"What're they doing on the road?"

"Where's the guerrillas?"

"How'sitfeel?"

"Hush," said Cass, "or I quit."

A silence fell over the pack. In the background, the minder whined, "Back to the bus."

Cass listened. "The trucks left them at a camp, he says, and drove off with their beds and cooking pots," she reported. "No, I got it wrong— there's no camp. They were promised one, but they were dumped in an open field instead. They were walking to town, he says, when they were attacked."

"Who attacked them?" asked Schuyler.

The old man spoke, more slowly now. "Bandits," Cass said. T.K.'s stomach went hollow.

For a long time Cass listened. "I can't translate this," she said.

T.K. felt her spine quiver under the vest. "We need to know," he told her.

"The bandits took everything they had." She hesitated. "That's not all."

"Focking beautiful," cried Rolf. "This wanker's focking beautiful." Rolf reclined on his side under the old man's face. His motorized Nikon whirred.

"They took turns raping his daughter, he says, and made her husband watch." Cass blurted out the rest. "Then they killed her husband in front of her."

"Get focking out of my frame," Rolf yelled at Kobus, who was zooming in from the rear.

Cass shook uncontrollably. The old man took her hands. She looked around, her face streaked with the tears. "He says war makes these things happen."

"Which one's his daughter?" Rolf rushed a fresh roll of film into his camera.

"Vultures, all of you," Cass said.

"Human interest, okay?" pleaded Rolf. "The world needs to know."

"Not this it doesn't," Cass said. She moved from one refugee to the next, gently inviting their stories into her tape recorder. In her wake, the other reporters strained to catch the words. The photographers kept shooting and reloading like combat riflemen.

Choking for breath, T.K. walked away on a story for the first time he could remember. He didn't know why, but he had no right to stand and watch this.

A shot froze them all. The minder had pulled a Makarov pistol from inside his shirt. "Back on your bus." His voice was hoarse. "I must have your film. Foreign friends may not stray from the itinerary."

The minder had a mutiny about to happen and he looked dumb enough to trigger it, until Cass marched over, fists clenched.

"Put away that ridiculous gun before somebody gets hurt," she said. "I never saw anything so unproletarian."

"Spit him out, Cass." Kobus, filming it, called encouragement. The other hacks cheered.

"My government will feed them," the minder said.

Cass was implacable. "If they waited for your rotten feeding program, they'd starve," she said. "It's in Swiss banks by now."

The minder retreated to the bus. Cass turned on her colleagues.

"We're taking these people with us," she said, "so double up, we won't turn away this time."

Cass could be pigheaded, but this time a righteous anger consumed her.

"Now that we've leeched off them," she said, "we'll start paying them back."

"Unprofessional," Rolf protested, "okay?"

"I want more than excuses," Cass said, "I want the candy bars in your pocket, Rolf. Who else? I see bananas. And some clothes." She swiveled on T.K.

"Ante up, Thomas," she said. "That shirt clashes with your eyes. Take your shoe off and shake it. No, the other one."

"We get paid to report on their problems," T.K. said, "not solve them." He sounded like Rolf.

"Read what Saint Paul wrote to the Corinthians," she said. "If you speak, or write, with the tongues of men and of angels—which I'm not saying you do—and have not charity, your stories sound like brass or tinkling cymbals—which I'm not saying they don't."

"I feel for these refugees too," T.K. said. "But reporters can't right every wrong we find in the world."

"You're not asked to right every wrong in this world," Cass said, "just the wrong done to these poor souls. It's an excellent start."

"I'll think about it," said T.K., though he was instinctively unlacing his suede boot.

"Take all the time you need," Cass said too sweetly, "in the privacy of your own room tonight, alone."

"Alone? You wouldn't, Cass, would you?" Her jaw was set. T.K. removed his boot and obediently shook it upside down.

* * *

It was past midnight when they reached the hotel. Cass alone was content, having extorted enough to leave the refugees they had dropped off with sustenance for another day. T.K. retired to his room, exhausted.

"Sa . . . wu . . . bo . . . " he mumbled, but without conviction. *"Sa . . . wu . . . bo . . . na?"*

"I wanted the singular," said Cass by candlelight, "not the plural."

"Sani . . . bo . . . na?" He stretched under the soothing caress of her fingers. King-sized beds couldn't compare with his single bed in these small nocturnal hours.

"Count to ten for me now." Cass massaged each muscle on his bare back. "Don't you want to understand the people you're covering?"

"Um, twea, tresa, quadra, cinca, please can I turn over now?"

"You pulled that one last night," Cass said, "and we never got past six. Go on."

"Sessa, setta, ocha, nova, dicha."

"B minus." Cass kissed him on the neck. "You may roll over now, very slowly, and improve your grade."

The telephone jangled. Calls after midnight invariably portended nightmares in daylight.

"About the buyout thing," the foreign editor said. "Publisher reserves the right to reject it."

His foreign desk had impeccably poor timing. "What buyout?" T.K. asked.

"This isn't our Moscow bureau?"

"What buyout?"

"Everybody got the letter—don't you read your mail?"

"Mail takes six, seven weeks. What buyout?" T.K.'s heart thumped, almost loud enough for Cass to hear.

"Rationalization, belt tightening, downsizing—in a word, layoffs. Publisher ordered a fifteen percent staff cut so they're starting with buyouts. Three weeks' pay for every year you worked here."

T.K. did a fast calculation—barely three months' wages. So a hack no longer worried just about land mines, malaria, and the testosterone levels of overarmed teenagers. Now he had to fend off attempts to bench him.

"I'm not old enough to retire." T.K. had visions of shuffleboard played against blue-haired ladies with wattles on afternoons when he belonged on deadline.

"Say so on the form and return it by the due date," the foreign editor said. "Now refresh me why you called?"

"You called me." T.K. looked at Cass, she was about to lose interest.

"T.K. is it?" the foreign editor said. "Yes, we're sending in our distinguished columnist Freddy Fern."

T.K. groaned. Calling a columnist distinguished certified that he was over the hill.

Cass whispered into T.K.'s free ear. "Tell him you're busy with your language lesson?"

Not at two a.m. T.K. lay on his back cradling the telephone. They were dropping a Bigfoot on him. What T.K. needed was a new laptop, not one of the self-appointed vestal virgins from the Washington press corps.

"Freddy Fern?" he said. "I thought he died."

"Not quite," the foreign editor said.

The malachite bangles clattered as Cass fished in the bedside drawer. He could make out the printing on the plastic packet she withdrew: *Safe Sex from the People of the United States of America.*

Cass slid down between the sheets until her bare back was invisible. T.K. struggled to make conversation. Was Freddy still writing those turgid thumbsuckers for the op-ed page?

"Freddy's traveling around the world to complete his book on the collapse of communism," the foreign editor said. "You're in one of the last countries where it's still breathing. Let Freddy sort it out for you, a great foreign correspondent in his day."

"Not now," T.K. said to Cass, who was licking a trail of wet kisses across his belly. She was still in motion.

"Your assistance isn't optional," the foreign editor snapped. "He flies down tomorrow from Frankfurt."

"Timing's terrible," T.K. called down to Cass rippling under the sheet. She had arrived.

"We can salvage this," she said, and set to work stroking him.

"Don't act such a smart-ass," the foreign editor was saying. "Freddy's a confidant of six Presidents, original Beltway insider, our syndicated mega-pundit, sources all over Capitol Hill."

"Frederick F. Fern." An alarm sounded inside T.K.'s head even as Cass concentrated his interests much lower. "Is he still drinking?"

"Only socially, no more blackouts."

"Just what I need, a fall-down drunk."

"Sit-down's more like it. He'll slide gracefully under your dinner table with an amusing anecdote. He dressed up as a lobster for the Gridiron dinner in Washington last year, a real pro. You just show him around, keep him out of trouble."

"Off the sauce, you mean."

"That too."

T.K. felt the condom pulled down snugly. He tried to stop her but Cass shoved him onto his back. She inserted herself firmly on top.

"Can he bring in my new laptop?" he asked.

"Freddy's old school," the foreign editor said. "Won't touch a computer, says they crimp his insights."

Holding the telephone was harder now that Cass had pinned his shoulders to the mattress. *"Una,"* she counted softly, *"twea, tresa, quadra."*

"We told him you'd file for him," said the foreign editor. "Freddy'll dictate his column, you dispatch it."

"Cinca, sessa." Her malachite bangles chimed as she rode him. *"Setta."*

"He's coming here," T.K. whispered to Cass.

"You first, precious." She laughed. *"Ocha, nova, dicha."* Her honey-brown hair tickled his nose.

"I can't wait," he gasped.

"That's the team spirit, T.K., you hang in there." And the foreign editor hung up.

T.K. dropped the receiver and hauled her down against him just in time.

* * *

Frederick Fern was the first to disembark from the Boeing 747, a perquisite that derived from his insistence on flying first class when hard times had banished ordinary reporters back toward the rear lavatories.

"Mr. Fern?" T.K. had waited two hours for the jumbo jetliner to land behind schedule and disgorge his Bigfoot.

"Place looks a lot dirtier since I last came through here with Maggie Thatcher," said Freddy. He removed a floppy golf hat and mopped his brow. "Or was it Kurt Waldheim?"

Dandruff clung to the collar of his sturdy Irish tweeds. Freddy wore trifocal sunglasses and carried a typewriter boxier than Cass's.

He sniffed the air with a veined nose. "What's that stink?" he said.

"Tear gas," explained T.K., who had run into another student protest, this time over UNEQUALFOR's tardiness in arriving.

"Can't represent our newspaper like that," Freddy said. "Personal hygiene's important in cultivating reliable sources. Get rid of those dungarees and have your tailor run off something smart. I have mine done in Hong Kong." A bouquet of vintage whiskey clung to him like a cloak.

Usually when a Bigfoot landed, you pointed him toward the good wines and the red light district and got on with your own story, but Freddy expected T.K. to dance more personal attendance. He lit the stub of a cigar and wheezed through a few puffs.

"When do I interview my old pal the President?" Freddy demanded. "First met him at that nonaligned conference in Colombo. He grew the beard later, you know, to cover up a weak chin. A rooster with the ladies, though not enough fire in his belly for a head of state. We got time for a beer? Throat's drier than a camel bitch in heat—aren't you dry?"

T.K. was pondering how to explain that no interview was scheduled and the bars hadn't opened yet, when Freddy saw Cass. She had been pouching her tapes off to Bush House in London, where the BBC would relay them by satellite.

Her fingers sought out T.K.'s hand. When he was alone, Cass tiptoed up and thrust her hands into the rear pockets of his jeans, but never before strangers.

"Say, we didn't have girls as pretty as you when Ed Murrow and I cut our teeth as foreign correspondents." Freddy grabbed Cass's hand and tickled it with his toothbrush mustache. "Except for Maggie and Clare."

"He knows Maggie Thatcher," T.K. explained.

"Not that Maggie." Fern looked annoyed. "Marguerite Higgins and Clare Boothe Luce. Sassy enough dames—they wouldn't brew us coffee or sew on buttons. Made the chaps do it ourselves."

Cass suggested that was so sexist.

"Couldn't agree more but the girls meant well enough, though they did complain about the cigars." Freddy chuckled over the memory. "Foreign correspondence is guys' work, isn't it, my dear."

Cass's neck reddened. "I'm a correspondent too."

"Bit of a lark until you catch a husband and settle down to have lots of babies?" said Freddy. "Don't try to carry my bags, honey, they're too heavy. T.K. can do that. Now T.K., be honest with me. Don't hesitate—"

"I won't."

"—to lean on me for this story as often as you need to. I did it for years, could teach you young pups a few tricks. Jack Kennedy, you know, told me during one of our touch football games . . ."

Freddy steered Cass out of the terminal with a succession of avuncular pats, leaving T.K. to the suitcases. Would he could end up like this, a windy old name-dropper overstaying his reputation, inviting the contempt of every young hack? Or would T.K. know enough to drop out of orbit and return to base before his fuel ran out?

* * *

Against T.K.'s advice, Freddy Fern demanded a suite on the top floor of the Hotel Turissimo. T.K. avoided upper floors of countries in rebellion, because of the nuisance of incoming mortar rounds.

"How do you dial room service?" Freddy fussed with the phone next to the sagging double bed.

"It got drafted into the army."

"Scruffy place you picked. Back when I joined Henry Kissinger on his shuttle diplomacy, we stayed at quite a gem called the Ritz, barman did a decent gin sling. Or was that in Paris? But we'll move tomorrow."

T.K. nodded. He would relocate Freddy anywhere, but he had no intention of moving away from Cass himself.

"I feel the urge to file," Freddy said.

"File?" said T.K. "You just arrived."

"A good journalist sniffs out his scoop and hits the ground running. They didn't call me Fast Freddy for nothing. Who's up, who's down, that's what the reader wants to know."

"I'll have to get my laptop," T.K. said.

"While you're at it, shag us a few beers, or Scotch—sun's over the yardarm."

Freddy was pummeling his typewriter when T.K. returned. The columnist had changed into a peach jumpsuit that strained against his paunch like a girdle.

"Where's the Scotch?" Freddy asked. The suite reeked of cigars. An empty fifth of Cutty Sark protruded from the open suitcase.

"I couldn't find any." T.K. handed across several brown bottles of local People's Liberation beer. Rumor had it aged with formaldehyde, which is why he didn't drink it.

Freddy snatched a warm beer, popped off the cap with an opener from a pocket of his triple-F-monogrammed jumpsuit, and emptied the bottle in a series of swallows.

"Have to do better than this," Freddy said. "Who heard of a two-fisted reporter without his Scotch?"

"Reporters don't drink much hard liquor anymore," said T.K. "The younger ones prefer designer water—Perrier, San Pellegrino."

"Bunch of pansies—a reporter isn't worth a bucket of warm piss without fire in his belly, and that's what Scotch gives you."

"Won't the warm piss put out the fire?"

Freddy ignored this. "Any green light from the presidency?"

T.K. hesitated to explain that Equatoria's President, or his advisers, had never heard of Frederick F. Fern. "He's chronically distracted these days," T.K. said.

"What the hell's that?"

"Habitually disengaged," T.K. said. "Senile."

"Don't believe that senile crap," said Freddy, "he's no older than I am.

202 / C H R I S T O P H E R   S.   W R E N

Keep pressing." He ripped the paper from his typewriter. "Get on it, we're fighting a deadline."

T.K. flipped open the old Tandy. His watch showed seven hours before the first edition.

Freddy put on his trifocals and adjusted the paper to arm's length.

"'Equatoria: Does Its Future Lie Ahead?' That's what we'll call this grabber."

"Its future can't lie behind," T.K. said.

"You'll never make columnist if you bog down in detail. Big thoughts, that's my burden." Freddy held his paper closer.

"As I forecast on my last trip," Freddy declaimed, "Communism as a deluded hope . . . salvation, yes . . . of ex-colonial countries . . . nations sounds more important . . . was poised . . . no, slated . . . to writhe like a what? . . . poisonous snake . . . make that beheaded venomous serpent . . . in this war-damaged . . . war-torn . . . war-ravaged . . . former . . . ex-Soviet   banana satellite I now find . . . Where's your goddam beer?"

Freddy drained another bottle.

"With the historic . . . no, stunning . . . hell, I used that yesterday . . . crushing . . . better, shattering . . . defeat sending the Soviet . . . Russian masters . . . overlords . . . and their armed . . . no, armed-to-the-teeth, rifle-toting, jackbooted Cuban henchmen . . . What the fuck's wrong with these glasses?"

Freddy buffed his trifocals with a handkerchief, which he then applied to his sweating forehead.

"Which is it," asked T.K., "rifle-toting, armed-to-the-teeth, or jack-booted?"

". . . missile-toting Cuban legions I last saw armed to a fare-thee-well . . . sailing . . . scuttling home, more vivid . . . has sparked . . . spawned . . . make that fueled . . . even better, triggered . . . a situation . . . crisis today . . . in this day and age . . . that I sense can only mount . . . flare . . . go with rampage . . . in ex-Red . . . ex-Communist . . . formerly Red . . . Equatoria . . . turning . . . transforming . . . this poor . . . feisty . . . hellish . . . land . . . country . . . nation in turmoil . . . into what I fear will become a hotbed . . . raging inferno's better . . . no, firestorm . . . of a predominantly what? . . . ideological . . . hatred . . . exclamation point. Jeezus, can't you find me a real drink?"

Freddy helped himself to the last beer.

"Yet I deny . . . flatly deny . . . any need . . . crying need for the West . . . NATO . . . the United States . . . Washington . . . to put this genie . . . toothpaste . . . back in the bottle. . . . tube . . . question mark? The controversial . . . no, crucial . . . better, unique . . . option . . . challenge, good word . . . that I believe this unsuccessful . . . failed . . . busted . . . experiment . . . scenario presents . . . poses . . ."

The computer keyboard clicked like an agitated cricket as T.K. piled one cliché upon another.

"Dispatch soonest," Freddy said when he was done. "Back it up by cable. And find us a bottle of Scotch—no reporter's worth a bucket of warm piss without his Scotch."

* * *

When T.K. met Cass in the lobby the next day, she looked so fair and tender in her sleeveless white dress that he was unprepared for the disaster that unfolded.

"Join us for dinner?" T.K. said. "He's driving me nuts."

"Your columnist's smutty, sexist, and your problem," said Cass. "He'd have his hand up my skirt before I finished my soup."

"Freddy chases women out of habit, like an old dog chases cars," T.K. said. "At his age he can't even remember what for."

Cass wasn't listening. "They're flying me to New York for an interview, Thomas—they liked my audition tape." She failed to sound casual about it.

"You only just learned radio," said T.K.

"Television seems more exciting, and it pays much more." Her eyes looked uncommonly bright.

"Don't take them too seriously," he said.

"The first-class ticket they sent shows they're serious," Cass said. "I won't have to ride sixteen hours with my knees against my chin, eh?"

T.K. warned Cass that she would be starting over with some affiliate out in the boondocks.

"Actually, they proposed I stop by their London bureau on the way, to see if I'd like that," she said.

"The problem with TV," he told her, "is it turns good print reporters into lousy celebrities."

"I'm radio, not print," she said, "and television has some terrific women reporters, just not enough of them. Don't act so upset, the network might not want me."

It was not T.K.'s favorite network. When its field producer arrived, he'd leased the hotel telex for a year so no one else could use it. He stopped letting print hacks view rough cuts, or unedited videotape, as Schuyler did. And the producer hired an armored personnel carrier from the Defense Ministry to follow his crew around for stand-ups.

"There's APCs all over town," Cass said when T.K. reminded her. "What's wrong with renting one? Everybody does it."

"Schuyler and his crew don't," T.K. said. "Your new network pays for interviews too—that's what some officials said when they tried to bill Schuyler."

"Why wouldn't overworked officials prefer talking to someone who values their time?" Cass said.

"When did you last see an overworked bureaucrat? You accused me of fiddling the exchange rate, and now you defend checkbook journalism?"

He struck a nerve. "It's not that simple anymore," Cass said.

"Because it never was. And a first-class plane ticket? I didn't expect you to sell out so cheap, traipsing off to New York to cast your pearls before swine in thousand-dollar suits."

His clumsy compliment, far from placating Cass, filled her eyes with tears, whether of hurt or anger.

"You don't want to understand," she said. "I'm being interviewed for the best job I could expect, more money than I hoped for, maybe international recognition. You expect me to turn that down?"

"You could marry me instead," proposed T.K., his libido aroused by the symmetry of her bare shoulders. She wasn't impressed.

"How?" Cass said. "I'd be on one side of the world and you'd be on the other. I need to travel, to prove I can do anywhere what I've done here. We'll put what we have on hold, deal with it later."

"Quickies in airport motels?"

Cass challenged him with ferocity. "Why must you always crush my self-esteem? The Bible talks of 'a time to every purpose under heaven.' Well, it's my time to find a purpose now."

"You always get depressed when it's your time of month—" Before he finished, T.K. had self-destructed.

"Get your own life. *Now.*" Cass shouted it so loudly that the other reporters in the lobby swiveled around.

She stomped off, colliding briefly with Barry of the A.P., while T.K. contemplated his knack for saying precisely the wrong thing to Cass.

"What got into her?" Barry said. "Your Bigfoot's on the prowl, wanted me to set up some interviews. I said it wasn't part of our service to subscribers, told him you'd love to do it though."

T.K. found a working telephone to call Freddy. Cass would come traipsing back, she had before.

"Get your computer up here," said Freddy. "I've got this urge to file."

Cigar smoke clogged the air of his room. Bedsheets spilled across the floor. A Scotch bottle lay in a corner where it was flung after Freddy tasted colored water inside.

"When's my background briefing with our ambassador?" Freddy said.

"He's back in Washington for consultations," said T.K.

Freddy harrumphed his disdain. "If we can't find us a story," he said, "I'll file another column."

"No no," said T.K. "How about a parachute drop scheduled for the U.N. tomorrow?"

Freddy brightened at this. "What falls out of the sky?" he asked.

"Excuse me?" asked T.K.

"Birdshit and paratroopers." Freddy's chuckle ended in a smoker's retch. "We'll cover the big jump. Blue-Helmets-to-the-Rescue."

"No Blue Helmets yet." T.K. said. "The Security Council can't agree whether to call them peacekeepers, peacemakers, peace enforcers, or peace builders. And China vetoed the acronym as offensive to its Uighur-speaking minority."

Freddy sniffed the empty Scotch bottle and flung it aside.

"So NATO's dropping some donated stuff for when the peacekeepers, or whatever they're called, do arrive," T.K. said. "Republican Guard'll fetch it and store it."

"We'll cover the dumb-assed drop anyway," Freddy said. "These Republicans drink mineral water too?"

"A local moonshine called lombo. Not bad over ice with crushed limes, but it leaves a nasty hangover."

"Get us some," Freddy said, "and send your girl here to tidy me up."

Freddy's voice dropped to a near whisper. "George Shultz has a Princeton tiger tattooed on his ass," he said. "I saw it when we went skinny-dipping at the arms control talks."

"So?" T.K. said.

"Fancied one myself," said Freddy. "They got a decent tattoo parlor here?"

* * *

T.K. only fathomed the depth of his rift with Cass when he was drifting off to sleep and the phone rang.

"Filing on this latest demand in your peace talks?" the foreign editor asked.

"What demand?" T.K. shook himself awake. There was a news blackout on the peace talks since they had been moved to a gunboat out in the harbor.

"This Benoit reports the Patriotic Alliance wants four ministerial portfolios in a coalition government."

"Out of thirty Cabinet posts?" T.K. doubted it.

Cass was punishing him, in flagrant violation of the nonaggression pact they had forged in bed. He was eating her dust again.

"She said the rebels demand, let's see," the foreign editor said, "the Ministries of Defense, Finance, Police, and Broadcasting."

With those portfolios, the rebels could control the country, but Cass couldn't know that, unless she swam out to the gunboat disguised as an oil slick.

"You were staying ahead of her for a change, which is what we pay you for, buddy boy," the foreign editor said. "Did I tell you a delegation of clergymen came by to deplore the violence in your coverage?"

"Violence goes with war."

"Deplored your language, actually. Saying people get slaughtered with primitive weapons struck them as culturally insensitive."

"What would you call clubs and machetes?"

"They proposed 'nonindustrial weapons.' Cheers."

* * *

When T.K. collected Freddy Fern the next morning, the columnist displayed symptoms of the lombo that he had ordered. He did not speak until the taxi left them at the drop zone, a trash-littered stretch of sand outside the capital.

"Light's blinding me," Freddy said. "Where's my sunglasses?"

"We couldn't find them," T.K. reminded him. "You said you'd do without them."

"My ass hurts and I can't see a goddam thing," said Freddy. "Have your gal find us my sunglasses. And some beer. My throat's drier'n a Bedouin's crotch—aren't you dry?"

But Cass was cutthroat competition again, and bound for New York. T.K. surrendered his own sunglasses.

"Bastards in the little red berets are hiding under their buses," said Freddy. "Not worth a bucket of warm piss, won't even fetch the gear."

"Fear of falling objects," T.K. guessed. "The Republican Guard's elite, you see, just not outstanding."

But Freddy was already wandering across the sand toward a red target flag at the bull's-eye of the drop zone. "We'll take a ringside seat," he said.

"Mr. Fern." T.K. chased after the columnist.

Freddy clung to the flagpole, blinking at the parachutes blossoming from the airplanes overhead.

"Haven't heard this roar since the Gulf War," Freddy said. "Jeez, but my ass is sore."

Trousers wobbled to his knees as he scratched. Something like an elephant had been etched large across the pudding expanse of Freddy's buttocks. Did his lombo supplier also do tattoos?

"Watched the old One Eighty-seventh jump once in Korea," Freddy said. "All guts and glory, and they knew how to drink."

A truck slid out the back of one transport and accelerated its descent, undeterred by a torn streamer.

"Stand in the door, airborne all the way." Freddy kept scratching. "Sock it in—"

T.K. reversed course. He was still running when the thud sent up a blast of sand that blew him flat. T.K. waited for the dust to clear, and opened his eyes. First he lost Cass, now he lost Freddy, next he'd lose his job.

Bits of metal skyrocketed in all directions. Some guardsmen were running toward the truck, but there was no sign of the red flag or the distinguished Frederick Fern, only a bush hat and some trifocals in the crater.

* * *

T.K. called his newspaper, the bearer of tragic tidings.

"Yeah, we saw it on CNN." The foreign editor sounded neither grieved nor irate. "Collected his body?"

"Not much left to collect," T.K. said. "In fact, I could fax Freddy back to you."

"Better plant him where you are, hero's funeral—Freddy'd like that."

T.K. inquired about next of kin.

"Four ex-wives," said the foreign editor, "they all loathed him."

"The publisher must be pissed," T.K. said.

"Between us, I doubt it. The masthead was sick of Freddy and his boring yarns at page one meetings. That's why they sent him around the world. Tops in his day, though—protect the legend, bury what you can find out in the bush, somewhere scenic under a tree. You can expense the booze for his wake. We'll pull Freddy's clips for the obit here, unless you want to write it."

"I'll plant him," T.K. said, "you write him."

"We'll say Frederick Fern was killed covering a military operation. True enough, isn't it? Needn't play up the truck crashing into him."

"On top of him," said T.K.

"Whatever. Be discreet and we'll owe you one."

* * *

Freddy would have enjoyed his funeral a few days later. T.K. billed the newspaper for all the imported Scotch he could pry out of the black market. That turned out the hacks. Ginny volunteered herself as the designated driver, or Schuyler's truck might not have found the way back.

"Freddy's had his last urge to file," T.K. told Vanessa a little sadly. She lingered behind when the others dispersed unsteadily from the lobby.

"He'll make a nice item for our Passages section," Vanessa said. "One of my editors even heard of Freddy, said he was quite a journalist in his day."

"A great professional, Vanessa, a lion among professionals, which is why Freddy wanted to be buried out there in the bush."

"Overlooking a lombo distillery?" Vanessa said. "It isn't much of a view."

"Don't mention the distillery in your piece," T.K. asked. "Professional courtesy?"

Vanessa regarded her torn fingernails with some disgust. "We piled enough rocks on him. Such a pity dear Cassandra couldn't make it." She watched T.K.'s reaction.

"Cass is still in New York," T.K. said, or so he assumed. She never said goodbye, but Vanessa knew that.

"Let me whisk you away from all this sadness, T.K." said Vanessa, who might have drunk less herself. So she did have an agenda. "Come upstairs and discuss it?"

"I promised to find gas for Schuyler's truck."

"Midnight then, my room," she persisted.

T.K. looked over the gleaming teeth and copper-colored hair in the busty package that Vanessa was offering. Why not, if Cass no longer needed him?

* * *

He appeared at her room well before midnight, but Vanessa had already changed into something flimsy. It did not take her long to proposition T.K.

"I'm promised an exclusive interview with the leader of the Equatorian Patriotic Alliance," she said. "That dear flack in Washington arranged it."

It was hardly in Vanessa's nature to share. If the interview was exclusive, why tell him?

"I'd be traveling through their underground to the Doctor's hideout," she said. "There are, well, risks."

"Risks?" T.K. laughed. "The Doctor dumps his enemies in crocodile ponds, he works them like slaves to mine his diamonds and golds. No thanks, Vanessa. You'd come back sitting on my coffin, smoking a filter-tip."

"But you've lived with his guerrillas," Vanessa said. "I heard how you even saved Cassandra. Take me up there and back and I'll share."

"Your exclusive interview?"

"That too."

Vanessa must have heard how Cass dumped him. A hotel full of hacks was like a college dormitory, in which nothing stayed secret for long.

T.K. would have enough to do here if the truce collapsed, but he did not dismiss the invitation. Vanessa would scheme to file first, of course, but a body as lush as hers was quite another kettle of fish.

She caressed his cheek. "What's needed here are confidence-building measures."

Only Vanessa could make sex sound like strategic arms negotiations. "Confidence-building measures are essential to any significant intercourse," she said, and divested herself of the flimsy nightgown.

A lacy red brassiere followed, baring breasts formidable enough for a centerfold in a glossy men's magazine. Nipples plump as a baby's pacifier protruded from creamy jugs so full that Vanessa must have had them stuffed. Comparing her superstructure to what he recalled of Cass's demure bust confirmed how overrated bosoms were.

The hard breathing was coming from Vanessa, who shed the matching red thong. A tattooed butterfly rode inside her thigh.

She was down to bare essentials. A tiny gold chain hanging from her neck matched another about her waist and more around her wrists and ankles. Enough glitter festooned her body parts to make a customs officer suspect Vanessa of smuggling.

"Shall I tie you down and rub guava butter all—"

"I don't much feel like it tonight," T.K. said.

Like a trainer housebreaking a shaggy dog, Vanessa started T.K. through his paces with a deliberation that left him wistful for the spontaneity that Cass brought to their lovemaking.

"Assert yourself," panted Vanessa, and coaxed him aboard with a lullaby of sexual expletives. Cass never talked that raw, even in French, though it seemed so long ago.

"What's wrong down there?" asked Vanessa.

"Nothing," T.K. said, because there usually wasn't.

Don't think Cass. Think mechanical sex, pounding pistons lubricating anonymous human machines, not the weightless emancipation of requited love but the grunting drudgery of an X-rated video. The more he tried to think dirty, the more he wilted.

Vanessa reached down. "My men don't usually deflate," she said. "Is there something you'd like to share with me?"

T.K. sat on the bed, too dispirited for excuses.

"Unless you're gay," she said. "That must be it."

"Vanessa, knock off the psychotherapeutics."

"I should have seen through your facade of macho vulgarity. It hides the vibrant inner child, so sensitive, so creative, so uncompromising in your loneliness."

Vanessa sat up too. "Why is it," she mused, "that the most rugged, attractive men always turn out to be gay? Even my Brazilian's bi. I'm willing to share, maybe the three of us could—"

"Give my libido a rest," said T.K.

Cass had emasculated him for quickies like this, taught him to find brains more erotic than boobs.

"Then I shall keep you safe in your brave little closet," said Vanessa, "safe from all those crude hacks downstairs who could never accept you as you are. In return, you shall take me to interview the Doctor."

"I've got a choice?"

"Is Cassandra aware of your sexual preference?"

"Yes." Cass had him pegged for a heterosexual recidivist.

"If you decide to swap orientations," Vanessa said, "expanding one's horizons is terribly important."

"Hand me my trousers?" T.K. said. "I gotta go file."

9.

POR?O PARADI!O, *qua?oria—?oday ?h* gov*rnm*n? and i?!
r*b*l oppon*n?! again accu!*d *ach o?h*r of *vading an
agr**m*n? ?o d*mobiliz* ?h*ir ?roop! and hand in ?h*
w*apon! a? n*u?ral !i?*! und*r ?h* quinin* ?r**!.

   Al?hough a ?*nuou! c*a!*-fir* !up*rvi!*d by Uni?*d Na?ion!
ob!*rv*r! con?inu*d ?o hold, *ach !id* charg*d ?ha? ?h* o?h*r
wa! . . .

Cass was returning tomorrow, the field producer explained, with some
Very Expensive Talent.

"Your network's dancing bear?" T.K. asked.

"That's what we call star correspondents like Beau Bradford." The producer had purchased T.K.'s attention with the beers they were drinking.
"He'll explain this place to the viewers back home."

"Why didn't the rest of us think of it?" said T.K., but he knew the difference. Americans cared now that GIs might be sent to help the United Nations police a cease-fire. This story had legs. But what had Cass to do with
it? T.K. ordered another beer at the network's expense.

"Why Beau's trying her out as a segment producer, breaking her in." The field producer wore the kind of smirk that wanted punching.

T.K. could not envision Cass, the public radio loner, running with the herd of TV producers—field producers, program producers, associate producers, senior producers, maybe producers' producers.

"What does a segment producer do?" he asked.

"Segments," said the field producer. "The usual reporting, finding people to interview, packaging stand-ups, scouting locations, arranging actualities—"

"What's left for your Talent to bring, besides his salary?"

"Charisma. And ratings. Beau can get us prime time every night," the field producer said. "Cass must have told you, in view of your mutual past?"

She hadn't, not a word in the few weeks since she left, not a postcard. T.K. missed her, the familiarity too, going back to those nightly rockets that had brought them together. When T.K. thought back to other women who crossed his life, counting them without completing his fingers, the memories flowed in grainy black and white, like a television movie after midnight. Cass filled his consciousness in wide-screen Technicolor. He'd meet her at the airport tomorrow.

"They're flying the Concorde through Paris but the last leg's a charter," said the field producer. "Commercial flights just aren't Beau. He's got four nations this week, then back to London for drinks with the G-Seven summit, which leaves barely three days here. We're bunching his stand-ups."

Cass had moved up to a higher caste of journalists then, more famous than the countries they covered, the sort who wallowed in limelight, not in polluted drainage ditches. Still, T.K. could afford to wait three days.

"Cass must have impressed the network suits or the Talent wouldn't be trying her out," the producer said. "Beau can be a demanding little prick. A demanding professional, I mean, but a wonderful guy. Excuse me, I've got to organize his cellular phones."

* * *

The next day, T.K. waited at the airport for Cass. A Lear jet taxied to the small terminal reserved for official delegations at the far end of runway. A faded red carpet was unrolled across the tarmac. Down the executive jet's foldout stairway bounded a fluffy blond head of hair atop a safari jacket.

T.K. had been abroad too long to recognize Very Expensive Talent.

He was trailed by a high-rent blonde with great legs, the Talent's personal assistant or maybe his mistress. A laptop computer dangled from her shoulder. She looked into the crowd, shielding her eyes with her hand, and T.K. saw the malachite bangles. He had been disloyally ogling the woman he loved. He waved but the police shoved him back and Cass, busy disentangling her laptop strap, didn't see him. She followed her traveling companion into a limousine—the ambassador's, judging by its American flag—and left in a cavalcade bracketed by police motorcycles. T.K. sat stalled in the traffic, clutching his bouquet of wilting flowers.

It was not uncommon for celebrity journalists to be treated like visiting heads of state if a government was dissatisfied with local correspondents and soliciting kinder coverage. But how could Cass cross the line? More than anyone else, she should know it was wrong.

Back at the hotel, hacks were bitching about the disruption in electricity, which had been disconnected to add a power line for a large air conditioner being installed in the top-floor suite. The Talent's entourage of producers, crews, and technicians were spending so freely on the black market that the dollar, for the first time that Alistair could recall, dropped against the dinar.

"Bloody bunch of seagulls, flying in, crapping over everything," said Alistair. "They even hired the Cafe Peri-Peri for the duration."

He had just returned from London, feeling ever so much better, thanks, with these smashing new miracle drugs. T.K. took him to eat at a dingy cafe run by an expatriate Indian family down at the port. They walked because the taxis around the hotel were hired by the network or now felt free to double their prices.

The food was greasy and the curry could not conceal the rancidity of the meat. They washed it down with stale beer served by a listless child to the blare of a television set behind the plastic curtain.

After they had disputed the bill and started walking back, Alistair spoke of Gunn, for the first and only time.

"Love isn't worth the bloody clap," he said. Then he shifted into an irrelevant tale about how he saw a cat scamper out of a restaurant in Beirut and the owner crossed chicken off the menu.

By the time Alistair wound up his story, they were at the Cafe Peri-Peri. Loud strangers had preempted the patio tables.

"Sod the wankers, they're eating real shrimp," Alistair said. "I hope they ordered the house salad."

"Nice gentlemen bring shrimp by plane," said Abednego. "Salad too."

The waiter flicked his soiled towel over the dishes. His grin suggested that the visitors were tipping well.

"Miss Cass is not here," Abednego said. His English had improved, thanks to her.

T.K. called to the nearest table. "Where's Cass Benoit and your Talent?"

"Yeah, where's the Flood Stud's latest producer?" said a technician.

"Stroking the Talent," quipped another, eliciting derisive mirth around the table. T.K. didn't like where this was heading.

"Cass could have me, or even you, by snapping her fingers," Alistair said as they continued back to the hotel. "What can this news presenter—"

"Americans call him an anchorman."

"—this news presenter offer her beyond his fame, wealth, influence?"

"Besides that?" T.K. said. "Nothing, zip, nada."

Back in his stifling room, T.K. set to work on an economic thumbsucker. But Equatoria's current accounts deficit, its vanishing exports and reckless imports were nudged aside by his preoccupation with Cass.

His imagination swept T.K. into the morass of self-inflicted misery, with despicable visions of the exquisite creature he cherished lying naked on the satin sheets of a double bed in the top-floor suite. The chill blast of the air conditioner was raising goose pimples on her breasts and belly, while the Very Expensive Talent fondled her swollen nipples and vagina preparatory to ramming himself home. Or Cass was whimpering through the ecstasy of an orgasm that T.K. had deluded himself into thinking he alone induced, but digging her fingernails and teeth this time into cologne-scented prime-time flesh.

No, promiscuity was not her style. But what if she were sedated with expensive whiskey, not the imitation rotgut from the market, and were drowsily revealing the pale hollows of her thighs to the Very Expensive Talent as the course of least resistance to her career? What if she had actually fallen in love and were proving her obsessive devotion on her knees, licking glistening strands of spent semen from her voluptuous lower lip, or crouched perhaps on all fours like a bitch in heat while her new master rutted bestially between her lubricious buttocks?

Impulsively, T.K. reached for the telephone and dialed. The first two rings confirmed his fears that Cass had indeed skipped dinner at the Peri-Peri for a baser form of intercourse, and was even now stroking the Talent like some fickle whore.

At the third ring, a prim voice scuttled his masochism.

"Cassandra Benoit," she said. A noxious wave of self-loathing washed over T.K.

"Beau?" she said. "Beau? Hello? Beau?" She hung up before T.K. could assemble his thoughts.

Beau? T.K. dialed again.

"Thomas, so much to tell you," she said.

"You weren't at the Peri-Peri," T.K. said, as if to justify his undecorous thoughts.

"We dined with the Prime Minister. Beau took me along to translate. Simply delicious, Thomas—the chef was trained in France."

Her voice conveyed an affectation, a crisper way of speaking.

"Can I buy you a beer in the bar, or something—hell, anything?" Having botched his opening gambit, he awaited the turndown.

"I really can't," she said. "Beau's playing poker at the American ambas-sador's—the air-conditioning in his suite isn't working yet."

It was the first good news T.K. had heard.

"I begged off," she said, "so Beau said he'd call about tomorrow's feed. Crumbs, if he heard I went off drinking with you hacks—"

"Just me, Cass."

"Bring some beer here?" Her giggle wafted a fresh breeze into his life. "You've made me thirsty, eh?"

Cass met him holding a black cellular telephone. "This doesn't work," she complained, as if he had been summoned to fix it. She was prettier than he remembered, but no smarter. Cass had yet to grasp that she ought to be in love with him by now.

He plucked a long fair hair from the collar of her tailored shirt. "I meant you to get over your jet lag."

"Lots of room to sleep on the flight, when they weren't pouring me champagne," she said. "First class is the only way to go."

It had only been a few weeks, yet she did not look the same. Her shaggy hair had been groomed into a sleeker, blonder pageboy.

"I had it cut in New York and he frosted a few strands," said Cass, "that's all."

"And what's changed your eyes?"

They seemed blue too, not just from the unfamiliar eye shadow. "New contacts," she explained.

"Once we agreed to keep no secrets," T.K. said.

"Beau suggested I try tinted contact lenses, if you must know, for the Q-rating."

"What the hell's a Q-rating?"

Cass fidgeted with her bangles. "A likability quotient with the viewers. Blue eyes make you more camera-friendly, Beau says."

"They don't make you a better hack, Cass. You're not a game show hostess, and where'd you get that?"

A new laptop computer, its backlit screen glowing in carnival colors, had replaced the clunky typewriter on her desk.

"You disapproved of technological fashion," he reminded her.

"Only when I couldn't afford it," Cass said. "Would you believe this costs five thousand dollars? Beau thinks the network may let me keep it when I sign the contract."

So she hadn't signed yet.

"Beau wants the network to make me a correspondent later, with a minimum guarantee of on-air time," she said. "It's lots of money."

"How much is lots?" he asked.

She went up on tiptoe and, slipping one smooth arm around his neck, whispered in his ear. Did they give her the perfume in first class?

"No hack's worth more than a hundred grand," T.K. said. How could reporters get paid more than the people they covered?

Instead of taking offense, Cass laughed. "I hated giving my radio editors notice, but there's no way they could afford to keep me."

T.K. leaned across, and stopped short of kissing the graceful curve of her neck. "I don't suppose you'd let me," he whispered, "just one last time . . ."

Cass did not encourage him. He would not court humiliation. What they had shared was already more than he deserved.

"Use your laptop sometime, I meant," he said.

She wasn't fooled. Cass stared into his eyes, searching for whatever they had lost.

"When we met, we loathed each other," she said at last. "Then we loved each other. Now, we still like each other. It doesn't happen often. Friends, best friends?"

T.K. watched Cass drifting away, as naturally as a boat yielding to the tide. He was resigned to losing her, but not to television.

"Best friends isn't the same," he said. "But we could be cutthroat competition again."

"Then we'll have to keep track of each other," she said, "eh?"

"That's what cutthroat competition's about."

She rewarded T.K. with a heartbreaking smile and gently shooed him out the door still holding his beer.

* * *

T.K. put it to his editor as delicately as he knew. "It's the dumbest frigging idea I've heard," he shouted at the telephone, "and you've come up with some real turkeys lately."

"Publisher suggested it," the foreign editor said. "Beau Bradford's hot, a rising star of network news. All we're asking is you follow him around, slam-dunk in a nice profile to lead the Sunday TV section. We could use something upbeat from you for a change."

"I thought war and famine were more important."

The foreign editor chuckled. "You correspondents think every story you cover is important, when it's only important because you're covering it. Give the readers what they want for a change."

It was demeaning. The Newspaper Guild ought to negotiate a rule exempting hacks from reporting on other hacks, but then the Very Expensive Talent wasn't a hack. He wasn't even a reporter, he was a news twink, which made him as ripe a target as a politician or a movie star. T.K.'s devastating profile might wake Cass up to the truth.

"Can I write this Beau Bradford the way I see him?"

"Sure, buddy boy," said the foreign editor. "Don't be influenced that our company's TV stations carry Beau Bradford's news magazine, or that he played golf in Bermuda last winter with our publisher. Hey, we all loved those inflation statistics in your request for a raise. Make your stories that well sourced. Cheers."

A note had been slipped under T.K.'s door reminding him that his telephone was engaged. The handwriting slanted like a Canadian wheat field in a windstorm. "Beau invites you for coffee up in his suite at seven A.M., please, for me?" She signed it, "Your faithful cutthroat competition."

* * *

T.K. woke early, his mind polluted with unworthy thoughts about where Cass spent the night. When he shaved, the mirror mocked him. His haircut was overdue; the gash that Cass had stitched up was lost in a road map of older scars and newer wrinkles. He confronted that age when the women he once lusted after were starting to look better with their clothes on, which was to say he wasn't getting younger himself, and Cass's Very Expensive Talent probably was.

He found Cass in the protective custody of the Talent and his claque, drinking coffee around a large table in the upstairs suite. She was wearing bluish eye shadow to breakfast.

"What's the visuals?" The Talent drummed fingers on the table.

"But the loss of authority among clan elders shows how war tore this society apart?" Her explanation concluded in a question, as if Cass sought permission now for her opinions.

T.K. spoke up. "Public radio gave your clan elders quite a run, didn't it," he said.

The Talent smiled at T.K. as though he had come begging an autograph.

"Twelve minutes forty seconds, actually," Cass said.

"Thirteen minutes on some old farts sitting around a campfire?" the Talent said. "Weird."

"Not for public radio," T.K. said.

"Beau, this is Thomas. You're my friends, so I know you'll hit it off," said Cass, wanting to believe it.

"Awesome. Love your stuff. Hey, I'm your greatest fan," said the Very Expensive Talent, and stretched out a manicured hand. The torso sculpted under his Brooks Brothers polo shirt rippled in synergistic harmony. Boutique muscles like those came from pumping Nautilus machines for lunch, not chopping firewood for supper. Whatever illusions T.K. had about wooing Cass back receded.

"Awesome," repeated the Talent. "Didn't you break that big scoop about—"

"No," said T.K., and made clear that what followed wasn't his idea. "My editors want me to follow you around."

"Awesome," the Talent said. "We professional journalists having our jobs to do. Tim is it?"

"T.K.," he said.

"Thomas," corrected Cass.

An old city editor taught T.K. to distrust anyone in designer jeans calling himself a journalist. T.K. accepted a steaming coffee mug emblazoned with black letters: *W.O.W.*

He shook out his notebook. "Now about your visit—"

"Jackson." The Talent snapped his fingers. "Can't you find me and Tom some quality time?"

His executive producer studied a clipboard loaded with yellow legal pads.

"Now's a no go. You're taking an audience with the President, Beau, then you're doing lunch for the diplomatic corps." T.K. envisioned the Talent in a chef's toque and apron, flipping omelets for ambassadors lined up in morning coats and striped trousers.

"Tonight, Beau, you've booked the bird," said the producer. "I could calendar him tomorrow between stand-ups. You've wheels-up the next morning."

That left T.K. barely a day to file for the Sunday edition, hardly enough time to skewer the Talent with enough wit or subtlety to get acquitted of verbal assassination. He might have to write this profile straight.

Then the Talent bestowed on T.K. a megawatt smile, the kind for which the network paid more than one million dollars a year. Briefly, T.K. basked in its radiance; maybe Beau Bradford wasn't so bad after all.

"Know why I respect you, Tom?" said the Talent. "Because you gave Cass that break she needed. Stringing for your paper. Takes an awesome guy to do that."

Cass blushed and looked down. True, T.K. offered her a chance but she had rejected it. What other corners was she cutting in her new career?

T.K. fumbled for a response. "We're sorry to lose her," he said. That, at least, was no lie.

Like a wolf urinating to define his territory, the Talent slipped an arm over Cass's shoulders. "I respect you, Tom," he said. "But I don't envy you."

T.K. sized up the blow-dried hair, the cobalt eyes, the dimpled jaw, the seamless skin toasted by a tanning parlor, not the blast furnace climate of the Third World. A thousand focus groups launched this face. The Very Expensive Talent looked as cute as Cass sitting beside him.

"Because you belong in ENG, Tom," the Talent said. "Electronic news gathering's sexier."

"Newspapering's where the big bucks are, Beau," T.K. said.

"Well, you deserve every penny, Tom. We're talking six, seven figures?" said the Talent.

"When we include our decimal points, Beau."

Cass moved to stifle T.K.'s sarcasm. "Beau and I were discussing ideas for my segment," she reminded him, and turned back to the Talent.

"The leader of the Equatorian Patriotic Alliance?" she continued. "They call him the Doctor but he isn't one? Hardly anyone's interviewed him, so I don't know about visuals?"

The Talent smiled on her, and Cass went small and appreciative.

"I want your segment character-driven," the Talent told Cass. "Research in New York checks him out. We ambush your Doctor for fresh visuals. Maybe he hangs around the U.N."

"Where your camera crew mugs him?" asked T.K.

"Hush," said Cass. "Just hush, Thomas."

"A little help, Tom," the Talent said. "What's the three most important things in ENG?"

"Accuracy?" T.K. said. "Speed, insight?"

"I'm talking ratings, ratings, ratings," the Talent said. "That's where visuals come in. Like, if the viewers can't see it, they won't watch it. So you've got to impact them. Something to knock their socks off."

"Even for what's really important?" asked Cass.

"Like what if Jesus had done the Sermon on the Mount as a stand-up," the Talent said. "Second camera zooming in for cutaway reactions. From hundreds of people fighting over that bread."

"Saint Mark's crowd count was five thousand," said T.K., "plus five loaves and two fishes. Have research in New York check it out."

Cass tried to look unimpressed.

"All I'm saying, Tom, is if Jesus did it on camera," the Talent said. "And an 800 number for call-in conversions. He'd change the course of history."

"Some people think He did," Cass coaxed, "with the Resurrection and all?"

"And that's awesome, truly awesome. But not quite for us," the Talent said. "Death grabs the ratings, God no."

The Talent consulted his gold Rolex. "Jackson, I'm talking to you. Calendar me."

"Running late again, Beau," his executive producer said. "You're too generous with your time. The President's limo's downstairs and you've got to dress."

"Tom, you stay, drink up my coffee. Keep the mug. What's with our cell phones, Jackson? Mine's accessing flyshit."

"Seems the guerrillas use our frequency too, Beau," his producer said. "We're negotiating with their liaison office in Washington."

"Why can't you just rent their dickhead frequency?" The Talent aimed his finger at Cass like a gun. "Power lunch at noon?" Bang. "Little black dress?" Bang. "And dump the tacky plastic bracelets."

"Malachite, actually," Cass said.

"They still look cheap. Gold's the power statement. Tom, let's treat her to Tiffany's."

Brandishing the gold rope on his wrist, the Very Expensive Talent swept out the door with his entourage.

"I won't wear them on camera," Cass said.

Very slowly, T.K. sipped the bitter dregs from the coffee mug, leaving her to fidget while he held his silence.

"In New York, they asked about newspaper experience, so I had to say something," Cass said. "You did ask me to string, remember? I need this job, Thomas, you were sweet not to contradict me."

He would have reminded her that fiddling résumés was no better than fiddling expenses, but embarrassing Cass would hardly win her back. T.K. changed the subject.

"Crumbs, your Talent is cuddly," he said.

"You're cuddly," she said. "Beau's gorgeous."

"Any hard news background?"

"Beau started out on weather in California, but he was so amusing that they made him local news anchorman," Cass said. "He won an Emmy, or is it a Grammy, for going up in a helicopter and reporting live on the flood devastation. It isn't so easy, Thomas, ad-libbing for an hour."

"That's why his crew calls Beauregard the Flood Stud?"

"Actually," said Cass, "his first name's Chester, but the Q-rating's low, so he uses Beau."

So Beau was a nom de tube. T.K. snickered.

"He didn't make it up, he was called Beau as a kid," Cass said, "and the focus groups struggle with a Chester. Come on, everyone had a childhood nickname."

"Including you?" he asked.

"Excepting me," said Cass, "which proves the rule."

"Beau's okay for someone paid to back-comb your hair, but a Beau telling you about the world's misery?"

"You're jealous," said Cass, "because you're afraid I want to sleep with him."

T.K. had to know. "Hasn't your Talent tried to bed you by now?"

Instead of denying it, Cass laughed. "For someone that famous, it's not about love or sex, it's trophies, acquisitions. Beau can have almost any woman he wants—why move on me?"

It was not what T.K. hoped to hear.

* * *

The next morning, T.K. found the Very Expensive Talent confronting a heavy schedule of stand-ups.

"Beau's doing it all over," his executive producer said. "He does it in front of Presidential Palace, then he does it on some monument to socialist martyrs, then down to the river to do it on some old ferry."

"You mean the new ferry," said T.K. "The old one was scrapped months ago."

"Scrapped old ferry, visual backdrop as metaphor." The producer consulted his clipboard. "Then some orphans' home, and Cass found us a squatter camp with disgusting squalor. And last, Beau does it in the army trenches."

The army didn't let anyone into its forward positions. The last television crew that tried was detained and forfeited a videocamera.

"We bought exclusive rights to the trenches," the producer said. "Hired the army's general staff as program consultants, easier than bribes—now don't print that."

Beau Bradford nodded at T.K. from a folding chair under a banyan tree, while an emaciated woman with vampire-blue lipstick and matching fingernails sculpted his makeup. Another woman dressed in the black of a cat burglar waited to tease his hair with a comb and hair dryer.

"We rented Beau a helicopter," the producer said, "until some dumbassed guerrilla shot it down last night. Beau won't wait for another—what a professional."

"Even if your Talent's Very Expensive," T.K. said, "how can he do a bunch of stand-ups before he knows what his documentary's about?"

"Plan ahead," the producer said. "We'll shoot more footage after Beau leaves, script some voiceovers and wraps for him to lay down when tape's edited in in New York—this is all off the record, right?"

T.K., who hadn't promised any such thing, scribbled more notes.

"Our viewers don't trust foreigners," said the executive producer, "so Beau's got a rule that anyone saying 'foreign' on camera gets fined a hundred dollars."

"Who gets the hundred dollars?"

"It goes into a pool to buy Cuban cigars. Beau's very influenced by Marshall McLuhan's global village."

"Your Talent reads books?"

"Research in New York did him an executive summary. Beau's schedule's tight."

The Talent summoned them over and threw down the cellular phone. "Why can't my people do anything right, Tom?" he said. "Piece of shit still won't access."

"Someone stole our base station last night," his producer explained. "We got the police tracking it."

"I think I saw it down at the market," T.K. said, "parts anyway."

"Buy it back," the Talent told his producer. "I can't dialogue without the cellular."

"Try the goat pen," T.K. said. "They were weaving baskets from electrical wire. And using something like a satellite dish to sort peanuts. They could teach us something about recycling."

The producer trotted off to deputize a posse of technicians.

"Like *W.O.W.*?" the Talent asked T.K. over the howl of the hair dryer, which ran from an umbilical cord clipped into a row of truck batteries.

T.K. pulled out his notebook. "Like what?"

"What my news magazine's entitled. *World of the Week. W.O.W.* Awesome, huh, Tom?"

The Talent turned one cheek, then the other to the makeup powder puff. "Reality-based news mags are hot," he said. "Because who's got time for long documentaries except some public TV dickheads. We got top-rated in our time slot. After my special report on how the I.R.S. victimizes white males. Did Cass tell you?"

"She forgot, Beau."

"Our debutante-sex-slave murder grew the show three points to a twenty-eight share. Want to know how we did it?"

"Not really."

"We dipped a leg of lamb in acid to show how she disposed of her lover."

T.K. hadn't a notion where this was leading. "So what's the point?" he asked.

"Nine hundred and fifty-nine thousand households," the Talent said. "Like, most news mags use only two, three segments an hour. We give five, six segments. Couch potatoes don't have time to channel-surf. No talking heads from Washington. Nothing in-studio. Just hidden-camera. Sound bites wrapped inside awesome computer graphics. We storyboard every reenactment so our viewers can't get bored. During the commercials, all they can do is sit there zonked. Like, '*W.O.W.*'"

T.K. scribbled more notes, state-of-the-tube stuff.

"Got to give the viewers what they want," the Talent said. "If we don't hold them, they'll roll right through us. There'll be five hundred channels out there. Interactivity. That's the buzz."

The Talent waved off the fussing of the hairdresser.

"Bottom line, Tom. Say production costs run four, five hundred thousand bucks per episode. My news magazine still costs less than a sitcom. Because there's no licensing fees. No royalties to pay those dickheads in Hollywood. We own the product. Recycle it. Reformat for video. Maybe repackage for distribution overseas."

The Talent pulled out a pocket calculator. "Now we bill our advertisers, like, fifty thousand for a thirty-second spot?"

T.K. forgot about his notebook. Who would pay fifty thousand dollars for thirty seconds?

"CBS gets three hundred thousand bucks for a thirty-second spot on its *60 Minutes*."

Ten thousand a second. T.K. calculated whether a hard sneeze on the air could consume his annual wages.

"We're talking audience maximization," the Talent said. "Expanding market share will drive our ratings. Because we know what viewers want. They're dumber than dirt, so it's not rocket science. What's your revenue stream?"

T.K. had never thought of his newspaper as a spreadsheet. "Quality comes first," he said.

"Hey, quality's our bottom line too," the Talent said. "If my news magazine got canceled, you can imagine the crap that'd replace us on the air."

"No, Beau," T.K. said, "I really can't."

The Talent bounded out of the chair, shaking his mane like a golden retriever in from the rain. A snap of his manicured fingers sent crews sprinting for the trucks.

"Action, Jackson," cried the Talent. He turned to T.K. "Interview me while we ride, Tom, to save time."

T.K. looked for Cass before he joined the Talent in the rear seat of a camouflaged four-wheel-drive Nissan hired from the Defense Minister.

"She's not here." The Talent fluffed a little more chest hair into the cleavage of his safari shirt. Why, when television correspondents removed their neckties, did they feel obliged to unbutton their shirts too?

"I sent Cass to advance the refugee camp. Do me some vox pops," the Talent explained.

"Vox what?"

"Street interviews," said the Talent. "I want to get Cass into stand-ups. The kid gives great camera."

"Helluva reporter," T.K. agreed.

"Like, foxy. Not just those cat eyes and cheekbones. Tight little package of boobs and buns. Cass could become heavy on-air talent. After she loses a few pounds."

It was then that T.K.'s grudging tendency toward feminism manifested itself.

"That's a sexist double standard," he said. "Women look better with some padding around their hips. Does your network weigh the beer bellies on you men?"

"Not the network, Tom. The camera. Makes her little buns plump. Camera never lies. I'll put my personal trainer on her."

The Talent mimicked a golf swing across the back seat. "Cass could end up coanchoring my magazine if she gets those bottom teeth fixed," he said. "She'd grow our ratings. Like, leave the other networks jacking off."

The Talent slapped T.K.'s thigh. "When do I okay your little feature?"

"My newspaper doesn't let us show stories before publication." T.K. didn't know if such a rule existed, but people demanding to see what was written about them usually tried to censor anything short of obsequious flattery.

"I played golf with your publisher. He won't mind." The Talent's smile thinned. "It's only to catch errors in quotes, like."

"Do people you interview get to choose their sound bites?" T.K. asked, but the Talent was no longer listening.

"Mimimimimi," he intoned, "momomomomo, moomoomoomoo, *Beau* Bradford here Beau *Bradford* here Beau Bradford *here,* mimimimimi . . ."

The Talent was warmed up for his stand-up by the time the convoy stopped. A detachment of field police jumped from the last truck to cordon off the road.

"We wanted the guerrillas in this too," the producer said, "but they didn't fax back in time."

A wardrobe assistant slipped an olive-drab Kevlar flak vest on the Talent. "The focus group liked the powder blue," he said.

"Too U.N.-ish, Beau," said his executive producer.

T.K. watched from behind the camera, impressed in spite of himself. Unlike Schuyler, who clutched a microphone like an ice cream cone, Cass's Very Expensive Talent gyrated with the restlessness of a rock music star, chopping at the air, flirting with the camera. His shirt had opened another button to accommodate a lavalier microphone.

"If your sons and daughters are sent to keep the peace in Equatoria. What'll they say when they phone home?" he intoned. "They'll tell you Equatoria is not the first right-wing dictatorship to be threatened by Marxist rebels. Communism is dead. But who can kill the dream? Back with an answer. After these messages. Until then, Beau Bradford here. Reporting to you live from the jungle."

Better than dead, like poor Freddy. But the Talent wasn't reporting, he was standing on a box with a hairstylist, a makeup artist, two television crews, and hired gunsels in attendance. And this is savanna, not jungle. Beau Bradford got it wrong and please, nobody tell him.

"Perfect, Beau," his producer said. "Just a small suggestion? It's the other way around—the guerrillas are conservative, the regime's Marxist. I know it's confusing."

"So who's these Shining Path dickheads?"

"Peru was month before last, Beau," the producer said, "but you're right, guerrillas running around the zoo and all."

"Can't research in New York check it out?" The Talent looked around at T.K. "My viewers don't care a rat's patootie. So long as we give awesome visuals."

* * *

T.K. followed from one stand-up to the next, filling his notebook.

"It looks like this war's turned the corner," the Talent was concluding. "But ordinary people like these are still waiting for it to go around the block. And what's this doing to the stalled peace talks? My highly placed sources tell me this much. Only time will tell. Whether it's the impossible dream. Or just another nightmare. Indeed"—a portentous pause here—"to everything there's a season. But whether the dawn arrives with a brass band. Or on little cat feet. Or fails to show up at all remains to be seen. A price must be paid. But must it take your tax dollars to pay that price? Back to you after some news about a breakthrough in another problem. Personal irregularity. Bran can't do it all, as any Equatorian will tell you. Until then, Beau Bradford here. On the scene for you."

"That's a tease," the producer explained. "Hooks the viewer so he'll be hanging in after the—"

"Commercial?" T.K. finished the sentence.

"Infomercial." The producer glared at him. "This is journalism."

* * *

"Can this country say yes to peace tomorrow after so many yester-days of war?" the Very Expensive Talent inquired of the camera. "No easy answers here. Because there are no easy questions. The fire may be out. But the embers of pain still burn. A sign of the times. And only time will tell. We live in a global village. But a global village is only as good as its global villagers. So there it is and here we are. Beau Bradford here in, Equatoria?"

"That's a wrap," said the executive producer.

"Jackson," asked T.K., "does any consenting adult in ENG use complete sentences?"

The producer distanced himself, as though T.K. were bringing cholera to the occasion.

"Busy schedules these days," the producer said. "And my name's Stanley."

* * *

The Talent juggled a hollow-eyed child on his knee. "Suffer the little ones to come unto me," he concluded. "Someone said that two, three thousand years ago. But in today's wars, it's little ones like this crippled lad who must suffer. For their fathers' refusal to beat machine guns into plowshares. And bury the hatchet. While innocent children fight for life, observers can only ask. Is their life worth fighting for? Back to answer that after these messages, Beau Bradford here. Sharing your pain at the Felix Dzerzhinsky Orphans' Home."

No sooner was the camera's baleful red eye extinguished than the Very Expensive Talent dropped the small boy, who ran off bawling.

"Pissed all over me!" The Talent shook out the puddle expanding across the soggy trousers of his poplin suit. "Can't you find a kid who's bled his lizard before you dump him on me? Now I've got to shower and change. We'll lose thirty, maybe forty minutes. Because you screwed up. Jackson. Any reason I shouldn't send you home to Bronxville?"

* * *

The government had cleaned the dirt streets at the squatter camp, where the Talent linked up with Cass. The potholes were filled, whitewash was slapped on the nearest shanties. A police truck blocked the path down to the sewage canal. The squatters had turned out for a holiday.

"I've spent two hours preparing Beau's two-minute stand-up," Cass told T.K., "done at least a dozen cutaway interviews. Beau calls them 'vox populi'—voice of the people. You didn't expect he knew Latin." She looked around. "Where's Beau?"

"Change of wardrobe due to precipitation."

Cass scanned the sky, but there wasn't a cloud.

"Beau's researchers found some footage of the Doctor shot by a Japanese crew," she said. "It's being pouched in so I can add the voiceover and my own stand-up."

"How can you let him take the credit when you're doing the work?" T.K. said.

"That's what a producer does," she said. "There's so much Beau can teach me—he knows how to woo a viewer. If I could learn that, what a difference I'd make."

She had, on public radio. Gratitude ill became Cass. It turned her soft and muzzled her sassiness.

"You aspire to the kind of inanities I've been hearing?" T.K. flipped open his notebook to prove his point.

"Television makes people, well, pay attention," Cass said. "Did you know Beau's name recognition earns him five thousand dollars a speech?"

"Journalists don't pontificate for hire," T.K. said.

"Everyone's doing it, Beau says. Crumbs, if someone paid me five thousand, I'd donate it to the dolphins."

"Why not hire yourself out for commercials?" Or were journalists stooping to that back home too?

A few freckles peeked through her makeup while Cass accused T.K. of not wanting to understand.

"Television lets you make eye contact, tell millions how you feel," she said. "You can't report that way for your paper."

T.K. told Cass it wasn't a reporter's job to tell people how you felt. You had to go out and quote someone who'd say it for you.

"Get real," said Cass. "Every time you choose what to cover, you massage the news. Whenever you decide whom to interview or what statistic to cite, you massage the news. Why not do it to make the world a better place? Who was it said the only thing necessary for evil to triumph was that good men and women do nothing? Why should journalists be excused from behaving admirably?"

So the network had discovered how to corrupt Cass after all. Had she been offered a less Faustian bribe, she would have bristled and walked away. Instead, they dangled before her the opportunity to do good for fame

and profit. Now he understood: Cass was indenturing her formidable talent
for a chance to save humanity on expense account.

* * *

The camera had been bolted onto the back of a truck. As it pulled away
slowly, the Very Expensive Talent kept pace, hands casually thrust into his
pockets, which some boys had been trying to pick without success. Behind
him more refugees gaped, clowned, and gave hi-Mom waves at the camera.
Those in back jumped up and down for a better view.

"This squatter camp is home to its inhabitants. So you can see the rage
seething around me. Your reporter tapping into their hope, their horror,
their heroism. . . . Yes, with the havoc and hangover of . . . Hypocrisy, hate,
hysteria, and now the . . . Humility and happiness. The hunger for . . . We'll
be right back after these messages."

The Talent looked for the producer. "Jackson, find us a sound bite there.
We'll do it voiceover later. With a soft-edge wipe or something visual-wise.
Running too late to reshoot."

They mounted again and headed for the army trenches along the National
Highway on the far side of the capital. The Talent took Cass into his camouflaged Nissan, leaving T.K. to hitch a ride with one of the camera crews.

Had Cass not proposed her shortcut near the docks, they might have gotten through. Instead, the convoy was brought to a halt at the port's main
gate by a ragged queue of day laborers that spilled across the street. But for
television and the Talent, so mundane a scene never would have galvanized
the world, or changed a nation.

"I want this tel-op." The Talent leapt from his command car. "I'll take a
stand-up here."

The crews deployed. At the sight of the cameras, the desultory queue
dissolved into a curious crowd, then a mob compliantly furious enough to
leave no stone unthrown.

The Talent hailed the protesters with a jolly thumbs-up: Screw the
masses of Equatoria.

Howling, they responded with volleys of garbage. The policemen, deter-
mined not to be left out of camera range, jumped from their trucks.

"I want this rage," the Talent yelled before an old tomato spattered
across his safari shirt. "I want it all."

Tear gas blanketed the rioters, followed by shotgun blasts of birdshot and the whack of riot batons. The mob scattered, chased by the cameras. A skinny youth, his escape cut off by police, collided with the Talent.

A policeman fired his shotgun. The Talent went down writhing, the skinny youth crawled off. T.K. rushed in, but two camera crews and Cass arrived first.

"Long shot first. Get the fucking significant long shot." The Talent waved everyone off. "Then zoom in on me. I'm not going anywhere."

The Talent winced, testing his buttock. Bits of tomato dangled from his shirt.

"Thank God they missed your face," his producer said. "We're getting you an ambulance."

"Not . . . until . . . I finish . . . my stand-up. Take one!"

The Talent lay on his side, one hand fondling his lacerated pants, and invited the camera's compassion.

"This"—he lifted the bloody hand and gestured across the horizon—"is a journalist's worst nightmare, finding oneself caught in the agony of a covering story that one is breaking . . . ouch, shit."

"You up to this, Beau?" the producer asked. "We'll airlift you to a hospital."

"I'm a professional," the Talent snarled through gritted teeth. "I want my viewers to smell my pain. Take two."

"Watch the four-letters, Beau," the producer said. "Blood'll get you prime time, 'shit' no."

"Take two." The Talent breathed deeply. "Beau Bradford here. Caught in a journalist's worst nightmare. The agony of the very breaking story. That I'm covering—"

"Beau, lean more into the camera and don't mess that gook on your chest?" the producer said. "Start again from 'caught in the agony,' et cetera."

"Can I help?" said T.K., hovering just off camera with Cass. "I know a little first aid."

"How about you enter with the natives," the producer said, "and carry Beau off as he finishes his stand-up."

"His lie-up," prompted T.K.

"Whatever. Take three, Beau?"

"Beau Bradford here. And this is a reporter's worst nightmare. Caught in the heartbreak. The agony of a breaking story. That I find myself covering—"

T.K. knelt by the injured Talent, squeezed his torn trousers. A small pellet popped out, then another.

"A little birdshot in the ass." T.K. displayed the metal pellets to the camera. "Take an aspirin and call me in the morning if the swelling's not down."

"Sonofabitch." The Talent struggled to his feet. "Who let this dickhead into my stand-up?"

"Praise the Lord, he's walking." T.K. held his ground between the camera and the Talent. "A television testimonial to the power of your prayers—"

T.K. ripped off the Talent's lavalier microphone. "Shit," he told it, "shit shit shit shit shit shit shit—"

Assorted technicians wrestled T.K. off camera. "Go screw up some other network," the executive producer said.

"There's a pellet or two left in his ass," T.K. said before he was hustled away.

"Take four," cried the Talent. "Beau Bradford here. Caught in a reporter's worst. Nightmare finding myself part of. The heartbreaking agony of this. Story around me—"

Cass looked on. "You thought that was funny," she said from under her sunglasses. The Nissan ride had smudged her lipstick.

"Your Talent got himself nicked in the ass and now he acts like he's facing open-heart surgery," T.K. said. "When ordinary people get blown away, it's too bad. When a celebrity bleeds, it leads the evening news."

"That's so pathetic." Without specifying what she had in mind, Cass left him to nurse her fallen Talent.

* * *

T.K. hadn't behaved much better. Once he filed his feature on Beau Bradford, he called Cass to make amends, but there was no answer. After several tries, he called the network suite.

"Mr. Bradford can't come to the phone right now," he heard Cass say.

T.K. hung up. Another hour passed, and he tried her room, again without result. He wouldn't jump to conclusions about Cass and her Talent. When the telephone roused him from bed, it had to be her.

"We can't run this." The foreign editor, instead, was shouting at T.K. from the American Midwest.

"Your profile's demeaning, buddy boy," the foreign editor said. "Beau Bradford got wounded in the middle of a war. We saw him hit on the evening news, it looked like the whole general staff was dragging him to safety, and you want us to make fun of a hero while he's under the surgeon's knife?"

"It's more complex than that." How often had T.K. tried to tell his desk?

"The network calls Beau's condition guarded," reported the foreign editor. "The doctors took three slugs out of him—we're getting all kinds of calls about him."

T.K. sat naked on his bed. He was in trouble.

"State Department briefing denounced Beau's shooting as regrettable," the foreign editor continued.

"Jeez, that bad?"

"Worse. White House condemned it as unhelpful to the peace process in Equatoria."

T.K. had reported long enough to know what that meant: Washington was pissed.

"Major policy implications," the foreign editor said. "Our Washington bureau thinks the White House will refuse to put our GIs in harm's way after seeing Beau Bradford gunned down in Equatoria."

Prudently, T.K. swallowed his response. Hacks rushed in where soldiers feared to tread these days.

"So we need a front-page story, buddy boy. You saw it, you rewrite it, or I'll have someone here do it from the wires and your next byline will be on your buyout papers." The foreign editor hung up.

T.K. worked into the night on a new story, hewing as close to the truth as he dared. He was back on the front page, but he couldn't go back to sleep.

The next morning, Schuyler stopped by, looking no less forlorn.

"I got a rocket from my network," Schuyler said. "They saw Beau Bradford shot on prime time, they're asking how I plan to match it."

"The wanker still around?" T.K. asked.

"Flew out this morning," Schuyler said. "Cass told Sipho that Bradford was heading back to London for surgery."

"Face-lift of the ass?" T.K. said. If Cass was still here, he mused, that was good news.

"You don't want the bad," said Schuyler. "Sipho went upstairs for a strobe light that Bradford's crew left us." Schuyler seemed to hold his breath as he spoke. "Sipho met Cass coming out of his suite, said she blushed and walked right past."

Cass once confessed to sleeping with lovers she didn't think much of afterwards. This time, T.K. had pushed her into it by mocking Beau Bradford. It was like Cass to cuddle the Talent to prove T.K. wrong.

Even Schuyler looked chagrined. "Looks like Cass spent the night up there. Sorry, but it ain't over."

10.

POR?O PARADI!O, *qua?oria—?h* !?a?* of ?h* fragil* c*a!*-
fir* in ?hi! war-?orn coun?ry !**m*d in doub? following ?h*
Uni?*d !?a?*!' d*ci!ion no? ?o commi? Am*rican ?roop*! ?o a
p*ac*k**ping forc*.

   Bull*?! again whi!?l*d ?hrough ?h* quinin* l*av*! a! fr!!h
figh?ing brok* ou? b*?w**n ?h* gov*rnm*n? and ?h*
in!urg*n?!, *ach of whom accu!*d ?h* o?h*r of viola?ing ?h*ir
c*a!*-fir* agr**m*n? . . .

Like other seasoned hacks, T.K. had started sleeping on the floor, his
mattress propped Beirut-style against the window to snag the mortar shrapnel that now slammed nightly into the capital, when the rumors about Cass
circulated through the hotel corridors.

Since that notorious night, they had talked once, when Cass telephoned
to ask T.K. to view her footage of the Doctor before it was shipped to the
network.

"It looks almost third generation," she said, as though nothing were
amiss. "Can you help sort it out?"

T.K. was in no mood. Her night with the Talent, let her sort that out first.

"That's so judgmental," Cass said, but she did not deny it. It wasn't clear who hung up first, but T.K. could not call back, she would mistake it for exoneration.

Within a week, Cass's reputation was unraveling as fast as the cease-fire outside the hotel.

"Bitch focked it up," Rolf said with the bitter satisfaction of a spurned swain. "Shows she's no better than the rest of us focking hacks."

Unable to pry anything more lucid from Rolf, who was stoned at the time and wearing his Walkman at full blast, T.K. looked up Schuyler.

"Cass hyped some visuals to get herself on the air," Schuyler said. "That's the buzz."

"She called it third generation."

Schuyler looked puzzled. "First generation's the original videotape," he said, "so a duplicate's second generation. Third generation's dupe of a dupe, pretty marginal—she didn't use that?"

T.K. didn't know. "I haven't seen her," he said.

Cass lay so low that T.K. wondered if she'd left the country. A postcard from New York confirmed it. Her writing overflowed the allotted space.

"Dearest Cutthroat Competition," she wrote. "They upgraded me to the Concorde. Arrived New York before I left London. Unhealthy for the ego to meet people who actually listened to me. I miss the real world, where you are."

She had signed off, "Fondest." Nothing more.

If she followed her Talent to New York, why send a card hinting at reconciliation? He turned the postcard over and scrutinized the Concorde photograph for some hint of her state of mind. Even there, he didn't know where Cass was.

So T.K. revisited the stations of his brief life with Cass, sifting for clues to their failed affair. One day he sat among the gasoline bottles in Phuqqa's tiny office, discussing the probability of a guerrilla assault on the capital.

"What makes them still fight after so many years?" T.K. asked, though he preferred to inquire about Cass.

"Faith," Phuqqa said, "that things can be no worse under a new regime."

"Then it's not just ethnicity."

"Most guerrillas are related by clan," said Phuqqa, "but some seek revenge for the murder of their families. Some are children rounded up in the villages and tutored in the Doctor's fanaticism. But his greatest ally has been our government's stupidity, like making peasants grow tomatoes all at once so we have glut for one month and shortage for the rest of the year."

"Cass told me about the tomatoes," T.K. said.

Phuqqa stopped a pile of papers from sliding off his desk. "Has she left without saying goodbye?" he asked. And T.K. had to concede his own ignorance.

He began to travel, leaving the capital to ferret out stories in the countryside, then throughout the region. He slept on unmade beds in a succession of deteriorating hotels, on the swept earth of remote huts, on stony ground. He was restless to move on once he had filed his stories, sloughing off his datelines because Cass would have used them better. At night, he numbed himself to sleep not with bad liquor but with the vocabulary sheets that she once prepared for him. Mastery of the exotic patois might woo her back if they ever met again.

Returning from across the river, where T.K. had interviewed refugees at a new hospital set up by Doctors Without Borders, he met Ginny on the ferry. She was back from checking out reports of a famine.

"You weren't away long," he said.

"Small famine," Ginny said.

He asked as casually as he could what happened to Cass, but it didn't fool Ginny. "I thought she wasn't your problem anymore," she said.

T.K. watched the brown river churning by the ferry's peeling hull. Cass had been his problem since she arrived. Did the news twink really fake a story? A bloated corpse—no, merely a dead pig—floated past.

Ginny sensed the suspicion in his silence. "Cass is ambitious," she said, without quite answering, "not dishonest."

They jostled down the ramp to the sun-bleached wharf with the other travelers and their livestock. Ginny retrieved her passport from the border guard and walked away as though the conversation was over.

It took T.K. longer to clear the border post. The guard puzzled over the passport, shook his head, and tried to call his superiors. He returned the passport after T.K. promised to report to the Ministry of National Guidance the next morning. T.K.'s new linguistic skills enlightened him on that much, though they failed to make clear whether he was summoned for a fresh scolding or merely because his visa needed renewal.

When he caught up with Ginny, she had found them a taxi among the jumble of trucks and carts.

"Remember the segment Cass was assigned on the Doctor and his guerrillas?" Ginny said. "The visuals were cooked, something about executing prisoners. You didn't know?"

"Her Talent found the film," T.K. said.

"And Cass didn't verify it," Ginny said. "Sure, the killings happened, but somewhere halfway around the world—seems the palm trees don't grow here." Ginny cringed as their driver sideswiped a bicycle.

Why, T.K. wondered, didn't Cass check it out with him? But then, she tried to, before they hung up on one another.

"She's in New York," he said. "She sent me this."

Ginny turned over the worn postcard he carried.

"She was around a few days ago," Ginny said. "Ask her yourself, bro, unless you'd rather she ran off with her Viking. That is why you haven't seen her around lately."

What Viking? T.K. sat up. "Not the Norwegian Refugee Council guy?"

Ginny nodded. "That blond hair and muscles—I can't blame her. Cass wants out of journalism and Lars wants Cass, offered to take her on as an aid volunteer. Only serves you right, if you're feeling too sorry for yourself to get off your butt and stop her."

"I'll call her," T.K. said, "after I've sucked up to the Ministry for my visa."

"Try the embassy reception tomorrow," Ginny said. "She'll be there if I have to drag her."

Ginny was a treasure. "If Cass won't marry me," T.K. said, "will you?"

"And hear you whine about turning fifty down the road?" said Ginny. "Cass'd put up with it, I guess. The two of you can't find your way downhill without each other."

* * *

T.K. overslept. He called Cass several times, without result. It was nearly noon when he arrived at the Ministry of National Guidance. No one bothered with his credentials. The guards who usually frisked him were busy filling sandbags. A solicitous welcome from the Deputy Minister fueled T.K.'s fears that something dire was about to unfold.

"We have seen too little of each other these many weeks, Mr. Farrow," said the Deputy Minister, speaking with an ominous civility. He waved T.K. to the usual chair in front of his desk. "I should have done more to spare you this meeting—a cup of tea, perhaps?"

Before T.K. could reply, the Deputy Minister picked up a typewritten statement and launched into the litany of accusations.

"We can no longer tolerate your shameless abuse of our hospitality and our patience. Since you arrived, you have been, let's see . . ." The Deputy Minister's voice fell conspiratorially, as if sharing an off-color joke. "Fanning social tensions of course, spreading baseless fabrications and slanders, trafficking in rumors calculated to offend the national dignity of the masses of Equatoria—oh, I like that one—insulting high personalities of state, promulgating neocolonialist distortions of our socialist reality—we know what that means, don't we?"

T.K. had no idea. The Deputy Minister hummed a little tune while he scanned the remaining charges. T.K. let his head drop in his hands, counted slowly to ten, and looked up.

"I acknowledge and bewail my manifold sins and wickedness," he said, "which I, from time to time, most grievously have committed, by thought, word, and deed—"

"On deaf ears, deaf ears," the Deputy Minister said. "Do not squander your last few minutes on useless prayer before we expel you."

The Deputy Minister gave a little whinny, the sort that earned him notoriety back when he was ripping out fingernails as a police interrogator.

"Expelled," said T.K., "for what I wrote?"

"No, Mr. Farrow, we're expelling you for"—the Deputy Minister consulted his manila folder—"currency speculation, tax evasion, black marketeering—that was what our consultant recommended, we do not want you parading around your expulsion."

Governments that threw out foreign correspondents for being too enterprising or unsympathetic had learned to do it more credibly. Slick lies about espionage, larceny, and moral turpitude, even when flung by the most disreputable regimes, tended to stick like cow pies on a barn door.

T.K. wasn't going without a struggle. "Where's your proof?"

The Deputy Minister shuffled through the sheaf of papers. "Only this week, you were seen trading foreign currency illegally on the black market. I have it here somewhere."

T.K. showed the stamp in his passport. "I was out of the country—"

"Where are your bank receipts if you're not changing money illegally? And you haven't paid any taxes."

Neither did any other hack. And nobody bothered with receipts. The authorities ignored his street transactions before Cass made him start going to the bank. Now they were punishing him for what he no longer did.

"Why me, why not other correspondents? Was it my reporting on dissidents like Dr. Phuqqa?"

"You Americans show more sympathy for one dissident who claims to be mistreated than for thousands of our martyred patriots," the Deputy Minister said. "We can't allow more hooliganism from you and Miss Benoit."

Was Cass going too? It would confirm that T.K.'s expulsion was fraudulent.

"We're not expelling Miss Benoit," the Deputy Minister said, "if she wishes to perform her penance by offering our hungry masses food instead of provocations."

Then it was true. Cass was staying on as an aid worker while T.K. left tainted by the stench of impropriety, whatever public support his newspaper professed.

"I'm fighting this," he said.

"And add espionage to our charges? No correspondent travels with a teddy bear—most suspicious," said the Deputy Minister. "But if you leave quietly, we're prepared to drop black marketeering and tax evasion, which leaves us just currency speculation."

"Freedom of the press is at stake here," T.K. said.

"Indeed it is." The Deputy Minister whinnied his agreement. "My government's right to be free of the press with its distortions, bullying, and arrogance."

"My readers will be outraged," said T.K. "Public protests outside your new embassy in Washington."

"I hardly think so—you reporters are more unpopular there than my government. We could flog you, and your fellow Americans would assume you deserved it."

The Deputy Minister consulted his gold Rolex. "Now you must excuse me," he said. "I'm late for lunch with your embassy's commercial attaché, to taste his cheeseburger delicacy. You have twenty-four hours to pack your suitcases and depart the sovereign soil of the Equatorian People's Democratic Socialist Republic. Give me your press card."

"How about forty-eight hours?" T.K. was mentally sorting through the outgoing flights. "I have to consult with my editors, pay my hotel bill—"

"Twenty-four hours." The Deputy Minister pocketed T.K.'s laminated press card. "Why consult your editors? We can arrange whatever evidence they need that you disgraced your newspaper."

"We're more of a product these days," T.K. said.

"As for your hotel bill, my rate compares favorably with the bank's." The Deputy Minister piled a stack of crisp new dinars on his desk.

"No thanks, I could get expelled for it," T.K. said. "When do your secret police drive me to the airport?"

The Deputy Minister swept the dinars into a desk drawer. "The People's Security Bureau are not chauffeurs. Hire your own taxi. Allow three hours to clear customs and immigration, they'll be thorough with your luggage."

Stand in line with the other passengers? It was the most insulting expulsion T.K. had experienced. When he got expelled elsewhere, the police customarily escorted him to the plane. One repressive regime even bought his ticket.

"Making us expel ourselves," T.K. said, "reflects poorly on your mistreatment of the press."

The Deputy Minister hesitated, as if reconsidering his decision. He rummaged through the file and held up a heavily underlined page clipped from T.K.'s newspaper.

"Your fabrication here about corruption among the so-called elite—malicious speculation, of course, but let's look at the other side." The Deputy Minister turned the page over. "Limited offer, it says, for this videotape cassette, *Become a Better Lover in Thirty Days: Satisfy Her Every Time.* Can your newspaper do that?"

"Make you a better lover? It's only an ad."

"No, send me this videotape, to facilitate your successor's accreditation. Have him carry it in—our mail's so unreliable."

"Give me forty-eight more hours," T.K. said, "and you'll have your cassette."

"Thirty-six hours," the Deputy Minister said, "but do not file stories after tonight. You may attend the press briefing tomorrow, but then you must go."

T.K. walked out of the Ministry. He'd have to tell his newspaper, but first he had to see Cass. Whatever she did, T.K. would not be with her, but Cass said it in the bush and she was right. Being enemies was a waste of time.

* * *

Schuyler looked up from the minicamera dismantled on the table in his hotel room.

"Expelling you," he said, "for what?"

"Currency speculation, committing journalism," T.K. said. "I plead guilty to the latter."

It hardly mattered, now that Equatoria was no longer the news flavor of the month. The Americans weren't sending GIs, so nobody at home cared. Cass's Talent had more clout than T.K. credited him for; once he got himself shot on prime time, the White House chickened out fast.

"My editors pouched me his stand-up," Schuyler said. "He had so much cutaway boom-boom edited in, it looked like the D-Day invasion."

"The Talent took some birdshot in the ass," T.K. said. "I was there."

"They're paying ten thousand bucks a speech for Beau's version back home," Schuyler said.

"Next thing, he'll be pitching it as a Sunday night movie."

"It's already sold." Schuyler put down his fistful of screws. "Don't turn out the light when they expel you," he said. "The network's pulling us out next month."

"To where?" T.K. said.

"Nowhere," Schuyler said. "They're doing it to save money. They'll buy visuals from agencies or free-lancers, assign the voiceovers to our correspondents in London and Tokyo. All the networks are downsizing, they think the viewers won't notice."

The viewers probably wouldn't. "Kobus, Sipho?"

"They're not on staff, so they'll have to free-lance somewhere," Schuyler said. "Me, I'm packing it in."

T.K. tried to visualize a breaking story without Schuyler and his crew. He couldn't.

"Network's putting me on early-morning radio news in Chicago till my contract runs out," Schuyler said. "I'll go back to rabbinical studies, that's what my wife wants."

"I'm sorry," T.K. said.

"I'm not. Sarah's taken me back, her biological clock's ticking. If I leave here in two weeks, I'll catch her about right—I've switched to boxer shorts."

"You, a rabbi?"

"I'm sick of wars. When did we last cover anything upbeat?" Schuyler turned to reassembling the minicamera. "It's time to celebrate life for a change."

* * *

T.K. usually avoided embassy receptions and the smug diplomats who inhabited them, but there would be enough food to spare him a last supper in the hotel. And Cass would be there. Though she was Canadian, the embassy listed her with the American press because she had worked for public radio.

The evening was mellow, with a soft breeze that wafted the wild scent of jacaranda, like the blue blossom that Cass had tucked in her braid. Lights twinkled on the freighters moored out beyond the harbor, while demurrage charges multiplied on their unloaded grain. He passed the small park where during the day, children played, and after dark, lovers retreated to find privacy from the overcrowded tenements. A couple was already grappling in the seclusion of a bush, and he thought of Cass.

But he could not inhabit the past. Life entailed change, even when it carried her away too. Without change, hacks like T.K. would have nothing to write.

From behind him, a small sedan cruised slowly down the boulevard, performed a tight U-turn, and passed again, its headlights dark.

It was a Russian Lada, driven by the crowd that bugged his telephone, but this time they were trolling for someone else. He recognized the roly-poly gait of a solitary pedestrian in the gloaming behind him.

On impulse, T.K. ran back. "Mukhtar," he called.

Before T.K. closed the distance, the Lada blinded him temporarily with its headlights and squealed off. There was no license plate.

"I owe much to you." Phuqqa would not let go of T.K.'s hand. In Equatoria, men walked hand in hand. Cass said it meant nothing more than friendship.

"The motorcar was parked in front of my office tonight, so I left by the back," Phuqqa said. "But these embassy invitations protect me. The police will not detain me if they see me dining with your ambassador."

"You're going to the reception too?"

From inside his jacket, Phuqqa uncrumpled a plastic shopping bag bearing the crest of Harrods of London. "Your ambassador lets me take some sweets home. It gives my nieces such a treat after porridge for supper."

Ahead, the United States Embassy sparkled like a cruise ship. The colonial villa had been refurbished for only slightly more than it would have cost to renovate an urban tenement back home.

"I'm being expelled," T.K. said.

Phuqqa tugged at the fake-pearl cuff links that dressed up his frayed white shirt cuffs.

"I will miss you, my friend," he said. "Our street talk is that guerrillas are infiltrating the capital. If you Americans won't join the U.N. force, I think our leaders will say the truce broke down and launch another offensive. The shops have sold out of grain and cooking oil; everyone expects the Alliance to strike first."

A cavalcade of limousines peeled off the boulevard and careened up the circular embassy driveway, past whitewashed columns floodlit like a national monument. Phuqqa identified the officials as they emerged.

"That tall gentleman is our Minister of State for Agriculture," he said. "When he took office, Equatoria exported sugar at a premium price. Now we import it from as far away as Thailand."

T.K. and Phuqqa shuffled down the reception line to be thanked for coming by a diplomat who had no idea who they were. The hall leading to the garden was stacked with teak tables, chairs, and other carvings waiting to be stuffed into the hold of the Boeing 727 that would carry the congressmen and their wives back to Washington. T.K. lifted a frosty Budweiser from a passing waiter.

"That woman looks like Jezzie Jerome," T.K. said, "though it's hard to tell without her guitar."

"A musician?" Phuqqa asked.

"She started out singing in coffeehouses with a trio called Jeffrey, John, and Jezebel. Went solo with a big hit called 'War Sucks.' Now she spends most of her time on causes. It looks like your government's hosting another conference of useful idiots."

Cass was in the garden with the American ambassador. Her tawny hair flowed loose; her bare shoulders glowed in the lamplight, though T.K. disapproved of her new black minidress because it displayed too much back and thighs.

"Why have a pool in Houston if you don't like to swim?" Cass was asking. The malachite bangles were back, clinking as she sipped from her chilled white wine.

"When I came home at night, Cassie," the ambassador drawled, "I'd pour a bourbon and branch water, sit by my pool, and tell myself, 'Tex, you're one rich sonofabitch.'"

Cass laughed politely.

"So you come skinny-dip in my pool here anytime," the ambassador said. "You don't need your bikini because I won't jump in with you—bring this scrawny little bastard if you have to. Now you build yourself another drink while I go work."

Galvanized by some new urgency, the ambassador drained his own glass and headed across the garden to intercept the Equatorian Foreign Minister, who arrived with a phalanx of bodyguards. T.K. turned but Phuqqa had gone, probably to fill his shopping bag with sweets.

"You're hardly scrawny or little." Cass watched T.K. through her wineglass. "About the bastard part, I can't make up my mind."

"Your postcard said you took the Concorde to New York," T.K. said.

Cass gave a brittle laugh and drained the glass. "That was six weeks ago. Mail's slow, eh?"

"I called you last night, several times," he said. "You never answered."

"I was at the warehouse till all hours, helping Lars and the drivers check the manifest," Cass said. "He sent another food convoy into the interior today, I could have gone too. Maybe I should have."

"You're not serious about giving up journalism?"

"You heard about the footage," Cass said, "very bloody visuals of young guerrillas cutting the throats of soldiers they captured. But someone in Washington complained that those guerrillas were fighting some other war. I don't remember the sequence but my voiceover covered it. I would never have used anything that gory, but it went on the air and Beau blamed me."

It was a reporter's first rule: If your mother says she loves you, check it out. "You've never been shoddy," he said.

"I was this time, eh? I overreached because I wanted to make things happen." Cass rubbed her bare arms. "It started when I said I worked for your paper—forgive me?"

"Nothing to forgive," he said. "The point is, you could have done it."

"That's not the point at all," she said. "I broke the Ninth Commandment—Don't bear false witness. Once you start bending the truth, where does it stop?"

A thought had crossed T.K.'s mind: the Talent hadn't shared his limelight so Cass could beat him in a beauty contest.

"Your lover set you up," T.K. said.

"What lover?" Cass was suddenly fierce. "Beau did hint that sleeping with him could help my career and maybe I considered it, until he stood up and unzipped—"

"That's sexual harassment."

"Vanity's the word," she said. "Beau wouldn't take off his trousers because he didn't want to show his derriere all bandaged up, he wanted me to service him kneeling. When I remembered how lived-in your body looks, I began laughing. Beau zipped up and walked out, so I went to bed alone, even locked the door. When I woke up, he was gone."

Cass wriggled free of T.K.'s celebratory pawing. "Not here, Thomas, people are staring."

"Go for the jugular," he told her, "go after the Talent's job. Tell the network it wasn't your idea, that I told you the footage looked legit."

"It's too late," Cass said. "Lars has offered me a chance to be useful again, helping people. I'm not going to sit back and watch anymore."

"But you're a hack, Cass, you've earned it."

T.K. knew how he wanted this to end, but no longer how to get there. The body that once nurtured him looked as unattainable as when they met. Begging wouldn't do any good.

"That's Jezzie Jerome over there," he said, trying to fill the silence. "From Jeffrey, John, and Jezebel?"

"I used to play her songs in college." Cass spoke in a hushed voice.

"Jezebel and I are both Vietnam vets," T.K. told Cass, "but she served her six weeks on the other side."

They were interrupted by a florid man with excessive sideburns and paunch.

"Cassandra Benoit? Congressman Willie Bob Walker." He spilled her wine as he pumped Cass's hand. "And this here's my bride of thirty years, Thelma Mae."

"Willie Bob and I listen to you all the time," said Mrs. Walker. "See, I told you she sounded darling."

Cass blushed.

"She sure is," Congressman Walker said. "Get yourself a TV program, Cassandra—you don't belong in that public radio pack of leftist perverts."

He noticed T.K. "You with the embassy? Oh, just a reporter. Do wish you media guys would get on the team and give those gutsy freedom fighters out there more credit."

T.K. smiled politely. One ideologue's gutsy freedom fighters were another's cowardly death squads.

"Why's the liberal media so afraid to tell the truth?" Congressman Walker said. "The Patriotic Alliance offers the only hope for this plucky little country."

"You newspaper people are always so negative," Mrs. Walker cooed.

Whereupon Jezzie Jerome backed into them. Her raven hair had been hacked away so unevenly that it must have cost a great deal of money.

"May I have your autograph?" asked Cass. She took T.K.'s notebook and ripped out a page. "I'm Cass Benoit."

"Cassandra Benoit from public radio? Why, I listen to you all the time," said Jezzie. "Your little reports are so progressive."

T.K. stepped in and introduced himself.

"You write that fascist garbage." Jezzie glared from the raccoon hollows of her eyes. "My political consultant sends me your crap, it's distorted, mean-spirited, petty—"

"Nobody's perfect," T.K. said.

"Always finding fault with this brave government," said Jezzie. "Can't you find anything positive to say?"

It was incumbent upon T.K. to complete the introductions.

"Congressman," T.K. said, "you've heard of Jezzie Jerome, who gave those wonderful concerts for our fighting boys over Radio Hanoi years ago. Ms. Jerome, do you know Willie Bob Walker, who cosponsored those bills on Capitol Hill opposing abortion, immigrants, AIDS research, school lunches—what have I missed, Congressman?"

They looked unamused by T.K., who had stepped back to referee.

"You don't know what you're talking about," the congressman said.

"Amazing how often the media gets it wrong," Jezzie said. "We artists wouldn't have to people the barricades if the media only did its job."

"Media's plural," T.K. said.

"That's your opinion," Jezzie said. "You journalists need to be licensed—"

"Like doctors?"

"Like real estate agents, isn't that right, Cassandra?"

But Cass had wandered off, autograph in hand, to look for Phuqqa.

"You and I may not see eye to eye on everything, Miss Jerome," the congressman said, "but we agree on that much. When Thelma Mae and I go off to Martha's Vineyard, we don't even buy a paper and we get along just fine." His wife stopped sidling toward the buffet table to nod agreement.

"My hideaway's on Martha's Vineyard," Jezzie said, "with picture windows shaped like peace symbols?"

"I know that big house on the bluff, it's perfectly beautiful," Mrs. Walker said. "Ours is nearer Edgartown."

"Where developers wants to tear down those big old houses to put up ticky-tacky condominiums?" Jezzie said.

"One of those historic houses is ours," Congressman Walker said. "We're mad as hell about it, never would have happened if the media was awake."

"Media's plural," said T.K.

"That's why I'm giving a concert to stop it," Jezzie said. "I don't suppose you'd like to serve on my hands-off committee."

"We'd be honored, wouldn't we, Willie Bob," said Mrs. Walker. "It's something all of us can support."

Congressman Walker was jotting down telephone numbers on a business card. "These are unlisted, Jezzie," he said, "but you call me anytime, day or night."

"And here's my unlisted numbers, Willie Bob." Jezzie was writing furiously herself. They went into a huddle.

T.K. looked on aghast. This tortured nation was about to blow apart, and they were forging an alliance against condos back home. In the end, it usually boiled down to whose tax shelter got gored.

Cass pulled T.K. aside. "I can't find Mukhtar."

"He probably got bored and went home." T.K. did not tell Cass about the Lada sedan. What could go wrong at an embassy reception?

Jezzie Jerome bore down and hustled Cass aside. "You must report on the new world information order that we're reshaping at our conference here," she said.

"Cass, can I take you—" T.K. never finished.

"Don't interrupt," Jezzie snapped. "Our limo's outside, Cassandra. I want to take you to our government guest house and play you the song I just wrote."

"I played the guitar," Cass said, "and wrote a few songs myself back in college."

"Injustice quakes before a guitar in the hands of a singer-songwriter," said Jezzie. "Play us one of your songs—I might record it on my next album."

"Might you?" Cass's eyes opened even wider.

"You must meet the rest of our delegation." Jezzie summoned a sullen youth with a bad beard and worse breath. "I bet you're a fan of this sensitive actor-activist—"

"It's my last night," T.K. pleaded before Jezzie cut him off. Cass gave a little nod as she was led away, though he may only have wished it.

It was time to take Vanessa to interview the Doctor. T.K. looked about but she wasn't to be seen.

"Can we trust them?" Thelma Mae Walker interrupted his thoughts.

"I doubt it."

"The shrimp, I mean." Her plate was piled nearly as high as her beehive hairdo. "Willie Bob warned me not to eat anything here, this country's so dirty, but I just couldn't resist these shrimp—what do you think?"

"Eat one and wait forty-five minutes. If you don't die, eat the rest."

Mrs. Walker smiled. "You reporters must meet such interesting people, is that right?"

"Oh yes," said T.K., watching Cass walk out of his life. "Other reporters."

* * *

Back at the hotel, T.K. telephoned his editors to put a salvaging spin on his setback before they read it on the Reuters or A.P. news wires.

"I'm getting expelled."

A massive groan carried back from his distant newspaper, testifying like a Greek chorus to his failure.

"Send this loser to the showers," screamed the foreign editor, "back to the Little League."

The distant chorus hooted its support, as though he were patched into the newsroom's public address system.

"Let me explain," said T.K.

"Explain?" the foreign editor roared. "We pay this bonus baby two million bucks and he gives away a triple, snotnose kid lobs it across the place like a wet kiss."

"Hello?" said T.K. "I'm getting expelled."

"Keep it low and inside, snotnose." The collective groan faded away, only to rise again.

"Should have yanked the kid in the first inning," the foreign editor said, "before he blew our pennant."

So the subject was baseball. T.K. thought they were still apoplectic over basketball back home, he'd been away that long. "Pennant race under way?" he said.

"All over TV," the foreign editor said, "whole newsroom's going ballistic—you on the moon?"

"Equatoria." It was the same thing.

"First shot at the World Series in eight, nine years, this town's not talking anything else, fourth game could wrap it up and the kid's pissing it away. Hey, hey, coach is sending in Morales."

"They're claiming it's for black-market currency violations," T.K. said, "but it's really for what I wrote."

"I didn't think they'd play old Morales," said the foreign editor, "that rotator cuff's benched him all season. Wish you could see him on the mound, grabbing his crotch, spitting—what a professional. Call in for the score, did you? Top of the seventh, we're trailing three–two."

"They're throwing me out tomorrow," T.K. said. A mighty cheer went up from the newsroom far away.

"Morales struck out the designated hitter—" The foreign editor's words were swallowed up in the cacophony. "Helluva racket here, speak up, T.K. is it?"

"I spell: Echo, X-ray, Papa, Echo, Lima, Lima, Echo, Delta. I'm expelled."

"Well, they tried that trick at Princeton, but I didn't budge," the foreign editor said. "You hang in there, T.K., tell them you haven't written anything worth getting expelled for, I'll back you up."

"Too late for that," T.K. said. "After I leave—"

"Great catch," the foreign editor said, "we got ourselves a team again."

"—I'll be filing you my farewell-to-Equatoria piece, hard-hitting, no holds barred."

"Give us lots of sweep, scope, color, voices, T.K.," the foreign editor said, "and hold it to four, five hundred words, space'll be tight if we take the pennant. Go, Morales!"

Half a column of type to sum up his career in this country. T.K. let the phone slip from his hand. He pulled the mattress down from his window and slouched on it.

Telephones, photographs, video—they had nothing to do with communication. A handful of demonstrators waving fists into a television camera could send the message that an entire nation was rising up. A banal photograph could be cropped to imply a threat that really didn't exist.

He dialed Cass's room but she had yet to return from her latest career as a singer-songwriter. He was about to call Vanessa when a knock sounded so softly at his door that he would have missed it were his editor still ranting.

She stood shivering in her maddening black dress, despite the heat.

"Where's your antifascists?" he asked.

"A fascist is someone who doesn't agree with them," said Cass. "When I explained how the government was stealing food from the refugees, Jezzie said you brainwashed me. Crumbs, she accused me of sleeping with you."

"Which you denied."

"I did not." Her laughter tinkled like wind chimes.

"Every time I think I'm over you, Thomas, you drag in looking like a drenched puppy and I tumble, eh?" Cass was looking at him. A black strap on her minidress had strayed wantonly over one shoulder.

"If you're being expelled," she said, "we deserve the last night together. I'd like that, if you haven't changed your mind, I mean."

* * *

In the muggy night air, T.K. lay on the mattress, reenacting a fantasy that had disrupted his sleep too often. In his mind she was riding him, a gentle, persistent mistress, gliding upon him. Her breasts skimmed his chest.

He opened his eyes. It was no dream this time. Her hair brushed his face when she bent to kiss him, shutting out the moonlight that washed the windowsill. Her breath fell harder when he thrust back.

"The last chap I did this to," she whispered, "looked just like you."

He rolled Cass over, tumbling her half onto the floor but without uncoupling or breaking the rhythm.

"Woman on top, you sexist." She was laughing.

"Lost your balance, what a klutz."

"Unfair." She nipped his shoulder.

"So's love, you taught me that." He was beyond restraint anyway and she hung on tight.

Afterwards, they held their embrace in silence. How naturally they finished together. What made him suppose that he had nothing in common with this woman? His hands drifted down her back to the dimples above her buttocks, just where he remembered them. In this darkness he could map her tiniest freckles as though he had stenciled them there. Her head conformed with geometric logic to the contour of his shoulder. Familiarity, not just passion, had brought him to orgasm, a knowledge that they shared, however impermanently, their private treasure in a world impoverished by cruelty and chaos.

"I want you to stay in television," he said.

"And what about you?" she asked.

He didn't know, he told her. He had invested in a career that fed on the kind of sudden change about to engulf them. Without change, hacks like T.K. would be reduced to covering fender-benders in parking lots.

"One never knows," she said, "does one?"

He pulled the ring gently from her right hand and slipped it on her left. "I'll settle for airport motels," he said.

His proposal was drowned in the stormy clatter of Hind-24 gunships above the hotel, circling like predators over a mortally wounded country. The cease-fire had grounded the helicopters; now they were flying on a new rendezvous with destruction.

Perhaps Cass did not hear him. When she said it again in French, it sounded more wistful:

"On ne sait jamais, qui sait?"

* * *

The turnout for the news conference at the Ministry of National Guidance was meager, considering the hard news that it promised of the cease-fire's collapse. Some hacks were away on a week's breather. T.K. hadn't expected to find Vanessa. Barry of the A.P. told him over breakfast that she was seen leaving the hotel around midnight with a stranger carrying her bags.

"Someone tried to rocket the Alliance liaison office last night," Barry said. "Missed and hit the Cafe Peri-Peri next door. And there's fighting on the national highway."

If the government had broken its cease-fire, T.K. would wind up his tour with a live story and file it from the first place his departing flight touched down.

Sometime after Cass slipped away, wearing his last clean T-shirt over her torn dress, Phuqqa's sister called T.K. to report that he had never come home. When she went down to his small office, she found it ablaze.

T.K. telephoned the Law and Order Ministry but no one answered. He called the police, which claimed to have no record of a Phuqqa in custody—or in the morgue.

T.K. was getting old. Last night with Cass had eclipsed his interest in everything else.

When he walked to the news conference, T-72 battle tanks rattled again through the streets, sending taxis veering onto cracked sidewalks. The vendors were gone.

The Ministry auditorium looked seedier than usual. The glass protecting

Lenin's portrait was cracked—T.K. had never noticed before. A muslin curtain was pulled across the stage. Sunlight filtered through grimy windows and flooded the rows of rickety wooden chairs.

Alistair was sitting in the last row, as usual, peeling an orange. "At last everything becomes clear," he said, though no officials had arrived.

"I thought the tanks were confined to base," said T.K.

"They'll tell you what you need to know about life, death, beauty, ugliness, good, evil, and the United Nations," said Alistair. "I've got proper news—my masters are giving me Beijing for my next post."

"Lucky bastard," T.K. said. New datelines were tearing apart his family—Cass, Alistair, Ginny, Schuyler. Hacks met, separated, and reconvened for successive disasters like itinerant actors. If everyone left, this violent war would go unreported, like the tree falling in the forest.

Kobus and Sipho had staked out their usual spot up front. Sipho held a piece of cardboard, while Kobus adjusted the white balance on his camera. Rolf sat cross-legged on the floor before the podium, stealing batteries from his Nikon motor to power his Walkman. The Deputy Minister walked in to survey attendance, shook his head, and walked out.

Cass used to settle in at news conferences early enough to set up her tape recorder and number the pages in her large black notebook. This time she rushed in late.

"Alistair's getting Beijing—" T.K. said, but she interrupted him.

"Schuyler left the reception early last night," she said. "He saw Mukhtar driven off in a black sedan with no license plates."

Cass clutched the recorder that T.K. had ransomed. She was wearing his tie-dyed T-shirt, his photographer's vest with many pockets, his belt with the Soviet Army buckle. She had expropriated most of his wardrobe along with his soul.

T.K. told her of the call from Phuqqa's sister. "You call the American Embassy if he's not released by the time I'm expelled."

"Mukhtar's one more foreigner to them," Cass said. "I'm tired of bearing witness to the misery of others."

"That's what a hack does," T.K. said. "Do you expect people will stop mistreating each other because you refuse to watch?"

"I guess that's why I put off signing the television contract," she said. "I want to make myself useful again."

"You'd be a good aid worker, but you're a better reporter." T.K. gripped her shoulders. "Stop trying to save humanity, we don't deserve it. Screw the rhinos, whales, and dolphins, Cass—go forth and save television, that's your destiny."

"What's yours?"

"Following you. I could try public relations, it pays better than newspapering."

"You, a flack?" Cass scoffed. "It's so ridiculous—you'd share your client's secrets with the first reporter who called."

"And your pigheadedness pisses me off, Cass, you're going to sign your contract as soon as this briefing's over."

"Bullying is totally unacceptable, we'll discuss it later, eh?" she said. "I promised to cover for Ginny, she's calling about a job offer. Can I trust you to hold my seat while I set up?"

"No, you can't," T.K. said. "You never could."

Alistair proposed they quarrel a little longer while he dashed for the loo.

Cass went to the front of the room and wedged her Sony alongside the other recorders. She pulled a roll of tape from her pocket, tore off a piece with her teeth, and piggybacked her microphone on top of Sipho's.

Cass turned, and her notebook snagged the cord, jerking her tape recorder to the floor. She looked at T.K. and melted his exasperation with a smile.

One hand on the table for balance, she bent low to retrieve the recorder, the same Cass in spite of herself—she would trip over television cables all the way to the top. If only he could be around to pick her up.

The room spun upside down and flew apart.

Thunder deafened him, the flash briefly stole his sight. He was slammed off his chair, hard onto his back. Matter whistled indiscriminately overhead, the windows evaporated, chairs whipped across the room and splintered against the walls. Then, a hush gave way to screaming.

Smoke billowed through the room. T.K., gasping for air, found himself on the floor among shards of glass and slivers of wood.

His ribs hurt again. Blood trickled from his hair into his eyes. His teeth stopped rattling but a high C kept ringing in his ears. He looked up. A concrete chunk dangled from the ceiling. His face dropped into rubble and vomit.

He opened his eyes again. A wedge of metal lay embedded in the pocked wall just over his head. He crawled forward on a discovery of the destruction. "Cass?" he called out.

A rocket grenade could not have wreaked such damage, no gaping holes revealed daylight through the walls. A mortar shell might have caused it, or more likely a bomb. But bombs often came in tandem, the second to finish the survivors and catch the rescuers.

Kobus, his bony arms varnished a slick crimson, was dragging someone who would have been Sipho. "No you don't, little bugger," Kobus was saying, "I won't let you." His artificial foot flopped askew. Others staggered toward a door buckled open.

T.K. stumbled over what was left of Rolf with his earphones, looking as though a chain saw had bisected him.

Schuyler was digging into the rubble, raising fresh cuts on his hands, sweeping a body clean of the debris that obscured any sign of life. It was Cass.

T.K. was again a teenage medical corpsman dodging through the trampled long grass. It's your best friend this time, too, remember how it's done, they bred it into you at Fort Bragg.

He rolled Cass tenderly onto her back, felt the moistness of her pale skin, cleared a clotted wad from her mouth and blew hard into her lungs. He was rewarded with a slight heave of her breasts. A pulse was there below her jaw, but coming weak and fast. Her breathing was shallow, uneven.

Briskly, he probed along the body he had held last night for broken bone and torn flesh. When he pressed against her ribs, Cass moaned. He satisfied himself that the brain paste on the tie-dyed cotton wasn't hers. So far so good, until he saw her left hand.

Dark blood gushed from a couple of her fingers, now scoured to bone. He ripped his shirt into strips, tied them around her arm, jammed his thumb against the artery.

"Hold her arm straight up," he told Schuyler, "and press hard here."

T.K. tore the shirt into more bandages, for her hand first, then her head. When he sopped up her cheek, Cass stared back with vacant pupils that usurped the gray of her eyes.

"It's stopping," said Schuyler. "How'd you learn this?"

T.K. cradled Cass in his arms and stumbled to his feet. Her head lolled against his chest; she gagged her way back to consciousness.

She announced she was thirsty.

Alistair offered to find water.

No, T.K. said, not while she was in shock. But he let Alistair help. Cass was too heavy for him now.

They put her in Schuyler's truck with Kobus and Sipho and set off for the Chinese hospital. Gunfire popped on the rim of the hill overlooking the harbor.

"The guerrillas are bloody grabbing the Martyrs' Monument," Alistair said.

T.K. nodded numbly. But who would bomb a news conference?

11.

POR?O PARADI!O, *qua?oria—?hi! ba??*r*d coun?ry *xplod*d in?o r*n*w*d warfar* ?oday a! a ?*nuou! c*a!*-fir* collap!*d b*?w**n ?h* form*rly Marxi!? gov*rnm*n? and in!urg*n?! who hav* wag*d a long !?ruggl* ?o ?oppl* . . .

Vanessa's exclusive interview with the leader of the Equatorian Patriotic Alliance had gone well. With a candor that she did not anticipate, the Doctor confirmed that the Alliance was selling diamonds and gold abroad. He explained how captured soldiers worked mining the wealth to finance his crusade against communism. And he said the Equatorian people would store America's toxic waste, but only until his nation recovered from the war.

"And this rumor that the United States wants the Stinger missiles back?" Vanessa removed her last cassette from the tape recorder. "Will you confirm or deny it?"

The Doctor sat on a carved chair, staring back through thick spectacles. "They offered only ten thousand dollars for each Stinger," he said. "I reject such an insult—we have paid more with our blood. If your country supports a free market, let us sell our Stingers where we choose, to other freedom fighters."

Having jotted this down, Vanessa found herself out of tapes and questions. She was right to leave T.K. behind; the Doctor was too good to share.

"What time is it?" she asked. Her watch had vanished while she napped after her journey.

"What time would you like?" the Doctor said.

When Vanessa arrived overnight, passed blindfolded from one guerrilla band to the next, the Doctor welcomed her with formal courtesy. But as she washed herself in the windowless room they provided her, she had a sense of being gazed upon from behind the cloudy mirror.

She tried to learn where she was, but guards turned her back. She heard men, guttural mercenary accents, arguing outside her room. When she called, there was only silence.

Now his eyes, under the heavy lids, followed her as she sipped a glass of tea served by an orderly. It was time to wrap up this prize-winning interview and file it before leaving on a topless holiday next week with her Brazilian.

"How much longer can you carry on this guerrilla struggle?" she asked. "Months, years?"

"Hours." The Doctor smiled and fingered the ivory-handled Magnum holstered at his waist. "We have abandoned our guerrilla struggle."

Vanessa grabbed for her notebook.

"For our final victorious assault," he said.

"Why didn't you tell me?"

The Doctor smiled. "You did not ask me."

"It's started then?"

"My fighters are storming the capital as we speak."

Her exclusive interview and the snapshots of herself with the Doctor, followed by her eyewitness account of the government's fall, should be good for another Overseas Press Club Award at least.

"Take me back," Vanessa said, though she didn't know where she was, certainly not up-country as she expected. She was missing out on the big story.

The Doctor shook his head. "My victory requires the sacrifice of every fighter I have."

"I cannot stay." Her schedule did not permit it; the magazine was closing its weekly issue tomorrow and Guido's extravagant holiday resort thereafter was nonrefundable.

A faint cannon muffle filtered through the concrete wall, or had a truck exhaust backfired?

"Stay as long as you like," the Doctor said. "Here you are safe."

The reporter's nightmare paralyzed Vanessa, finding herself mired in the wrong spot while real news was breaking elsewhere.

"I must file this marvelous interview," she said. "My magazine's researchers need time to check the facts."

The Doctor grabbed her wrist, painfully. It was the first time he touched her.

"What facts? We check your article together, there must be no mistakes, journalists lie about me because my enemies pay them to—no more time to lose, so much to do."

What was he babbling about? Vanessa felt dizzy, too much was happening. Where was T.K.?

"Have you never wanted enough time for the perfect interview?" The Doctor squeezed her arm harder. "I give you that chance now to write the perfect interview of my life, of my call to reunite all men as brothers, with all women as their sisters to wait upon them in joyful submission. Our task will transform humanity."

"Transforming humanity sounds heaps of fun," Vanessa said, "but I am merely a senior magazine correspondent."

"Stop pretending to be stupid." The Doctor was standing over her. "You must prepare thoroughly for our next interviews—do not insult me with more silly questions."

The Doctor picked up a handful of her copper curls. "But your hair and limbs must be covered while we work. You were invited here not for a beauty contest but for your talents as a journalist."

Vanessa looked for the lecherous wink but there was none.

"We will find as many weeks and months as it takes for you to interview me properly," he said. "Your questions must be more perceptive."

Weeks, months? Years? For the first time, Vanessa felt out of control with a man. "But my deadline—"

"Do not demean our task with deadlines," he said. "We finish when we have finished, when we are satisfied with each question you ask and every word you write. No lies, no split infinitives."

Vanessa looked to the door, but it was shut. It would take every stratagem she knew to get out of here—with a story too dated to use.

"My editors'll wonder where I've gone," she said. "They'll drop me from the masthead."

"Let us fool them," the Doctor said, "and make your editors think your boat capsized in the rapids. Then we will have all the time you need to write an interview so perfect that they will fill their magazine with me many times over. For they must learn, as you do, that joy cannot truly exist unless it is preceded by pain."

* * *

Ginny skipped the news conference because Cass had promised to fill in. When Ginny called the United States, the secretary put her on hold. She was about to hang up when the middle-aged white male news executive called her name.

"About the reporting position in your letter," she told him, "I'd like to accept it."

"Right," he said. "We'll need to discuss salary and such before you start." A pause followed.

"Next week won't do," he said, "because the American Society of Newspaper Editors is meeting, then our managing editor's off to Asia, so it'll have to wait till next month. You can't come this week?"

Take the cookies when they're passed, her Aunt Edna taught her, because there may be nothing but crumbs left when the plate comes around again.

"This week's fine." Ginny studied the airline timetable. If she caught a flight tonight, with a change in Paris, she'd be there by Friday morning.

An explosion somewhere in the capital rattled the windows. Ginny would have to leave soon for the airport.

"Friday noon for lunch?" he said. "And we take our deadlines very seriously here, diversity or not."

Patronizing bastard. "I'll be there," Ginny said, restraining her anger. "If I'm not, you can offer my job to someone else."

"Noon it is," the news executive said. "You would start on our metro staff, but if you do well, there may be a foreign posting down the road. Or do you still want my job in five years?"

"Oh, no sir," Ginny said, "not at all."

She could wait a little longer.

* * *

"In your window," asked the network, "on the bird?"

Schuyler had no emotion left. "We don't have any bird because I don't have any visuals to feed you because I don't have a crew anymore."

"They were in the bombing?" The voice sounded almost human. "Legal can check our liability for contract crews."

"They were up front where you paid them to be when the bomb went off. Now Sipho's dead and I need a plane to fly Kobus out fast, not a lawyer."

Schuyler could hear artillery now, out near the international airport.

"There's an old airstrip by the river," Schuyler said. "The charter outfit we use knows it. Fly me in a fresh crew when you take out Kobus and you'll have all the A-roll and B-roll you want. By tomorrow, there'll be nothing left to this disaster but visuals."

"You're going through an awful lot of cameras and crews," the voice said. "Guys in the goldfish bowl won't be happy."

"Tell the pilot to take Kobus to that new French hospital," Schuyler said. "He'll know where to find it."

* * *

The Irish nursing sister bustled into the hospital's admitting room, her apron spattered with blood, to declare that Cass must have a guardian angel.

"She missed the full blast when she bent down." The sister recited the diagnosis. The bones in her hand were all broken, but Cass was stable for now, despite a risk of sepsis from the shrapnel inside her.

"Your lass is plucky enough," the sister said. "She hardly cried when we took off her two fingers."

"Then you'll have to operate again," T.K. said.

The sister shook her head. "Our blood supply's gone and we're almost out of anesthetic. You'd find bandages in the black market, but without a transfusion, the trauma of another operation could kill her."

"Take my blood, as much as Cass needs. I'm type A."

"She's type O, you could only use hers," the nursing sister said. "Can you move her? Médecins sans Frontières has a new hospital on the other side of the river."

"You mean Doctors Without Borders?" he said. "I was there last week."

"When we started sending patients across the river for surgery, the border guards looked the other way, but the river's too treacherous at night. The French surgeons would mend her if you could cross her over."

The sister hesitated. "There's another problem. Some soldiers came to count our foreign patients. The officer wants to put Cassandra under the army's protection. I think they might move our foreigners to the military hospital to keep the guerrillas from storming it."

"Cass, a hostage?" T.K. had to see her.

The nursing sister nodded. "Only for a few minutes—she's sedated. I'll prepare her to travel tonight."

She led him down a corridor overflowing with numbed civilians. A young mother rocked on her heels, squeezing a lifeless infant. A nurse walked among the casualties with a ledger, performing a triage that divided those battling for survival from others likelier to live or to die. Orderlies pushed bloodstained stretchers through the crowd. Over the commotion hummed a diesel generator.

"Contact lenses kept the splinters from her eyes," the nursing sister said. "Pity about that sweet face."

She beckoned T.K. through a side door into a small room. The windows had been taped over to stop the glass from shattering, which only added to the gloom.

Cass lay on the nearest cot, a tube running from the bottle of saline drip down into one arm. Bandages swelled her other hand into a white mitt. More bandages across her cheek obscured her right eye. Some rosary beads rested in her free fingers; the nuns must have placed them there.

He knelt beside her. "Recognize me?"

Her lips forced a smile. "You're the hack who grabs my fax and my bed," she said, "and my life whenever I need you, like now, Thomas."

"Then you ought to marry me," he blurted. Cass never looked more desirable.

"Cutthroat competition can't marry each other," she said. The bandages on her hand were sodden with blood.

"What competition?" he said. "You won. Okay, maybe we just live in sin."

"I dropped it," she said, but groggily. She meant the tape recorder. Her unbandaged eye glanced about with a desperation that belied the listlessness in her voice.

"You're a klutz," he said, "and it saved your life. I'm taking you to a hospital where you can drive them crazy in French—can you travel?"

"I'll try for you."

The nursing sister pulled at his sleeve.

"Rest up," he said, "because I'm coming back."

The door flung open. A blinding glare washed the room, illuminating Cass and the comatose patients in the other cots. A television cameraman scanned the faces frozen in his halogen searchlight.

"Howdoesitfeel?" The correspondent thrust his microphone at Cass's bandaged face. She bit her lip.

"Howdoesitfeel?" T.K. once asked it himself, now the intrusive question disgusted him.

The cameraman panned pruriently along Cass's body, lingering on her face, waiting for the composure to crack.

The correspondent looked at T.K. "She dying?"

"No," said T.K., "but you'll be if you don't—"

"Gotta be professional." The correspondent prodded the other patients, who showed even less life than Cass. "Speak English?" he asked them while the cameraman recorded the damage.

"Out, the lot of you," said the nursing sister.

At least the field producer had the decency to wait out in the corridor. "I heard every wacko group around the world's claimed credit for the bomb," he said, "but nobody here. Too bad about your girlfriend."

T.K. stifled his rage. Cass's survival came first. "You haven't reported she's dead?" he asked.

"Cable on our up-link got stolen, so we can't feed," the producer said. "Millions of dollars of technology gone dark because some raghead carries off a hundred bucks' worth of copper. We're chartering our tapes out."

They had a plane then. "Take Cass?" asked T.K. "Give the nuns an hour to change her bandages, sedate her?"

The field producer shook his head. "We got to catch the bird. If it was up to me, yeah, but we're competing head-on against the other networks."

The producer dropped his voice. "I don't know why we bust our butts," he said. "Airliner crash in Pakistan today, another Arctic oil spill, more fighting in the Balkans, some wacko in Texas shoots up another fast-food joint, and now the World Series is under way. Our bombing could end up on the shelf, but staying competitive's part of the job."

"You're not bugging out?" T.K. said.

"We're leaving our local drivers the minicameras," the producer said. "We'll buy whatever they can get."

And whatever they got depended on which side they backed in this war. T.K. remembered Cass's network contract; he had to find it fast.

"I thought your network hired her," he said, "or is there a clause nullifying her contract if a bomb goes off?"

"If Cass signed it, I guess they'd owe her," the producer said, "but we can't find her a hospital before we feed the bird. Didn't she fake that footage?"

"Your Very Expensive Talent faked it. Cass doesn't recall the execution and I don't either. But I do recall how Beau got himself shot in the ass four times on camera—I was there and have it on tape." T.K. didn't, but it didn't hurt to let the bastards think so.

"I'll pass the word." The producer did not seem reluctant. "But what's Cass going to look like now?"

"What's that got to do with how good a reporter she is?" T.K. said.

"Sure," said the producer, "she'll be terrific if . . . I mean, maybe stand-uppers from a wheelchair, a profiles-in-courage kinda stuff?"

"Shrapnel missed her legs."

"We'll run it by the focus groups, grow the ratings, the suits on the twenty-sixth floor just might go for it—here's my card, let's do lunch some-time." The producer sniffed over T.K. like a dog checking out a fire hydrant.

"Love your stuff," he said, "got to split before the airport blows, the crash of civilization, shame it's gotten too complicated for our viewers."

* * *

T.K. left the hospital and made his way back through streets snarled with a gridlock jumble of tanks and honking trucks. In the hotel lobby, the television set flickered, the Doctor's face leaned into a hand-held video camera. The rebels must have seized the television center across town and were showing home movies.

Once in his room, T.K. scrubbed off what he could of the bombing's grime and called his newspaper. The overseas lines were jammed. T.K. tried the embassy.

"The United States Embassy is temporarily closed because of the political situation," a recording announced. "If you are calling about the softball game, press one; about the prayer supper, press two; to reserve a frozen turkey at the commissary, press three; to book a table for Fiesta Night at the snack bar, press four. For an emergency, press five . . ."

There was nothing to press on T.K.'s phone, only the same old rotary dial.

". . . and leave your name and telephone number," the recording said. "The embassy duty officer will try to get back to you. Have a nice day."

T.K. was about to hang up when a youthful drawl broke in.

"Marine guard, sir."

"Help me," T.K. said. "I need the ambassador."

"His secretary isn't available, sir."

"I don't want his frigging secretary."

"Embassy's closed, sir."

"Then give me the press attaché. I'm an American reporter."

"I'm not authorized to give out home numbers. Have a real nice day." The line clicked.

The Boeing jetliner that ferried in the congressmen must still be at the airport. If the embassy doctor put Cass on that plane, she'd be safe.

He set out on foot for the embassy. A convoy of trucks rolled by packed with soldiers looking as though they expected to die. A van with combat policemen slowed down to watch him run down the boulevard, then sped off.

He cut through the park to save time, past the sandpile that local children used as a playground. The air was pungent with a unique stench of burned rubber, roasted flesh, and spilled gasoline.

A body sprawled crablike in the sand, the tire draped over the blackened neck still smoldering. T.K. found a branch and poked at the remains. The face was badly charred, the hands and elbows taped tightly behind the back. A cheap cuff link with the stone missing had fallen from the shirt. He rolled the corpse over and pulled a melted green plastic bag from the pocket. The tire's heat had not obliterated the gold label: *Harrods of London.*

No one deserved this death, but T.K. could not afford the luxury of mourning his friend. His hip throbbed as he raced for the American Embassy.

The gates were locked. At T.K.'s shouts, a marine stepped out in camouflage fatigues and helmet. He carried a grenade launcher.

"Embassy's closed," the marine said.

"I'm an American citizen," T.K. said.

A second marine in camouflage emerged with an M-16 rifle. T.K. passed his passport through the metal fence.

"This says Irish." The marine thrust it back. "You one of those I.R.A.s?"

"I'm an American," T.K. said. A dumb American who outsmarted himself with the wrong passport.

The marine retreated to consult his comrade, who was pointing the M-16.

The first marine ducked inside and fetched a crew-cut civilian. "You're supposed to be expelled," the spook yelled.

T.K. conjured up a smile. The C.I.A. must have its covert flights moving in and out. Before he could explain about Cass, the spook cut him off.

"You hypocritical bastards come sucking up to find out how much we know and then you print it like you invented it," the spook said. "So let me peel the onion, you got no chips to call in."

The spook walked inside without a backwards glance. A revolver protruded from the waistband of his trousers.

The marine rifleman chambered a bullet. "Back off," he said.

T.K. stood his ground, hands shoulder-high—and nearly got sideswiped by a black Chevrolet. Behind the wheel sat the consul who had issued him the new passport.

"Jeez, you're a mess, T.K., get in." The consul looked haggard himself.

The marines saluted as the Chevrolet carried T.K. inside the embassy.

The consul rummaged through the first-aid kit in his office. "I wish I could help," he said. "We have a crisis getting our congressmen out. Their plane took off when the airport came under fire, left half the delegation behind."

"Buying souvenirs, I'll bet." T.K. let the consul stick bits of tape over his cuts.

"Teak carvings. My consular section's combing the market for them. Now some show business types showed up with American passports and demanded we stop this war. We'd bring down a plane from Frankfurt but we don't know who's got the airport."

T.K. asked about the embassy doctor—he could look after Cass.

"Congressman Walker's wife got food poisoning at the reception. The doctor flew out holding her hand."

That left driving Cass across the border, but the consul shook his head. The guerrillas had mined the highway.

"We'll try a land convoy once the road is cleared," the consul said, "but the congressmen and celebrities won't ride on the same bus. Hell, they won't share the same room."

"Her stretcher would fit in the aisle," T.K. said.

"Trouble is," said the consul, "Cass doesn't qualify for evacuation priority, she's a foreign national."

"The ambassador qualified her to go skinny-dipping in his pool last night."

"I'll do what I can after we shovel the first lot out—they're banging their spoons against the high chairs, all demanding to leave first. You want to go too?"

"Not without Cass."

The consul handed T.K. the rest of the bandages. "I'll bend the regulations however I can—she's not married to an American or anything, is she?"

"We plan to be," said T.K.

*　　*　　*

When T.K. returned to the hotel, Schuyler was looking for him.

"I have a charter flying in a new crew," Schuyler said. "It can take Cass out with Kobus."

"Consul told me the guerrillas grabbed the airport."

"Not that old strip near the river—you know it. The pilots'll try that if we can get there by midnight. Will your newspaper split the cost?"

"Sure," said T.K., who didn't know. "But a plane can't land in the middle of the war."

"These guys were bush pilots back in Canada. I'll light up the strip with the truck headlights. They'll be in and out before anyone can shoot."

Schuyler handed him a printout. "Ginny wrote you some B-matter, you've got less than an hour to file."

The crazy thing about hacks was that they'd cut each other's throats over a story too trivial to make it past the want ads, then share shamelessly if someone was in trouble.

"After we collect Cass and Kobus," Schuyler said, "it'll take about an hour to the strip, if we don't run into any roadblocks."

T.K. climbed the stairs to Cass's room and jimmied the door open. Her blue Canadian passport was buried under a heap of underwear in the bottom drawer. He found the network contract inside her desk with the first-class airline ticket. He signed the contract as a witness and backdated it by a week.

He opened her passport and peeked: thirty-one years old next month. So less than a decade separated them. T.K. stuffed what he had gathered into his jacket. For himself, he took the photograph of Cass with her schoolkids and a silk scarf because it smelled of her.

One task remained. T.K. found the telephone number in her address book. He dialed it over and over. The voice that finally answered sounded like Cass.

"Mrs. Benoit," he said, "I'm a friend of your daughter."

"Thomas, is it?" her mother said. "She wrote us about you. Is she there?"

A hack reported the truth without exception, not even for this. "There's been a bombing," he said. "Cass caught some shrapnel."

The other end of the line went silent before he could share the rest: So far, your daughter lost a couple of fingers, but before we're out of this, she could lose her hand, her eye, maybe her life.

"Not serious," he said instead. "She's scratched up a little."

Still no response. Had her mother hung up?

"Hello," he said. "Just her cheek and hand, she's looking fine. I just left her at the hospital."

"Cricket's in hospital," her mother said. "What's her phone number?"

"There isn't one," he said, "so I'm moving her to a nicer hospital across the river. Just for observation."

"Her father's a cardiologist, you know—he'll want to consult with Cricket's physicians on her X-rays."

Cricket? What cricket, T.K. asked.

"Her brothers called her that as a baby, all arms and legs and too tiny for 'Cassandra,'" her mother said. "When she went off to McGill she insisted on Cassandra. Then Marc called her Cassie, now it's just Cass. I try to keep up, but my husband says she's still his Cricket. Here I'm telling you family secrets."

"If you can't trust a reporter with a secret," T.K. said, "whom can you trust?"

Cass would not cheat him of the pleasure of throwing "Cricket" at her tinted contacts, he was keeping her alive.

His window shattered, the hotel shook with the blast outside, big enough for a 120-millimeter mortar. Guerrilla gunners must have sighted in on the cathedral spire.

"Quite a wedding celebration here," T.K. explained. "The hospital where I'm taking Cass will be quieter."

"I worried about her going so far away," her mother said, "but you know how stubborn Cricket is, always entered ski races when she wasn't very good—now don't tell her I said so."

"Cricket can be competitive," he agreed.

"I begged her to come home, but she felt safe with you, she said, you remind her of Marc, but without his wild streak."

That's right, I'm merely abducting your daughter from the hospital through the carnage of a civil war to a plane that may never arrive.

"I don't mean to pry, but I thought something was happening between you two," her mother said. "You do sound more reliable than Marc, God rest his soul. It's hard to forgive him for leading her into that avalanche, I don't know how she found the strength to dig out. Will the bombing be on television, or in the papers here?"

"Don't believe what you read or hear, Mrs. Benoit. You know what the media's like—are like."

"I'm relieved it's not serious. You'll have Cricket call us from the new hospital, eh?"

"Cricket'll be fine," he said, "I promise."

Having copped out on journalistic integrity, T.K. hung up. Before leaving, he weighed Cass's new laptop computer against her old typewriter, and scooped up both. If the war got any worse, he'd be filing his stories on a rock with a chisel.

* * *

Back in his own room, T.K. sat down with her laptop. The keyboard felt strange and he could not decide how to begin, but he wrote anyway. There wasn't time to think.

"The battered country of Equatoria exploded into renewed warfare tonight as a tenuous cease-fire collapsed between the government and insurgents of the Equatorian Patriotic Alliance, which has waged a fifteen-year struggle with covert American assistance to topple the nation's pro-Marxist regime."

Write what you know. Write it and get back to her.

"Under cover of nightfall, heavily armed guerrillas swept into the outskirts of this former colonial capital, dislodging confused defenders who fought back with tanks and artillery. There were reports that some elite units from the Republican Guard mutinied and looted their own stores."

The words were flowing now, faster than he could punch them into the computer, as habit overrode his worry for her. There was no time to read what he wrote.

"The attack followed the surprise bombing of a news conference called by the government, ostensibly to comment on the United Nations' decision not to send troops to supervise the cease-fire and new elections in Equatoria."

He searched the strange computer for the key to save what he had written.

"The bombing, which the government and the insurgents promptly blamed on each other, killed a South African television sound engineer and a Dutch photographer." If Rolf hadn't been Dutch, the luckless bastard was now. "Nine other foreign journalists were injured, including Cassandra Benoit, a Canadian who formerly reported for public radio . . ."

Hell, why not? ". . . and is this reporter's fiancée."

But Cass explained why things happened too.

"The latest fighting, which escalated through the night, perpetuates an ideological and ethnic struggle that began shortly after Equatoria won its independence from colonial rule, when the liberation movement's Marxist faction seized power with Soviet and Cuban backing . . ."

In another ten minutes, T.K. had finished. He saved his story on a floppy disk and printed out a copy. By the time he picked up the telephone, the line was breaking up too badly and he called instead.

"Foreign desk," chirped the news clerk.

"It's T.K.," he said. "All hell's broken loose."

The foreign editor picked up. "We were watching until CNN lost the picture—you anywhere near that bomb?"

"I can't file out electronically," T.K said.

"Come home," the foreign editor said, "and join us here on the desk, regular hours, lots of meetings, your own ergonomic work station."

After larking for years out with the poachers, he was being asked to defect to the gamekeepers. Becoming an editor meant wearing matching socks and a necktie.

"Is the shopping mall beat open?" he asked.

"Filled two minutes after the managing editor posted it," the foreign editor said. "Come home, T.K. I'll sponsor you for my health club—we'll treadmill together."

And T.K. struck his own Faustian bargain.

"I'm packing it in on one condition," he said before the telephone went dead. "That you split the cost of a plane charter out of here."

He was late. From under his bed T.K. pulled out the flak vest, twenty-two pounds of ceramic armor plates from RPR Ltd. in London. With a felt-tipped pen, he crossed off his blood type, A, taped on the front and wrote in O.

Laden with his flak vest, her typewriter and laptop, T.K. ran out of his room. He never looked back.

12.

SOMEWHERE IN EQUATORIA—This nation ceased to exist after its capital was overrun last night and reduced to rubble by rampaging guerrillas who unleashed an orgy of ethnic bloodletting unprecedented even in this civil war.

The mass flight of frightened refugees swelled to tens of thousands by daybreak, according to a hasty estimate by a couple of foreign reporters who remained behind. . . .

As T.K. left for the hospital, the hotel lights failed for good. He collided in the dark lobby with one of the cyberwonks.

"My NiCad died," caterwauled the wonk, as though a relative had passed away. "How can I access my hard drive when my NiCad's deceased?"

"File by forked stick," T.K. said. "They did it in the old days."

Schuyler's old truck was waiting outside. T.K. placed Cass's new computer alongside her typewriter on the front seat and climbed in.

"Alistair's meeting us at the hospital," Schuyler said. "Ginny too—did you hear her job came through?"

Driving without lights, Schuyler pulled into the deserted street. Rifle shots cracked from across the park. Some looters were peeling the steel shutters off a shop with crowbars.

T.K. watched a rocket whistling overhead shear off another chunk of the cathedral's unfinished tower. The only way he'd beat Cass on a story like this was to ship her out.

"Get through to your paper?" Schuyler asked.

T.K. nodded. "They want to make me an editor." He waited for his friend to recoil with the horror of betrayal.

"You might be good at it," Schuyler said instead. "You've been out in the field and know what it's like. We can't go around forever taking chances, T.K.—I've promised Sarah to get out while I'm still intact."

"You'd rather be a rabbi?" T.K. asked.

"It's communications too, isn't it," Schuyler said, and mumbled something about walking through the valley of the shadow of death and fearing no evil. Everyone T.K. cherished seemed to have gotten religion.

"You never told me what T.K. stands for," said Schuyler.

T.K. dodged the question. "You'd tell Cass."

"Hack's honor, I won't."

"Something my folks called me as a kid."

"Something corny like Tommykins?"

"One word, Schuyler, and I'll rip your heart out and piss on it."

"Cass'll find out anyway—you're going out with her?"

"Yes, maybe. I don't know."

T.K. felt for her network contract still inside his jacket. If it disappeared in this war's confusion, he could take Cass back to the halcyon way things used to be, and no one would think to blame him for stunting her career.

Schuyler braked for what looked like corpses in the road, but he did not stop.

"You're expelled," he said, "and the bomb cut you up. Why stay around for more killing?"

"You first," said T.K. "Your Sarah's waiting."

"I've got to set up my incoming crew," Schuyler said, "then I'll be gone once the airport reopens. No one at home cares, now that American troops aren't coming."

"I'm choosing between the best woman in my life," T.K. said, "and the best story."

"What kind of a choice is that?" Schuyler scoffed.

"I know, I sound unprofessional," T.K. said. Once he left, he could find himself deskbound, but if he hung in to redeem himself with this war, he might never see her again. "Is any story worth Cass?" he wondered aloud.

"I can't think of one," said Schuyler. "Maybe the collapse of the Soviet Union, but it's been done." He parked the truck behind the hospital. "Don't leave her laptop here—I don't trust that kid."

The scrawny young watchman who had opened the gate stretched out a beggar's hand. He looked lost inside the army greatcoat. A snubby Kalashnikov, metal stock folded, dangled from his neck.

"Hungry, please." He mimed feeding himself.

"Fifty dollars for your AK," T.K. said. "It can feed your family for weeks."

The watchman shook his head. "So hungry, please."

T.K. pulled his last fifty-dollar bill from his money belt and unfolded it in front of the boy's widening eyes. "This," he said, "for that."

The boy said nothing until T.K. moved to put the bill back. He snatched at the bill, but T.K. held tight.

"Bullets too."

The boy pulled the metal crescent from his pocket and showed the cartridges gleaming inside. He slammed the magazine into the Kalashnikov, handed it to T.K., and grabbed the money. And the boy ran out the open gate.

T.K. checked the magazine. Damn, it was half empty. He flipped the selector through automatic, single shot, and back to safety, then tossed the rifle in the back of the truck.

"You nuts?" said Schuyler. "They'll blow us away if they find that at a roadblock."

"They might blow us away anyway, it's that kind of night," T.K. said. "I bought her travel insurance."

Isn't there anybody you care about, she once asked him, enough to commit yourself without reservation? Yes, Cass, there is now.

* * *

Alistair was waiting inside the hospital with the nursing sister. "The soldiers are here," she said.

The sister led them down the teeming corridor. Cass, freshly sedated, only nodded when they shifted her to the stretcher. In the drawer beside the bed, T.K. found her dented bangles and slipped them into his pocket. Alistair helped him carry Cass to the back door of the hospital. A soldier barred their exit with his rifle.

"He was told to keep all foreigners inside," the nursing sister translated.

"I'm our embassy doctor"—Alistair feigned importance—"and this patient is a British subject."

The soldier, reeking of sour lombo, jammed his rifle into Alistair's stomach.

"We can negotiate," gasped Alistair.

An army major with twin stripes and a star on each epaulet waved them back with his pistol.

"Help us." T.K. pointed to the stretchers holding Cass and Kobus. "And we help you." A few dollars usually satisfied underpaid soldiers; bribing an officer was trickier.

"A gift of friendship between our two nations."

A flicker of the major's eyes betrayed his curiosity. "What gift?" he asked.

T.K. had no idea. The major could always confiscate money, but T.K. had nothing else to offer. His hand brushed the computer case slung over his shoulder.

"A gift," he announced. Teasingly, he slipped her gray laptop from its case. He opened it, touched a button. The screen glowed in colors that grew more and more vivid as T.K. dialed maximum contrast.

The major pressed a key, mesmerized by the new colors blossoming in tidy columns across the screen.

"Spreadsheet," said T.K., "with twenty interactive ladies inside, nineteen interactive costumes."

The major pushed more keys. "Give me," he said.

T.K. heard the whining crescendo. Incoming mortar rounds always terrified him, but not this time.

In the courtyard, the diesel generator spewed a meteor shower of sparks. The lights dimmed and died. There followed panic in the dark corridor. Either the shell fell short, or the guerrillas were softening up for an assault.

The only light was emanating now from the laptop; it illuminated the major's panic before T.K. pushed the glowing screen into his face.

Five thousand dollars in silicone and molded plastic shattered into shards on the tile floor. In the darkness, the major groaned.

T.K. crawled back down the corridor and found Cass. The intravenous drip was already pulled from her arm in anticipation of the journey.

"That bloke traded Cass for the computer?" asked Alistair, who was kneeling alongside.

"They don't make these new laptops to last," T.K. told him. "He's not happy—let's move."

They maneuvered Cass out the door. Schuyler and the nursing sister followed with Kobus.

"I'll pray to Saint Jude to intercede," the sister said.

"Just ask Saint Jude to get us past the roadblocks," T.K. said.

"Of course," said the sister. "He's our saint of hopeless causes." And she bustled back inside.

Ginny was waiting, out of breath as though she had been running. She clutched a wad of floppy disks and paper.

"We'll have to pigeon these out," she said. "The hotel lines are out, and the army's fighting each other downtown."

They slid Cass into the back of the truck alongside Kobus. There wasn't time to retrieve Sipho's body. Alistair had joined Schuyler up front. T.K. climbed into the back with Ginny, alongside Cass.

He opened the flak vest up like a poncho and covered as much of Cass as he could. Then he chambered a bullet in the Kalashnikov and flipped it onto safety.

"Schuyler said you got a new job," he told Ginny. "You can take Cass out."

Ginny hesitated. "I'm in no hurry, you go first."

T.K. held the rifle, but where could he hide it? He looked around the bare truck and finally handed it to Ginny, who sat on it.

Pedestrians had vanished by now from the unlit streets. A few lanterns flared and dimmed in passing houses, which looked otherwise deserted. A heavy tank rumbled past with soldiers clinging desperately aboard. A volley of shots erupted to the right, then somewhere off ahead.

If T.K. had accompanied Vanessa to her interview, he might not have seen Cass again. But he put this out of his mind. Vanessa could fend for herself better than T.K. and his fellow travelers. If a rocket grenade crisped the truck, their obituaries would merit a few lines back with the want ads, or maybe not, with the World Series under way.

"Roadblock." Ginny saw it first.

Schuyler at the wheel had overlooked the armored car protruding beyond the overturned bus at the intersection.

Its machine gun locked onto the truck before Schuyler could turn around. From both flanks, soldiers drifted in like ghosts, looking unpredictable and scared, the kind that T.K. dreaded most.

The soldiers examined Schuyler's press card under a flashlight, then Alistair's. T.K. no longer had his card; if he climbed down, they might let the others through. But the turret gunner would see the AK-47 behind Ginny.

A very young soldier, his oversized helmet bobbing, swung onto the back of the truck. The boy shone a flashlight into T.K.'s face, at Ginny, and down the bodies of Kobus and Cass. Her unbandaged eye stared back at the flashlight.

"Cass?" he asked, "from Canada?" The boy leaned forward, forgetting his rifle. "She feeds soup to us street children," he told T.K.

"My older sister's youngest daughter is very sick," T.K. said.

"Cass is your older sister's youngest daughter?" The soldier expressed delight. "You speak our language."

Once again, T.K. mangled the vocabulary that Cass had drilled into him. But the young soldier, talking too fast now for T.K. to follow, summoned an old man with a stripe down the back of his helmet.

"Will she die?" he asked.

"If you do not let her go," T.K. said.

The old soldier stepped back and waved the truck through.

Schuyler swerved left into a maze of back streets to avoid the next roadblock. T.K, sitting in the back, cradled Cass's head in his lap. Her closeness offered small comfort. This journey was foolish; she might have fared better under guard at the hospital.

But they could not turn back. From the roadblock behind them came the clatter of the big machine gun, the rattle of Kalashnikovs, and the explosion of a grenade. He had heard it before.

Wars like this ended in exhaustion, not cease-fires. Or they never ended. The same old horrors kept turning up under new datelines.

T.K. stroked her bandaged head. "Nearly there," he told Cass. He had no notion where they were.

The truck corkscrewed over the potholes and ditches like a boat in a storm. Cass was speaking in a small voice:

"We have erred and strayed from Thy ways like lost sheep." Her prayer came fast, mechanically, like her pulse. "We have followed too much the devices and desires of our own hearts. We have offended against Thy holy laws . . ."

"Scared?" he asked when she was done. Cass nodded.

"Me too," he said. "But we're saddled up and moving anyway."

"Made that up for me, did you?"

"John Wayne did."

"Same thing," she said.

The road ahead began to undulate in the gloom. As they drove on, it came alive with furtive travelers not waiting for first light to stream out of the capital for sanctuary somewhere, anywhere. They toted or dragged pitiful bundles, trundled bicycles and carts piled high, carried and swept ahead children, mingling with and indistinguishable from the world's flood of millions dispossessed by tragedy.

Had Cass been lucid, she would have made them stop the truck to take aboard as many refugees as possible, enough to cost her the rendezvous with the plane. Schuyler knew the danger of compassion. He swung the truck off the road and into the fields, keeping wide of the refugees.

Cass moaned. T.K. searched his jacket for a loose malaria pill and placed it on her tongue reverentially, like a Communion wafer.

"This will kill the pain," he told her.

Either she had forgotten the deception that he confessed to as an army medic or she wanted to trust him, for she swallowed the tablet.

"Yes," Cass said, "that does feel better."

Beside her, Kobus lay ominously still. Ginny felt for his wrist, but said she found nothing.

They had broken free of the city, lost in fields that opened around them in darkness like some vast sea.

"Where now?" Schuyler called out. T.K. had no idea.

But Schuyler found a road and swung onto it, still without lights, guessing at each turn of the rutted dirt. Using headlights would make the truck a target. A war zone after dark was always dangerous, yet darkness offered the best cover.

"My hand hurts," said Cass, more out of discovery than complaint.

"You lost a couple of fingers," T.K. told her, "the ones with more smarts than I've got in my entire body. We're evenly matched at last."

What other scars would she carry? But he did not dwell on this; it was Cass he loved, not what she looked like.

He was staring into the future, not of mathematically precise electronic technology and computers that failed once the lights went out, but of atavistic ethnic hatreds, sectarian grudges, and tribal rivalries fanned by warlords and hatemongers, of civility deteriorating into anarchy till nothing remained but thuggish guerrilla armies in sunglasses, unebbing tides of refugees—and the hacks who hung in to cover them.

"All will be well," he said, "Cricket."

"Crumbs, never love a newspaperman." The sedation *was* wearing off. "What did they call you?"

"You won't find out," he told her, "if you don't hang in."

In contrast to the clamor of artillery dueling in the capital, an uncanny silence prevailed. Off to the left, the whitewashed buildings of the United Nations Development Program remained incongruously lit up. A little closer, T.K. discerned the compound of the Catholic Relief Services.

Even so, the truck seemed adrift, rolling north when the river boundary lay east of the city. He was about to bang on the cab, when Schuyler turned right onto a smaller dirt road. T.K. had traveled this one before, with Alistair and then with Cass.

Suddenly, the truck braked hard for a tree across the road. Shadowy highwaymen rushed from the barricade. Out of the dark, sinister hands grabbed at the truck.

The truck shuddered when Schuyler sideswiped the tree, plucking off someone clinging to the cab. A rifle fired up front. The truck careened into the field. Another highwayman had scrambled into the back of it.

Ginny aimed the AK-47 low like a shotgun and squeezed off a shot. The highwayman dropped from the truck. She pitched the rifle to T.K. and flung herself across Cass.

T.K. flipped the Kalashnikov to full automatic and sprayed the shadows, trying to keep the barrel from climbing up. More bullets ricocheted off the truck. Ginny groaned as though a horse had kicked her.

A second intruder, machete in hand, was crawling forward. He whacked Kobus, flung him overboard. T.K. pulled the trigger but the AK-47 no longer responded.

The intruder brought his machete down on Cass. It clinked against the ceramic armor of the flak vest and she cried out. The truck lurched forward.

T.K. blocked the next blow with the Kalashnikov, and it clattered onto the floor. The intruder, too wiry to stop, was on top of him now. Sweat dropped onto his face. Sinewy hands pressed the machete against his throat. T.K. fought back, twisting and pushing until his strength failed.

And the discarded Kalashnikov smashed over the intruder's head. Ginny swung it again, one-handed this time.

T.K. broke loose, slammed the intruder's nose flat with the back of his hand, whipping the clenched fist like a wrecking ball. Then he drove the splintered bone upward under the heel of his hand, again and again, until Ginny tugged him off.

"She's safe," Ginny said, "he can't hurt her anymore."

Together they rolled the intruder over the side. The truck gained speed as it wobbled along the road. The muzzle flashes from the ambush receded.

The truck stopped short of the big ditch. Alistair jumped out and sprinted to the driver's side.

"Schuyler's shot," Alistair said. He leapt in, shifted back into gear, and picked up speed.

T.K. flung the spent rifle into the bush. He had taken no pride in shooting desperate drifters.

Alistair did not slow down until they saw the airstrip. It looked hollow against the horizon of the squatter camp. The truck stopped, and they dragged Schuyler from the cab.

"Don't quit on me, because you're not on camera," T.K. said. "Too many stand-ups left in your contract."

Schuyler no longer answered. T.K. laid him on the grass and bound up the hole sucking from his abdomen. Cass tried to help them when they lifted her from the truck.

"Was Kobus dead?" asked Alistair.

"I hope so," T.K. said. Then he heard the plane.

What was it Schuyler told him, hit the headlights three times and leave them on? He flashed the signal and the plane overhead banked into the landing. In the truck lights, the airstrip looked too short, much too narrow.

Ginny leaned against the truck's muddy wheel. When T.K. touched her arm, the one she'd broken months ago, his hand came up bloody.

"My interview in the States," she said, "is going to have to wait."

"No it isn't," T.K. said while he wrapped up her arm, "because you're taking Cass with you. Barry's sent a stringer to the hospital to file our stories—mine's first."

"Sure," Ginny said, "right after mine."

"Check Schuyler's passport for a home address, sis—try to reach his wife before she hears it on the news."

Into his own jacket, he tucked Cass's eyeglasses, her passport and airline ticket, and some tapes salvaged from her room. He added his last dollars to her remaining traveler's checks; she would need them. He folded the jacket around her shoulders and under her head.

He shaped her fingers, the good ones, around his ballpoint pen and guided it across her contract. She'd be rich and famous now.

"The network won't want me—" she said.

"If they don't, they'll lose a lawsuit—you're better than they deserve." He looked for Ginny. "Mail this, don't give it back to Cass. Or me."

The plane had arrived, not the big Cessna but a lighter Pilatus, following the trail of light thrown by the truck down the grassy strip. It seemed too small for the evacuation as it rolled to a stop just beyond the truck's headlights. A camera crew jumped out with a Betamax and aluminum cases of gear.

"Can you carry out three?" T.K. asked the pilot, who was clearing a storage hatch. "The guy's about gone, but his wife still needs him."

"We'll just about make this," the pilot said, kicking at the airstrip. He boosted Ginny aboard, then handed out two stretchers. "French hospital's not fifteen minutes. I'll radio them to light up the field."

"Aren't you coming too?" Cass stared up with an entreaty that shamed T.K., a proposal he couldn't refuse, though he did.

"Too risky," he told her. "This plane can clear the strip with just you, Ginny, and Schuyler."

"Come anyway, please," she said. "Please, it doesn't matter for Schuyler anymore."

"He promised his wife he'd come home," T.K. said, "and I'm keeping that promise. I'm a hack, Cass, and now I wish I weren't."

"Do stop babbling, Thomas, and don't you dare get yourself—" She started to cry. "I can't replace you," she said.

T.K. stroked her face. He hoped it was wet from the rain, he was terrified of her tears.

When Cass was grateful, she turned docile and compliant, as she had with the Talent; she yielded that competitive edge, wilted into a damsel in distress. But she might hang in out of spite.

I was so scared, Cass told him the night they first made love, and you made me stick it out just to spite you.

"I'm staying, yes," he told her, "but then I'll be coming after you with so many rockets that you'll wish you never heard of journalism or me."

"So pathetic," she murmured.

"I'm sick of begging you to marry me." He could taste the long night's exhaustion and the drizzle salted with his unaccustomed tears. "But beat me again and I'll marry you instead, on any terms you want, only because I want to wake up next to you for the rest of my life."

"Yes," said Cass, "I'd like that. But let's not compete anymore, I don't want to humiliate you."

"Who's humiliated?" he snapped. "Your exclusives were all beginner's luck, Cricket, so if you're a one-trick filly, better quit now. Isn't that how you Canadians lost the War of 1812?"

"That's wrong," said Cass. "I can do it again." She reached for his forehead. "And you're not marrying me until we find you a proper haircut. I'm not taking home a hoodlum."

They handed her up and the pilot slammed the door. There was no time to kiss her goodbye. T.K. backed away reluctantly as the Pilatus pivoted for takeoff. He might never see her again.

The truck lights flashed on, defining a ribbon of escape. The plane hurtled down the dirt at full throttle, straight for the liquid darkness of the river.

No, it was climbing, just in time to clear the tree line. Alistair cut the headlights. The small plane banked toward the river and disappeared with a wiggle of the wings, the pilot's promise that all would be well.

The weight of her fell from T.K.'s shoulders. The camera crew, wearing flak vests now, threw the gear into the back of the truck before climbing in themselves, and one was a woman. Hell, what was unusual about that?

"This ride'll cost you one of those," T.K. told her.

"We brought extra." She pulled another flak vest from a cargo bag.

T.K. slipped his own over the rain-soaked T-shirt with the quadrilingual appeal: *Foreign Press. Don't Shoot.* He tied Cass's silk scarf around his neck; it would have to protect him.

It had rained this hard when Cass arrived. He jumped into the truck and dumped the spare flak vest on Alistair's lap.

"No thanks, mate," said Alistair, and kicked it under his feet. "Never wear them."

From within the squatter camp, he sighted the sparks of an assault rifle, and another. "Rock'n'roll behind us," T.K. said.

"What a royal wanker you are." Alistair shifted into gear. "If she asked me, I'd be gone."

"Plane couldn't have taken off with me, too."

The loss of her numbed T.K. Staying here was the dumbest thing he'd ever done, unless it was the smartest. Whenever she leaned on a man, Cass got herself screwed in more ways than one.

"Cass can't handle gratitude," he said. "She needs us like a dolphin needs a tuna net. If I'd gone with her, she'd maybe die apologizing for the inconvenience. She's got to fight back, recover that fast mouth of hers, decide whether she can do better than me . . ."

Besides, how could you walk out on slaughter like this? Who cared anymore? Not news twinks or pundits or bottom-liners, only mushroom journalists. Outside the cab, the rain pounded down, lightning charged the sky. T.K. felt for his missing press tag; he was no longer legal here.

"I'll renew your visa with a government stamp I nicked," Alistair said. "It's back in my room."

"This government won't be around tomorrow," T.K. said, "or your room."

The truck paused where the rutted tracks intersected in the mud. "Pick a fork," said Alistair.

"We came in from the left, so I'd guess the right."

Alistair turned the steering wheel and accelerated into a shroud of flame. The blast sent the truck rocking back on its rear axle like a startled warhorse. It slammed down.

T.K. threw up an arm to cushion his head before the windshield shattered. Her silk scarf had protected him.

He climbed out and inspected the broken axle. The truck must have hit some kind of land mine; an antitank mine would have incinerated them all.

T.K.'s arm ached when he hauled Alistair out of the wreckage with his torn flak vest. "Bloody thing saved my feet," Alistair said.

"How you feeling otherwise?" asked T.K.

"Don't know, can't see much," Alistair said. "In fact I can't see a bloody thing."

T.K. sat Alistair down and turned his bruised face to the rain. Droplets trickled from the corner of his eyes and mouth. "Just a little concussion," T.K. said, "it'll clear up." He didn't know what else to say.

The cameraman crouched moaning over his shattered minicamera. His sound engineer, oblivious to a gash across her scalp, coaxed sounds of life from her recorder.

"Did I tell you it's your network's truck?" T.K. said.

The cameraman stumbled to his feet and hugged his Beta before discarding it.

"No story without bleeding visuals," he lamented in an Australian accent, "and no visuals without a bleeding minicam, is there, Sheila?"

Alistair rubbed at his eyes, without result. "You better hike it to Catholic Relief Services."

"U.N. looks closer," T.K. said.

"Catholics got a telex," said Alistair. "You can update the story, doss till it's safe to look around."

"You mean us, good buddy."

"I'd slow you down," said Alistair. "Leave me here, come back tomorrow or so, I'll be right as rain."

"You're a pain in the ass again, Alistair," T.K. said. "Just shut up and take my hand."

The Catholics would have a medical kit, too. T.K. led Alistair off the road, into the rain-soaked grass. There were more mines than the one they'd just set off.

The cameraman and the sound engineer followed close behind. "Can we help carry your recorder?" asked Alistair.

"Shove your sexism—I look helpless?" Sheila snarled in a New York accent.

"I'll bet she has dark eyes big enough to drown in," Alistair whispered. "I think I'm in love."

A hard rain was hiding them as they cut through the fields. T.K. held Alistair by one hand, and by the other, Cass's boxy old typewriter; it was state-of-the-art again.

Ahead, the city skyline exploded with a thunder that moved the ground. The airport fuel depot must have taken a direct hit, or maybe the Hotel Turissimo. There was nothing to draw him back. By now his roots lay beyond the river.

The horizon glowed with apocalyptic fire. A clatter of machine guns added to the cacophony of pandemonium. T.K. recognized the boom and slam of the heavy self-propelled howitzers. He had to get out of this one alive, even as he stumbled toward the blazing skyline with the blind faith of a moth lured into a candle. Flashes from the big guns spotted his night vision, making the soggy walk harder.

Maybe editing wasn't so bad. Would his lunch break be long enough to shop for dinner, have it waiting when Cass got home from her network?

The thought distracted him only for a moment, then the adrenaline surged. It looked like the end of the world ahead, and T.K. and Alistair had this exclusive to themselves.

"Thanks, mate," Alistair said. "Chasing rock'n'roll by ear wasn't what I signed up for."

"We're hacks," T.K. said. "We'll be filing our guts out when the world's forgotten how to read."

She must be landing about now. T.K. imagined his cutthroat competition lying inside the pitching cabin, biting into her succulent lower lip to mask the pain, her bandaged face ghostlike in the muted glow of the instrument panel, while the pilot eased into the final descent and touched the rain-slick runway, rolling toward those who would make Cass and whatever else T.K. loved well again.

She was still his problem: now he owed her his survival.